T0365693

HAMMER

—— OF ——

GOD

LOU SCAFIDI

iUniverse

HAMMER OF GOD

iUniverse books may be ordered through booksellers or by contacting:

iUniverse
1663 Liberty Drive
Bloomington, IN 47403
www.iuniverse.com
1-800-Authors (1-800-288-4677)

Because of the dynamic nature of the Internet, any web addresses or links contained in this book may have changed since publication and may no longer be valid. The views expressed in this work are solely those of the author and do not necessarily reflect the views of the publisher, and the publisher hereby disclaims any responsibility for them.

Any people depicted in stock imagery provided by Thinkstock are models, and such images are being used for illustrative purposes only. Certain stock imagery © Thinkstock.

ISBN: 978-1-5320-1614-1 (sc)
ISBN: 978-1-5320-1615-8 (e)

Library of Congress Control Number: 2017901363

Print information available on the last page.

iUniverse rev. date: 02/06/2017

CHAPTER

—————— 1 ——————

Timbre stood on the dock in San Francisco waiting for his cargo to be unloaded. He was taking deep breaths of the cold salty air, listening to the sea gulls squawking while they tried to steal the fish that were coming in on the fishing boats. This was the first time in six years that Timbre was back on American soil, except for transferring ships in New York, and it felt good to be back.

"Hey, Timbre!" the Captain yelled from on top of the gang plank. You want to get your ass up here and help us get this crazy damn horse of yours off my ship before he kills someone?"

Timbre smiled as he made his way up the gangplank wondering for the hundredth time why he ever bought that crazy horse.

When Timbre was making his way home from the Far East he'd stopped to visit the Netherlands. In the hotel that he was staying at he met and struck up a friendship with one of the young local girls that worked at the front desk. She was no more than sixteen, blond hair with blue eyes and spoke passable English. Hilga, that was her name, was one of those people that always wanted to improve herself. In Timbre she saw her chance to advance her mastery of the English language and to learn more about the mysterious America so she offered to be his guide, which Timbre readily accepted.

After taking him on a tour of the city she then insisted on showing him the beautiful country side. While touring they came across a ranch that was raising, what the natives called, Friesian horses. To Timbre, who had never seen one before, the big black horses were the most majestic horses he'd ever seen.

They stopped to admire them and while doing so the owner of the ranch came out to greet them.

"You are English, no?" The tall blond man asked in bad English.

"Yes Sir. I was just admiring your horses. I hope you don't mind?" Timbre asked, while noticing a big stallion standing alone in a separate coral.

"How come you got that one separated from the others?" Timbre asked the owner.

"That one, what's the word" he asked the girl in Dutch and she said. "Born crazy."

His face lit up with a smile and he repeated. "Yes, born crazy. He try to kill other horse that come near him and any human too. He try kill about anything that move. We thinking of putting him down but would be such a waste. He magnificent, no?"

"Yeah. Magnificent yes. You mind if I walk over and take a closer look?"

"Sure, but you remember, he killer. You do not get close to him, he bite you in face."

Timbre walked slowly towards the coral, not wanting to spook the big black. Timbre always had a special way

2

with animals, especially with horses. And, the time he spent in Tibet, studying with the monks made him even more proficient in bonding with animals. It was all part of his gift, that his Mother used to call it and the reason he traveled to Tibet in the first place. He always wanted to explore his strangeness, as he called it.

While he was touring Asia he had heard vague talk of Holy men that lived high up in the mountains and the things they were able to do with just the power of their minds. It sounded to him like the very thing he was searching for all his life. As hard as he tried he couldn't ignore what he'd heard and the pull it had on him. Something about it kept nagging at him, so after much soul searching he finally sought them out, which wasn't an easy thing to do.

He first had to travel to Katmandu in Nepal, from there to a village in the mountains called Namche. The monks in that temple had refused him entry into their Monastery. After begging them for entrance for over a week they suggested that he move further up the mountain to a temple in Khumjung Gompa a couple of thousand feet further up the mountain.

At first the head monk was very wary of him. Although the head Lama spoke broken English and was very polite he didn't think that Timbre was suited to their way of life. After a couple of days of trying to persuade the monk to give him a chance Timbre finally wore him down with the promise of a big donation to his temple. Since the Monastery needed a lot of repairs, which the monks couldn't afford to have done, the head Lama reluctantly agreed to take him in and give him a try. He wasn't exactly accepted with open arms by the other monks but they did what the head Lama instructed them to do without complaining about it.

In the two years that Timbre spent with them he learned a great deal through the guidance of the Master and some of the other monks who were instructed to teach him. He never did catch on to the religious side of their teachings, at least not all of it. He understood their thinking but he never could accept their pacifism, although he did learn to control his temper. When he finally decided he'd learned enough and now understood most of his gifts and how to control them, he said his good-byes.

As he got closer to the big black, the horse took note of him and just stood there glaring at him with his ears pinned back. He looked like he was getting ready to fight. Timbre relaxed his whole body and cleared his mind, letting his calmness drift into the Stallion.

"So what's your story big feller?" Timbre asked him in a soft voice as he got closer. "Are you stone cold crazy like they say you are?"

Timbre saw the look in the blacks eyes slightly change to a calmer state as he asked the question. "I bet you're not crazy but just plain mean. You know they plan on making you into a dog stew?" The blacks ears perked up and his eyes softened a little more.

"Damn, big boy, I do believe you understand me. If you understand me come over here to the railing."

The black edged slowly to the railing until he was staring Timbre in the face. "Listen, and believe what I'm telling you. I don't want to see you dead and I don't think you want to be dead, so if you agree to calm down some I'll take you home with me. It won't be a soft life but it will be a free life and a much more interesting life than you have here. And, you won't become puppy chow. But if you still want to act crazy I'll just walk away and let them do what they will with you. You decide."

The black stared at him for a couple of minutes, but not in a hostile way, then reached his head over the railing and nuzzled Timbre's neck.

"That is damest thing I ever saw," the owner said from behind Timbre. "How you do that?" he asked.

"I have no idea, but the son-of-a-gun seems to understand everything I say to him. And I bet he's never even heard English before. This is even a first for me. I've always been a fair hand with horses but this goes far beyond anything I've ever experienced. I'm even a little spooked by this," Timbre told him, scratching his head. After a couple of minutes passed with Timbre staring at the horse and contemplating, Timbre asked, "Would you consider selling him to me, and if yes, how much do you want for him?"

I give you fair price to take him. There nothing I can do with him," the rancher happily agreed. "I just glad to get that crazy horse off my property before he kill someone." And so with the help of Hilga the deal was struck.

The journey wasn't an easy one and there were times when Timbre regretted buying the crazy bastard, but for the most part the big black stood by his bargain and behaved himself--- most of the time. He was a very moody horse, sometimes he was docile and at other times meaner than a wounded bear. As hard as Timbre tried he couldn't figure him out.

"Hey!, any of you guys know where there's a stable around here?" Timbre shouted to a few men standing around on the pier as he led the Black off the gangplank.

"Yeah, about four blocks down and to your right," one of the rough looking men yelled back over his shoulder.

"Thanks," Timbre yelled, as he lifted his duffle bag and threw it over his shoulder.

"You know, you should be carrying this bag and not me. In case you don't know it, you're the beast of burden." The big black slightly turned his head toward Timbre and snorted. "Screw you too," Timbre mumbled under his breath. By now he was used to talking to the black as if he understood him---and maybe he did.

The stable was roughly were the dock worker had said it would be. Sitting out front was an older man smoking a pipe. He didn't look like he'd shaved in a week and he smelled a lot like a horse. When he stood Timbre could see that he was short and was going bald. It was hard to judge his age because although his face was wrinkled he had the sharp eyes of a younger man.

"You looking to board that big black of yorn?" He asked Timbre as they walked up closer to the barn.

"Yep, if you have an empty stall I'd like to leave him here for maybe a week or so."

"That will be two bits a day which includes food and a rub down."

"Sounds fair, but I have some stipulations."

"What the hell is stip--- whatever?

"It means that I have some rules that you would have to follow."

"I'm listening," the stable owner said, suspiciously, squinting his eyes.

"One: keep him separated from the other horses--- and humans too while I'm thinking about it. Two: I'll come by every day and feed and brush him. He don't take to kindly to strangers. Three: Don't get into the stall with him, he hasn't been house broken yet."

"He's that mean, hey?"

"Meaner."

"In that case the price went up to a dollar a day and you pay for any damage he causes."

6

"Deal," Timbre agreed handing the old man a dollar for the day.

"There's an empty stall in the back of the barn you can put him in and there's food up in the hayloft."

Timbre led the black to the back stall and then guided him in. Leanin' in close to his head Timbre told him: "Listen to me. I have to gather supplies and buy a saddle for our trip. It's going to take me a couple of days to gather all we'll need so you'll have to stay here for a while. I'll be by every day to feed you and see that you're doing alright. So for God's sake behave yourself. I mean it. Don't cause any problems for me. He promised to leave you alone and so you do the same with him. We don't need any trouble."

"You always talk to your horse like that?" the stable owner asked from behind Timbre.

"I didn't hear you walk up," Timbre told him turning around. "I guess I do. Don't know if he understands me but it calms him down some to hear my voice."

Timbre didn't feel like explaining the connection he had with his horse, besides who would believe it, he hardly believed it himself so he left it at that.

"If you say so," the older man said. "I heard you say something about a saddle and some supplies."

"You know where I can get them?" Timbre asked, already knowing that the older man knew where he could get whatever he needed.

"You can get a saddle and bridle right next door here. Tell my brother I sent you. Two blocks down you can get all the supplies you need at the Emporium, just tell my cousin I sent you."

"Sounds like your family has the horse trade all sewed up."

"Not quite but we're working on it. Tell you what young feller, since you're going to give my family so much business

I'll save you some time and climb up to the loft and throw some hay down to your horse. Don't worry I won't get in there with him, you convinced me he's nuts. You can feed him some oats when you get back"

"Nutso? That sounds like a good name for him," Timbre pondered. "Thanks for the information. I'll see you later. With that Timbre backed out of the stall and headed next door.

There was no sign on the door but a saddle hung from some ropes in front of the place letting the people know, the ones that couldn't read, what was sold in there. Timbre eased the door open and stepped inside. It wasn't lit as well as he would've liked but he could see well enough once his eyes adjusted. There were all sorts of saddles and bridles strewn around the place and off toward the back of the room was a near duplicate, except for being a little older, of the stable owner next door.

He stopped his work at a bench when he spotted Timbre and laying down his tools he came around the bench.

"Welcome young fella. And what can I interest you in today?"

"The old timer next door told me you were his brother but didn't mention that you were twins."

"Careful with that old timer shit, boy. His name is Roger and I'm Pete and we ain't twins. Now what can I do for you?" Pete asked sounding a little miffed.

"First off, I want to apologize for the old timer remark, I certainly didn't mean any offense," Timbre told him, not wanting to get on the bad side of him right off. After all he had to do business with him.

"Apology accepted. So what do you need?" Pete asked, softening up a bit and getting right down to business.

"I'll need a saddle and two halters."

"I think I can accommodate you. What kind of saddle you looking for? A roping saddle or just a comfort saddle?"

"A comfort saddle. I don't plan on doing any roping."

You'll find them at the front of the store and to your left. Have a look at them and tell me if any of them suit you."

Timbre turned and took about ten steps and turned to his left. There were about six or seven saddles lined up on wooden horses that he thought would suit him. After examining them he settled on one. It was just a bare bones saddle, nothing fancy.

"You think you could customize this saddle if I told you what I want done to it?"

"Probably, but it will cost you extra," Pete said, shrewdly looking Timbre over.

"That's fine. Just so it don't cost me too much extra," Timbre told him, noticing how Pete had looked him over.

"So what is it you want me to do to that saddle?"

"First: I'd like a little extra padding on the seat. I have a long ride ahead of me and don't want a sore backside when I get there. Second: I'd like a couple of hooks placed here and here he told him pointing at spots on the saddle. Third: I'd like you to put a couple of compartments here and here so that they're not very noticeable. Think you can do all that?"

"Can and will, if you're a mind to pay for it."

"How much will it cost me?"

The old man contemplated on it for a couple of minutes and then gave Timbre a price. It was much higher than it should've been and they both knew it. Timbre could see that Pete was expecting him to haggle over it and how surprised he was when he didn't.

"It's a deal under two conditions. One: You have the saddle ready in two days, and Two: You make me a belt for my pants to my specifications, and three: I'll bring you a pair of boots and I want you to put knife sheaths in them," Timbre counter offered.

"Agreed," Pete quickly shot back before Timbre could add anything else. "Now where's the horse so I can measure it for the saddle?" Pete asked, anxious to get to it. "And, when you bring me the boots bring me the knives you're going to put in them so I can measure them to fit. You want me to put the sheaths on the inside of the boot facing the legs or the outside facing your pants?"

"On the outside. And my horse is next door with your brother but you can't measure him. You'll just have to eyeball him and do the best you can."

"What's wrong with him that I can't get any measurements?" Pete asked, suspiciously.

"Ask your brother when you get over there, he'll explain everything to you. Now, where's the Emporium?" Timbre asked, in a hurry to get on his way.

"About six or seven blocks straight down from here. It'll be on your right. You can't miss it. And tell…."

"Your cousin you sent me," Timbre finished for him. And don't forget to talk to your brother before you mess with that horse." Timbre reminded him as he walked out the door.

Timbre turned right when he came out of the saddle shop and headed toward the Emporium. On his way he noticed a bank on the left side of the street and decided he was going to need more spending cash. He had been going through his pocket money mighty quick lately. Entering the bank he noticed that it was nearly empty at this time of day and had a clear shot to the teller behind the counter.

"What can I do for you, Sir?" the middle aged man who was wearing spectacles and reading something asked Timbre, looking up at him.

"I'd like to write out a draft for five-hundred dollars, drawn from the Los Angles Bank of Commerce in Los Angles. If you will be so kind to oblige me?" Timbre answered him, writing out the draft.

"I'd need to see some sort of identification first and of course I'll need to wire for approval from your bank in Los Angeles, which won't get here till early afternoon tomorrow. If all goes well you can pick up your money around two o'clock. Is that agreeable with you, Sir?" The teller asked expecting Timbre to turn around and walk out. After all not many rough looking men came in and asked for that large amount of money.

"Here's a letter from the bank manager in LA introducing me," Timbre told him, reaching into his jacket and pulling out the letter.

The teller examined the letter carefully and then asked, "Do you have anything else to verify that this is you?

Timbre looked at him and thought that it was a good thing he had learned to control his temper in Tibet because this weasel was starting to get on his nerves

"Let me see," Timbre said to himself out loud in an annoyed voice while searching through his pockets. "Will this do?" he asked producing his ticket from the ship that had brought him into Frisco.

The teller examined the ticket for a while then looked up and was about to say something about the ticket but thought better of it when he saw the look in Timbre's eyes.

"This will do just fine. Come back tomorrow at two and we'll have your money ready for you, if everything checks out of course. Oh, and in case you're not aware of it there will be a five dollar charge for the transaction. Is that agreeable with you?" The teller asked in a subdued voice.

"That will be fine," Timbre told him in a gruff voice. He figured if the teller was a little afraid of him things would go much smoother tomorrow.

"Thank you for your business," the teller said as Timbre left the bank. Glad to see the dangerous looking man leave.

Timbre continued on to the Emporium looking into the shops along the way. When he came within a half block of the Emporium he spotted it, which wasn't very hard to do. All sorts of goods lined the sidewalk in front of the store and of course the big sign that hung from the porch said it all too. SELLERS EMPORIUM.

Timbre walked through the open front doors and the first thing he noticed was that it was a lot bigger inside than it looked from the outside. Glancing around he was sure that they'd have everything he needed--- and a lot of things he didn't need.

As he walked around the store he picked things off the shelves, mostly clothes at first. He needed a whole change of clothing, his European cloths wouldn't do very well on the trail.

"May I help you, Sir?" A man that looked a lot like Roger and Pete but younger and taller asked him.

"I believe you can. Your cousins, Roger and Pete, highly recommended your establishment to me. I'll be needing a passel of supplies. I already have the clothes now I need boots and some guns. Do you sell guns? Timbre asked, handing him the clothes he had gathered.

Of course. I believe I can supply you with everything you'll be needing," he told Timbre, handing over the clothes to a clerk that seemed to magically appear by his side. "Bring these to the counter then come back while I escort this gentleman around," He told the clerk. Turning back to Timbre he motioned him to follow him.

"By the way, my name is Carl, and you are?" Carl asked, sticking out his hand.

"Timbre," he answered, taking the offered hand.

"Nice to meet you," Carl told him. "Now let me see," Carl pondered with his hand on his chin. "Ah yes, the guns are this way. We have the finest selection of all the latest firearms available."

Timbre examined the display case that Carl led him to and was impressed by the selection of guns that were displayed. After looking them over thoroughly he said to Carl, "I'll take two of these new Colt 45's, that Henry 45 repeating rifle, that Greener shotgun, ten boxes of 45 ammunition and two boxes of shotgun shells. Also, two holsters, a scabbard for the rifle and an ammunition belt to put the holsters on. I'll also take that Bowie knife and two of those skinning knives." Timbre said, pointing to them as he walked down the knife display. "You have any of them folding knives that I've heard about?" Timbre asked, looking in the cases for one.

"I believe we just got a shipment in. I'll send one of my clerks to fetch a couple for you to examine," Carl said, motioning to the clerk behind the counter to go in the back and fetch them. "You see anything else you'd like while my clerk is fetching the folding knives?" Carl asked, anxious to sell more good to this stranger. This was turning out to be one of the biggest single sales he'd had in quite a while.

"Yeah. How about that bullwhip hanging there? You got a 12 footer?" Timbre asked eyeing a couple of them hanging from the ceiling.

"We sure do. If you don't mind my asking, do you know how to use one of them?" Carl asked, curiously. "They can do you a lot of damage if not used properly."

"I worked as a bull whacker for a time and learned how use one fairly well. I don't plan on roping anything but if I do need a rope the bull whip will do just fine," Timbre told him.

"Ahh, here's your selection of folding knives," Carl exclaimed as the clerk appeared with a bunch in his hands.

Timbre examined them and chose three small ones and one bigger one. By this time there were two clerks carrying all of Timbre's stuff.

"Now, what else can I show you?" Carl asked.

"Boots, some camping gear, and food stuff for the trail," Timbre told him as Carl made for the boot section.

"What kind of boots would you like?" Carl asked. Would you like the ones with the high heels or would you like the ones with the lower heels? The lower heels are more comfortable for walking, that is if you plan to do a bit of walking."

"I'll take the ones with the lower heels, if you have them in my size?"

"Very good," Carl answered him. "I'm sure we have your size, we have most sizes."

Thirty minutes later one of Carl's clerks was tallying up the damage while Carl looked on.

"That will be three hundred, and---oh hell let's just call it three hundred even since you've been such a good customer to my family. How would you like to pay for it? We take cash or check. Of course in order to pay by check you'd have to have an account with the local bank," Carl smiled.

"I'll pay cash. Half now and half when you deliver all this gear to your cousin's stable."

"And when would you like it delivered?" Carl asked, as he watched Timbre peel off $150.00 from a roll of bills.

"Let's say around ten AM three days from today." Timbre told him. "I'll take the clothes, the boots, and the knives with me now. If you don't mind?"

14

"Not at all I'll have my man wrap them up for you immediately. Carl said, gesturing to his clerk who was already wrapping them up. "Everything else will be at the stable on Friday morning at ten. In fact I'll deliver your goods personally," Carl assured him, shaking his hand again.

"Nice doing business with you," Timbre told him.

"The pleasure was all mine," Carl answered, and meaning it, as he still pumped Timbre's hand.

"One other thing," Timbre said, pulling his hand loose. "Can you direct me to the closest decent hotel?"

"I sure can. When you go out the front doors make a right and then go down three blocks. At the intersection of the third block make a left, two blocks further down you'll see the Grand Hotel on your right. It's a decent hotel with reasonable rates. Tell the man at the desk I sent you."

"Is he your brother or your cousin?" Timbre smiled.

"Neither," Carl laughed. "I own it."

"Well that's a new one," Timbre chuckled, as he waved goodbye and left.

The hotel was just where Carl had said it would be. After checking in he carried his own duffle bag and packages up to his room. After throwing everything on the bed he gave the room a quick look over. He had to admit that Carl hadn't been lying. The place was clean and looked comfortable. Plus, the rates had been very reasonable. Feeling hungry Timbre left the room and went looking for a restaurant.

For the next two days Timbre examined the town and found it to be very interesting and exciting, just as he'd remembered it. The food was excellent and the night life was entertaining. The money that he signed a draft for had arrived just as the teller said it would and he collected it with no trouble. He also made sure that he took a trip to the stables every day to feed and check up on Nutso who seemed to behaving himself nicely. Timbre also took the time to shoe Nutso. He thought it was going to be a nightmare, but the big black surprisingly cooperated. He also stopped to check up on how his saddle was coming along and to buy a couple of pack bags to carry his stuff in. He also purchased a saddle tree and two pads, one for Nutso and one for the pack mule he planned to buy, if he could convince Nutso into not killing it. He also dropped off the boots and knives so Pete could fit them properly.

On the third day Timbre showed up early in the morning at the saddle shop wearing his new trail clothes, which still felt kind of stiff to him. He was there to pick up his saddle, the belt, his new boots, and the rest of the gear he had ordered from Pete.

Pete presented him with his modified gear with a proud look on his face. Timbre carefully checked over everything and concluded that they were exactly what he had ordered. While Timbre paid Pete the money he owed him he complemented him on his craftsmanship, which made Pete beam with pride. Then he put on his new boots, which felt comfortable even with the two knives hidden in them, thanked Pete, picked up his stuff and left.

Carrying his gear next door he entered the stable and nodded to Roger who was mocking out a stable.

"Hey Roger, can you clear out that corral out back? I want to put Nutso in it for a while."

"Sure thing," Roger answered. Timbre thought that asking Roger to do that for him was going to cost him extra but Roger looked more than anxious to accommodate him. "You going to try and ride that beast?" Roger asked as he headed to the corral. "This I gotta see," he chuckled.

Timbre walked behind Roger till he came to Nutso's stall. Placing his gear down he walked into the stall and started talking to his horse.

"Listen, today is a very special day. I don't think you ever had a saddle put on you before, much less someone on your back, so we'll start out real slow. And, I would appreciate it if you didn't try to kill me. The sooner we get through this the better it will be for the both of us. Do we have a deal?" Timbre asked, hoping that this time the big black really did understand him.

Nutso turned his head slightly toward Timbre and if Timbre didn't know better he would have sworn the horse smiled at him. "You're not going to make this easy on me, are you?" Timbre mumbled as he put the halter around Nutso's head. He then backed Nutso out of the stall and lead him to the empty corral. Once in the corral Timbre went back and got the saddle and blanket while Nutso stood there watching him closely.

"Okay. First I'm going to put this blanket on you and see how that goes." Saying that Timbre placed the blanket over the big blacks back. "Now that wasn't so bad, was it?" Timbre asked, as he reached down for the saddle. As Timbre was straightening up he saw the blanket fly over his head. "What the hell?" Timbre shouted. "Come on, stop screwing around. Let's try this again," Timbre told him retrieving the blanket and placing it on his back again. "Now leave it there," Timbre told him as he started to bend over for the saddle again.

Halfway bent over Timbre quickly stood up straight just in time to catch Nutso about to rid himself of the blanket again. "Stop right there!" Timbre shouted, stopping Nutso before he could rid himself of the blanket.

"I'm only going to tell you this once," Timbre said to him angrily. "If you don't let me saddle you and ride you you're of

17

no use to me. We had a deal and if you're not going to honor it I'll dump your butt right here and take the next stage out. Which, by the way would be way more comfortable and faster than riding your ass all the way South. I'm just doing all this so I can take you along. You might think that what you're doing is funny, but I don't. We got a lot of miles to cover and no time for clowning around. Now let's try this again." With that said Timbre bent down, grabbed the saddle and placed it on the black's back. Nutso stood still as Timbre cinched the saddle, but Timbre could tell that the horse was becoming nervous. As smart as Nutso was, he was still unsure of this new experience.

"Okay, I'll let you walk around until you get used to the new feeling of having something on your back." With that said Timbre led the black around the corral by his halter until Nutso got comfortable with the saddle on his back. "Now comes the hardest part," Timbre crooned to the black while stroking his head. After he was sure that Nutso had settled down, he told him. "Now I'm going to get on your back. Hold still," Timbre whispered as he mounted him.

At first the black just stood frozen in place not knowing how to react to the weight on his back. Timbre thought to himself that everything was working out fine, that is until he put his heels to the black's flanks to get him to walk, that's when all hell broke loose. Timbre held on for dear life as the black went berserk and tried to lunch him into the air---which he did about thirty seconds later.

Timbre got lucky and landed feet first before going into a forward roll and then slamming hard onto his back, knocking the wind out of him. It had been a long time since he'd been thrown from a horse and as he lay there trying to catch his breath it came back to him how painful it was.

As Timbre lay there staring at the sky, getting his breath back, the black walked over to him and nudged him with his nose. "I'm still alive no thanks to you," Timbre gasped, grabbing on to the Nutso's lead and pulling himself up. "You rest up while I take care of some things," Timbre told him sarcastically as he limped out of the corral.

"That horse of you'rn sure has a lot of spirit," Roger told him laughing. "You going to try that again? I sure would like to see that. I'm guessing your voice ain't as soothing as you thought," Roger said, still laughing, as he following him.

"Piss off," Timbre told him, while rubbing his leg and walking to the front of the barn. That made Roger laugh even harder.

As Timbre reached the front of the barn, the wagon with his supplies pulled up with Carl and one of his clerks sitting up on the wagon seat. "What the hell happened to you?" Carl asked, looking down at Timbre, noticing the dirt on his clothes and the limp.

"He had a little run in with his horse," Roger answered from behind Timbre. "Guess who won?"

"Don't have to guess, I can see from here who won. Where do you want this stuff?" Carl asked, as he climbed down and his clerk jumped into the back of the wagon.

"You can set the stuff down by the door," Timbre told him as the clerk started to hand things down to Carl and Roger.

When they finished unloading Carl said to Timbre, "Would you like to check it over and make sure everything you ordered is there?"

"Don't mind if I do," Timbre remarked as he started sifting through the packages. "Seems to me that everything I ordered is accounted for," Timbre told him satisfied, while he dug into his pocket for the money he owed Carl.

"Nice doing business with you," Carl smiled, as Timbre handed him the $150 he owed him. Timbre threw the clerk a silver dollar as Carl placed the money in his wallet. "You going to try to ride your horse again? Word is he's plum loco. If you are I'd like to hang around and watch, that is if you wouldn't mind?" Carl asked, smiling.

"I ought to charge you guys an admission fee to watch," Timbre said, as Pete walked up.

"Am I too late for the show?" he asked his brother.

"Well brother, I'm afraid you missed the first half of it. It was short but exciting. Maybe the second half will be longer now that this young fella is getting the hang of it," Roger chuckled.

"How did that saddle feel ta you, young fella," Pete asked Timbre. "Were you on it long enough ta tell?" He chuckled, making everyone else laugh, except Timbre.

"It was like sitting in my ol' Ma's lap," Timbre told him, shaking his head and heading back to the corral. He had thought of a couple of things to say to them but instead decided to ignore them. He knew that they were just funin' him, but it got on his nerves never-the-less.

The big black saw Timbre coming and walked over to greet him with his head hung down, looking like he was feeling guilty for throwing Timbre into the dirt.

"We are going to have to try this again. Now you know what to expect so try not to panic because I have no wish to eat dirt again."

Timbre slowly mounted the big black and could feel the tension running through his flanks. Gently he touched his heels to the horse's sides and held on tight. Instead of going crazy, as Timbre expected, Nutso slowly moved forward.

"That a boy," Timbre softly said to him, patting him on the neck. "A little bit faster now," he told him as he dug his heels in a little deeper.

Nutso responded and picked up the pace until he was trotting around the corral at a goodly pace. It felt like the horse was enjoying himself after being cooped up for so long. But what really was surprising to Timbre was how well Nutso was responding to Timbre's nudging of his knees. If Timbre pressed with his right knee and gently tugged right on his halter line Nutso would turn right. The more pressure Timbre would press with his knee the sharper the turn. By the end of the hour it seemed like they were moving as one. It was like Nutso could read his mind.

"Good boy," Timbre said as he dismounted. "I guess I don't have to use a bit on you after all. I'm relieved that I don't have to try and put one in your mouth. I'm pretty sure that will save us both a lot of pain."

"Well, that was disappointing," Roger exclaimed, from the edge of the corral.

"You can say that again," Pete chimed in. "That was a big waste of my time."

"Sorry to disappoint you fella's but I'll try harder next time to break my neck so you two can have a good laugh," Timbre smiled, walking out of the corral.

"I for one was not disappointed," Carl said walking up beside Timbre. "I never saw a horse respond to a rider the way that big black responded to you. In fact I've never seen a horse like that period. He's magnificent. Would you consider selling him?"

I think not. I put too much work into him to part ways with him now. But if I ever do decide to sell him I'll keep you in mind," Timbre told him, knowing that was never going to happen.

"If you wont sell him can you at least tell me where you got him? Maybe I can buy one just like him," Carl asked.

"I bought him in the Netherlands, that's overseas in case you're wondering."

"Never been there but I've heard of it. A little too far for me to travel for a horse though. Well, you know where to find me if you ever change your mind about selling him. "I'll give you a good price for him," Carl smiled. "Nice meeting you, and thanks for your business. Anytime you're back this way come in and see me. I'll even give you a discount, even though I'll lose money doing that."

"You lose money? I highly doubt that," Timbre smiled.

"You know me all to well my friend," Carl laughed, while climbing up onto the wagon seat beside his clerk. "You have a nice trip and take care of yourself," Carl waved as the wagon pulled away.

Timbre watched Carl slowly roll away, then started to load his packs with all his new gear. The guns he strapped on, then fished out the ammunition from the pack and loaded them. He hefted them in his hands and found them to be well balanced. He couldn't wait to try them out. The pig sticker he stuck in his pant belt, he'd get around to adjusting that later. The bigger folding knife he put in his front pocket and the littler ones he placed in the secret compartments that he had Pete sew into his belt.

"You fixing to leave now young fella?" Roger asked.

"In a while. First: How much will you take for that mule over there?" Timbre asked, nodding toward a big gray mule in a stall that Timbre had been eyeing.

"He's a good one, but ain't you afraid that horse of yours will try to do him in?" Roger asked.

"Let me worry about that."

"Okay, no skin off my back if you want to waste your money. I'll take seventy-five dollars for him, and that's a bargain," Roger added.

"Fifty dollars and it's a deal," Timbre countered, digging into his pocket for the money.

"You drive a hard bargain but I'll take the fifty," Roger agreed, still feeling like he got the best of the bargain.

"I'll be right back," Timbre told him, handing him the money and heading for the corral.

Nutso was standing by the railing waiting for him, anxious to see what came next. "Okay, here's the deal. I have a lot of gear to take along with us. You have a choice: You can either carry me and all the gear or I can buy a mule to carry it for us. If I buy the mule you'll have to get along with him. No biting, no kicking, no rough stuff. What say you?" Timbre waited for some sign from Nutso, hoping he agreed to his terms. After all he already bought the mule.

Receiving no sign from the big black and so not knowing what the big black was thinking Timbre had no choice but to bring the mule to Nutso and see how he reacted to him. Walking back into the barn Timbre saw that Roger had already backed the mule out of the stall and had put the halter on him.

"Thanks Roger," Timbre told him taking hold of the mules lead. "Well, here goes nothing," He said and walked the mule toward the corral, all the while not taking his eyes off Nutso, looking for any sign as to what the big black planned to do.

Timbre brought the mule right up to the fence post and stood there waiting for Nutso to make a move. The big black stared at the mule for a bit and then walked up to him and smelled him. After sniffing him a couple of times he then backed off and calmly walked away.

"I thought you said that horse was mean? He doesn't seem very mean to me," Roger said from behind him. "Seems like he accepted that mule without much of a fuss."

"That he did. Mm mm, maybe I better change his name," Timbre thought out loud. "He sure ain't the killer that he used to be. Okay, let's get this mule loaded up and I'll be on my way."

With Rogers help, putting the saddle tree on the mule and loading all his gear onto it only took Timbre thirty minutes. "Well, thanks for everything Roger, see you around," Timbre waved, after mounting Nutso and leading the mule out.

"Drop by anytime if you're in the neighborhood," Roger waved back.

CHAPTER

2

Timbre had decided to take the stage road that led to Los Angeles instead of going across country which was the shorter route. The stage route was well trodden, with the ocean and white beaches on his right and the rolling hills to his left. Every twenty-five miles, take or give a couple of miles, there were rest stops where the stage changed horses. It also gave the customers a chance to eat, take care of their personal business, and stretch their legs. Timbre planned on taking advantage of those rest stops. He was going to try and avoid sleeping on the ground as much as possible. He thought to himself how soft he had become traveling through Europe and Asia. Even the monastery, where he spent a couple of years, had beds. Not real comfortable beds, but at least they were off the ground.

After clearing the city and traveling some miles beyond it Timbre dismounted, walked a ways off the road and checked his new pistols. He wasn't as fast as he used to be, he was out of practice, but the pistols shot true and that was good enough for him. He figured with some practice he would be able to handle them quicker but for now he was satisfied with his performance.

Going back to Nutso, who was a might skittish from hearing the gunshots, he pulled out his new Henry. He noticed that the mule was still calm enough and figured the mule had been around gunfire before. He walked back to where he had shot his pistols and shot the Henry a number of times and concluded that it was right on the mark. Except for the elevation controls it had fixed sites.

Walking back to the big black who had calmed down, he told him, "Smell this," and placed the barrel of the rifle under his nose. The black nickered and pulled back a little. "That's gun powder. You should get used to the smell and the sound of a gun. We might be needing to use it some time."

With that said, Timbre took hold of Nutso's lead and with the big black watching him closely let go with another round from the rifle. The rifle bucked in his hand, the recall sending the barrel towards Timbre's head. At the same moment that the rifle went off Nutso reared up pulling Timbre off balance and saving him from a nasty smack in the face from the rifle barrel. Nutso had pulled loose from Timbre and backed away from him a bit.

"Well, nobody ever accused me of being overly smart," Timbre said to the big black. "That wasn't one of the brightest things I've ever done. But you get the idea now of what this thing sounds like. Okay, it's time to go before I do something else stupid."

With that Timbre re-sheathed the rifle and climbed on board of Nutso. He took hold of the lead of the mule, who was just standing there studying both of them, and continued on at a slow walk. Every couple of miles Timbre would dismount, tie the mules lead to the saddle, and walk in front of the big black. It felt good to stretch his legs once in a while.

"Sun's going down, doesn't look like we'll make the station tonight, we'll be camping out doors," Timbre stated, looking around for a good camping site. "That looks like a good place to camp. Up on that clump of grass."

Timbre led the pair about thirty yards off the road to a plot of grassy land. He unsaddled the big black and unpacked the mule. He then hobbled the mule but left Nutso alone. For some reason he didn't think Nutso would wonder off, or step on him while he slept.

Making a small fire he cooked himself a pan of beans and a couple of slices of bacon while his animals grazed. After dinner he scraped his dish and pot clean, rinsed them with a little water from his canteen and then laid out his bedroll. When he was satisfied that nothing was going to poke him when he laid down he pulled out a feed bag and put some oats into it. He fed Nutso first and then the mule.

"Tomorrow we'll make better time now that you have your legs under you and I'm more or less used to the road again," he told Nutso.

His first night sleeping on the ground after so many years of using a bed was not a pleasant one and he was up earlier than the sun. He had cooked and eaten his breakfast, saddled Nutso, repacked his gear on the mule and was ready to travel twenty-minutes after the sun came up. As promised they made better time the second day. Nutso took to the road like he was born to it and the mule kept up with him with no problem. By noon they hit the first stage stop. He stopped there and had lunch and chatted with Fred, the station manager.

By the time he finished with his meal and talked some it was late in the afternoon. Timbre asked Fred how far the next station was. Fred told him that the next stage stop was about twenty-two miles further on and he didn't think that

27

Timbre could make it before dark. After dark the place was locked up tight and he doubted that the manager there would take too kindly to Timbre disturbing his rest. He suggested to Timbre that it would be better for him to stay the night and that he and his animals could sleep in the barn. He also stated that he would really appreciate the company so they'll be no extra charge for the use of the barn.

Timbre accepted his offer and stabled and fed his animals. The rest of the night, until it was time to turn in, was spent sitting around swapping tales with Fred who had led an interesting life before settling down here at the station. Fred also filled him in on what was going on in the country since Timbre had left.

That night Timbre slept in the hay loft and had a decent night's sleep. The next morning he had breakfast with Fred, said his good-byes and was on his way again.

After that Timbre was on schedule to hit every stage depot before dark. As he worked his way South he occasionally met up with some of the stages at the way stations and chatted with some of the passengers over lunch. All in all it was a pleasant journey for him. That is until he came to a small town that was close to the end of his journey. He was more than familiar with this town and had some old friends there. He immediately headed for a small tavern at the end of the main street that he had bought for an old buddy that he'd once trapped with.

Timbre tied the mule to Nutso and then left Nutso untied. He then looked around at the few people walking the streets. It was high noon and siesta time so the few stores that were open were kinda deserted. Timbre walked through the front rickety doors of the tavern and just stood at the entrance letting his eyes adjust to the dark room. The first thing he noticed, when his eyes adjusted to the dim light, was a slim gent all dressed in black with a six gun strapped to his leg sitting at the corner table and sipping a beer. His black hat sat low on his forehead so his face was in shadow but Timbre could tell that he was watching the front door from beneath the brim of his hat. He wore his gun like a shootist would wear it and that made the hairs on the back of Timbre's neck bristle. Everything about the man screamed trouble. Also, there was something about that gent that looked very familiar to Timbre but before he could place him he heard a familiar voice that he hadn't heard in many a year shout at him.

"Is that really you, Tim," the heavy set bearded man that was behind the bar shouted. Only his closest friends called him Tim.

Coming from around the bar the heavy set man with big beefy arms and a beer belly lumbered up to him and gave him a big bear hug.

"Yeah, it's me you big buffalo. Unhand me, your breaking my ribs," Timbre huffed trying to push the bartender away.

Letting him loose the bartender joked, "How can I break your ribs, I could hardly get my arms around you? Seems like you've been eating your way around the world. When did you get back? How long has it been, five, six years?"

"More like seven. I've been just traveling around the world tasting its culture. If you think I'm bad now you should've seen me when I first landed in Frisco. I've lost a good deal of weight since being on the trail, can't you tell by my clothes. Look how loose they fit," Timbre told him pulling at the waist of is pants. But enough about my fat, how have you been? It looks like you've been eating regular yourself," Timbre laughed, patting him on he belly.

"I'm getting by. This ain't no gold mine but it puts food in my belly. Hey, I'm sorry I don't have the money I owe you but I can give you part of it," Frank said, looking down, feeling a little ashamed.

"Did I ask you for anything? I'm not here to collect any money from you Frank. I just stopped by to say hello. Besides, what I gave you wasn't a loan, it was a gift. Now I don't want to hear anything else about money, but I will take a beer."

"Maria! Bring my friend a beer," Frank shouted over his shoulder.

As if she was just waiting for Frank to yell for her an older but attractive Mexican lady appeared from behind a curtain that hung behind the bar. Grabbing a mug from under the counter she filled it with beer and brought it over to them.

"Timbre, meet my wife Virginia,' Frank proudly smiled.

"Nice to meet you, Ma'am," Timbre half bowed removing his hat.

"Virginia, this is the man I told you about. The one who made this all possible.

"Won't you sit down, Senior?" she asked, indicating the chair to his right and setting the beer down on the table in front of the chair.

"I'm sure you two have a lot to catch up on so I'll leave you two alone for now while I cook dinner. You will join us for supper, Si'?"

"My pleasure," Timbre smiled sitting down.

"Nice meeting you Senior Timbre," she smiled, as she turned and walked away.

"Same here." Timbre replied to her back as she walked away. "When the hell did you get married and how did you find a woman who would want you?" Timbre jokingly asked Frank.

"I married her about five years ago. I was quite a catch especially since I was a business owner. And I owe this all to you."

"Again, you owe me nothing. Have you heard from Jake lately?" Timbre asked, sipping his warm beer.

"Me and Jake went fishing about three months ago. Haven't seen him since but I'm sure he's alright. You going to visit him?" Frank asked.

"I was planning to stay a couple of months with him, so yeah. Hey, why don't you come down once I settle in and we'll all go fishing just like ol' times?"

"That sounds like a plan. You can count on it," Frank smiled. "I'll be right back," Frank told him, sliding back his chair and standing up. "I'm hungry. I'll check on our dinner. You're going to love it. Virginia is the best cook in the county."

"Sounds good, I'm a bit hungry myself. I hope she made enough to fill us fat guys up," Timbre laughed.

On his way to the back Frank stopped at the strangers table and Timbre heard him ask, "Can I get you another beer before I go into the back?"

"No thanks. I'll be leaving in a minute or two," the stranger told him in an soft oily voice while staring at Timbre in a strange way.

"Okay. Thanks for dropping in. Come back soon," Frank mumbled, forcing himself to smile. Timbre could tell that the stranger had made Frank nervous and Frank was relieved that he was leaving.

Once Frank disappeared behind the curtain the man in black stood up and walked to the bar. He then turned and faced Timbre. Timbre looked into the strangers dead black eyes and realized that this man's intentions toward him was not friendly.

"Do I know you?" Timbre asked him, tensing up.

"Not directly, but I know you. I've been looking for you for a good number of years but I never thought of looking for you out of the country. Maybe you should of stayed out of the country," he hissed.

"Do I want to know why you were looking for me?" Timbre asked.

"Probably not, but I'll tell you anyway. I've been paid to find and kill you," he smiled.

"May I ask why?" Timbre asked, placing his hand on his belly gun.

"I guess you have a right to know. You pissed my boss off when you shot him up those many years ago up in Wyoming territory."

"I don't remember shooting anyone up there. You sure you got the right man?" Timbre asked, not remembering shooting anyone in Wyoming.

"Oh, I have the right man. Let me refresh your memory: My boss had just finished with having a little fun with some Indian squaw when you came along and shot him in the back. Now do you remember?"

It all came back to Timbre in a flash and he asked, "He lived?"

"Obviously, no thanks to you. After he recovered, and it was touch and go there for a while, he's spared no expense to find you. You know, I'm kinda sorry I did find you. Looking for you was an easy payday. But all good things must come to an end," he frowned.

"How did you find me?" Timbre asked. "If you don't mind telling me?"

"Oh, I don't mind. After searching for you so long I'd like to savor this moment anyway," the gunfighter smirked.

"My boss found out who you were and what you looked like, which wasn't very hard to do, he then hired men from all over the country to keep an eye out for you. Kinda like a bounty but without the posters.

You must really love to travel because every time someone reported seeing you by the time I got there you were gone again. Then you disappeared for all those years and nobody knew where you'd gotten to. We kinda figured that you were dead. Then, out of the blue, as luck would have it, one of those hired men just happened to be on a stage that ran into you at a way station, just outside of Frisco. While he was having coffee he heard the manager there call you by name. Timbre isn't a common name so at the first stop they came to with a telegraph line he wired the information to my boss, who then wired it to me. And, as fate would have it, I just happened to be in this vicinity. Well, maybe just happened is stretching it a might. You see, I was on my way to question your friend Jake, but lucky me, you saved me a trip and most likely saved Jakes life in the bargain. I heard that he's a feisty ol' shit that most likely would've tried something stupid and got himself killed. The strange thing is I didn't know about Frank here being your friend, I just stopped in for a beer. And lo and behold, guess what, fortune dumped you right into my lap"

"What if I pay you double what your boss is paying you to forget you found me?" Timbre asked, trying to bargain with him. Timbre knew that this man was extremely dangerous and wanted no part of trying to best him in a gun fight, especially since Timbre was so out of practice.

"That's a tempting offer but a contract is a contract. Besides, I really like killing people and I've been having a dry spell lately. So anytime you're ready, make your move," he told Timbre, moving his hand slightly toward his gun.

Stalling for time, trying to figure a way out of this mess, Timbre asked him, "I would imagine that there are a lot of people you could be killing. Why the dry spell?"

"Hell, I don't kill just to kill, there's no fun in that. I like to see the look in a man's eyes when he realizes that he's about to loose his life. It's harder than you think to find a man stupid enough to face my gun, unless he's drunk of course; and there's no fun in killing a drunk. They're dead before they know they're dead."

"You must know that your boss is an insane monster and more than deserved to die? The only thing I'm truly sorry for is that my bullet didn't put that sick bastard in the ground for good," Timbre stated, starting to get angry just thinking about that twisted freak.

"Of course I know that he's a sick bastard, but a sick bastard that pays extremely well," the gunfighter smiled

"But are you aware that you're just as sick as he is by doing his dirty work?" Timbre shouted, remembering who this guy was.

Timbre suddenly sprang to his feet while drawing his gun at the same time, hoping to catch the gunman off guard. But even before Timbre cleared leather he felt a bullet smash into his chest like a sledge hammer. The stranger had drawn and fired faster than his eyes could follow.

"Now you've gone and hurt my feelings," the killer said to Timbre's prone body. "By the way, that was most satisfying watching the light go out in your eyes. In that split second you knew you were dead, didn't you?" he asked, not really expecting an answer from a dead man.

Sam came rushing out of the back room at the sound of the shot just in time to see the man in black go out the door.

CHAPTER

3

"Hello Son," the voice of his Father whispered into Timbre's ear.

Timbre snapped open his eyes and the first thing he saw was his dead Father's smiling face.

"I guess this means that I'm dead?" Timbre asked, feeling around for the bullet hole. For some reason he wasn't even a little surprised to see his Father. Somehow he knew that he had died.

"Mostly, but not quite," his Father told him. "You'll be going back shortly but the boss man wants you to know some stuff before you do and I was elected to fill you in."

Timbre was about to say something when a full grown lion came into view and just stood there staring at them for a few seconds before just calmly walking away. Timbre automatically reached for his gun, but it wasn't there.

"What the hell was that," he asked, still startled.

"Oh that," his Fathered laughed. "That takes some time to get used to. You see there's no death up here since we're already dead, by human standards that is. Nothing has to eat, and there's no need for money, in fact just about all human emotion is pointless here, except love that is, so there's no reason for hostilities. It's a little more complicated than that but we don't have time to go into long explanations right now. You'll learn more about this place the next time you come back."

"Is Mom up here too?" Timbre asked, anxious to see her.

"Yep, but the big man thought it wise for you not to see her at this time, something about being too hard to let go when you have to leave again. You'll realize in time that he knows best."

"So what is it that you have to tell me? And couldn't you find an easier way to communicate with me besides having some asshole shoot me?"

"You getting shot wasn't part of the plan. You weren't supposed to run into Fargo for quite a while yet. But, the bosses took this screw up and turned it into a positive experience," his Father told him, looking a little embarrassed.

"Fargo, so that's the asshole's name," Timbre mused, then went on. "You know, whoever is in charge of planning stinks at it. The big boss should fire him and get a new planner. Who's in charge of this place anyway, God?" Timbre asked angrily.

"No, this place isn't heaven. It's close to it but not the real thing. It's more or less a peaceful rest stop so I'd curb your temper up here. What we called the arch angels are in charge of this place. Mostly they do a good job but by God giving people a free will it sometimes messes up their well made plans. And that's where you come in."

"Me? I'm dead. Remember?" Timbre asked, surprised to be part of a plan.

"Let me explain," his Father continued. "Every five-thousand years or so some people are born with powers far beyond what's normal. The Angels keep a close watch on these men, or woman, to see how they handle their gifts. Some choose to ignore their gifts, some use them for evil, and most don't even know they have a gift. And then there are those that use their gifts for good. You my boy have not only used your gifts for good, but enhanced them. So congratulations, you've been chosen to be one of God's hammers. Meaning that your job will be to try and right the screw-ups in God's plans," his Father explained, studying Timbre closely for his reaction.

"I have a couple of questions," Timbre said, thinking on what his Father just told him.

"Fire away, but be forewarned, I don't have a whole lot of answers. After all, I'm relatively new here myself," his Father smiled.

"Okay. First: How are these people chosen to receive these gifts?"

"That's beyond my paygrade, Son. What's your next question?"

"What if I refuse the job?"

"Again, beyond my paygrade. I don't know. Next."

"What am I supposed to do next if I accept the job?"

"That I know," his Father laughed.

"Finally," Timbre laughed with him.

"For now we're going to send you back to your body before they bury you. Then after you're well you go about your life just as you had planned to do. Then things will unfold around you just as they were meant to. Just remember to use the gifts you have when the time comes. When you reach the end of your trail again you'll come back here and you'll be trained to handle other assignments. Oh, and one more thing: That horse of yours isn't crazy. He was placed in your path to help you. And yes, he does understand when you talk to him. Maybe you should change his name, he is a wonder you know? One more thing you should know: The angels have placed other things in your path to help you to survive what's heading your way."

"What's heading my way?" Timbre asked, a little apprehensive.

"Can't tell you. The only thing I can tell you is that it's extremely dangerous so you're going to have to stay sharp at all times."

"Why can't you tell me, especially if you guys want me to survive it?" Timbre asked, confused.

"Because if you knew what's coming you would try to change it and then maybe screw everything up. Is that enough of an explanation for you? You always did have to know everything," his Father said, getting frustrated with all his questions.

"That's part of my gift," Timbre laughed.

"Yeah, yeah," his Father smiled. 'Well, it's your decision, in or out?"

"What do you think?"

"I think it sounds like a lot of fun," his Father smiled.

"Then I guess I'll give it a shot'" Timbre agreed, nodding his head in the affirmative.

"OK then, it's time we got you back. Ready?"

"One more thing, Dad, say hello to Mom for me and tell her I'll see her soon. And Dad, I sure do miss you," Timbre told him with tears in his eyes.

"I've missed you too, Son. I love you. See you soon. And say hello to the boys for me and that I'll see them soon," his Father told him, waving good-bye as Timbre faded away.

CHAPTER

4

Timbre jerked awake and tried to sit up but the pain that shot through his chest caused him to fall back and loudly moan. He heard a door open and turned his head toward the sound and saw Jake entering the room.

Jake had aged some since Timbre had last seen him. His hair was completely gray now, as was his shaggy beard, and his eyes had heavy wrinkles all around them. The color of his eyes were now a dull brownish color and he stood a little hunched over.

"You awake boy?" Jake asked. Timbre tried to answer him but his throat was as dry as a Cactus and all that came out was a croak.

"Don't try to talk just yet. Let me get you some water." Jake told him while walking to the side of the bed and fillin' the empty glass that sat there by the water pitcher. Here, just take little sips at a time," he told him, gently holding the back of his head and putting the glass to his lips.

"How?" Timbre whispered.

"How are you still alive, or how did you get here?" Jake asked, not sure as to what Timbre was asking.

"Here," Timbre barely said.

"After you were shot Frank came running out of his back room just in time to see that gunman walking out the front door. After checking to see if you were dead or alive he ran for the Doctor. At least what they call a Doc in that town. All she was an old mid-wife and not a true Doc. Anyways, that ol' lady said you wasn't breathing and pronounced you dead. Then, Frank being Frank set you into his wagon and brought you here to be buried. Halfway here he heard you starting to moan and reasoned that the old witch had been wrong and that you weren't as dead as she thought. Right away he put the whip to his horse and got you here pronto. Damn near killed that horse too.

'Once here I sent one of the boys lickety-split for a real Doctor. When the Doc got here he took one look at you and couldn't figure out why you were still alive. He told me it was a miracle that you weren't dead. Then he commenced to remove the bullet from your chest, which by the way was a gnat's hair away from your heart. Then he sewed you up and told me it was up to God now whether you lived or died. You've been asleep for about a week now and it was touch and go there for a while. Still is I'm guessing, but it looks like it's now leaning to more alive than dead. You go back to sleep now and I'll have some soup made up for you so when you're ready you can eat something. And boy, it's good to have you back," Jake smiled with tears in his eyes.

"Hey Jake, Timbre rasped. "Thanks, and Dad said to tell you hello." As Timbre drifted off to sleep once again Jake looked at him queer like, wondering if Timbre had really seen Sam.

Months passed while Timbre healed and renewed his strength. It wasn't an easy healing, he suffered through a lot of pain. But finally he was starting to feel like his old self again. Winter had come and gone, if you can call the weather in Southern California winter.

It was a nice warm day with a slight breeze and Timbre was sitting on the porch watching the cow hands working around the place while also observing Nutso and his mule wondering around the corral. He also saw Jake coming toward the porch after his brief trip to town.

"Whatcha' got there?" Timbre asked Jake as he climbed the steps of the porch.

"A letter, for you, and it came all the way from Afreeka," Jake informed him, holding the envelope in the air and waving it at him before handing it to him.

"All the way from Africa? I'll be damned!" Timbre exclaimed, shaking his head in wonderment.

"Who da ya knows in Afreeka?" Jake inquired.

"Can't say until I read it," Timbre told him watching Jake lower himself down onto the empty rocking chair beside Timbre and making himself comfortable.

Jake watched Timbre carefully open the envelope and extract a folded sheet of paper from it. He didn't look away until Timbre started to read it. Jake then leaned back in his rocker, gazed out at nothing in particular, and waited patiently for Timbre to finish reading.

As Jake rocked he thought of how much he loved this season---Spring. He enjoyed watching the rebirth of the land and often times wished that he too could be rejuvenated at the end of every winter. Jake knew that time was running out on him and that he was now a whole lot closer to the end than he was to the beginning. He felt that he had only a couple of more winters left in him and consoled himself with the fact that at least his last winters would be spent here in Southern California where the weather was somewhat tolerable for

41

a man of his years. Jake was grateful that he didn't have to spend his remaining years roaming the mountains in the Northwest. Not that the years he'd spent their weren't good ones, but Jake had been younger then and the winters had been easier for him to take.

Jake's mind wondered back to his youth when he'd been able to travel all night and still be able to stand and fight most of the next day. He smiled when he thought of some of the epic battles he'd taken part in and got to missing the old days again. Jake glanced over at Timbre, who was still reading, and marveled at how much he resembled his old friend Sam, Timbre's Father.

Like his Dad, Timbre stood well over six-feet, with wide shoulders and a barrel chest. He was a big man and had no excess fat on him after his recent ordeal. And, like most men who spent their lives outdoors Timbre wore his hair long in the back, mostly to keep the weather off his neck. The only clue one had to Timbre's thirty-eight years was the strands of silver in his otherwise jet-black head of hair. Even his bushy mustache, which trailed down a couple of inches from the end of his chin, was starting to show some signs of gray in it.

His chin, which was shaped almost perfectly square, had a small indentation in it that was slightly to the right of center. It gave the illusion that his face was slightly crooked. His jaw slightly jutted out, as if it were daring anyone who had a mind to try and put it back in center. Jake believed that if it wasn't for Timbre's bold chin his nose would have remained straighter. As it was Timbre's nose took funny little turns here and there thanks to all those who'd missed his jaw and broke his nose instead. But, the biggest difference between Timbre and his Pa, Jake thought, was their eyes. Timbre's eyes were the color of volcanic soil, while Sam's eyes had always brought to mind a bubbling blue stream.

Sam had told Jake that Timbre favored his Mom in that area. Jake had taken Sam's word for that because he'd never had the pleasure of meeting Sam's wife. Jake didn't consider Timbre a very handsome man but just an attractive one that most people took notice of.

Anytime that Jake daydreamed of the old days, and that was happening more and more frequently, his thoughts would always drift back to Sam and he would miss him terribly. How many times they'd fought together against the Crow, Blackfoot and even against renegade whites, Jake couldn't clearly remember. What did stand out in his thoughts though was the first time he laid eyes on Timbre. Timbre was about seven-years old at the time when Sam had first shown up with him in the Rockies. When Jake had inquired why he'd brought the boy with him this time Sam's answer had been a sad one.

Sam had relayed to Jake how on his trip home he'd found his beloved Valda dead and the boy being looked after by strangers. Since there were no living relatives on either side of their family to watch after the boy Sam stated that he'd be traveling with him from now on. Sam also had given Jake the option of pulling out, with no hard feelings on his part, if the boys presence bothered him.

There'd been a lot of sorrow in Sam's voice when he'd talked about Valda's death. Jake had been touched by Sam's tale but couldn't find any thing to say about it. Jake wasn't big on expressing his emotions: He simply stated that he saw no reason to break-up their partnership. He figured the boy would fit in just fine. Sam had smiled sadly, nodding his gratitude and walked away to attend to their horses.

It was true, Jake had no desire to terminate their friendship. To him Sam was a special human being, different than any other man he'd ever known. There was something about Sam that made decent men trust him with their lives and lesser men want to stay clear of him. Sam had the ability to always know when he was right and was never afraid to act on it regardless of what others might have thought.

Years ago, while the other trappers headed for their annual rendezvous on the Platte River, near the Wyoming-Nebraska border, to sell their winter catch to the representatives of the Eastern fur companies, Sam had always headed East to St. Louis to spend his summers with his wife and son who resided there. On those trips home Sam always took along their winter catch of furs and sold them directly to the cutters, thereby eliminating the middle men. It was no secret that Sam and Jake were getting much more for their furs than the other trappers who were trading on the Platte and this didn't sit well with the furriers who were buying the pelts at the rendezvous. They were getting nervous, afraid that Sam might start a trend that the other hunters might want to copy and that wouldn't be good for their business.

Late one summer, a representative of one of the big fur companies approached Sam in St. Louis and attempted to point out to him the folly of his ways. He told Sam that he didn't think it was a good idea for him to continue with his current way of doing business. He also told Sam that it would be much healthier for him to let Jake do the trading for them on the Platte. After all, it wouldn't do to make the other trappers feel as if they were being cheated. Sam, being Sam, patiently explained to him that he didn't give a damn what the other trappers did. Where they did their trading was their concern and where he did his was his business. Sam made it clear that all he wanted was to be left alone. Of course it's never that simple, nothing ever is when money is involved. It was then that the traders decided that they had to make an example out of Sam and Jake so as to keep the other trappers in line.

The next winter, while Sam and Jake were doing their Trapping, they were set upon by the fur companies' bully-boys. Men that were employed to enforce their rules. These men were killers and cut-throats, most of them bordering on the insane.

Now there was a battle, Jake snickered to himself. They'd fought on the run for three days and on the third day after they'd put a number of those bad boys under, and the odds were slightly more even, they'd stood their ground and fought. The battle soon deteriorated into a knife fight and ended with three more of those cut-throats lying dead and the remaining two making fast tracks for home. After that no one disputed Sam on where he could or couldn't sell his furs. Jake chuckled again, thinking of that little set-to.

"What are you cackling about you old fool?" Timbre asked, folding his letter neatly away.

"I were just rememberin' the first time I lay eyes on yare ugly puss," Jake commented, coming back slowly from the past. "It were right aftar yar pour mother had passed aways. Rest her soul."

"So what's so funny about my Mother dying?" Timbre asked, not taking offense because he now knew that she was happy were she was.

"Nutin', but ya knows how one thought leads ta anothor. I were led ta think of yore Pa an' some of tha good times we'd accumulated togethar."

"Yeah. He was something, wasn't he?" Timbre agreed, putting his hand on Jake's shoulder. "We all had some good times together."

"I'm jus' sorry I warn't with him at tha end'. If I were maybe I coulda stopped those damn savages from layin' him under," Jake said, looking away.

"There was nothing you could've done to save him, besides you had your squaw to look after," Timbre smiled.

"Now ther' wer' a fine woman," Jake told him, "But she warn't much on havin' fun, not like you an' yar Pa was. But, in all fairness ta her, I got to say that she wer' a whole lot more comfortin' durin' the winter months than you and yore Pa was. The winters became mighty unsatisfying after she went under," Jake reminisced.

"You always were a horny old goat," Timbre laughed.

"That may be, but I can still learn you a thin' or two when it comes ta tha ladies."

"I don't doubt that," Timbre laughed.

"Ye best not. Now, what's in that letter?" Jake asked, not able to contain his curiosity any longer.

"You remember that English fella, the one I guided for about ten years ago? We stopped here for a while. Sylvester Remy was his name."

"Oh yeah. He were that crazy fella that talked funny. Tha one who almost got ya kilt about a half dozen times. What's he want?"

"Seems he's in Africa and wants me to join him there."

"What's that fool doin' in Afreeka, and whys he wan' you thar far?" Jake asked, suspiciously.

"He says that after he returned home to England to claim his inheritance he had to stay and put everything in order, then he had to make sure everything was running smoothly. Well, it seems that after all these years he's feeling restless again and figured he was now entitled to another adventure. Says Africa is the perfect place to do some exploring and hunting. Also said that he'll pay me handsomely if I join him there and track for him. He also says that he found me to be a fine companion. Seems he misses my good company," Timbre smiled.

"Well, at leas' he's got tha good sense to realize that yar the best damn tracker that ever lived, although you do cheat a might with that gift of yourn, but that might be tha only sense he's got. Ye take my ad-vice and stay away from that thar lun-tic, he'll get ya kilt far certain."

Timbre smiled inwardly when Jake referred to his gift. Jake was one of the few people still living who knew he had a sixth sense. Jake had become aware of it about the same time Sam had. Timbre had been a boy at the time and had not yet learned how to conceal his special talents like his Ma had warned him to do.

Timbre's mother had been the first to become aware of his strange talents about a month before she'd come down with the mysterious illness that she had succumbed to. Valda started to suspect that Timbre wasn't like other children when he began to predict, and with unfailing accuracy, the arrival of visitor's, or what the weather was going to be like, or any other half a dozen little things like that.

After observing him for a while Valda came to the conclusion that Timbre wasn't aware that he was doing anything out of the ordinary. He was just doing what came natural to him and didn't give any thought to the fact that nobody else could do what he was doing. Valda was still in the process of trying to determine the extent of Timbre's powers when she fell ill. The doctor was called in by the neighbors when she became too weak to get out of bed one morning and Timbre, not knowing what to do, had gone to them for help.

After weeks of probing and administering foul tasting medicines to her the doctor came to a conclusion that she was dying. Why she was dying, he had no idea.

Timbre could still remember the warning his mother had given to him just days before she'd passed away. She'd told him: "Elmo," she always called him by his given name, "people are not yet ready to accept your special talents. They'll not understand them and what folks don't understand they'll fear and that fear will make them a danger to you. So learn to conceal your special gifts from the world. I don't know where or how you acquired your gifts but I'm certain that they were not born of evil. Don't ever neglect them and use them only for good--- or at least don't do harm with them. As soon as I'm strong enough to get out of bed I'll help you to learn how to do that," she'd promised, hugging him tightly to her.

Valda never did get any better and a short time later, with winter barely half over, she passed away in her sleep.

If Timbre dwelt on his mother's passing for too long he would actually start to hurt and the feeling of abandonment he'd felt on that cold winter morning would come flooding back to him.

He remembered how their neighbors, the Cumby's, had been more than kind to him. After they saw to Valda's burial they took him in until Sam would come and fetch him. It was the longest winter that Timbre could remember spending, but finally it came to an end.

Shortly after the ice melted Sam came paddling down the Missouri, busting to see his wife and son. To say that Sam was shocked and crushed when he learned of Valda's death does not do justice to what he actually felt.

At first Sam couldn't accept the fact that his Valda was gone. She'd been fine just a short six-months ago when he'd last seen her. He couldn't understand how anyone so healthy could take ill and die so quickly. But in the end Sam had no choice but to accept his wife's death. What else could he do?

Those were the bleakest days of Timbre's life. Sam had gone on a drinking binge that'd lasted over a month. He totally ignored the existence of Timbre and Timbre had never felt so alone-- not even when he had roamed the great plains of the Southwest by himself. Then, just like that, one morning Timbre stumbled into the Cumby's kitchen for breakfast and there was Sam sitting at the table having a cup of coffee and waiting for him to get up. Sam's mourning had come to an end. He figured it was time to get on with their lives again.

Sam would always love Valda and would forever mourn her loss but somewhere in his drunken state he had come to realize that he had a son, that he loved, and still had to help him to grow into a man. Now he had to make a decision, what to do with Elmo while he was away trapping during the winter?

The idea of leaving Elmo in a boarding school entered Sam's mind but then the thought of coming home and possibly finding his son had also expired from an unknown ailment was too much for Sam to contemplate. He discarded that notion as quickly as it had come to his mind. The next idea that he had was to give up trapping, but the only other thing he was qualified to do was to sail a ship-- and that too would entail leaving Elmo behind. That idea was also quickly scrapped.

Although Sam didn't believe that the wilds were a proper place to raise a civilized boy he loved Elmo too much to leave him behind. After doing a lot of pondering on the matter Sam came to a decision: He decided he would take Elmo with him trapping. After extracting a solemn oath from Timbre that he would keep up with his studies Sam agreed to take him along with him.

Of all the possibilities that Sam had considered the one logical possibility that had never occurred to him was to stay in St. Louis and learn a new profession. Sam was an intelligent and educated man and could've learned a new trade easily, but freedom and adventure was deep in his blood. Not even the great love that he'd felt for his wife had been strong enough to keep him from his wonderings. He was a man who needed adventures to make him feel alive. It was a trait that he passed down to Timbre.

Timbre smiled to himself when he remembered the first thing that he'd demanded of Sam as they paddled away from St. Louis. Timbre was sitting in front of the Canoe, while Sam guided it down the Missouri. He was feeling like an honest-to-God frontiersman. No one had ever felt braver than he had at that moment as he helped paddled down the river toward the great unknown. Putting all the force in his voice that he could muster, he'd yelled: "Dad!"

"What is it Elmo?" Sam had asked, sensing the importance of the moment.

"I don't ever want to be called Elmo again. I hate that name," he'd blurted out.

When there was no immediate response from Sam, Elmo had figured that he'd overstepped his bounds. After all, his Mother had chosen that name for him. So, in a more subdued tone, almost a whine, he added, "All the kids at school make fun of my name."

"Truth be known," Sam stated, after a couple of tense moments had passed, "I was never partial to that name myself. It was your Ma's daddy's name and she loved him enough to want to honor him by naming you after him. He was a good man and it was a fine gesture so I went along with her, though I didn't particularly like the name. You got something in mind that you want to be called?"

"Yes Sir, my friends at school call me Timbre. I sorta got used to that."

"Timbre?" Sam paused, mulling it over. "I suspect it's short for our surname, Timbrewilken?"

"Yes Sir," Timbre had answered, with his voice filled with hope.

"It's got a pleasant enough ring to it. I reckon it will do as well, or better than most, but would it offend you if I still called you Son now and then?"

"No Sir!" Timbre had beamed, throwing out his chest proudly. He now had a new name to go with his new life.

"You listenin' to me?" Jake demanded to know, pulling Timbre back to the present. "Why da ya hav' that silly grin on yar puss for?"

Timbre found that the more he was around Jake, like Jake, he tended to live more and more in the past.

"I was just thinking back to the first time Pa took me with him and how young and ignorant I was back then," Timbre answered.

"Ya might've been young but I don't recollec' ya havin' ever being ignorant. But that's not ta say that ya still can't prove me wrong, 'specially if you decides ta go runnin' off ta Afreeka ta join that thar mad Englishman," Jake told him, getting back to the letter.

"He isn't a madman," Timbre smiled.

"What'd ye call a man who'd hunt Grizzly with a bow if'n he did'n hav' to? Or how 'bout goin' after big cats with a pistol? Or just plain dragging you all over injun territory beggin' ta have your scalps lifted?"

"We didn't do anything that you and my Pa didn't do at one time or another, and we sure as hell didn't drag a kid along with us while we were doing it," Timbre reminded him.

"That's so, but we'd don' it 'cause it were our job, not far tha fun of it. And ya knows it!" Jake loudly stated, beginning to get angry.

"Are you going to sit there and tell me that you and Pa didn't have fun doing what you did?" Timbre asked, smiling.

"No I'm not, but that ain't the point, ya youn' smart alec!" Jake yelled.

"Okay, okay, calm down. I get your drift," Timbre told him, trying to pacify Jake, not wanting him to get all worked up. "Think of me going to Africa as a job. A man needs to work and the pay is good."

"You don' need the money," Jake stated. "You and yar Daddy foun' enough gold ta last ya tha rest of yar lives--- an' then some. I might be tha onliest one who knows that far shor so don' try ta buffalo me with that lame excuse about needing a job. Besides, even if ya were flat busted ya could come live hare with me far tha rest of yor life an' never need another red cent. An I knows of a few others who'd be more than willing ta give ya the shirts off thar backs, so don' go telling me 'bout jobs"

"Thanks for the offer," Timbre sincerely said. "If I ever find myself broke I'll know where to come."

"No need far thanks. It's tha leas' I can offer ya. If it warn't far ya giving some of us ol' trappers the money ta purchase these hare spreads after the Beaver market run dry a lot of us would've gone belly up far shor'."

"You all payed me back with interest, one way or another," Timbre told him. "None of you owe me anything."

"It ain't about paying back, Bub. You gave ta us without a thought of ever getting yar money back. Ya didn' know, or ask, if we could make a go of ranching or shop keeping. Ye gave because ya cared about us. An we'd be glad ta give ta ya for the same reason. Hell, I had ta force ya ta take back tha money ya lent me. Ya knows yar like tha son I never had. When I rolls over all this is going ta be yours anyway," Jake finished, with tears in his eyes, while his hand swept across the horizon,

"If you're going to start bawling I'm getting the hell out of here," Timbre joked, not knowing how to respond to Jake's generosity.

"That'll be tha day when ya sees me bawl, ya Fat-Headed Jackass!" Jake yelled.

"What happened to: "You're like the son I never had?" Timbre laughed.

"Times achange fast, Bub," Jake answered, grinning. "An' talkin' about changin' times, is it safe yet far ya ta tell me where you and yar Pa found all that gold? I've been meanin' to ask ya that question far some time now."

"How come you never asked before?"

"Never thought it were my business. Still don', but I'm too old now ta care 'bout mindin' my own business anymore. I guess curreyiosity is gettin' tha better of me in my Ol' age."

"Black Hills," Timbre simply stated.

"Tha Dakotas?" Jake asked, unbelievingly.

"You know of any others?"

"Ya means ta say that 'cep' far you an yar Pa it ain't been foun' yet?" Jake asked, ignoring Timbre's smart remark.

"Yep. And if I were you I'd keep it under my hat. If word got out it would mark the end of the Sioux nation."

"Yar sure enough right 'bout that, but it's boun' ta be discovered sooner or later," Jake informed him.

"Better later. Things are changing fast enough as it is," Timbre commented.

"I'll be damned. You knows me and 'bout a dozen other boys hunted them hills far years an never come across any sign of gold. I even roamed them with you and your Pa," Jake said, still finding it hard to believe.

"Were you looking for any?"

"No, but I 'spect neither were you an' yar Pa."

"You're right, we warn't. I guess we were just luckier than most."

"Ya know what else has got my curreyiosity up?"

"What's that?"

"How come after you an' yar Pa squirreled all that gold aways you two still felt the need to kept comin' back ta tha mountains?"

"You know how Sam was. After a month or so in the big cities he was ready to hit the trail again. The man couldn't stay put in one place for very long. A yern for the wild country and the danger it represented always dragged him back."

"Not like you, eh Bub?" Jake laughed.

"No, not like me," Timbre smiled.

"So. When ya leavin' far Afreeka?" Jake asked, turning serious.

"What makes you think I'm going?"

"By tha look in yar eyes. I've seen tha' thar look too many times, in too many men not ta rec'nize it when I sees it," Jake told him "I would think you'd had yar bellyful of boats by now. Didn' ya sign on a clipper an' sail half way 'round tha world after ya Pa was kilt?" Jake asked, knowing full well what Timbre had done.

"You know I did, but I never got to Africa. I always wanted to see Africa, ever since I read about it in a book."

"I always warned yar Pa that youse were readin' too many books, an' that all of them words would someday clog-up yar brain," Jake mumbled. "I also knows that thar's no sense in tryin' ta talk ya out of goin'. Yar like your Daddy was. Once ya make-up yar mind on somethin' it's easier tryin' ta get a mule ta learn ta dance then to change your mind. Speaking about mules, what do you plan to do about that mule and horse that followed you and Sam here? I never seen such a dedicated animal as that ther' horse of yourn.

Ya know, he would come to the back window where you was recovering and peek in the window every morning to see if you was still breathing. I never seen anything like it. Did you ever give that ill tempered beast a name? Jake asked.

"I've given it some thought and decided to name him Thor. He's been a good companion, a real pal, and he was sent to me by the God's--- and he's Norse."

So, how're ya plannin' ta get ta New York ta catch yar boat?"

"The easiest way would be by ship, if I was going. But before I make up my mind there's some people in Montana that I want to see. Besides, who said I was going. All I said is that I always wanted to see Africa," Timbre answered him, giving the matter some thought.

"That's good news and bad news," Jake told him.

"Why do you say that?"

"Becaus'n, if'n ya stops in Montana tha chances of ya goin' on ta Afreeka are mighty slim," Jake smiled. Timbre looked at Jake and could see that the years hadn't dimmed his memory. Jake still remembered Cat.

"You don't forget much, do you?"

"Ya wouldn' ex-pect a horny old goat like me ta forget a beauty like that one, would ya?" Jake chuckled. "If'n ya did yar dummer than I thought ya was. If'n ya want my advice, I'd hitch-up with that one. Yar a fool if ya don't. She ain't going to wait forever."

"You're probably right, but how can I expect her to wait for me every time I get the itch to do some traveling?"

"Ya couldn', so stop yar wonderins. You've seen jus"bou everythin' worth while ta see. Ya might even des-cover that she's worth givin' up your saddle sores far. Or, you might even consider taking her along with ya."

"That's a lot to think about. So what's the bad news?"

"The bad news is that ever since that darn war started the Injun's have been acting up somethin' fierce. Now that it's ended they're starting to send more troops in to quiet things down. But for now it's still dangerous country out there."

"I always got along with most of the tribes and the ones that ain't very friendly I can always avoid. I'm not that much of a tender foot yet," Timbre smiled.

"If you say so. Oh! While I was in town I bought you some new duds because you lost so much weight while you was healing. Your old clothes are falling off you so I bought some things that will fit. And here's something else I picked up for you", Jake told him pulling out a Derringer from his pocket. Handing it over to Timbre, he told him, "It may be small but a .45 slug coming out of that little thing will pack quite a punch. I don't know if I'd ever want to shoot it. Most likely it'll make my old hand numb but I figure you can handle it just fine. I also figured that if you ever have to use it it would be because you were in desperate need of it."

"Point taken. And I surely thank you for all this, Timbre told him examining the small gun.

"Tell me true," Jake said seriously, staring Timbre in the eyes. "You plan to go after that pistolaro who put that bullet in ya? Because if ya ar' I'm going with ya."

"What are you crazy? I plan to stay as far away from that killer as I can possibly get. I'll never be able to best him in a gun fight no matter how much I practice. I never seen anybody as fast as he is. As a matter of fact I'm changing my name to just plan Tim. I don't want anybody reporting back to that crazy bastard that I'm still alive," Timbre stated truthfully. "But sadly," he continued, "I have a strange feeling that I'll be meeting up with him again somewhere down the road."

"You think he's what your Pa warned you about?"

Timbre had told Jake what he believed had occurred while he was dead and Jake not knowing of Timbre ever lying to him had believed his story whole heartily.

"I think he's a big part of it. Either way I'm going to do my best to avoid him. Hey, you heard from Jessie lately?"

"Not a word for some years now. I was hoping he would've showed up when you, me, and Frank went fishing. Now that would've been a fine gathering. But the truth is I haven't heard from him for years. Last I heard he was working on a ranch, I believe somewheres in Texas, but I won't swear to it," Jake reported.

"I'll ask around for him and maybe I'll run into him during my travels," Timbre told Jake.

"While I'm thinkin' on it, I'd like ya ta do me a favor," Jake more or less asked.

"Name it," Timbre told him, glad to be changing the subject. Jessie was like a brother to him and it never sat well with him when Jessie turned down his offer to sail away to Europe with him those many years ago.

"There be a little town in Texas called Cotton Grove, I'd appreciate it if ya could' stop off thar on yar way ta Montana an drop off a horse far me. It's only a couple of hundred miles or so out of yar way."

"What the hell for?" Timbre asked, not imagining why Jake would make such a request of him.

"Oh 'bout fifteen or so year ago I borrowed a horse from this hare gent an' I never got aroun' ta returnin' it. Now I rec'on it's time ta pay him back before I pass on. I don' want ta leave this here earth an' hav' people think that I owed them somethin'. I'd return tha horse myself but my ol' bones don' fancy makin' that long ride. Since yar goin' that way anyways...," Jake trailed off.

"How do you know that this gent is still in Cotton Grove and that he's even still alive if you haven't seen him in all these years?"

"A mutual friend rode through hare 'bout a year or so ago. He toll me he bumped inta Lucas, that's tha gent I owe tha horse ta, in Cotton Grove. Seems Lucas owns a small spread thar. Also said that Lucas were wonderin' when I was goin' ta get 'round ta re-turnin' tha horse I borrowed."

Timbre shook his head with wonder. It still amazed him at how these old timers did things, but he didn't doubt Jake's story for one minute. Time meant nothing to men like Jake when it came to paying back or collecting a debt.

"If it's that important to you I'll drop the horse off," Timbre relented with a sigh.

"Cous' it won' be tha same horse that I borrowed but I don' think Lucas 'spec's that particular horse. Do ya?" Jake asked, worriedly.

"I wouldn't think so," Timbre told him, not really knowing what Lucas expected.

"When yar plannin' on leavin'?" Jake asked him.

"Day after tomorrow. I got a lot of traveling to do and I might as well get to it sooner than later," Timbre told him, starting to stand.

"One other thin'," Jake said, holding Timbre down by his arm. "I probably won' be hare when ya gets back so I wants ta tell ya somethin' before ya leaves. I already toll ya once today how I feels 'bout ya, but I want ta add this: You've been a good frien' an' it makes me fierce proud ta say that I've wintered with ya. And here's a little somethin' extra to take with ya," Jake told him placing a shell in his top pocket. "Just in case."

Timbre sat and stared at the sky. It was a beautiful sky, pale blue and dotted with big fluffy snow white clouds that just seemed to go drifting on forever. He knew what Jake had placed in his pocket but it was too beautiful a day to think about death. But, on the other hand, he knew that Jake was right. Jake didn't have much farther to go and the chances of Timbre coming back this way again while he was still alive were mighty slim. Timbre hoped that what he told Jake about the after life would sooth his passing. It wasn't the dying that bothered Timbre, it was the how of it.

Some time passed before Timbre was able to talk and with tears in his eyes, he said: "We had some good days together Jake and I guess you know that if it wasn't for you risking your own life to pull my fat out of the fire more than once I wouldn't be sitting here today. You always treated me like kin and I always loved you like you were my kin. You and my Dad taught me just about everything I know about staying alive. It's me who's been honored to have wintered with you. Now if you don't mind, I'd rather not talk of dying anymore," Timbre finished, looking away, with a tear on his cheek.

"If'n yor goin' to start bawlin' I'm gettin' tha hell out of hare," Jake declared, in a choked voice.

"That will be the day when you see me bawling, you Old Fart," Timbre whispered, starting to get-up.

"Before you walk away, listen to me," Jake demanded, grabbing Timbre's wrist and stopping him from leaving. "I'll have one of the boys restock your supplies and get your rig ready for you. When you leave, and I suspect it will be early in the morning, there's no reason to be waking me up to say your good-byes. I don't much like good-byes," Jake told him, letting go of his wrist. Timbre just nodded and walked away not trusting his voice to say anything more.

The next day Timbre and Jake kinda avoided each other, each not knowing what else to say. Timbre spent most of the day checking his gear and talking to Thor. That night, before turning in, Timbre walked over to Jake, who was sitting on the porch rocking, and without saying anything, hugged him. Jake hugged him back and then both men parted with tears in their eyes and went to bed. The next morning Timbre rode out, and true to his word Jake didn't watch him go.

CHAPTER

5

"What can this guy do that you can't?" Walter Sloan asked Jesse for the hundredth time as the town of Cotton Grove came into view.

"Hopefully he'll be able to pick up the trail where I lost it back at the stream," Jesse answered him, for the hundredth time.

"So you keep saying," Sloan said, doubtfully. "He better be as good as you say. We've wasted a lot of precious time coming here to get him."

"He's special. You got my word on that. I've seen him follow sign that even Cheyenne trackers couldn't locate. I can't rightly say how he does it, but he does, and that's what's important right now. Jesse knew of Timbre's gifts but had sworn years ago to keep it to himself.

"And you're sure he's in this here town?" Sloan asked again.

"No Sir, I'm not," Jesse answered, patiently. "But you heard what ol' Pete said as well as I did."

"I remember him saying that it'd been a long time since he last saw this fellow and that he couldn't be absolutely certain that it was him that he spotted. It seemed to me that Pete liked the sound of his own voice a little too much. A fella like that tends to make things up just so's he can hear himself talk. For all we know he mighta sent us on a wild goose chase."

"I tend to believe that Pete saw what he saw. He mighta added some to it, he always did like to drag on a story, but I do believe that he saw him. Besides, what other choice do we have but to gamble on the fact that Pete was right? This is the only chance we got on getting back your wife and daughter," Jesse stated.

"Well then, if he's our only chance let's stop gabbin' and get a move on," Sloan ordered, urging his tired mount on a little faster.

Walter Sloan was a hard straightforward man. He was the sort of man who was always convinced that his way was the only way to get things done and he never wavered an inch, no matter what the cost. Sloan had been that way for all of his sixty plus years and as a result of his self-righteous attitude he'd never been able to make many friends. The fact that Walter had no friends never bothered him. He believed that the majority of people were weak and didn't possess the inner-strength to do the right thing when the need arose- as Sloan judged the right thing to be. And the one thing that Walter Sloan had no use for was any sort of weakness.

Sloan was a strong man mentally and physically and rarely, if ever, ran across his equal. The fact that he couldn't find anybody to live up to his standards gave Sloan the feeling of superiority and the right, in his eyes, to live by his own set of rules.

Walter Sloan lived by his own laws and if it wasn't for the fact that his laws basically corresponded with the laws of the land he no doubt would've been an outlaw instead of a rancher. So, being the way he was Walter lived his life alone-that is until he met Evelyn. Walter realized the moment he saw Evelyn walking alongside her Father's wagon heading West, across his land, that living alone was something he could no longer endure. From the moment they locked eyes Walter knew that he had to have her. Living alone was no longer an option.

Evelyn's long brown hair had been blowing in the warm breeze and her worn print dress had pressed up against her willowy body in a way that made Walter ache all over just by looking at her. No one can say, not even Evelyn, why she had felt the same way about Walter as he felt about her, even though he was fifteen years her senior. Both of them knew instantly that if there was such a thing as destiny it had caught up with them. They were both aware that they were destined to spend the rest of their lives together the moment they locked eyes on one another. A week after they met, they were married.

It didn't take Evelyn long to create a new Walter Sloan-well almost new. It wasn't that Walter still didn't think that he was right about everything but with Evelyn's help he learned to be more tolerant towards other people. He even went as far as to try and overlook their weaknesses.

During their first year of marriage Sloan's ranch flourished. Between Evelyn and his new found prosperity, Walter didn't think life could get any better- that is until the birth of his daughter, Teresa. For a man who hadn't thought he'd want, or need anybody, Walter had more than his share of love.

Sloan aged stately under the careful eyes of his wife and daughter. They made sure that he ate right and refused to let him worry too much about his ranch. Not only did Walter gain control over his life but it seemed that he'd gotten Old Man Time under his control as well-- that is up until the time he'd received the devastating news about his wife and daughter.

Walter was on roundup when the news that his ranch had been raided reached him. Evelyn and Tess had been abducted by Comanches. Within six-hours of receiving the news Walter and seven of his best men were on their trail. Two-weeks later, after Walter realized that they weren't gaining any ground on the fleeing Comanches, his years finally started to catch-up with him. And, as if for spite, for all those years that Walter had eluded it, time got even with him with a vengeance.

Sloan's neatly trimmed hair and beard had turned completely gray, not the silvery gray it had been slowly turning to, but a dull dirty gray that made him look as if he were unkept and dirty. His face, that had been almost free of wrinkles now looked like an old gully after a heavy rain. His hard lean body, which he used to carry ramrod straight, now stooped over. It was the almost broken Walter Sloan, now in an old body, who was now heading for Cotton Grove to seek help from a man he'd never met.

"Where do you think we'll find him, Jesse?" Sloan asked, without turning around.

"At this time of day most likely in the saloon."

CHAPTER

6

Jesse Horran was Sloan's right-hand man. Jesse had hired on as a wrangler when Teresa was about ten years old. Before a year had passed Jesse had become Walter's foreman. Some say that Jesse was the chief contributor to the success of Walter's ranch, besides Walter's wife that is, but as far as Jesse was concerned he'd just done what he'd been paid to do.

Although Jesse worked for Sloan for about seven-years they rarely spoke of personal matters. Yet, if Walter could call anybody friend it would be Jesse.

In many ways Jesse and Walter were cut from the same bolt of cloth and in other ways they were complete opposites. For example: Jesse, like Walter didn't talk much and when he did have something to say he kept it short and to the point. The reason being that Jesse had learned at an early age that it was safer to be a listener than it was to be a talker. Walter, on the other hand, didn't talk much because he didn't like people well enough to spend his time conversing with them. Jesse and Walter had other similarities, but the main one that drew them together was that they were both tough, hard men.

Jesse was a man who expected nothing but the worst from life. If now and then something good did happen to come his way he had a hard time enjoying it. He never expected his good fortune to last for very long, he had learned that lesson at an early age.

Jesse had always been small for his age and even after he was full grown he was never considered to be a big man. He stood about five-foot-six inches tall but like most smaller men Jesse had learned to fight for every ounce of respect that he felt was due him. Those who knew him swore that Jesse was the toughest five foot six man that they'd ever run across- or any man for that matter. Once he had met Kit Carson, the famous scout and Indian fighter, and was shocked when he had to look down at him. From that day on Jesse knew that his size didn't matter and that any man could command respect no matter what his size.

Jesse's life started its downward turn when he was only nine and both his parents were killed in an Indian raid while heading West. Jesse was sent back to Chicago to live with his only relative, a distant female cousin. After a brief stay with her his cousin decided that she didn't need, 'no damn kid to look after,' so she shipped Jesse off to a workhouse, which was disguised as an orphanage.

For two-years Jesse endured being worked to exhaustion in suffocating heat, freezing cold, and near starvation. He was constantly beaten and ridiculed by some of the older boys as well as by some of the overseers who favored the stronger boys who they could get more work out of.

One day Jesse received a particularly nasty beating from one of the older boys. The bully had decided that Jessie being so small didn't need all of his food he was getting and so started helping himself to half of it. Jessie, who was half starved to begin with, made-up his mind that he wasn't going to be bullied anymore, he'd had enough.

A couple of nights later, after everyone was asleep, someone hit the greedy bully in the head with something hard, placing him into a coma. Of course everyone suspected Jesse right off. Some of the injured boy's friends even went as far as to report their suspicions to the authorities- but no one could positively say that it'd been Jesse who'd done the clobbering.

Even though Jesse knew that the boy had been asleep when he had bashed him and hadn't seen anything he had no doubt that sooner-or-later he'd be punished for it. If not by the authorities then by the bully himself when he woke-up. So at the tender age of twelve Jesse snuck out of the workhouse in the middle of the night and started on his way West again--- only this time he was traveling alone.

Because of his size and age Jesse found it hard to get work because nobody thought he was big enough, or strong enough, to handle any of the hard work that was required around a farm or ranch. When Jesse was able to find employment it usually consisted of all the dirty jobs that nobody else wanted to do. Jesse's position in life made it easy for people to take advantage of him so he was constantly being cheated. But Jesse always found a way to get even. There was always something laying around for the taking, something he could sell along the way. He didn't consider this stealing, he considered it getting what was due him.

Slowly, Jesse made his way across the country, stopping only long enough to work so he could eat and buy some of the necessities of life. He had no idea where he was going but felt that he would know the place when he got there. It was a year and a half later when a hungry, cold, and tired thirteen-year old wondered into a small Missouri town. The first thing that Jesse did was to look for work. He was lucky, if that's what you want to call it, to find a job that very same day- swamping out the town's only saloon.

Jesse had gotten the job because of his good looks. He had grown some and his body had become hard. His hair was the color of dirty hay and his eyes were the color of a clear blue lake. One look at his face and one could tell that this wasn't an ordinary thirteen year old, that Jesse possessed wisdom beyond his years. One of the working girls in the saloon, not much older than Jesse, had taken a fancy to Jesse's looks and had begged the owner to hire him.

Jesse worked in that saloon through the summer, just barely making enough to survive. In that time, the girl who had gotten him the job, also made a man of him. It was toward the end of the summer when the three trappers, who'd been drinking steadily there through the warm months asked him if he wanted to work for them.

The men were looking for someone to tend their camp while they were out trapping. In return for cooking, cleaning, skinning, and cutting the fire wood, they would give him ten-percent of their profits-- and all the food he could eat. Although the job they offered him sounded too good to be true the thought of breathing fresh air again sounded wonderful to Jesse-- and too tempting to pass-up.

Although Jesse knew better than to trust the three men he also knew that he couldn't survive much longer doing what he was doing. The pay that he was receiving, when the owner felt like paying him, barely kept him alive- and he sure as hell didn't have anything left over to save. Jesse needed a stake if he ever hoped to move on. He didn't particularly like those trappers, but it was the best offer he'd had so far- plus it was the only offer he had so far. So against his better judgement, Jesse took the job.

Everything went smoothly for Jesse for the next three-months. The work was hard, but Jesse was used to hard work. He kept out of the trappers way as much as possible while doing his job. The mountain air and the good food made the hard work all worth while. Most of Jesse's time was spent alone, puttering around the camp and listening to the trapper talk at night.

The three men would leave early in the morning and not return until nightfall. If they had caught anything they would throw it at Jessie when they returned and tell him to skin it and cook it. In the evenings, during and after dinner, the men would sit around the fire and talk about their past adventures and Jesse would listen attentively. Jesse tried to absorb as much as he could from these men because he planned to come back and trap on his own after his job with them was finished.

Through the winter and early spring the furs kept piling up and although Jesse didn't know what they were worth he figured that he'd receive more money from them than he had from all of his other jobs combined.

It was in early May when one day the three men came back to camp early and the leader of them, who was called Bear, informed him: "We'll be breaking camp in the mornin' and moving-out."

"Yes Sir." Jesse was elated to hear that he was about to come into money and that he could finally move on.

Although none of the men had ever physically abused him Jesse still feared them. None of them were overly civilized and Jesse figured that the only reason he hadn't been cuffed was because of the outward show of respect that he heaped upon them.

"Isn't there any more critters left to catch?" Jesse asked, collecting the dishes after dinner.

"Too warm. Their furs ain't no longer any good," Bear grunted.

"Then we'll be going back to town to sell what we got?" Jesse asked, trying to keep his eagerness of finally being shuck of them out of his voice.

"Most of us will," one of the other men laughed, slapping Bear on the back.

"Shut ya yap!" Bear yelled, glaring at the man.

Jesse asked no more questions but continued on with his chores as if nothing had been said. He knew by what had just transpired that the three men had no intention of giving him his share and that they might even do away with him. Jesse figured that the only chance he had of staying alive, at least till morning, was to play dumb.

Bear watched Jesse closely as he went about his business. When he was convinced that the dumb boy hadn't caught on to their plans he relaxed a bit.

Jesse lay awake all night waiting for a chance to sneak off into the darkness, but every time he was ready to make his move he would see one of the men watching him. It was as if they were taking turns guarding him. Why they didn't just kill him so that they could all sleep was something that Jesse couldn't figure out but was grateful for non-the-less.

Too soon morning arrived, its weak rays finding Jesse still laying bundled in his bedroll. He hid beneath his blanket and prayed that the three men would just forget about him and move on.

"Boy! Ya bes' git out of that bedroll an do yar chores." Jesse heard Bear bellow at him.

Bear's harsh voice dashed all of Jesse's hopes. He realized that they had no intention of ignoring him and leaving him be. Jesse lay still, stalling for time, hoping for an idea to come to him.

"I ain't agoin' ta call ya agan, Boy!" the gruff voice called out.

"Yes Sir," Jesse answered, mustering up all of his courage and climbing out of his bedroll. He couldn't stall any longer.

"I'm sorry I over slept. I'll have breakfast ready in a minute."

Jesse quickly started to gather together the cooking utensils, trying to act as if nothing was wrong.

"No need far that," Bear said, beckoning him over with a wave of his hand. "I knows ya ain't as dum' as ya puts on ta be--- an' I tain't neither. I knows ya knows that we ain't plannin' on takin' ya back with us, so ya can stop ya play actin now."

"Listen, I been thinking. I don't really want any part of the furs. I figure the food and what you taught me is plenty enough pay. You can keep my share," Jesse told him, in a shaking voice, as he walked over to where the man was sitting.

Although Jesse needed the money that was owed him, he needed his life even more.

"It tain't that easy, Boy. Ya sees I sorta promised ya ta someone and this hare person 'tain't someone ya breaks ya promise ta."

"Promised me? To who?" Jesse asked, surprised, and a little relieved because it didn't seem as if he was going to be killed after all.

Jesse was doing some fast thinking and figured out that he was going to be sold into slavery. He had heard of such things but he thought it only happened to dark skinned people. The thought of being a slave didn't much appeal to him but it was better than what he'd thought was going to happen to him. Besides, he could always escape later on. Whoever bought him couldn't watch him forever.

"Nary ya mine 'bout who. You'll be knowin' soon enough."

"Are you selling me? Am I to be someone's slave? I don't think the law allows for no white boy to be a slave," Jesse told the man, still hoping to change Bear's mind.

"I don' knows what ya ar' ta be used far, an' I ain'ts one ta ask questions. Ya just be still now before ya gets me riled."

Jesse didn't rightly know why but he felt that Bear knew exactly what he was going to be used for and didn't have the heart to tell him. That bit of realization scared the shit out of him almost as much as thinking he was going to be killed did. Before Jesse could worry on it any longer a shout rang out from the edge of camp.

"Riders comin'!" one of the men yelled.

"That be him now," Bear said, getting to his feet and grabbing Jesse by his collar so he couldn't run off.

The trappers, and Jesse, watched as three riders rode into camp. Jesse could tell, even though they were mounted, that they were big men. As they came closer Jesse could see that one of the riders was a boy like himself. He judged the other teenager to be about one or two-years older than he was. But whereas Jesse was small for his age this boy was big for his.

"Damn!" Bear muttered, under his breath, then said louder in a friendly manner: "Howdy Sam-- Jake."

The three men stopped their horses directly in front of Bear and the one in the middle, the one called Sam, asked: "What are you doing with the boy, Dunlap?"

That was the first time that Jesse had heard Bear's real name used and so guessed that this man knew Bear from a long time back. He also guessed that these men didn't like each other much- even though Bear was trying to act as if they were long lost friends.

Jesse could feel the fear and tension in Bear's body as Bear pulled him closer to him. He sensed that death was no more than a flicker away. Instinctively Jesse knew that these warn't the men that Bear had been expecting. For the first time that morning Jesse felt hope. Then out of the corners of his eyes he saw Bear's two partners slowly start to circle behind Sam and his friends while Bear kept Sam's attention by talking to him.

Jesse was contemplating shouting a warning but before he could the mounted teenager spun his horse around and walked him a couple of yards away. He positioned himself at his companion's backs facing the two stalking hunters who were up to no good. It was as if he'd been aware all along on what the two men were planning on doing.

Jesse smiled when he saw that the boy's sudden move took the two ruffians by surprise and taking the heart out of their plan. He near laughed out loud when he saw Bears men slink back to the edge of the camp.

"Nutin'. He be our camp boy. I were just shakin' him out a mite. Ya knows how neglectful these scallywags can be," Bear lied, deflated and not able to look Sam in the eye.

"That true, Boy?" Sam asked, while placing his hand on the butt of his gun.

"No Sir!" Jesse hollered in relief. "He says he's going to sell me."

"Is that so?" Sam asked, looking at Jesse and studying him close.

Jesse felt as if Sam's eyes were examining his soul. After a few seconds Sam turned his eyes on Bear again and asked: "To who?"

"Ye ain't agoin' ta believe what this har' little beggar tells ya?" Bear pleaded, shaking Jesse by the collar.

"I might not know the boy but I sure as hell know you- so naturally I'm believing the boy. Now, I'm only going to ask you one more time. To who?" Sam demanded, drawing his flintlock and aiming it at Bear's head.

"Now wait up, Sam!" Bear begged, letting Jesse go and raising his hands. "No need far that. I were agoin' ta sell him ta Mountain. I didn' wan' ta, him bein' such a fine boy an' all, but ya knows how Mountain gets if he dosn' get his way?"

"So, that big slob is still selling whites to the Indians?" Sam said, more than asked.

"I don' knows that. Ya knows I wouldin' have anythin' ta do with anythin' like that."

Jesse's heart raced just thinking about being sold to Indians. Although he hadn't yet seen any, he'd always been fearful of them showing up in camp while he was alone. Jesse still remembered what they'd done to his Mother and Father- and didn't even want to think about what they were going to do to him.

"I'll tell you what I'm going to do for you, Dunlap," Sam told him. "Since you didn't know what Mountain was going to do with the lad-- and now that you do know and don't want any part of it-- I'm going to do you a favor and take the boy off your hands. That is if it's all right with him?" Sam finished, looking down at Jesse.

"Yes Sir," Jesse said, feeling a smile cover his face. "It's sure alright with me."

"Ya can't do that!" Bear screamed. "Ya jus' can't come riding inta a man's camp an' takes what ya wants. It ain't proper- or lawful."

"Are you figuring on stopping me?" Sam asked, cocking his gun.

"No. I rec'on I ain't, but Mountain will hav' something to say 'bout this when he gets here," Bear threatened.

"Well, you tell that lard of shit that I took the boy and if he wants him to just come and fetch him. You come along too if you have a mind to."

"Maybe I will," Bear said, feeling as if he had to say something, for the benefit of his men.

"Maybe mules will sprout wings and fly," Sam said, and then turning to Jesse, he asked: "Boy, you got a name?"

"Jesse, Jesse Horran."

"Well Jesse Horran, my name's Sam and this here is Jake. That youngster covering our backs is my son, Timbre. Now that you know everyone I suggest that you get your gear, saddle your horse, and come along with us."

"Yes Sir, but I don't own a horse," Jesse told him. "They let me borrow one of theirs."

"What did they promise you for being their camp boy?"

"Ten-percent of the furs," Jessie answered quickly.

"Mighty generous offer, considering they had no intention of paying you. But, a deals a deal. I'd say judging by that stack of furs that a horse and saddle would just about cover your ten-percent. Wouldn't you agree, Dunlap?" Sam asked, with a mean look in his eyes.

"If ya says so," Bear agreed, angrily, knowing first hand of Sam's, Jake's, and even the boy's fighting abilities. Bear knew that if push came to shove him and his men didn't stand a chance against them.

"Good. Then it's settled. Saddle yourself a horse Jesse-and pick yourself out a good one."

Jesse rode out of camp with Sam, Jake, and Timbre that day and kept on riding with them for the next six-years. They taught him how to trap, follow sign, and even how to read letters. They even showed him a whole new side to the Indians. Jesse found that once he came to know the Indians that he liked them and admired the way that they lived. By the time the three of them parted company Jesse was a man- more than able to care for himself.

The summer that they parted was a turning point in Jesse's life. Jesse had come to the conclusion, after many months of soul searching, that it was time for him to take his leave of Sam and Timbre. Jesse knew that it was time that he struck out on his own if he was ever to amount to anything. He realized that he couldn't hang on to their coattails forever. It wasn't fair to them and it wasn't fair to him. Sooner-or-later he'd have to try it on his own and the longer he put it off the harder it would be to do.

Jake had already left them a while back and had taken up with a Cheyenne woman and was living with her at her Father's village along the Platte. Jesse figured that living there, close to Jake, was a good place for him to start out on his own. If he got into trouble at least he'd have Jake close-by to turn to.

Parting with Sam and Timbre was hard for Jesse to do, even though Jesse knew that he'd miss them terribly-- and he was pretty certain that they'd miss him too. But no matter how hard it was to leave them he also knew that it was the right thing to do; so, after much hugging and sadness Jesse took his leave of the two men he'd grown to love. Jesse stayed on with the Cheyenne for a year or so, learning as much as he could from them, until it was time for him to move on.

Occasionally, Jesse would run into Sam and Timbre and they'd hunt together for a month or so before drifting apart again. The three of them remained close friends throughout the years, but like all traveling men they lost touch with one another for long stretches at a time.

Years later, when the news of Sam's death reached Jesse, he was shocked. He never thought that death could ever catch hold of Sam. The hurt ran deep in Jesse and he felt guilty over Sam's death. He figured if he had stayed on with them he could have prevented Sam's dying.

He searched for Timbre throughout the Northwest so he could ask him for forgiveness but with no luck. He finally ran into an old trapper that informed him that Jake was now living in California and owned his own ranch. He figured if anybody knew where Timbre was Jake would be the one.

As luck would have it Timbre was there when Jessie arrived and was about to depart for San Francisco. After a joyous reunion Jessie told him how guilty he felt about leaving Sam. He was surprised to hear that Timbre felt the same way because Timbre had left Sam to attend to some business that had to do with some gold that they had discovered.

Timbre offered Jessie some of the gold that they had found but Jessie turned it down. Then Timbre asked Jessie to accompany him on his trip around the world-- and again Jessie turned him down.

Before Timbre left, he again begged Jessie to come with him. Jesse turned him down again, telling him that he had no desire to see Europe, that he felt his destiny was here in America.

After Jessie had declined Timbre's offer once again Timbre pulled out a wad of money and forced Jessie to take it, informing him that there was a ton more where that came from. Jessie, who was feeling bad in declining Timbre's offer again, took the money, hoping that would some how that would make up for his refusal to travel with his friend.

Soon after Timbre departed for San Francisco Jesse left Jake's ranch, promising to stay in touch with the old timer. Jesse never went back to the high-country but just wandered throughout the West-- and for the first time in his life he didn't need to worry about money for a while.

Even though Jesse had only occasionally seen Sam and Timbre after they had parted company just knowing that they were somewhere's around had made Jesse feel safe. He always knew that if he ever ran into trouble and needed them that they would come running to his aid. Without any hope of running into either one of them again the mountains didn't appeal to Jessie anymore. The wilderness became a lonely place for him.

Jessie took odd jobs here and there as the mood struck him and while in Texas he hooked up with Walter Sloan. It was either that or get mixed-up with the war that had started between the states. Sloan was a hard man but also a fair man. He was the type of man that Jesse could relate to, a man he could trust and give his loyalty to. And so a bond was formed between them, a bond that lasted for many a year.

CHAPTER

7

Timbre sat at a back table in the near empty saloon facing the front doors. His wide-brimmed hat was tilted down on the front of his head, shielding his eyes from the afternoon sunlight that streamed in through the front windows. His feet were propped up on the chair in front of him and half a glass of beer rested in his left-hand, which in turn rested on the table.

Timbre had dropped off Jake's horse to his friend hours ago. All Jake's friend had said to Timbre when he dropped the horse off was, "It's about time," and nothing more. No thanks, or come in and have something to eat or drink—-just, "it's about time." Timbre just stared at the old man and a powerful urge to smack the crap out of him came over him. Biting down hard he just mounted-up and rode out before he did something foolish.

Timbre rode into Cotton Grove around mid-afternoon. He planned on spending a week in a real bed and to drink a couple of gallons of beer. It had been a long hard ride from California to Texas, most of it consisting of desert. Like most travelers Timbre hated desert crossings. If the sun didn't drive a man crazy then the boredom of looking at the same scenery, day after day, did. Once you've seen one grain of sand you've seen them all. There's never anything to look at in the desert unless you make a real effort to do so and even then it's usually something boring. Without color and new landmarks a traveler has no way of judging how far he'd traveled. Without any reference points there never seems to be a beginning or an end to the miles of endless sand. The only guide that the desert offers to the wary pilgrim is the silhouettes of the mountains that seem to keep floating farther and farther away on the distant horizon; but no matter how hard you ride they never seem to get any closer.

Then, when you don't think you can take another day of the desert without going mad you look around and you're surrounded by cactus and beautiful high-desert flowers. It takes a while before you realize that they're real and that you've beaten the desert.

The bones of many a man and woman litter the desert floor. There were plenty of bones of people buried in the ever shifting sand that didn't perish from lack of water, or any illness, but simply were overwhelmed by the emptiness of the seemingly endless land. The desert has a way of robbing some of their will to live. Just giving up and laying down to die seemed the natural thing to do for some.

It takes a strong and determined person to survive a desert crossing. Most of those who survived it swore that they'd never try making that crossing again. This was the fourth time that Timbre had crossed one desert or another and each time he'd completed a trip he'd sworn that he'd never do it again- and each time he had meant it. So there he sat swearing that there was nothing on Earth that was going to get him to move from this town for at least a week.

Timbre was about to nod-off when a loud bang abruptly awoke him. His right-hand automatically reached for the butt of his gun. Except for his right-hand and slight eye movement Timbre remained motionless. It took him a second to realize what had caused the bang. It had been the front doors being shoved open with enough force to bounce them off the walls.

His eyes trained on the front door, Timbre saw two men standing just inside of the entranceway. They were temporarily blinded by the dimmer light inside of the saloon and were waiting for their eyes to adjust. Timbre recognized Jesse Horran immediately, the older man with him he didn't know. Timbre relaxed and took his hand off his gun.

Jesse hadn't grown much in height, but the growth through his shoulders and chest more than made up for his lack of height. Timbre could see that Jesse's arms were putting a considerable strain on his buckskin shirt and his face was tanned to the color of worn leather. His light colored hair, or what Timbre could see of it poking out from under his tan hat was turning gray and he was now sporting a mustache. Timbre saw Jesse's sharp blue eyes dart about the room as they tried to pierce through the shadows. Timbre guessed, by Jesse's posture, that his old friend was under a lot of pressure.

Jesse's eyes adjusted to the light and he quickly spotted Timbre sitting in the back of the room. Timbre let out a low moan as Jesse and the other man walked toward his table. It wasn't that he wasn't glad to see Jesse but by the way Jesse was acting Timbre knew that this wasn't a chance meeting--- Jesse had been specifically looking for him and that could only mean one thing---trouble was on its way.

"Long time. How ya been?" Jesse asked, in his soft voice, smiling down at Timbre.

"No complaints," Timbre answered, pushing up his hat so that he could see Jesse better. "How 'bout yourself?" Timbre asked him, removing his feet from the chair and pushing it toward Jesse with the toe of his boot.

"Same. No complaints," Jesse said, sitting on the offered chair.

Before Jesse could say anymore, Sloan blurted out: "I hear you're the best tracker alive?"

"I take it you have a problem?" Timbre asked, ignoring the man's rudeness. Timbre was used to people with problems being rude. "Have a seat and we'll talk about it over a beer."

"We don't have time for sitting and socializing. We'll talk in the saddle."

Timbre didn't let his anger show at the older man's belligerence, but instead turned his head so that he was facing Jesse. Timbre needed to know whose side Jesse would choose if it came to choosing.

Seven-years ago Timbre wouldn't even have to have contemplated that kind of thinking but people go through a lot of changes in that length of time. He didn't think that Jesse would ever turn on him, no matter how much time had passed, but one can never be absolutely certain about anything, or anybody.

Jesse knew by Timbre's look what he was asking and without saying a word answered him by slightly shaking his head negatively, and at the same time shrugging his shoulders. Those gestures told Timbre all he needed to know, he wouldn't have to guard his back against Jesse.

"Since you're in such a rush, I suggest that you hurry along your way," Timbre told Sloan, turning back toward him.

Sloan stared hard at Timbre and for a minute Timbre thought that he was going to be foolish enough to draw on him, but then something in Timbre's coal black eyes made

Sloan think twice about it. Walter Sloan was not a man given to back away from anything, or anybody. He'd never feared dying, but lack of fear didn't mean lack of intelligence. Even if he did beat Timbre in a gun fight he'd be risking killing the only man who could be of any use to him. Sloan had his wife and daughter's lives to consider. Walter did the only thing he could do, he swallowed his pride and collapsed onto the nearest empty chair. Sloan cursed Jesse under his breath, he blamed him for this mess. If Jesse hadn't been so incompetent and lost the trail they were following he wouldn't have to be here now begging this stranger for help.

After working for Walter for so many years Jesse instinctually knew what the man was thinking- and it hurt him. He'd always done the best he could for Sloan but ever since they'd started on this chase Sloan had treated him, and everyone else, like dirt.

Jesse understood that Walter was under a lot of emotional strain and for that reason alone he'd overlooked his bad manners and had remained loyal to Walter and their quest- that is until he was almost forced to choose between his dearest friend and his boss.

"Timbre, meet Walter Sloan," Jesse said, the tension leaving his body. Although Jesse was tired of Sloan's attitude he was still glad that nothing more than Sloan's pride had been hurt. He had no doubt that Walter was no match for Timbre and didn't want to see his boss killed.

Sloan offered his hand to Timbre, acting as if nothing unpleasant had transpired between them. Timbre realized that the man was trying to save face by acting as if their altercation had never occurred, so he took his hand.

"Is Timbre your surname or your given name?" Sloan asked, forcing himself to be cordial, knowing that trying to bully this man wouldn't work.

"Both. That's the only name that I go by," Timbre answered, keeping it short, knowing that Sloan was busting to get on with what he came for.

"Jesse has informed me that you're the best tracker alive," Sloan said, having had enough of small talk. "If you're half as good as Jesse claims I can sure use your help."

"Go on," Timbre prompted, leaning back and sipping his beer. Before Sloan could comply, Jesse jumped in: "Sorry to interrupt, Mr. Sloan, but while you're telling Timbre what happened, you mind if I tell the boys that it's alright to come in and have themselves a beer? They've been on the trail a long time."

Sloan's eyes narrowed and for a second it looked as if he was going to scream at Jesse, but after a brief internal struggle with himself he regained control. Digging into his pocket he pulled out a handful of money, throwing it on the table, he said, "I'm buying- and while you're at it, get us one too."

"Yes Sir," Jesse said, picking up the money and heading for the door.

While that brief conversation was taking place between Jesse and Sloan Timbre had the chance to study Walter more closely and what he saw he didn't like. Sloan was a man on the verge of exhaustion---and just as about ready to crack wide open. He needed sleep badly, but sleep or no sleep, their was something in Sloan's eyes that warned Timbre that he was not dealing with a totally rational man. He would have to watch Sloan very carefully.

"Like I was saying," Sloan continued, as Jesse walked away. "I need your help. My wife and daughter were abducted by Comanche."

"Where's your ranch located?"

"About six days hard riding north of here."

"And Jesse is sure it was Comanche?" Timbre asked. "I ask because Comanche's haven't raided that far north since the Rangers had put a hurting on them many a year ago. They've mostly been operating way South of here. But then again, I could be wrong about that because I've been out of touch for a while."

"Comanche---that's what Jesse said, and he claims he knows his Indians," Sloan told him, with a trace of sarcasm in his voice.

Before Timbre could defend his friend the saloon doors swung open again and Jesse stepped through them followed by six dusty tired looking cowboys. Even though they couldn't make Walter out, sitting in the dim light, they all nodded in his direction anyway as they filed toward the bar.

Timbre watched as Jesse put the money on the bar and the bartender started to distribute mugs of beer to the men. Jesse waited until everyone was served before handing two of the mugs to a tall young man. Then, picking up two of the glasses himself, both men started back toward the table.

The first thing that Timbre noticed about the young man accompanying Jesse was that he was wearing his Navy Colt strapped down onto his right leg--- like a shootist would. Timbre smiled at that because in all probability the youngster considered himself to be very deadly with a six-shooter, even though he most likely never shot at a man.

Timbre wiped the smile off his face as the young man approached because he had no wish to offend him. The lad was only acting normal for his age. Every man who's ever owned a gun, at one time or another, wanted to be thought of as being dangerous hombre. As youths, Timbre and Jesse, had both gone through that phase.

"Timbre," Jesse said, handing him a beer, "This here is Curtis Sloan."

"Son?" Timbre asked, as the young man put a beer in front of Walter and then extended his hand toward Timbre.

"Nephew," Curtis answered, as Timbre shook his hand. Curtis' hand was well calloused, telling Timbre that he was a working relative.

Timbre looked Curtis over and guessed him to be about eighteen or nineteen-years of age. He was a tall boy, standing about the same height as Timbre. Curtis' hair, which he wore long like the rest of the cowboys, was light brown, almost bordering on a dirty blond. He kept his long lean face clean shaven. Timbre figured that with his light features it would've been difficult, especially at his age, to have grown a beard or mustache, even if he'd desired to. Curtis reminded Timbre of a young and taller version of Jesse. If he didn't know better he would've guessed that Curtis was related to Jesse and not Sloan. But what caught Timbre's attention the most was the way that Curtis' bright green eyes looked directly at him without wavering when he shook his hand. Most young people that Timbre encountered had the tendency to avert their eyes whenever they were introduced to an older person. Underneath all that dust and dirt Timbre judged Curtis to be a bright and handsome young lad.

"Are you going to help us, Mr. Timbre?" Curtis asked, sitting in the chair directly across from him.

"First off, my name is Tim now, no mister: And second, I haven't yet heard what I'm needed for."

"Didn't my Uncle tell you that my Aunt and Cousin were taken by the Comanche's?" Curtis asked, with surprise in his voice.

"Yes, he did, but you already got the best tracker in the territory with you. Jesse doesn't need me to show him how to do his job."

"Then why did he drag us here?" Walter Sloan asked loudly, no longer content to just sit and listen. "He's the one who lost their trail and then claimed that you're the only one who could possibly find it again."

"I'm afraid that's true, Tim," Jesse said, picking up on the name change. "I tracked them to a crossing about twenty miles east of here and that's where I lost them. I saw where they went into the water but I couldn't find any tracks leading out. We searched both banks, upstream and down, for over a day and couldn't find any sign. I tell you, it sure is mystifying."

"Are you certain that you were trailing Comanche and not Kiowa, Jesse?" Timbre asked. "It's hard to tell the difference sometimes."

"Kiowa or Comanche, what difference does it make what kind of Indians we were trailing?" Sloan exploded. "Whatever kind of Indians they are they got my wife and daughter!"

"It makes a big difference," Timbre explained, patiently. "If they're Kiowa they'll double back and head Southeast, if they're Comanche they'll most likely head Southwest."

"They were Comanche," Jesse told Timbre. "At first I didn't think so because there hasn't been a Comanche raid that far north in years. My first pick was Kiowa, but after examining the evidence I knew it was Comanche that'd staged the raid."

Timbre had too much respect for Jesse's knowledge of Indians to ask him what his evidence was, so instead he asked: "So you don't believe that they doubled back from the crossing?"

"Tell you the truth, I don't know what they did. Who knows what a Comanche will do-- or why? They could've gone just about anywheres. That's why we need you."

"How far is it to Sloan's ranch from here?" Timbre asked Jesse.

"It's about an eight-day hard ride from here," Sloan answered, becoming impatient with all the questions.

"No offense Walter but you told me six days the last time I asked you," Timbre told him. "You're tired and confused, which is understandable, so I'd rather Jesse answered my questions. He understands where I'm headed with them better than you do."

"One tracker to another, ay?" Walter asked, sarcastically. Then without waiting for an answer, he added: "Go ahead and answer him Jesse. But six days or eight days what difference does it make?" he mumbled.

"Jesse?" Timbre asked, ignoring Sloan's remarks.

"Ten, ten and a half-days. That's counting the time it took us to start on their trail, the time we spent at the stream, and the time it took us to get here," Jesse answered looking sideways to see Sloan's reaction to his answer.

"Where's the ranch located?"

"It's about fifty miles north of Fenton. We followed their trail East from there, that is until it turned sharply South missing Lubbock by no more than twenty-miles. About twenty-five miles past Lubbock the trail changed direction again and headed West, but in a more Southerly direction."

"How many ponies you figure you were tracking?"

"Seven—--maybe eight, counting the ladies."

"Only seven warriors staged a raid so far north and then had the guts to ride through populated areas. Something just don't seem right about that," Timbre pondered.

"But the one fact that's undeniable is that they definitely got the women," Jesse stated.

"What is it that you're thinking?" Walter asked Timbre, seeing his troubled face.

"I don't rightly know. I'll tell you when and if I ever figure it out," Timbre answered him.

"Does that mean that you'll help me?" Walter asked, sitting up straighter in his chair.

"With certain conditions attached," Timbre stipulated.

"If it's money, you'll be well paid," Walter told him, assuming that's what the delay was all about.

"That's not one of the conditions," Timbre said.

"Well state them," Sloan demanded, "so we can get on with it."

"From here on I'm in complete charge. You and everyone else will take orders from me," Timbre told him, while looking him right in the eye.

After a couple of seconds had passed, and Sloan had given no verbal reply, Timbre started to see flashes of anger and hate surfacing on Walter's face. Timbre had no wish to have another confrontation with the man, so in a softer tone, he said: "I know this isn't easy for you to swallow Walt, but it has to be this way. They may be your wife and daughter but you have no experience when it comes to this sort of work- and I do. I've handled jobs like this before and I can promise you that one mistake can cost you dearly. Now, before you fly off the handle, think about what I just said to you."

After some minutes passed, Sloan reluctantly consented. "Okay, I'll agree to that--- for now. What's your next condition?"

"I want you and your men to get some sleep."

"Sleep! We don't have time to sleep!" Sloan yelled, jumping to his feet.

Sloan placed his hands on the table and leaned menacing toward Timbre. When his face was only about a foot away from Timbre's, Sloan spit out: "If that's the stupid kind of orders you plan on giving, the deal is off!"

Timbre watched in silence as Sloan's face turned red with rage and his jaw muscles tightened with anger. Timbre knew that it would be of little use for him to try to explain his reasoning until Walter blew himself out and calmed down.

"Uncle Walt," Curtis said softly, placing his hand firmly on Sloan's arm and pulling him slowly down onto the chair. "Listen to what Tim has to say before making your mind up and throwing his help away. He must have a reason for not wanting to leave until tonight."

Sloan stared at Curtis and slowly his nephew's words sank into his feverish brain. Nodding, he turned his attention back to Timbre; ordering: "State your reasons."

"Okay," Timbre said, even though he wasn't sure that Sloan was ready to listen. "You told me that you lost your wife's trail six hours due West of here?"

"I didn't say that I lost the trail. What I said was that Jesse lost the trail," Sloan interrupted, pointing an accusing finger at Jesse.

Timbre's quickly turned his gaze toward Jesse and he briefly caught the flash of anger in Jesse's eyes before Jesse looked down. The look in Jesse's eyes told Timbre that Jesse wasn't going to take much more of Sloan's abuse. In fact, Timbre was surprised that Jesse had let Sloan go this far. The Jesse Timbre had known would've stopped Sloan in his tracks long before he'd reached this point.

"Uncle Walt," Curtis said, in his soothing voice. "You know it ain't Jesse's fault, he did everything he could. He wants to find Aunt Eve and Cousin Tess as much as we do."

"You may be right," Walter agreed, sounding almost sorry for his outburst against Jesse.

Jesse knew that it was the closest thing to an apology that he was going to get, so for the sake of the two women Jesse once again swallowed his pride and overlooked Walter's rudeness--- but it was getting harder and harder for him to do that.

"Regardless of who did what, the fact is the trail was lost six hours hard ride from here," Timbre continued, making it clear by his tone that he didn't care to be interrupted again. "If we leave now we won't arrive at the stream until well after sunset--and no matter how good Jesse thinks I am I know that I wouldn't be able to find a trail at night that Jesse couldn't find in the day. On the other hand, if we leave tonight, say about midnight, we'll reach the stream around daybreak with your men and mounts rested. Rested men don't make as many mistakes as tired men do."

"That makes sense to me, Uncle Walt," Curtis agreed. "What do you think?"

"I don't like the idea of waiting around and doing nothing, but I can see that I don't have much of a choice about it. If he can't find the trail in the dark it wouldn't make much sense leaving now," Sloan said, struggling to his feet. "I guess we leave at midnight."

"Good," Timbre said. "But there's one other thing before you leave."

"Now what is it?" Walter asked, irritated by yet another demand.

"There's something that's needed to be said-- and believe me I don't relish saying it," Timbre hesitated.

"Just say it straight out," Sloan told him, anxious to be on his way.

"If that's the way you want it. The Comanche's have had your wife and daughter now for well over a week. I believe your relentless pursuit of them has prevented them from taking the time to do whatever they'd been planning on doing with your woman folk. But--- you've not been on their trail now for almost two-days-- and...," Timbre trailed off, spreading his hands and letting Sloan come to his own conclusions.

Sloan's eyes bulged and Timbre could almost feel the heat emitting from them as his words sunk in. With a voice that sounded as if it were coming from deep inside of a well, Sloan said: "Don't you think I know that? Why do you think I wanted to leave right away instead of waiting until tonight? You're not telling me anything that I'm not aware of. But let me tell you something that you might not know. If I don't get my wife and daughter back alive then I want the heads of the murdering devils who took them- and I don't care what the cost is. Do we understand each other?"

"Perfectly," Timbre said, seeing Sloan's intense hatred rise to the surface.

"Good, as long as we understand each other," Sloan told him, before turning to Curtis. "Curtis you see to the horses and supplies, also see to the rooms and some hot food for the men."

"Yes Sir," Curtis answered, as Walter left.

Timbre studied Sloan as he made his way toward the door and knew that he was watching a man who would live the rest of his life mourning and hating. Timbre didn't deny Sloan his right to hate, and even if he did he wouldn't know how to go about talking him out of it. It's one thing preaching forgiveness but it's a whole different story trying to live it. If the man wanted vengeance, and Timbre figured Sloan had a right to it, then Timbre would help him to get it.

"Sorry I got you into this," Jesse said, intruding into Timbre's thoughts. "If there was another way I could've done this I would've. I know this ain't fair to you, but those women are like family to me."

"You of all people should know that ain't ain't a word, Jesse. Besides, what the hell is fair in life? Somethings just have to be done and fair has nothing to do with it. One question though, how the hell have you put up with that man all these years? No offense, Curtis," Timbre added, remembering that Walter was Curtis's Uncle.

Jesse had smiled when Timbre had said ain't ain't a word. He remembered that was one of Sam's favorite sayings.

"I know it's hard to believe, but he used to be a likeable man, well at least a reasonable man. He just isn't thinking clearly anymore-- and I can't say that I blame him," Curtis said, defending his Uncle.

"The boy's telling it straight," Jesse agreed. "I can't say what kind of a man he was before I signed on with him but since I've known him he's always dealt with me fairly- until now that is. But I'm willing to overlook his rudeness for a bit longer. I guess I figure I owe him that much."

"Fair enough, Jesse. I guess I can put up with his short comings for the women's sake, and for old time sake--- as long as he doesn't push too hard."

"I'm obliged. It seems my debts to you just keep piling up," Jesse said. "I only hope that someday I can pay you back a little of what I owe you. I'm just sorry that I never got the chance to payback your Dad for what he done for me."

"He never wanted any thanks. He just did what he believed to be the right thing to do. Besides, he knew how you felt about him, he didn't need you doing anything to prove it. As far as I'm concerned, I'll take your friendship as payment."

"You'll always have that," Jesse replied.

"I want to offer you my thanks too," Curtis said, taking advantage of the lull in the conversation between the two men.

"I havn't done anything yet to be thanked for," Timbre told him.

"You didn't tell my Uncle to go to hell and you've also agreed to try and help us. For that I thank you."

"If you really want to thank me you can start by keeping a tight rein on your Uncle. It seems to me that you're the only one who can control him. Stopping him from doing something foolish can mean the difference between getting your Aunt and Cousin back or losing them."

"I'll try my best but I can't guarantee you anything. He's getting harder and harder to reason with," Curtis told him while standing. "I better go and tell the men to get to the hotel and get some rest. Then I'll see to the supplies. You need anything? Curtis asked Timbre.

"Nothing I can think of."

"Then please excuse me," Curtis said and walked off.

"He's a good boy," Jesse said, when Curtis was out of ear shot.

"Seems to be. He's well mannered, that's for sure," Timbre said, sure that he and Curtis would get along just fine.

"Now that we're alone what's with the name change and how long you been back?' Jesse asked.

"Kinda a long story. You really want to hear it?"

"Fire away. I'll just enjoy my beer while you flap your lips," Jesse smiled.

Timbre told Jesse the whole story, starting from when he first landed in San Francisco until he left Jake's ranch.

You really believe that you talked with Sam?" Jessie asked, not knowing what to make of Timbre's tale.

"Yep. I believe it but I don't expect you to," Timbre answered, seeing the doubt in Jesse's face.

"I really don't know what to make of it, but the one thing I'm certain of is that you believe it happened just the way you told it and I can see the change it made in you."

After a moment on pondering over the story Timbre just related to him, Jesse asked: "Let's say that everything you told me is true, and I'm not saying it isn't, do you think this has anything to do with what your Dad warned you about?"

"Your guess is as good as mine, but I wouldn't doubt it. Too much of a coincidence—--don't you think?"

"One thing Sam never believed in was coincidence and he taught us to question such things. So, I've a mind to question this chance meeting of ours and lean toward this being connected to your destiny," Jesse concluded.

"Yeah, me too," Timbre agreed. Changing the subject Timbre asked: "were you in the war Jesse?'

"No. Seems the South needed beef worse than they needed soldiers so they left us cow punchers to our business of supplying them with cows."

"How come you never contacted Jake to let him know that you were alright and where you were?" Timbre asked, curiously.

"I sure meant to. But, you know how it goes. Time kinda slips away from you. Before you know it years have rolled by. How is the old codger anyway?"

"He's getting old but when I last seen him he was in good health. Told me to tell you hello if I bumped into you."

"That was nice of him. I'll be sure to drop him a line as soon as I can. Well, as much as I'd like to sit around and catch-up on old times I best be helping Curtis get things ready for tonight," Jesse stated, gulping down the rest of his beer. With a little moan, Jesse made it to his feet.

"You better get some sleep yourself. We ain't as young as we used to be. We'll talk later," Timbre told him.

"Ain't ain't a word. Remember?" Jesse smiled, before he hurried away to catch-up with Curtis.

Timbre watched Jesse leave while wondering if any of them knew the sorrow and the horror that awaited them. Timbre had been on these kind of hunts before and none of them had ended happily. When Comanche's and woman were involved----it wasn't pretty.

Most Indian fighters claim that the Comanche is the toughest and cruelest Indian that ever rode the plains. The word mercy has no meaning in their language--- they neither show it nor do they expect to receive it. Even the Apache, who once called the Northwest part of Texas home and was considered by some to be the fiercest Indians in the West, were beaten and driven out by the Comanche.

Just thinking about what the Comanche's did to their captives sent a shudder through Timbre's body. Most men who'd dealt with the Comanche would eat a bullet before allowing themselves to be taken alive by them.

Timbre had learned about the special bullet that the Texas Rangers carried when he was tracking a Comanche raiding party for Captain Walker a lot of years back. It was under much the same circumstances that he found himself in today. Each Ranger in Walker's outfit carried a forty-four shell filled with cyanide and capped off with melted wax. If the time ever came when it looked as if they were going to be overrun by hostiles--- they bit the bullet. Swallowing cyanide was preferable to what the Comanche's had in mind for them.

Timbre unconsciously patted the cyanide shell in his shirt pocket. Ever since that time with the Rangers carrying one had become a habit with him. Most of the time he even forgot he had it on him. He wished that he could've given one to each of the woman before they were captured. He hated to think of what they were going through and what he was going to find at the end of the hunt. For a moment Timbre selfishly wished that Jesse had not located him and that he didn't have to get involved in somebody else's heartaches.

Timbre wallowed for only a few seconds in self-pity before he allowed himself to think about those poor women again. The picture that formed in his mind was a sobering one and he put his mind to solving the dilemma that was confronting him. Where could they have disappeared to?

Timbre couldn't afford to let himself become emotionally involved with those women. Emotions would only mess up his thinking, so he forced the picture of their agony out of his head. He'd have only one shot at rescuing them and he'd need all the skills at his command to accomplish that.

After putting aside all of his sentiments, Timbre started to focus his mind on the job that lay ahead of him--- and only the job. He'd learned in Tibet how to control his feelings in most situations. He couldn't afford to make any mistakes in tracking the Indians. The Comanche were very unforgiving when it came to making mistakes.

Taking one last pull of his beer, Timbre put the glass down, and stood. He shook off the feeling of dread that had come over him like a cold wind and headed for the door. If he was to leave tonight, and leave he must, he had things to take care of.

CHAPTER

8

The sun was just peeking over the horizon when Jesse turned to Timbre and said: "We're almost there. Their trail disappeared about a mile further along."

"Tell me Jess, how did you know I was in Cotton Grove?" Timbre asked, curious on how Jesse knew where to find him.

"I'd of thought you'd would've asked sooner," Jesse smiled."

"I had other things on my mind. So?"

"You remember Pete Withers?"

"Yeah. I ran into him as I was coming into town," Timbre answered, already knowing the answer to his question.

"Well, we ran into him the other day while we were searching for sign. After he inquired into what we were looking for he informed us that he saw you heading into Cotton Grove and that maybe you could be of some assistance to us."

"I told that ol' fraud not to tell anybody he saw me but I guess that was too much to hope for. Now don't get me wrong, I like a good conversation as much as the next man but 01' Pete would talk you unconscious if you gave him half a chance; And lie, he'd tell you the sun was shining while standing ass deep in a raging blizzard. I'm surprised that you believed him. I thought you knew better than that."

"Pete did tell me that you asked him to keep mum about seeing you, but since he knew we were like brothers he didn't see any harm in telling me your whereabouts. Besides, I had no choice. I had to take the chance that he was telling the truth for once in his life," Jesse said, defending himself. As he gently reined in his mount he pointed to a spot a little further along the trail, towards a wide stream. "There's where I lost the trail."

Timbre stopped a little ahead of Jesse and dismounted, leaving Thor behind he walked slowly the rest of the way to the stream, examining the ground carefully to where Jesse had indicated he lost the trail.

The stream was about fifty-feet wide and ran at a leisurely pace, Southwest. The water was clear and cold, which was normal for this time of year. Later into the summer the stream would dry up considerably and turn muddy.

"How deep is it in the middle?" Timbre asked Jesse, who had walked up beside him.

"Four, five feet the most."

The two Sloane's dismounted and joined Jesse and Timbre while the rest of the men remained mounted, but within earshot. As of yet Timbre had not met or talked to any of the mounted men. They'd ridden a little ways behind him all night, preferring to keep to themselves, which suited Timbre just fine. Working with them was only temporary and Timbre neither had the time, nor the inclination, to make any new friends.

"What now?" Walter asked.

"Now, I think it's time for me to get my ass wet," Timbre told him. Turning to Jesse, he asked: "Tell me Jesse, what exactly has been done so far, except messing up all the tracks that were here?"

"Me, Sloan, and some of the boys headed downstream and searched both banks for tracks. Curtis and the rest of the men went upstream looking for sign. According to them, they followed the water until it disappeared into a canyon where the horses couldn't go."

"You a fair tracker?" Timbre asked Curtis.

"I've got a lot to learn," Curtis answered, shyly. "But Camilo there," Curtis continued, nodding toward one of the mounted men, "He tracked Apache down in Old Mex when he was younger. Jesse sent him along with me."

Timbre turned toward the mounted cowboys when Curtis nodded his head toward them. He immediately spotted the only Mexican among them. Except for the glint in the old Mexican's yellowed eyes, his stoic face gave no indication that he had heard what Curtis had said, although Timbre was certain he had. Timbre stared intently into the old man's eyes and even though they weren't what they used to be, they were still the eyes of a tracker.

Timbre very faintly nodded to the old Mexican; one tracker acknowledging another. After a few seconds passed the old Mexican very faintly nodded back to Timbre.

"Well, it's time to get wet," Timbre said, turning to look at Walter. "Why don't you and your men go have breakfast by that grassy knoll. I'll call you as soon as I find anything."

"How long you figure to be?" Walter asked.

"As long as it takes. I also need to be left alone so I can concentrate on what I'm doing.," Timbre told him, unbuttoning his shirt. "And keep the fire small, No sense advertising where we are."

"Okay, we'll give you room," Walter said. "You heard him men, go make yourselves some chow."

The men turned their horses and headed toward the hill, with Walter following on foot.

"You want me to take your horse for you?" Curtis asked Timbre.

"No thanks, he'll be fine where he is. It's best to keep away from him, he doesn't take to being touched," Timbre warned him, sitting down and pulling-off his boots.

"We'll leave you be now," Jesse said, pulling Curtis away before he could ask any more questions.

Timbre stood and stripped to his underwear. He then walked back to Thor and draped his clothing over his saddle. He hung his gun belt on his saddlebags and stuffed his boots under his bedroll.

"Go wait over there for me," Timbre told Thor, pointing to a patch of tall grass about ten-yards away from the stream.

Timbre watched his horse walk over to the lush grass and begin to eat. When he was sure that his mount was going to stay put, Timbre tentatively entered the water.

The water was so cold that it made Timbre suck in his breath and grit his teeth. He wished that he had time to wait for the sun to warm it up a bit but he knew that time was one thing he was short on. Tensing his body Timbre willed himself to get on with the task at hand.

Sloan's men, who were sitting around sipping hot coffee and eating biscuits watched fascinated as Timbre bobbed up and down in the water as he wadded back and forth in the freezing stream. They were speculating on just what in the hell that crazy tracker was up to. Jesse, who knew what Timbre was about, didn't volunteer any information. He just sat patiently and waited for Timbre to finish.

"What the hell is he doing?" Walter yelled, running out of patience. "He's been at that nonsense now for over an hour."

"What you're looking at is a master tracker applying his trade," Jesse told him, with pride in his voice. "Just give him a little more time."

Before Walter could respond, Timbre came sloshing out of the stream with his hands full of rocks---shivering. He quickly walked over to where Thor was still grazing and set the rocks down beside him. He then removed a towel from his saddlebags and started to dry himself off as he watched Sloan walking toward him.

"What've you found?" Sloan yelled, while he was still a good fifteen-feet away.

Timbre ignored Sloan's question until he had completed drying himself, which didn't make Sloan happy.

"Are you going to answer me, or not?" Sloan demanded to know, standing right in front of Timbre.

Before Timbre could tell him to back-off Jesse appeared carrying a bright red blanket, which he wrapped around Timbre's shoulders.

"Thanks Jess, that water was colder than an Apache's heart," Timbre told him, as the rest of the men who were following Jess, gathered around. Bending over, Timbre recovered the rocks he had placed on the ground.

"What's with the rocks?" Walter asked.

"See these scratches?" Timbre asked Walter, handing him a couple of stones.

"Yeah," Walter answered, closely examining them and then passing them along to Curtis, who was now alongside of him. "So?"

"Those rocks were kicked over by your horses while you were searching the stream. You can see where their metal shoes marked them. Now look at these," Timbre said, handing Walter some more stones.

102

Walter looked at them and then again passed them along to Curtis, saying: "I don't see any scratches on them."

"Me neither," Curtis said, looking at Timbre, confused.

"That's because there aren't any marks on them, but never-the-less they also were kicked over by horses."

"Unshod Indian ponies?" Curtis asked.

"Yep."

"So what? What's the big deal, we already know that the Indians entered the stream here," Walter remarked, disappointed that that's all there was.

"They're rocks all up and down the stream with scratches on them, but these rocks," Timbre explained, taking the unmarked stones out of Curtis's hand. "were confined to a small area."

"I don't get it! Spell it out!" Walter bellowed, getting frustrated with the way Timbre seemed to be dragging out the explanation.

"Okay," Timbre said, getting to the point. "The Comanche's entered the water here, but they didn't cross the stream, nor did they go down it, nor up it. They came out of the water a few feet away from where they entered it. Then they covered their tracks and doubled back the way they'd come."

"If they did that don't you think Jesse would've spotted it?" Walter asked, not quite believing him.

"No. When the Comanche came out of the stream they backed out and covered as much as their tracks as they could. When your men rode up and scattered about, while Jesse was looking for sign, they managed to wipe out any sign that might've been left. That's why Jesse couldn't find their trail. This was mighty slick even for Comanche. It would've fooled anybody."

"But it didn't fool you," Jesse said, feeling foolish.

"It didn't fool me because you'd already done most of the work."

"How can you tell that these rocks were kicked over?" Curtis asked, still examining the stones.

"Feel both sides of the stones--- with your eyes closed. Can you feel how one side is smoother than the other?" Timbre asked.

"No," Curtis answered, closing his eyes and feeling the stones.

"Don't let it concern you," Jesse told him. "Very few people can tell the difference, and only one in God knows how many, can do it while in freezing water."

"What now?" Walter asked, despondently.

"It's not as bad as you think," Timbre told him. "I believe that while you were searching the stream the Comanche's were close by watching you."

"But they had all that time with the women, without us pushing them." Walter said.

"That's true. But what could they do? If they did anything to the women they would've given away their position. My guess is they just sat, doing nothing, waiting for you to leave. I don't believe you lost as much time as I first suspected. I'll even bet that they aren't moving as fast as they were before."

"Are you telling me that I was in eye shot of my wife and daughter and didn't know it?" Walter asked, almost in tears.

"That's my guess. If it makes you feel any better, they would've killed your women, and probably most of you, if you had stumbled onto them."

"What now?" Walter asked, pulling himself together.

"The first thing to do is to find out where they were holed up and then which way they headed after you left. I suggest that you split the men up. A third of them search the hills to the East, a third take the middle, and the rest search the knolls to the West. And tell them if they find anything to make sure that they don't mess up any tracks that are left."

"What are you going to be doing?" Walter asked.

"I'll be waiting here having breakfast. Whichever two finds their trail can send one man back while the other stays put."

"How will the other men know when the trail is found?" Curtis asked.

"You stay here. When word is sent back that the trail has been found you stand on top of that hill and wave this red blanket," Timbre told him, referring to the blanket he was wearing. "The rest of you men keep an eye out for this blanket. When you see Curtis waving it hightail it back here."

"Why can't I just fire a couple of shots? Wouldn't that be easier?" Curtis asked.

"If you can tell me exactly where the Comanche's are go ahead and fire your shots. If not, why risk letting them know where we are?"

"I see your point," Curtis said.

"You heard him men!" Walter yelled. "Keep an eye out for this blanket!"

"Another thing," Timbre told them. "I don't think they bothered to cover their tracks this time so it shouldn't be to hard finding where they camped."

"Camilo, you and Pike go to the East. Jim, you and Frank take the middle. Me, Jesse, and Glen will go west," Sloan ordered. "Okay, let's get mounted and ride."

As the men left, Timbre walked around to the other side of his horse and then threw the blanket he was wearing to Curtis. He then took off his wet underwear and changed into dry clothes. As he was finishing strapping on his guns Curtis emerged from behind his horse.

"Those are mighty fancy shooting irons. Mind if I ask where you got them?" Curtis asked.

"I bought them in San Francisco. They're the latest thing in six guns."

"Are they forty-fours?"

"Nope, they're forty-fives. They pack a punch and are easier to get back on target after you fire them. Didn't see a need for forty-fours."

"I've never seen six-shooters like those before."

"They're modeled after the Dragoon forty-fours. I believe there was only a thousand or so of the Dragoons made. Seems Colt designed them for the Mexican American war. They did have a nasty habit though of the cylinder falling out when least expected. When Walker, the head of the Texas Rangers, got his hand on one he loved it so much that he went back East and had Colt make him a couple of hundred of them, but without the flaws.

They were a little on the heavy side but the good thing about them was that when you bashed someone on the head with one the barrel didn't bend. From then on they were known as the Walker Colt. I once owned one of the original Dragoon's but I gave it away just before I left the country. They're still a well sought after pistol. But anyway, Colt didn't stop there, he then went on to design these to handle the new self contained bullets," Timbre explained, taping the butt of his gun. "I see you carry a .36 caliber Navy Colt. That's a fine weapon.

"It's okay, but it doesn't have the stopping power that yours does. Nor does it reload as fast. I sure would like to own me one of those new Colts."

"They're mighty rare for now but I'm sure they'll be all over the place mighty quick. As far as getting your hands on a Walker Colt, a Ranger has to die before one becomes available, then it's usually passed on to another ranger."

"How come you carry your second gun in a belly holster and not stuck down your pants like most do?"

"If you ever tried to sit with six inches of steel shoved down your pants front you wouldn't have to ask that question," Timbre smiled.

"Besides, it slides out quicker from a holster and has less chance on catching on a piece of cloth."

"Yeah. I imagine it would. By the way, what's with your horse? How come nobody can touch him? He's probably one of the finest looking horse's I've ever seen, I'm guessing that most who see him can't help but run their hands over his silken looking coat. You'd think he was used to being touched," Curtis rambled on.

It took Timbre a moment to adjust to the abrupt change of subject. Curtis reminded him of a kid in a candy store who didn't know what he wanted to taste first.

"He can be dirt mean when he has a mind to. Not all the time but who knows when something will set him off. So it's better all around if people just stay away from him."

"I haven't seen him act ornery," Curtis said, looking at the big black.

"He's okay as long as he's left alone, but if he's touched no telling how he'll react".

To demonstrate his point Timbre smacked Thor on his rump. Immediately the big black's head whipped around, his teeth snapping shut at where Timbre's arm had just been. Before the black could try to bite him again Timbre smacked him hard on the nose. The black's eyes glared at Timbre for a moment and then shaking his head he went back to cropping grass.

"I see what you mean," Curtis said, backing away. "Why do you keep him?"

"One reason is I don't have to worry about him being stolen. Also, he's the strongest, fastest, and one of the smartest horses I've ever owned. As you can see I don't need a bridle to ride him. And once you get used to his ways, and him trying to take a chunk out of you now and again, he ain't so bad," Timbre laughed.

"How do you control him without a bit?"

"Muzzle pressure and leg pressure. As you're probably already aware, Indians use hackamores to train their ponies with and then switch to War Bridles after the horses are easier to handle. I personally wouldn't try to put a bit in his mouth unless you want to feed him your fingers."

"I don't believe I've ever seen a horse with such a smooth coat, nor one with a head shaped quite like that."

"And chances are you never will again. He's called a Friesian and comes from the Netherlands."

"Neitherlands? I don't think I ever heard of that breed. Curtis said."

"The Netherlands is a country over the ocean, not what kind of horse he is. I told you the name of the breed. Didn't you learn where that was in school. Did you go to school?"

"Yeah. I went to school all the way to the sixth grade. I can read, write, and even do numbers," Curtis smiled, proudly.

"Good for you. You went to school a lot longer than I did," Timbre smiled, starting toward the small campfire that was still smoldering by the knoll.

"Can you read and write?" Curtis asked. tagging along behind Timbre.

"That's a mighty personal question. In some places a question like that could get you a broken jaw," Timbre told him.

"I'm sorry," Curtis apologized, not intending any harm by the question. "I didn't mean to offend you."

"You didn't. I can read and write."

"Where were you headed when we found you? There's nothing much around here," Curtis asked.

"I was thinking on going to Africa before I ran into you fellows, but first I have some business in Montana."

"Isn't Texas a bit out of your way. As I recall, Montana lies North of here and Africa is somewheres across one of them big oceans. I don't believe you can sail to there from here."

"I wasn't waiting for a ship in Cotton Grove, I was their because I had just finished doing someone a favor. I had planned on resting up some before moving on to Montana. Does that clarify it for you?" Timbre asked, with a slight edge to his voice.

"I reckon it does," Curtis answered sheepishly, knowing he was on the edge of pushing Timbre too far with his questions. Changing the tone of the conversation, Curtis asked: "What do you figure it's like in Africa?"

"You sure do ask a lot of questions, and I've answered most of them for you because I like you, boy. But if you want to know more read a book."

"I have read books but it's not the same as learning first hand. I grew up on my Uncle's ranch and this is the furthest I've ever been from it. Oh, I've talked with Jesse but getting more than three or four sentences out of him at one time is like trying to pull a bull out of the bog. Besides, you're the most interesting person I've ever run across. Why hell, you've been almost darn everywhere. I could learn a great deal from you," Curtis gushed.

Timbre was flattered by what Curtis had said and resigned himself to help the boy out as much as he could--- before he snapped and shot him. "Okay son, I'll try and answer most of your questions, but only if you promise to give your mouth a rest once in a while," Timbre smiled.

Although Curtis didn't find Timbre's remark all that amusing he joined in and smiled with him, saying; "I'll try but never have been able to before."

Timbre looked at him and when he realized that he was serious started to laugh out loud. Curtis joined in realizing what he just said, releasing the some of the tension he was feeling.

Thor hearing their laughter walked over to where Timbre and Curtis were sitting to investigate the ruckus. The sight of the horse standing over them and staring down at them made Timbre and Curtis laugh even harder.

When their laughter finally subsided, Curtis said, "I better wash these pans and cups before the men get back."

"Here, let me help you," Timbre offered, grabbing the coffee pot. "Lead the way."

Curtis was walking ahead of Timbre and Thor and had only taken about fifteen steps when he heard Timbre shout to him, "Curtis! Don't move!"

The urgent sound in Timbre's voice made Curtis freeze in his tracks. He stood, as if rooted to the ground, the only part of him that he moved was his eyes as he searched for the danger. When he didn't see any he started to relax and ask Timbre what the problem was--- and that's when he heard the problem start to rattle.

Curtis immediately recognized the unmistakable sound that a Rattler makes just before it strikes. He slowly looked down and to his left and spotted the coiled snake about two-feet away.

"Just take it easy and don't move," Timbre warned him, in a soft soothing voice.

"Shoot it," Curtis hissed, beads of sweat forming on his brow.

"In a second, just relax," Timbre's soothing voice told him, as he removed something from his saddle.

Curtis couldn't take his eyes off the snake. It took every bit of nerve that he possessed not to move. He couldn't understand what was taking Timbre so long. If his hands weren't so filled with the dishes he would've tried to shoot the Rattler himself. Curtis felt, more than saw, the Rattler start to strike. In desperation he started to jump to the side, but just before Curtis's feet left the ground and before the Rattler could sink his fangs into his leg, Curtis heard a loud crack.

"You're okay," Timbre told him, as Curtis regained his balance and looked around, wondering where the snake was. Curtis spotted the Rattler a few feet away, minus its head. It's body was writhing around in its death throes.

"Why didn't you shoot it?" Curtis demanded to know, in a panicky voice, as Timbre calmly coiled his bullwhip.

"Couldn't risk the noise. We still don't know where the Comanche's are, besides a shot would've unnecessarily brought everyone hightailing it back here," Timbre explained.

"Jeez! I could've been bitten!" Curtis exclaimed, still visibly shaken and looking at the snake which was lying still now.

"That's always a possibility with Rattlers. Damn snakes are a pain in the ass-- but I guess they have their uses," Timbre said, tying the whip back onto his saddle and then picking up the pot he'd set down. "Come-on, we better get these things cleaned."

"Where did you learn to use a whip like that?" Curtis asked, continuing on to the stream, but still visibly shaken.

"Some old bullwhacker taught me to use it a long time ago. It comes in handy at times."

"I'd sure like to learn how to use one," Curtis stated, as they reached the edge of the stream and he started to rinse the cookware.

"It takes a bit of practice," Timbre told him, bending over and washing the pot he was holding.

"How did you know a Rattler was there? You couldn't see it from where you were standing?" Curtis asked, now that he was thinking clearly again.

"Thor smelled him first and let me know something was there by the way he was acting, then I got a brief whiff of him myself after testing the air more closely. My nose isn't what it used to be or else I would've spotted him sooner," Timbre told him, matter-of-factly.

"How could you smell him?" Curtis asked, not believing him, thinking that he was funning him. "Snakes don't smell."

"The hell they don't. Have you ever tried sniffing one?"

"No."

"Well try it someday and I guarantee you that you'll never miss that odor again."

"I will. You know I've never known anyone like you. That's why I'm sure that you could teach me a lot," Curtis said, envying the adventures that Timbre must've experienced. "For instance: How come you sit an army saddle and not a regular saddle? Although, I must admit that I've never seen an army saddle quite like that one."

"For starters: You don't recognize my saddle because it's closer to being an English riding saddle than it is to being an army saddle. Plus, I've had some changes made to it. The reason I don't use a saddle like yours is because I'm not a cowboy--- and I don't ever intend on being one. Since I'm not punching cows I have no use for all that extra leather that you carry."

"What changes have you made to it?" Curtis asked, straightening and shaking the water off of the plates.

"For God's sake, go and look for yourself and stop bothering me. I don't mind you asking questions but don't annoy me with questions that you can find out the answers to for yourself. When you're finished examining my saddle you best get your butt up that hill and start looking for any riders heading this way."

"What are you going to do?" Curtis asked, hoping that Timbre would pass the time with him on top of the hill.

"I'm going to lie on this patch of grass and take a nap. It's been a long night. Try not to wake me until you see someone coming," Timbre told him, lying down and pulling his hat over his eyes.

"Wake up, riders coming," Curtis announced a short time later, shaking Timbre by the shoulder.

"Okay, I'm awake," Timbre grumbled. "Stop poking at me. Were they close enough for you to make out who they are?" Timbre asked, sitting up and rubbing the sleep out of his eyes.

"It's Uncle Walt and Jesse. They'll be here in about five-minutes."

"I kinda thought they'd be the ones who'd find the tracks. Help me up," Timbre requested, stretching out his hand towards Curtis, who grabbed it and yanked him to his feet. "Thanks. I'll be right back, I'm goin' to wash the sleep off and relieve myself."

"What made you think they'd be the ones who'd find the tracks?" Curtis asked, when Timbre got back from the stream.

"I figured the Comanche's had holed up somewhere to the West of here and that's where they were searching," Timbre explained, as Sloan and Jesse galloped into camp.

"Go wave that blanket, Boy!" Walter yelled to Curtis, as they quickly dismounted.

113

Picking up the red blanket Curtis ran to the top of the hill and began to wave it.

"We found where they'd watched us from," Jesse said, breathing hard. "You were right, they were camped about a mile and a half to the West of here."

"Which way did they head from there?" Timbre asked.

"Their tracks lead off in a Northwesterly direction, but more West than North," Jesse answered, as Curtis came stumbling down the hill, tripping over the blanket that he was dragging and plowing into Jesse almost knocking him over.

"Sorry," Curtis apologized. "Did I miss much?"

"That was fast," Walter said, surprised to see Curtis back so soon. "You sure all the men saw the signal."

"Yes Sir. Most of them were already on their way back. I suspect they spotted you and Jesse riding for camp."

"Good," Walter nodded. "We were telling Timbre that he was right about those Comanche's doubling back. We found their camp about a mile West of here."

"You say the tracks go Northwest from there?" Timbre repeated, deep in thought, not paying attention to Walter's and Curtis's conversation.

"It doesn't make sense. What do you make of it, Jesse?"

"You're right. It doesn't make sense. I'd have bet my saddle that they would've headed South and not back the way they'd come."

"And I believe you'd be making a safe bet," Timbre told him. "I think they did head South regardless of what the tracks say."

"But the tracks plainly go Northwest" Walter protested.

"And I'm sure that if you follow those tracks you'll eventually discover that it's a false trail. I believe they split up and went in different directions. I have admit that they're being overly cautious for Comanche's. It makes me wonder..."

114

"How can you be so sure that it's a false trail?" Walter asked, interrupting Timbre's line of thought.

"I can't. I just got a hunch that you'll find somewhere along the way that they changed direction on you again."

"What if your hunch is wrong and we go off chasing in the wrong direction?" Walter asked, not knowing what to do.

"I've given that some thought," Timbre explained. "You and your men keep on their tracks and I'll head South. If my hunch is right I'll cut across their trail somewhere along the way and hopefully gain some ground on them."

"And what if you're wrong?" Curtis asked.

"Then no harm done because you'll still be on their trail. Once I'm convinced that I'm wrong and that they're not heading South I'll turn around and catch-up with you."

"If your hunch is right, and I'm inclined to think that it is, and you do catch-up with them--- do you think you're up to handling seven Comanche's all by yourself?" Jesse asked.

"You got a point there," Timbre said, contemplating the question. "But there won't be seven, remember they split up. But, I guess it wouldn't hurt to have another man with me, one who can shoot straight. You got any suggestions on who that could be?"

"Me, or Jesse," Walter interjected. "Either one of us can shoot."

"No. You two are out. Jesse has to do the tracking and you have to lead your men," Timbre said, half telling the truth.

Walter's men didn't need him to lead them, Jesse or Curtis could handle that. The truth was that in Walter's state of mind he'd get them both killed if they ran across the abductors of his wife and daughter.

"I'd like to go with you," Curtis jumped in, before Walter could suggest anyone else.

"Can you shoot straight?" Timbre asked.

"He's an excellent shot," Jesse answered for Curtis. "I taught him to shoot myself."

"Have you ever shot at a man?" Timbre asked Curtis

"No, but those aren't men we're hunting, they're Comanche's. I won't have any trouble shooting them," Curtis declared, confidently.

"You won't, will you?" Timbre asked, angrily, not waiting for an answer. "Well Buster, you best get one thing straight; Those are men that we're after and right now they're more man than you are. And here's something else you can chew on: If and when we do catch-up with them I plan on back shooting them if I get a chance because Comanche's scare me to death. You think you're up to doing that?" Timbre concluded, studying Curtis's face closely. Timbre over dramatized his fear of Comanche's but he did it to drive home a point to Curtis.

"Yes Sir," Curtis said, contritely, lowering his eyes.

"And another thing," Timbre continued, figuring he might as well get it all out of the way while he was at it. "I know you like to ask questions and I'm not faulting you for that. Asking questions shows me that you're willing to learn. If I have the time I'll try and answer your questions, but if I don't you do what I say when I say it, without hesitation. Got that?"

"Yes Sir," Curtis secretly smiled, trying to hide the excitement that was building up in him.

Timbre's sharp eyes saw the beginning of a smile forming on the corners of Curtis's lips leading him to believe that Curtis wasn't taking the dangers that lie ahead of them seriously. Hoping to drive his point home, Timbre continued: "I want you to pay close attention to what I'm about to say, Curtis. First: I don't plan on getting myself killed because of

116

you. If you go off on your own and get yourself into trouble don't look to me to get you out of it. You get yourself into trouble, you get yourself out of it. Second: If you endanger my life by not following my orders you won't have to worry about the Comanche's killing you---I'll do that myself. Do I make myself clear? If I don't, say so now."

"I understand you perfectly and I give you my word that I'll do exactly as you tell me."

"Good. Then maybe we'll both get out of this alive."

"Right. When do we leave?" Curtis asked, his voice filled with excitement.

"Right away. Get your gear together- and bring along plenty of food and water. No telling how long it will be till we run into someplace to stock up again."

"Yes Sir," Curtis said, hurrying away to gather their supplies.

"Jesse," Timbre said, turning his attention to his friend. "Something's not right about this whole thing so you be sharp and keep an eye out for anything out of place. I don't know how but I'm certain that they'll try and trick you again. When, and if, I cut their trail I'll leave you plenty of sign so you can follow me."

"Don't worry about us. They won't fool me again. I'm wise to them now. You just take care of yourself and the boy. Good-luck," Jesse said, sticking out his calloused hand.

"Thanks, we'll need all we can get--- and then some," Timbre told him, taking his hand and squeezing it.

"You take care of my nephew," Walter ordered, as Timbre released Jesse's hand.

"If I had any other choice I wouldn't be taking him," Timbre commented. "He's awful green but I'll do my best to get him back to you safely."

Timbre liked Curtis but what he didn't like was taking along an inexperienced kid on such a dangerous job.

"I understand. Do your best. I'd wish you luck but I don't believe in it. I believe each man makes his own luck," Walter stated, walking away to find Curtis.

"If memory serves me right," Jesse smiled, "I do believe that I heard that same speech, the one that you just gave Curtis, from your Dad. That's the one he gave to me when I first joined up with you three. But, as near as I can recollect--- he never did get around to killing me."

"Yeah, but Curtis doesn't know that," Timbre laughed, putting his arm around Jesse's shoulders as they walked toward the pack horses.

"He's really a good boy," Jesse informed him, as they walked. "and one hell of a shot. Just remember when he pisses you off, and he will, that you were young once too- and don't be too hard on him."

"I'll keep that in mind--- but that was a helluva long time ago," Timbre said, sneaking a shovel out of the supply pack when Walter and Curtis weren't looking.

"You figure on needing that?" Jesse asked, with a frown, as Timbre hid the shovel under his bedroll.

"I hope not, but---."

"I'm ready to go," Curtis interrupted, riding up to the two men.

"You say your good-byes?" Jesse asked him.

"To my Uncle, but not to you," Curtis said, bending over and extending his hand toward Jesse, who then grabbed it with both of his.

"You listen to what this man tells you. You can learn a lot from him--- and even possibly stay alive while doing it," Jesse told him, while squeezing his hand. "Make me proud of you, Son."

"I'll do my best--- and Jesse, in case I don't make it back, thanks for everything you've done for me. You've been a great friend and teacher. I couldn't have asked for better."

"Don't sound so final, I'll be seeing you again," Jesse told him, letting go of his hand. "Just do as Tim tells you, he knows his business."

"Will do," Curtis assured him.

"See you at the end of the trail, Partner," Timbre winked at Jesse, as he turned Thor toward the hill.

"You got that right!" Jesse yelled, as they rode away.

CHAPTER

9

The two men rode for the rest of the day without a break, eating in the saddle and only stopping long enough to relieve themselves. The further they got from the stream the dryer the land became. No longer was the grass abundant and lush, but instead the ground changed to rocks and shrubs with only an occasional patch of green spattered around. The country was now what the Easterners referred to as scenic--- and the Westerners referred to as crap.

It was well into the night before they stopped. Thor was still strong enough to have kept on going but Curtis's horse looked like she needed to rest--- besides, it had gotten too dark to look for tracks.

"Doesn't your horse ever get tired?" Curtis asked, dismounting and looking at Thor who seemed to want to go on.

"Probably, but I haven't seen it yet. I always poop out before he does," Timbre confessed, slowly sliding out of the saddle.

"How far you figure we come?" Curtis asked, unsaddling his horse.

"Somewhere between twenty or thirty-miles," Timbre guessed, while trying to work the kinks out of his back.

"It feels like a hundred," Curtis moaned, while making camp.

"If it feels like a hundred-miles to your young body imagine what it must feel like to these old bones," Timbre chuckled, rubbing his backside with one hand as he unsaddled Thor with the other.

"Are you going to help me setup camp?" Curtis asked, as Timbre sat on his saddle.

"I just did," Timbre yawned.

"Would you mind gathering the wood while I get the coffee ready?" Curtis asked, pulling out a coffee pot from a big sack that had been hanging from his saddle

"Don't need any wood, even if there was any around to gather. There won't be a fire. We'll be running a cold camp from here-on-in. We'll just have beef-jerky, soda-crackers, and water for supper. I hope you brought plenty of water?" Timbre asked, worried that Curtis might not have.

"I brought four full canteens. I wish that you'd of told me that we'd be running a cold camp, I wouldn't have lugged along the coffee pot. It's just extra weight if we're not going to use it," Curtis said, putting the coffee pot back into the sack and getting out the food.

"We'll make use of it in the morning when the glow of the fire won't light up the sky," Timbre told him, as Curtis handed him his food.

"I can't wait," Curtis mumbled.

As he ate Curtis kicked away rocks, smoothing a space on the ground for his blanket.

"That should do us for the night," Timbre told him, finishing his food, and also clearing away some rocks so he could lay out his bedroll. "Before we leave in the morning transfer some of that gear you're carrying to my horse. If you don't lighten your load your mount wont be able to keep up."

"Right. Speaking of horses, I'm going to water and hobble mine before I bed down. I'd offer to do the same for yours but I like my bones the way they are," Curtis informed him, while pouring water into his hat and offering it to his horse who lapped it up greedily.

"When you're finished watering your horse just put some water in your hat and set it on the ground. He'll smell it and come and get it himself."

"Aren't you going to hobble him?" Curtis asked, putting his hat on the ground and filling it with water.

"No," Timbre stated, lying down and setting his guns within easy reach. "Chances are he'll be there when I wake up. Least ways he always has been."

"What if he isn't?" Curtis asked, as he watched Thor drink from his hat.

"Then I guess I'll just have to take your horse," Timbre mumbled.

Before Curtis could ask him if he was serious he heard Timbre begin to snore. Curtis shook his head and waited for Thor to finish drinking. Retrieving his hat he then removed his gun belt and laid down. He fell asleep while still wondering if Timbre had been serious about taking his horse.

Curtis awoke to the smell of coffee brewing. Opening his eyes he could just make out, in the pre-dawn light, Timbre moving around the camp.

"Get-up. It's almost time to be moving," Timbre told him, handing him a cup filled with coffee.

"Where did you get the wood for the fire and how did you know I was awake?" Curtis asked, taking the hot cup from Timbre.

"When you sleep do you dream of questions to bug me with? But if you must know I knew you were awake by listening to the rhythm of your breathing," Timbre explained, as he walked away. "As far as the fire goes I found some sticks scattered around. You couldn't spot them in the dark but when I looked hard enough in the light I was able to find a few."

"Awwww!" Curtis moaned, as a rock dug into his rump. "Do you ever get tired of sleeping on the ground?"

"All the time," Timbre answered, watching Curtis shake out his boots before putting them on. "When I was younger I didn't mind it so much but now my old bones scream at me every time I wake up on the ground. Do you know what else I get tired of?" Before Curtis could answer Timbre answered for him. "You asking me questions every two seconds."

"Just how old are you?" Curtis asked, gulping down his coffee and then rolling up his blanket.

"Don't know for sure. My guess is somewhere around forty, give or take a few years. I stopped keeping track a long ways back."

"Wow! You are old!" Curtis exclaimed, not able to suppress a smile.

"Didn't your Mother teach you better manners? Don't you know it's not polite to agree with someone who says they're old?" Timbre informed him, going along with Curtis's attempt at humor. "And don't wear your spurs today, they make too much noise," Timbre instructed, while saddling Thor.

"My Mother never taught me anything that I can remember," Curtis told him, in a serious tone, as he removed his spurs. "My Aunt and Uncle raised me since I was two. They told me that both my parents had died of Cholera so they took me in and raised me as their own. You think we'll get my Aunt back?" Curtis asked in a chocked voice.

"We'll find her. But prepare yourself to find a totally different person then who you knew. Now, pack your gear and let's get moving."

"I see your horse didn't run off during the night. Do you want to transfer some supplies before we leave?" Curtis asked, while saddling his horse---ignoring what Timbre had just told him.

"I've already taken care of that while you were sleeping," Timbre informed him, while double checking the camp for anything that he might've overlooked. He left the fire smoldering in case Jessie was following his trail.

"Ready?" Curtis asked, vaulting into the saddle.

"Yeah," Timbre answered, climbing onto Thor. "We'll take it a bit slower today. I don't want to take the chance of missing any sign."

"Do you think we took the right trail?" Curtis asked, gently nudging his horse forward.

"They're definitely heading South like I figured they would. There's plenty of sign telling me that we're on the right trail."

"You think we're getting close?"

"No telling yet how close we are. Just keep your eyes open."

"What am I supposed to be looking for?" Curtis inquired.

"Anything that doesn't belong, or anything that doesn't feel right to you. You'll know it when you see it, or don't see it."

"I will? How would I know it when I see it, especially if I don't see it--- whatever that means?"

"You'd be amazed at what you know without knowing that you know it," Timbre chuckled, finding the explanation amusing.

"Huh?" Curtis exclaimed, not quite understanding what Timbre was getting at.

"For instance: Let's say you've had a wooden post in your yard for a number of years. The post was never used and it was in a place where it wasn't in your way. As each day passed the more unnoticeable the post became, until eventually you didn't see it at all anymore. Now mind you, the post was still there but it had become so familiar a sight that your lazy brain didn't register seeing it anymore. Then one day somebody comes along and removes that post without informing you. Now, the next time you enter the yard something inside of you senses that something's been changed, but you can't put your finger on it. Your brain can't tell you what's changed because you stopped seeing that post a long time ago--- but instinctively you know something isn't right and it nags at you. It's that same nagging feeling that will take hold of you when your brain says something ain't right. When you get that feeling stop and take stock of everything around you. A big part of being a good tracker is nothing more than recognizing those feelings when they creep up on you. You have to train your eyes to see, not just to look, but to really see. If you take things for granted you'll never be a good tracker."

"You make it sound easy," Curtis said, studying the ground, as they talked.

"Very few things in life are easy. If you want to be good at something you have to work at it. The better you want to be-- the harder you have to work for it. Given enough time though most anybody can learn to track. How good you get at it is another story."

"Will you teach me what you know?" Curtis asked, looking at Timbre with school boy eyes.

"I'll teach you what I have time to teach you," Timbre smiled. "But it would be impossible to teach you in a couple of days what it took me over thirty-years to learn. That's asking a lot-- even from me," Timbre smiled.

"Then I guess I'll have to ask a lot more questions," Curtis beamed.

"Oh crap, what did I just get myself into?" Timbre mumbled to himself. "For now just shut up and move a ways to your right. No sense both of us studying the same piece of ground."

Timbre had ordered Curtis to do that just to get him away from him for a while. He highly doubted that there'd be any sign where he sent Curtis to look. He just needed some time to himself before Curtis' questions drove him to suicide.

After five-hours of steady riding and not seeing anymore sign, Timbre was starting to get frustrated. He was about to call it a day when he spotted a crushed twig on the ground. Stopping his horse Timbre dismounted to take a closer look.

"What is it?" Curtis wanted to know, riding over to where Timbre was knelling.

"This twig was crushed buy a horses hoof--- and it's still a little sticky. I figure it was done sometime early this morning."

"Who do you figure broke it?" Curtis asked.

"Who else? Our friends most likely," Timbre told him, examining the twig carefully.

"But I don't see any hoof prints around anywheres," Curtis told him

"The ground is too hard for unshod ponies to leave any marks, but those rocks over there have recently been kicked over. See the difference in color? But how many horses and who was riding them is anybody's guess."

"Or which way they were headed," Curtis added.

"If you'd get your ass down here and take a closer look you wouldn't be inclined to make such dumb remarks. You'll see that they were traveling South," Timbre sharply corrected him.

Curtis was a typical cowboy. It would never have occurred to him to get off his horse. The only time a cowboy gets off his horse is when there's no way around it—or he's too sore to stay in the saddle.

"How can you tell which way they were heading?" Curtis asked, reluctantly dismounting and kneeling beside Timbre.

"The crushed twig is here, the kicked over rocks are a few feet south of it, and we've been trailing South all this time," Timbre explained to him. "My instincts and reasoning tell me that they're still heading south."

"I see," Curtis mumbled studying the twig.

"Wait here," Timbre ordered, leaving Curtis with the horses while he walked on ahead.

Timbre examined the ground carefully as he sauntered along. After about thirty-yards he knelt and formed a mound with a bunch of rocks.

"Mount up!" Timbre yelled, as he stood.

"Son-Of-A-Bitch!" Curtis screamed, as Thor clamped down on his shirt, his teeth just lightly grazing his arm.

"I warned you," Timbre smiled, after seeing what had happened.

"I was only going to fetch him for you," Curtis whined, examining his torn shirt.

"He don't need to be fetched, he'll come by himself," Timbre told him, as Thor trotted over to him.

As Timbre mounted Curtis could've sworn that he saw a smile pass over the black's face, but he quickly dismissed that notion---horses can't smile.

"Why did you pile those rocks up like that?" Curtis inquired.

"So when Jesse and your Uncle get here they can follow us. We'll be doing that every mile or so from now on."

True to his word, every mile or so, Timbre made Curtis dismount and pile a bunch of rocks together. They'd gone about five-miles when Timbre stopped them and dismounted.

"How far ahead do you think they are?" Curtis asked Timbre, who was kneeling on the ground examining a bunch of hoof prints in a soft patch of dirt.

"Not far. They got sloppy and made their first mistake by riding through this soft dirt. I'd say that these tracks were made maybe six hours ago, give or take an hour," Timbre told him while mounting.

"They're starting to get getting careless. I guess they figure that their little trick back at the stream worked and that they're in the clear."

"There's a second possibility," Curtis added. "They might not care anymore if we find them."

"I thought of that too, and that possibility has me worried. We'll just have to be cautious from here on out. If they stopped early their camp may be close by."

"How can you be sure when those tracks were made?"

"By how sharp their edges are. You compare the clearness of the rims of the tracks with how hard the wind was blowing and you should get a pretty accurate time of when they were made. See how those prints are a little faded around the edges. The wind has been mild for the last couple of days so I'd say that they've been there long enough to have been worn down some but not long enough to have become blurred. So I'm guessing six hours old--- eight the most."

"How long did it take you to learn that?" Curtis asked, amazed.

"Most of my life--- and I'm still learning."

"And you're sure that these were made by the same Indians that we're after?" Curtis excitedly asked.

"They were made by unshod ponies--- and see how much deeper those two sets of prints are compared to the others? Those two ponies were carrying double. I'd say that these are our boys."

"Then let's go get them before they get away!" Curtis yelled, digging his heels hard into his horse's flanks.

As Curtis spurted off at a gallop, Timbre yelled: "Asshole!"

Timbre reached into his saddlebag as Curtis faded from sight and pulled out a piece of beef-jerky. Shaking his head he began to chew on it.

For over an hour Timbre followed the faint hoof prints. It was difficult going because Curtis had galloped over most of the Comanche's tracks. Then suddenly, the Comanche's tracks veered to the West, while Curtis's tracks continued on South.

"That asshole will probably be in Mexico before he discovers that he's no longer chasing anybody," Timbre said to Thor as he dismounted to mark the cutoff for Jesse.

For the next two-hours the rocky ground gradually turned into grassland, making the tracking easier. Timbre knew by the greening of the landscape that there was water nearby.

Looking up Timbre spied a stand of rocks ahead, shaped like a horseshoe. The tracks were leading him directly toward them. Dismounting, Timbre slowly started to circle the boulders. He had gone no more than twenty-yards when he ran across another set of hoof prints coming from the East, also going into the horseshoe. Another six feet, or so, more tracks appeared leading away from the rocks.

"Some of them made camp in there," Timbre said to Thor, who was following him, "Then this other bunch joined them and they all rode out together--- I figure no more than two hours ago--- but only one was carrying double this time. We better have a look."

Although Timbre was sure that all of the Indians had departed he still used extreme caution on entering the horseshoe. With his gun at the ready he inched along the boulders and into the half-circle of rocks. The interior of the natural fortress ran about a hundred and fifty-feet from side to side and about two-hundred feet from the entrance to the furthest boulder. Running near the rear of the conclave was a small stream.

Timbre had a clear view of the whole interior from where he was standing and even with the sun starting to go down he was able to confirm that the camp was indeed deserted---except for a body that had been left staked out on the other side of the stream.

Holstering his gun Timbre slowly walked toward the corpse. He was in no rush to see the mess that the Comanche's had left behind. As Timbre was about to jump the small stream that separated him from the dead woman--- he saw the body twitch. Seconds later a long soul wrenching moan accompanied the twitching.

"Damn! She's still alive!" Timbre gasped, as he ran back to where Thor was grazing.

Grabbing his canteen Timbre hurried back, jumping over the stream and to the woman's side.

"God!" Timbre exclaimed, closing his eyes tightly when he saw what was left of her.

What the Comanche's had left behind wasn't pretty. She had been slowly skinned and then hot rocks has been placed on her exposed flesh. If that wasn't enough they'd also forced red hot stones into her body cavities. Her face, which at one time might have been pretty, was now minus a nose, ears, eyelids, and lips. There were other parts of her body missing as well but Timbre refused to look at them.

She had no right to still be alive and Timbre wished that she wasn't. There was nothing he could do for her but to watch her die in intense agony. Timbre took a deep breath and opened his eyes. He cut the bonds from her hands and feet, or what was left of them. Lifting her head he pried the now cooled stone out of her mouth and taking his canteen, Timbre slowly poured water into her burnt and blistered mouth. As her wildly insane blue eyes tried to focus on him she strained to utter one word.

"Daughter--," she strained, through a charred mouth and a throat ripped raw by screaming. Timbre had to put his ear close to her mouth to hear and understand her. "Save- her."

"I will. Your husband is on the way, hold on."

"No----- mustn't----- see---- me," she pleaded, squeezing his arm with her burnt fingers. "Promise----- me."

"How can I stop him?"

"Kill---- me---- bury---- me---- please---- can't---- bear---- pain----- kill----- me----save----daughter," she begged, trying to cry through dried up eyes.

Timbre knew that there was no way that she could live. Every minute that she stayed alive was pure hell for her. Not being able to stand seeing her suffer anymore, Timbre nodded his head. Reaching into his top pocket he pulled out his cyanide shell. Laying her head down he took out his folding knife and wedged off the covering of wax. Lifting her head again, he explained to her: "This is cyanide. I don't think it will be very painful but it will do the job quickly."

"Five---- Indians---- two white!" she moaned, staying Timbre's hand from administering the poison so she could tell him that.

"Did you know them?" Timbre asked, not as surprised as he should've been. Something about this whole thing had been nagging him since the beginning---- now he knew what it was.

"Stop---- at----- ranch---- for----- water-----strangers," she grimaced.

There were a lot more questions that Timbre wanted to ask but he knew that she wasn't in any condition to answer them. Her eyes told him that she had reached the end of her rope and the pain was making her slip quickly into total insanity.

Tilting her head back Timbre poured the cyanide down her throat.

"Daughter----- don't----- forget----- God---- bless----- you," she whispered, as her face contorted and her body spasmed.

"I won't forget," Timbre vowed to the dying woman, holding her tight. "Don't you worry--- I won't forget. They'll pay for this, I promise you that. And Ma'am, I know it's hard for you to believe now but there is a God and a beautiful after life waiting for you. I don't understand it all, but trust me, I've been there. Please, don't be scared." With tears rolling down his cheeks Timbre gently lowered the dead woman's head to the ground. He then staggered to his feet to get the shovel. He couldn't remember the last time he'd shed tears as he buried her wrapped in his extra blanket.

CHAPTER

10

Sloane's men were spread out, riding in pairs, searching for sign.

"Over here!" Camilo yelled to Walter and Jesse who were riding about twenty-five yards to his right.

"What've you got?" Walter asked, as he, Jesse, and the rest of the men, rode over to investigate what Camilo was yelling about.

"Maybe a marker, Senor," Camilo answered, pointing to the pile of rocks on the ground.

"What do you make of it, Jesse?" Sloane asked.

"That's Timbre's sign. He found their trail and marked it out for us. There should be a pile of rocks like this one every mile or so."

"Then let's make some time," Sloane ordered, kicking his horse into a gallop.

The men raced off after Sloane but Jesse knew it was a mistake to run their horses without knowing how far ahead Timbre was but there was nothing he could do to stop them. Shaking his head, Jesse put his spurs to his mount and took off after them.

Timbre was patting down the last shovelful of dirt when Curtis entered the horseshoe at a full gallop. At the last moment Curtis saw the stream and yanked back on his reins sharply, causing his mare to sit back on her hunches and come to a sliding stop.

Vaulting out of the saddle Curtis hit the ground running. Leaping over the brook he continued his sprint until he was standing beside Timbre. Staring down at the freshly turned earth, he breathlessly asked: "Who is it?"

"Your Aunt," Timbre informed him, before walking away to leave Curtis to grieve in private.

While Curtis sobbed out his pain Timbre unsaddled Curtis's horse and rubbed her down with his saddle blanket. When he finished he set him loose to water and graze.

As the horse wondered away Timbre picked up Curtis's gear and carried it to the opposite side of the semi-circle, to the right of the entrance.

Searching through Curtis's supply bag Timbre located the coffee pot and coffee. Starting a small fire he brewed a pot of coffee. Timbre had almost completed drinking his third cup of coffee by the time Curtis joined him.

"I'm sorry," Curtis apologized in almost a whisper, as he sat by the empty cup that Timbre had put out for him.

"What for?" Timbre asked, noticing Curtis's red swollen eyes.

"For running off like I did. I acted like a fool," Curtis sheepishly admitted, while pouring coffee into his cup. "After I cooled down I stopped and waited for you. When you didn't show I doubled back. If it hadn't been for those rocks you marked the trail with I might not have found you."

"Don't feel too badly, it turned out for the best," Timbre consoled him, feeling too empty to be mad. "There was nothing you could've done here; and besides, your Aunt didn't want you to see her."

"What did they do to her?" Curtis asked, staring into the fire.

"Why ask a question that you really don't want me to answer?"

After thinking about it for a couple of seconds, Curtis agreed: "You're right. I really don't want to know."

Both men went back to studying the fire, lost in their own thoughts.

"What was her name?" Timbre asked, minutes later, looking up at Curtis.

"What?"

"Her name, what was it?"

"Evelyn. Her name was Evelyn. Why do you ask?"

"When someone spends their last moments in your arms you should at least know their name."

"You mean she was still alive when you found her?" Curtis asked, shocked. "Why didn't you tell me that?"

"I did. Didn't I tell you that your Aunt didn't want you to see her?"

"Yes, but I didn't think she actually said that. I thought it was something you made up to make me feel better. What exactly did she say?"

"She asked me to bury her so that nobody would see her," Timbre informed him, mater-of-factly. "She loved you all too much for that. She wanted your last memories of her to be nice ones. She also asked me to save her daughter."

"Did she linger on for long--- after you found her?" Curtis asked, with tears forming in his eyes.

"No, just a few minutes."

Timbre didn't lie, but neither did he tell Curtis the whole truth. Timbre knew that few people would understand what he'd done for her, unless they'd been there at the time.

"Are you going to go after Tess? And if so---when?"

"In about four-hours," Timbre answered, assuming that Tess was Curtis's cousin.

"I'm ready to leave now. Why wait?" Curtis asked, anxiously.

"You're not going with me."

"Why? Is it because I ran off before? I swear that won't happen again. I learned my lesson. From now on I'll do exactly as you say," Curtis pleaded.

"It's too late for that," Timbre told him, sipping his coffee. "The damage has already been done. You've run your horse into the ground. He's played out and needs at least eight hours of rest before you can push him hard enough to stay up with me. If you push him sooner then that he'll be dead before you make fifteen-miles."

"Damn!" Curtis exclaimed, angry with himself for being so stupid, realizing that Timbre was right. "Okay, but what about you? Why aren't you leaving now?"

"Because, I'm played out too and need the rest. I can't ride all day and night anymore. Those days are behind me."

"But what about Tess?"

"I'm going to give it to you straight because I'm too tired to think of a way to soften it up for you. Those Comanche have a four to six-hour lead on me, which means that in all probability they've already stopped for the night. If they're going to do your cousin like they did your Aunt it's probably to late to help her. Her only hope is that they'll be content from doing your Aunt and will save Tess till morning---- and by morning I'll have caught up with them. I know that sounds cruel but that's the way it lays out."

"Are you sure that they won't hurt Tess till morning?"

"The only thing I'm sure of is that we can't do anything to help her tonight. Make sure you wake me in three-hours," Timbre ordered, laying back on the soft grass and pulling his hat down over his eyes and cutting off any further conversation.

Timbre knew that for the next couple of weeks that he would have to be nearly exhausted to sleep; And, if he was lucky enough to get some sleep he knew that it would be filled with nightmares. He had gone through experiences like this before and was aware that it would be some time before the image of Evelyn would leave his dreams alone.

Timbre slid in and out of sleep restlessly for a while until suddenly the sound of approaching horses pulled him out of his nightmares.

"Curtis!" Timbre yelled, jumping to his feet and looking around.

"Right here!" Curtis yelled, running toward him.

"Quick, behind these rocks," Timbre told him, drawing his six-shooters and squeezing in behind a boulder.

"Who do you think they are?" Curtis asked, in a frightened voice, squeezing in behind him.

"How long have I been asleep?"

"About three hours or so."

"Then I'd guess it's your Uncle and his men, although part of me hopes it's not."

"Why do you say that?"

"Because if it's them that means they damn near killed their horses getting here this fast."

Minutes later Timbre's fears were confirmed. Sloan and his men rode into the conclave with Walter in the lead.

"Damn! Look at those horses. They're damn near rode to death," Timbre cursed, stepping out from behind the boulder, and holstering his guns, with Curtis following close behind.

Seeing Timbre and Curtis Walter dismounted and threw his reins to one of his men, "Take care of him," he ordered.

As Walter approached them Timbre could see that he was even crazier now than when he was when he last saw him.

"Where are they?" Walter bellowed.

"Your wife is over there," Timbre told him, pointing in the direction of the grave.

Sloane turned his head toward where Timbre had indicated and squinted his eyes, trying to pierce the blackness.

"I don't see her," Sloane said, walking toward where Timbre had indicated.

"You better go with him," Timbre told Curtis.

"Yeah," was the only reply Curtis made before falling into step behind his Uncle.

"Dead?" Jesse softly asked, as he dismounted.

Timbre nodded and walked away--- returning to the glowing campfire.

"I'll see to your horse," Pike, the one who was taking care of Sloan's horse, offered while reaching for Jesse's reins.

"Thanks," Jesse said, handing them over and following Timbre.

As Timbre was relighting the fire, Jesse asked: "Coffee still hot?"

"No, but it'll only take a minute to heat it up. Sit down while I relight the fire."

"Rough?" Jesse asked, sitting.

"Yeah," Timbre answered, placing the coffee pot on the fire once it was lite again. He then sat across from Jesse.

Without saying another word Timbre reached into his pocket and removed the empty shell casing. He looked at it for a second and then threw it to Jesse. Jesse caught the shell and examined it. It only took him a second to realize what it was--- and what it had been used for. Looking at Timbre, he nodded and threw the shell casing back to him. Timbre caught it and then threw it into the fire.

Before the two men could say anything more an angry voice yelled: "Why did you bury her? You had no right to do that."

"She asked me to," Timbre said, looking up as Walter walked out of the darkness and into the glow of the fire.

"Curtis told me all that, but that still didn't give you the right to bury her. She didn't know what she was asking. She'll be buried at the ranch where she belongs," Sloane told him in an angry and loud voice. "Jesse go tell some of the men to go an fetch her. We'll be taking her home with us."

Timbre looked at Jesse and shook his head from side-to-side, then he rose slowly to his feet.

"Nobody is going to fetch her. I'll shoot any man who tries---and that includes you Sloane," Timbre threatened. "I gave Evelyn my word that nobody would see her and I plan on keeping it. In a year or so if you still have a mind to take her home, be my guest--- but you're not going to do it now."

"You got no right to tell me what I can or can't do with my own wife," Sloane threatened him, placing his hand over his gun butt.

"Evelyn gave me that right. If you want to be buried alongside of her go ahead and pull that gun."

"Uncle No!" Curtis yelled, grabbing Walter's gun hand as he started to draw. "It's what Aunt Evelyn wanted. You know you wouldn't want to go against her last wish."

Sloane stared at Timbre---- and for the second time in three days he backed down. It was becoming a habit that Walter didn't like. Right or wrong he'd never back watered this many times to the same man.

"You win again," Walter hissed. "You can thank Curtis for your life."

"I'll be sure and do that," Timbre told him, sitting down again. "If you're a mind to, you best sit and listen to a few things that I have to say."

"Is it important? I want to get back to Eve and make a marker for her," Walter asked, angrily. It was evident that he didn't want to talk to Timbre anymore.

"It has to do with your daughter. You decide if it's important or not," Timbre told him, not particularly wanting to talk to him either.

"For her sake I'll listen, but I don't know what you can tell me that Curtis hasn't already," Walter said, squatting. "But you go ahead."

"There's one thing that your wife told me before she died that I didn't tell Curtis."

"And what was that?" Walter asked, impatiently.

"That some of the men who did this to her were white."

"Are you telling me that white men had a hand in this?" Walter asked, dubiously.

"I sorta suspected something like this," Jesse, who had been quiet up till now, joined in. "It all fits. That's why they had the nerve to ride so close to the towns and how they were able to raid so far north without being detected. I felt something wasn't quite right about this raid from the beginning; and the feeling just kept getting stronger and stronger as we went along."

"Is that the only thing that made you suspicious, or did I miss something?" Timbre asked.

"You didn't miss anything that I'm aware of. No, it was something else that happened after we split-up that made me start to think along those lines. About ten-miles from the knoll, where we parted we ran across a fresh grave. It had been covered over with brush but I spotted it anyways. Whoever tried to hide the grave must've been in a hurry because they did a lousy job of hiding it. Thinking it might be one of the woman we dug it up. What we found in it was Ol' Pete Withers. He'd been beaten pretty badly and then killed. That made me ask myself: Why would Comanche's on the dodge, with two white women in tow, run down an old man, beat him, kill him, and then try and hide the body?"

"They wouldn't," Timbre answered.

"That's the way I saw it. They must've seen us talking to him when we rode away from that creek and were curious as to what our next move was going to be. Again, I asked myself: Why would Comanche's go to all that trouble? Indian's don't think that way. It's something they just wouldn't do."

"What did you come up with?"

"Nothing then. We just continued following their tracks till they lead us to a stand of rocks. I figured that if they were going to change direction that would be the place to do it. It would've taken us forever to follow their trail on that hard ground."

"So you turned South and hoped to pick up their trail when they left the rocks," Timbre interrupted.

"Yep, but I didn't know if I'd made the right move until we ran across your marker. But how did you know what I'd done?

"Because you couldn't have gotten here this fast if you hadn't done something like that. You took a big risk. You could've been wrong."

141

"No. The more I thought about it the more I was convinced that whoever killed Pete found out from him that we were going after you for help. The ones we were following must've stayed back and watched us from a distance and saw you heading South and the rest of us heading for them. That's when I figured that they'd circle back as soon as they got the chance in order to warn those that had ridden South that you were coming for them."

"That's when you figured that one of them had to be White," Timbre nodded.

"I got the strong impression by the way they were acting that they were getting mighty worried about something. I figured that it would be highly unlikely that a Comanche would be aware of your tracking skills, so why would they be worried about you? Indians would've figured they'd lost us at the stream. I reasoned that it had to be someone who'd heard of you--- and your skills. Putting that all together it more than pointed at a white being involved."

"Excellent reasoning, Jesse," Timbre nodded at him. "But I'll take it a step further: I've got a strange feeling about this one," Timbre continued, "I'm pretty sure that I've tracked this monster before. And, if it's who I'm thinking of my Father's warnings are coming to past."

"Why didn't you tell me of your suspicions before?" Walter asked Jessie, interrupting the conversation while feeling betrayed.

"Because, that's all they were---- suspicions. I didn't want to believe that white men would have a part in anything like this," Jesse told him.

"You did good, Jess," Timbre complimented him, proud to have been one of his teachers.

"Thanks, but a lot of it was luck," Jesse said humbly.

"So you two are saying that there were three white men involved? Two here and the one Jessie was tracking?" Curtis asked.

"No. I'm afraid that the one Jessie was tracking got here before your Uncle and warned his partner, the one that was doing the evil deed. That's why your Aunt was still alive when I found her. They cut out in a hurry knowing I was close behind."

"If you two are finished, I'll go and say good-bye to Eve. Then we can be on our way to get my daughter back," Walter interjected, standing up.

"Weee- are not going anywhere. I'll tell you what I told Curtis," Timbre stated, bracing himself for another confrontation. "Your horses are in no shape to be rode. They need at least eight-hours of rest, and even after that they'll have to be rode gently."

"You don't really expect me to stay here and do nothing when my daughter is so close, do you? And if our horses are spent, which I ain't saying they're not, why aren't the horses of the bunch we were chasing not just as spent. You said they rode out of here on the double, so maybe they'll be on foot in a couple of miles or so."

"That's a question that I can't answer with any certainty. The only thing I can come up with is that they had fresh mounts waiting for them somewhere along the way. I've seen seven or eight sets of tracks leading out of here but I can't be positive of the exact number because they were all messed up. But, if there were eight, that means they picked up an extra rider along the way.... and most likely that someone was waiting for them with fresh horses."

"It's all guessing, isn't it? Well maybe you're wrong and that half of them are on foot now. Maybe I'll just take my men and go have a look."

"You know what? I really don't give a damn what you do," Timbre sighed, also standing, as the rest of the men gathered by the fire to listen. "You might be able to bully these men into going on but you won't be able to bully those horses. You do what you want, but you try pushing those ponies and you and your men will be strung out on foot from here to Mexico."

"Tell me this, how do you expect to rescue my daughter from seven or eight men all by yourself? You're goin' to need help," Walter glared.

"I have no Goddamn idea," Timbre yelled. "But I'll have to think of something. Did it ever occur to you that I'd appreciate a little help--- or do you think I'm suicidal? It wasn't me who rode my horse into the ground. You want to follow along and help--- fine, but I guarantee you that when I catch-up to them bastards I'll still be alone."

"He's right, Walter," Jesse agreed. "The horses are done in--- and so are the men. There's no sense in running us all into the ground for no reason."

"I'm not a complete fool. I'm aware of all that. But we got to do something," Walter lamented, in frustration.

"If you want to do something useful--- pray," Timbre told him, walking away.

Once he was out of ear shot from Walter and his men Timbre gave two short whistles, and as if by magic Thor appeared by his side.

"Damn fools," Timbre muttered to Thor, as he tightened his cinch. "There isn't a lick of sense among the whole lot of them."

"You'll get no argument from me," Jesse agreed, coming up behind Timbre.

"I didn't mean you," Timbre said, without turning.

"Why not? It's true. I could've tried to stop him from running the horses into the ground--- but I didn't."

"Then why didn't you, if you knew better?"

"Maybe it's because I've worked for him so long that I've gotten use to taking his orders, or maybe I knew it would be useless to try," Jesse explained. "Whatever the reason, I'm sorry that I got you into this mess. If you'll lend me your horse I'll handle it from here. I got no right to ask you to get yourself killed for our foolishness."

"If I thought that this mean-spirited fleabag would let you ride him I'd be more than happy to lend him to you, but he won't, so I guess I'm stuck with the job. Besides, I'm not doing this for Sloane, or you for that matter. I'm doing this to fulfill the promise I made Evelyn."

"The moon looks bright enough for night tracking," Jesse said, looking toward the sky, knowing there was nothing more to be said.

"Soft ground, three-quarter moon, I shouldn't have any trouble following their tracks."

"No, no trouble at all," Jesse agreed, watching Timbre yank on his saddle to test it.

When Timbre was satisfied that the saddle was firmly secured, he turned to Jesse and asked: "Do you remember saying the other day that you owed me and hoped to repay me someday?"

"I remember and still stand by it," Jesse answered, knowing that Timbre was about to hold him to it.

"Well I'm calling you on it--- and I warn you it won't be easy. If you want to back out of your offer say so now and no hard feelings."

"I already figured that it wasn't going to be easy. What is it you want?"

"Two things. The first one is the toughest. If Walter tries to dig Evelyn up I want your word that you'll try and stop him, even if it means shooting him."

Jesse was silent for a moment, then he replied: "That is a tough one---- but you got my word on it. What else you want me to do for you?"

"If something happens to me I want you to go to Montana and let her know that I won't be coming back and that she should get on with her life--- if she hasn't already."

Jesse didn't have to ask Timbre who he wanted him to notify, he knew exactly who Timbre was referring to. He also didn't tell Timbre that everything was going to be alright. In fact, he'd be surprised if it turned out that way. The best Timbre could hope for was to maybe sneak the girl away from the Comanche's during the night. And, accomplishing that little feat didn't seem very likely.

"I would've gone to Montana without you having to ask," Jesse informed him, a little disappointed that Timbre felt he had to ask.

"I figured you would've, but it's comforting to hear it," Timbre said, making Jesse feel better.

"Do what you must," Jesse told him, as Timbre mounted. "But don't get yourself kilt doing it. I'd feel mighty poorly if you went and done that."

"I'd feel mighty poorly about that myself. See you at end of trail," Timbre smiled, riding out.

Timbre knew that time was running out for Tess. The unexpected arrival of Walter had delayed his departure--- putting him behind schedule. Having to lean out of his saddle, in order to make out the tracks, would slow him down even more. To makeup some time, since the tracks were heading straight South again, Timbre decided to take a big chance.

"If we expect to save the girl we've got to get a move on," Timbre told Thor, urging him into a trot.

Timbre no longer bothered to look for sign, he had no intention of burying anyone else this night. Timbre kept Thor at a steady trot for nearly three-hours. Then, for no explainable reason, a strange feeling came over him and he brought Thor to a halt. Dismounting, he frantically examined the ground all around until he found some tracks.

"Somethings wrong," Timbre said.

Grabbing his canteen, he took a swig of water. Then, while giving water to Thor, he said to him, "They split up again. Four of them are still riding South and the other four went off in another direction. Somewhere's back there I missed the trail where they cut away. It also looks like that the ones that I'm still following no longer have the girl. None of their ponies are riding double. Damn! We don't have time to backtrack and find which way the others went."

Timbre put his canteen up and then walked a couple of yards away from Thor before sitting down.

"Okay," Timbre said to himself, "Take a deep breath and relax." Timbre learned in Tibet that by relaxing and breathing deeply he was able to tap into his special talents. It felt like talking to a wise old friend when he shut out the outside world and went deep into his mind.

Right after Timbre's mother's death, when he began traveling with his Father and Jake, Timbre would constantly talk out loud to himself. At first, his Father, had passed off the cause of Timbre's strange behavior to the death of his Mother. Sam figured that as soon as the missing of his Mother wore off Timbre's chattering to himself would stop; But, as the weeks went by and Timbre continued to talk to himself Sam began to worry.

He feared that Timbre had become permanently touched. It had been Jake who had helped to eliminate Sam's misgivings about his son.

One day, after noticing the worry on Sam's face while Timbre was talking to himself, Jake asked: "Hav' ya ever really listened ta what tha boy is sayin'? If not may be ya ought ta, before ya go's an' worrys yourself inta a lather."

Sam took Jake's advice and payed closer attention to Timbre's ramblings. To his amazement Sam discovered that Timbre was actually predicting their immediate future. Nothing big, just where game was, or if danger was near. Surprisingly, Sam soon discovered that Timbre was right more often than not.

That evening, while they were sitting around the campfire, Sam asked Timbre, "Tell me Son, why do you talk to yourself?"

"I don't?" was Timbre's innocent reply.

"It sure sounds that way. But, if you're not talking to yourself, then who are you talking to?" Sam asked, puzzled.

"I have somebody who lives inside of my head that talks to me. Sometimes he warns me of what to look for, or helps me solve a problem."

"That may be, Son," Sam told him, not knowing what to make of Timbre's answer. "But if others heard you talking to your friend, him being out of sight and all, they'd think that you're touched in the head," Sam explained.

"Well I'm not," Timbre declared, defensively. "Mommy knew about him and she didn't think I was touched."

"Did she?" Sam asked, surprised that Valda had never mentioned it to him.

"Yes Sir."

"Do you actually hear a voice?"

"No. It's sorta like just knowing what it's saying, without really hearing it. It's hard to explain. Don't you have someone inside of you that tells you what to do?"

"Well, I guess my conscious has spoken to me once or twice, but I don't think that's what you mean," Sam answered. Then, turning to Jake for help, he asked: "Do you understand what he's trying to say, Jake?"

"Can't rightly say I do, but that don' mean tha boy don' know what he's talkin' 'bout. Hell, we both seen stranger things in these hare mountains. I say that we don't question his peculiarities an' just sit back and reap in the re-wards of them. Hell, I never bagged so many furs, in so short a time since I've been alistenin' to him."

"I didn't know you were listening to him," Sam said, surprised.

"Hell yes. I thought youse were too, else I would've spoke up sooner."

"That may be all well and good for us, but I don't want people to go around thinking that Timbres not right in the head. It isn't something that should be hung on him."

"Then let him pre-tend he's talkin' to his horse. Hell's bells, mos' of us do that anyways."

"That might work. You understand what Jake means, Son?" Sam asked, turning to Timbre.

"Yes Sir. You want me to pretend to be talking to my horse so people won't think I'm crazy."

"That's it. You think you can remember to do that when people are around?"

"Yes Sir. I'll try," Timbre replied; and from that day forth, Timbre was always careful not to be caught talking to himself.

As Timbre grew the voice inside of him became fainter and fainter, until one day he couldn't hear it unless he sat down and cleared his mind of everything else and listened for it very closely---like he was doing now.

Timbre had never heard of the word meditation before he studied in the temple, but he also learned that you don't have to know what something is called in order to be able to do it. Timbre was floating in a state of neither sleep nor consciousness. He was in what he referred to as his half world, where knowledge and ideas drifted into his mind with the aid of a tiny voice. He remained suspended in that state for a while before forcing his consciousness back to the surface.

It was always easy for Timbre to fall asleep while meditating, especially if he was tired. He was now struggling not to drift off when the answer suddenly came to him. After stumbling to his feet and getting himself orientated back into the real world he whistled for Thor. Within seconds his horse was by his side.

"We got lucky," Timbre told Thor. "Those dumb ass Indians got drunk yesterday and forgot to refill their water skins back there at the stream. They're headed East with the girl, toward water. The two whites accompanied by two Comanche are still heading South. What puzzles me is why the two whites left the girl with the other four. They went through a whole lot of trouble to get her so why let her go now? That puzzles me, but I'm not about to question our good fortune."

Climbing onto the saddle, Timbre pointed Thor East and dug his heels into his flanks. They galloped through the night at a reckless pace. Once or twice Thor stumbled, causing Timbre's heart to momentarily stop beating. He had visions of himself flying through the air and hitting the ground with a thunk, snapping his neck. Running his horse at night was fool hardy and it scared the shit out of him, but if he wanted to save the girl he had no choice but to trust his life to Thor's instincts. After two-hours of none stop terror Timbre joyously brought Thor to a stop.

"They're close bye, I can smell water," Timbre whispered, dismounting.

Timbre didn't want Thor wondering into the Comanche camp in search of water while he was trying to sneak up on them, so he let Thor finish all the water left in the canteen.

"You stay here until I call for you," Timbre ordered Thor while removing his bullwhip from the saddle.

Timbre trotted, keeping close to the ground, heading for a brush covered hill. By the time he reached the base of the incline he was winded. Waiting a couple of minutes to catch his breath he then silently ascended the hill. Halfway up, Timbre dropped to his hands and knees and crawled slowly the rest of the way to the top.

Timbre expected a sentry to be posted at the summit and was pleasantly surprised when he didn't find one there. Inching his way along the crest Timbre reached the far edge of the hill and found himself looking down into the Comanche camp. Between the three-quarter moon and the fire that was burning brightly Timbre had no trouble in seeing inside of the camp.

He immediately spotted two of the Indians at the far side of the camp, close to a stream. The third one was passed out among the rocks. They were sleeping Comanche style, with their horses tied to their wrists. Seconds later, the third Comanche walked into view, carrying more wood for the fire. When the buck came within three-feet of the blaze, he threw the wood into it. The sudden flare of the fire enabled Timbre to get a brief look at the Comanche's face. It was completely painted yellow and had a big smile on it.

Timbre watched as the smiling Comanche walked around to the other side of the fire and kicked at something on the ground. For the first time Timbre spotted the girl. She was staked out--- naked.

Timbre couldn't make out what the Indian said to her, but he did see him rub his crouch and heard him laugh.

Still laughing, the Indian turned and started up the hill. Timbre slunk further into the bushes and as the Comanche drew closer he could see that he was no more than fifteen or sixteen-years of age---- and still drunk.

His age and drunkenness explained why he was being so careless. His sexual desires were stronger than his desire for doing his duty. As the Comanche drew closer Timbre willed himself to become part of his surroundings. Having lived so long with nature Indians evolved into being instinctively one with it. They learned, out of necessity, to immediately sense when something was out of place and when danger was lurking nearby.

Timbre watched the boy from the corners of his eyes. He was afraid that if he focused his full attention on him the boy would sense his presence.

The young Comanche scanned the horizon in search of any possible enemy that might be still trailing them. As of yet Timbre's presence hadn't been felt by the young buck so the youngster didn't bother to scan the hill top for any danger.

After Yellow-Face had satisfied himself that no enemy was within sight he lifted the front of his breech-cloth and proceeded to relieve himself. Turning to his right and then to his left he playfully sprayed everything within his range. When the young Comanche finished with watering the hill top and started to cover himself he suddenly felt something twist tightly around his neck, cutting off his air supply. He tried to scream but the only sound that he was able to emit was a low grunt.

His air supply almost depleted the youngster desperately clawed at whatever it was that had him by the neck. He was still struggling fiercely with his unknown assailant when he was yanked violently backwards. The last thing that he ever felt was a mind exploding pain ripping through his body.

Timbre quietly lowered the dead Comanche to the ground. There was a look of total surprise on the dead teenager's face but Timbre felt no remorse for having killed the boy. The youngster had been a warrior who'd chosen to go on a killing raid. He'd wanted to kill and torture and do what the older men did. If they hadn't prepared him for the possibility of being killed, they should've.

Unwinding his whip from around the boy's throat, Timbre hung it back around his left shoulder, he then pulled his knife out of the young warrior's kidney. He then wiped the blade clean on the Indian's breech-cloth and then replaced it in his right boot. That done, he slowly and silently made his way down into the enemy's camp.

Timbre decided to leave the naked girl where she was for the time being, there was no telling what she'd do if he cut her loose. He couldn't take the chance that she'd do something to wake-up the three men. Picking up an old dirty blanket that smelt as if it had belonged to Yellow-Face's horse, Timbre wrapped it around himself to mask his scent. He then silently walked over to the Indian sleeping by the rocks and covered his mouth with one hand and with the other he slit his throat. The older Comanche had made it easy for him, Timbre could smell the liquor on him.

Moving on to where the other two Comanche's were bedded down Timbre did what few men were capable of doing. He stealthily removed their rifles by their sides and then squatted a few yards away without disturbing them, or their horses. The horse blanket that he had wrapped around him had reassured the horses that he was friendly. Drawing his guns, Timbre settled down to wait for sunrise, which he judged to be less than an hour away.

The faint glow of dawn lit the landscape as Jesse knelt on the ground studying the tracks.

"What's the matter now?" Walter asked impatiently, from the top of his horse?"

"These tracks I've been following were made by only four ponies and none of them were carrying double."

"Which means?"

"Four riders split off somewhere behind us- and the ones we're following don't show any signs of carrying double."

"How far behind did they cut off, you reckon?"

"I can't say," Jesse answered, standing and scanning the landscape.

"Do you think Timbre caught on to that?" Walter asked, becoming frustrated with this new turn of events.

"Must've, his tracks are nowhere to be found around here. My guess is he's on the trail of the four that got Tess."

"Thank God for that," Walter sighed with relief. "Where do we go from here?"

"We can either stay with this trail and try to catch the four that's headed South, or we can backtrack and pick up the trail of the four that have your daughter," Jesse informed him, knowing full well what Walter's answer was going to be.

Even though Jesse was fairly certain as to what Walter would choose he believed that his job was to read sign and to give his boss the facts and then to let him make the decisions.

"As much as I hate to see those four murdering scum get away I'd rather have my Tess back. Let's get started back, we've lost enough time."

"Yes Sir," Jesse said, mounting and heading back in the direction in which they'd come.

Jesse was mad at himself. He should've spotted where the men had parted company. His only excuse was that it was dark and he wasn't expecting them to do that. The years he'd spent cowboying had dulled his tracking instincts.

"How come Timbre didn't leave us a marker when he left the main trail?" Curtis asked, pulling up beside Jesse, who was concentrating on watching the ground.

"I don't know. Maybe he missed where the four cut-off just like I did and had to double back--- just like we do. If that's the case he probably didn't have time to stop and mark the trail," Jesse speculated without taking his eyes off the ground, wishing that Curtis would let him be.

"If he had to doubled back how come we don't see his tracks?" Curtis asked.

"I don't know! Stop asking so many damn questions and keep your eyes open--- instead of your mouth!" Jesse snapped, not wanting to make conversation.

"Yes Sir!" Curtis said, giving Jesse a wide berth. Curtis knew Jesse well enough to know when to keep his mouth shut and to leave him alone. While growing up he'd acquired a lot of lumps learning that lesson the hard way.

Trying to spot the Indian's tracks among their own was tiring work and after a couple of miles of straining his eyes Jesse stopped his horse to rest them. Jesse rubbed his eyes, stretched, and was about to continue when he heard the faint sounds of gunshots coming from way off in the distance.

"That sounded like gunfire," Walter said, riding up between Jesse and Curtis.

"That's what it sounded like to me too," Jesse agreed, standing in his stirrups and looking toward the direction from which the shots had come.

"How many you count?" Walter asked.

"Two or three. I'm not sure," Jesse answered. "How many you count, Curtis?"

"I think there were three, could of been four."

"You think Timbre caught up with those murderers?" Walter asked, visibly becoming excited.

"Could be hunters, but I doubt it. Too much of a coincidence, and I don't hold with coincidence. I'm betting it's Timbre, but I could be wrong."

"If we ride over to investigate and it does turn out to be hunters how much time do you rec'on we'd lose?" Walter asked.

"Those shots were fired—----I'd say from at least thirty minutes ride from here, give or take a few minutes. Sound travels far in this flat country. There and back---mmmmmmmm, I'd say we'd lose around an hour or so," Jesse guessed.

"That's a lot of time to lose," Walter pondered. "What would you do, Jesse?"

"It's not up to me. It's your daughter," Jesse told him, caught off guard by Walter's question. It was the first time since this all began that Walter had asked his advise on anything besides tracking.

"But it's also your friend out there," Walter reminded him, putting Jesse on the spot.

"Put that way, I'd have to say we take the chance and head straight for those shots," Jesse answered.

"What do you say, Curtis?" Walter asked.

"The way I see it, if it was Timbre doing the shooting chances are he lost the battle. Don't forget, he is up against four killers. If he did lose then Tess is still in a lot of trouble and the faster we get to her the better. But, if it wasn't Timbre who fired those shots then chances are he's already rescued Tess or at the very least he's still on her trail. Either way I think we should take the time to investigate. So I agree with Jesse."

"Sometimes you really do amaze me," Walter told Curtis, looking at him with new found respect.

Young men on the threshold of manhood sometimes have moments of pure genius, but more often than not their moments are filled with sheer stupidity. It's just a matter of chance as to which one will surface at any given time. This time it was Curtis's turn to shine and he knew it.

"Sometimes I amaze myself," Curtis beamed, feeling proud of himself.

"Lead the way, Jesse. Let's go see what all the shooting was about."

"Yes Sir--- but let's not run the horses into the ground this time, we still might need them after we get there."

"Fine, you set the pace, but let's not dawdle either," Walter ordered, not pushing the issue. He'd learned his lesson about rushing into things the previous day.

"Yes Sir," Jesse said, urging his mount into a slow but steady ground-eating trot.

Timbre felt, more than saw, the Sun start to rise as he watched the two Comanche's for any signs of consciousness. Even though he was facing East he wasn't worried about the rising Sun blinding him. By the time the light became strong enough to impede his vision the fight would be over.

The first thing that Timbre had noticed about the two Indians was that they were still wearing their war paint like the young Buck back on the hill had been. The one furthest from Timbre had his face painted black and the one closest to him had his face painted white. The paint made it difficult for Timbre to see their eyes clearly so he couldn't tell whether they were really asleep or if they were faking it. That was one of the reasons why he'd decided to keep his distance from them.

Getting too close to men that might be lying in wait for you, even if you knew what they were up to, was a dangerous and foolhardy thing to do. Timbre had no desire to shoot it out with the two Comanche in the dark, besides, he needed to capture at least one of them alive. He'd judged that his best course of action was to wait and let them make the first move.

As Timbre studied the two small, bandy-legged, Comanche he was amazed that these physically nondescript people had become the terrors of the Southwest. At one time the Comanche had been just an ordinary tribe of Indians roaming on foot for food on the outskirts of the Great Plains. Ordinary that is until the Spaniards introduced the horse to the Southwest.

The Franciscan monks who'd built their missions throughout the West in the 1500's had regarded the natives they encountered as Godless savages. They believed that it was their duty to indoctrinate the heathens into Christianity and thereby save all those poor ignorant soul's from the fires of hell; and, for that act of supreme kindness it gave them the right to utilize them as slaves.

One of the responsibilities that the Franciscans' thrust upon the Apache and Pueblo Indians was to care for the Spanish soldier's horses, when they stopped at the missions to rest. The Indians, not being as dumb as the monks believed them to be, shortly figured out the benefits of being mounted, over the disadvantages of being on foot; And, after having had that revelation they set out to remedy that situation by stealing the Spaniard's horses.

When the Comanche nation migrated to the Southwest, in the early 1700's, the other tribes were already familiar with the horse and were utilizing it in a limited way. It only took the Comanche a short time to realize the full potential of the horse. It was right after he acquired his first mount that a strange metamorphosis took place. The Comanche and the horse became as one. He was able to do things astride a horse that no other tribe had ever dreamed of doing. The Comanche totally ignored the fact that it had been the other tribes that had first introduced them to the horse, they came to believe that their God had created the horse just for them.

Once the Comanche mastered the art of making war from astride the horse he became the most proficient killer the West has ever seen. So proficient in fact that they were able to drive out the Franciscan monks, the Spanish soldiers, and later the French soldiers from Texas. Once they accomplished that, they then turned their talents toward the other tribes that shared the plains with them.

Along with their allies, the Kiowa's, the Comanche commenced to drive the Apache, Ute, and Navajo, out of central Texas and Eastern New Mexico. Eventually, Texas and most of the Southwest belonged to them. That is until the Cheyenne wondered upon the scene. The Southern Cheyenne more than held their own against the Comanche and Kiowa's and in 1840 the Comanche and Kiowa were forced to make peace with them. They needed to concentrate their forces toward a new more powerful enemy. An enemy that called themselves Texans.

For years the war between the Indians and the Texans raged, neither one of them gaining the advantage, that is until the six-shooter was invented. With all that firepower the Texans were now able to push the Comanche South until he become a fugitive in the land that he'd once so fiercely ruled.

As Timbre studied the two Comanche's he tried to understand their propensity toward cruelty. Other Indian tribes tortured their captives, but they had reasons for doing so. Granted, it was reasons that white men found impossible to understand but never-the-less, they were reasons.

The Apache killed their captives slowly in order to absorb their vital life force as it left their dying bodies, thus, making them stronger. Other tribes tortured their captives in order to test their enemy's courage. The more pain their enemy could withstand the greater the warrior he was judged to be. If they deemed their enemy to be great warrior then how much greater were they for defeating him. But, it was only the Comanche, as far as Timbre knew, that tortured their victims, woman and sometimes children, just for the pleasure of it.

Timbre's mind wondered for a second thinking of what they'd done to Evelyn---- and a second was all it took for all hell to break loose. One minute the two Indians were sleeping and the next minute they were moving like lightning bolts. How long they'd laid there awake, watching him, waiting for him to make a mistake, Timbre had no idea. Finally, their chance had come and they didn't hesitate in taking it.

White-Face, who was the closest one to Timbre, sprang to his feet and charged at him with his knife poised in the air. Jumping to his feet Timbre snapped off a shot. The bullet hit White-Face in the arm, shattering his elbow and causing him to spin away from him. Then, without hesitating Timbre fired a second shot at Black-Face who'd just vaulted onto his pony.

Timbre got lucky, his bullet passed through Black-Face's knee and into his mount, but before Timbre could see what effect the bullet had on Black-Face, White-Face completed his spin- and while spinning had somehow managed to transfer his knife into his left-hand and was now charging at Timbre again.

That move took Timbre totally by surprise and damn near cost him his life. The Comanche was no more than a foot away and his knife was rapidly descending toward Timbre's throat when he snapped off another shot without aiming. His bullet ripped through White-Face's left wrist and the Comanche's knife and most of his wrist went flying over his head. That did it, the Comanche fell to the ground, writhing in pain.

With White-face down Timbre turned his attention back to Black-Face. The struggling Comanche was pinned under his dead horse and Timbre could see blood and bone seeping out of a hole in his knee. His gun held at the ready, Timbre slowly approached the trapped Indian. He had only taken a few steps when White-face, despite the pain he was in, tried to bite him in the leg. Timbre jerked his leg back and then quickly brought it forward again, kicking the Comanche in the face. Looking down at the now unconscious Indian Timbre saw pieces of bone sticking out of the Comanche's right elbow. He could also see that his left-hand was just dangling from his tattered wrist.

"Tough little bastard," Timbre mumbled, stepping over him and approaching the pinned Indian once again. "If I had been two feet closer to you, you bastard, I'd have a knife sticking out of my throat by now."

From his angle Timbre couldn't tell if Black-Face was concealing a weapon under his body or not. Aiming his revolver at the Comanche's head Timbre cautiously walked up to him. As he bent over to search him the Comanche spit on him.

"Aren't you a bundle of joy," Timbre commented, back-handing the Indian across the face before finishing searching him. Finding nothing, Timbre told him: "You look nice and comfy so I'm going to let you lie there and rest for a while. It's been a hell of a tough morning for you so we'll chat later when you're better rested."

Leaving the Comanche, Timbre went around the camp collecting any loose weapons. Once he was satisfied that he'd rounded them all up he proceeded to the girl.

"How much further?" Sloane asked Jesse, after they'd been riding for an hour.

"Can't be much longer," Jesse answered. "Curtis! Ride to the top of that hill over yonder and see if you can spot anything. We'll wait here and rest the horses."

"Yes Sir," Curtis said, riding toward the only hill in sight.

Everyone watched Curtis in silence as he reached the hill and began to ascend it.

"I think he's spotted something," Jesse said, as Curtis got to the top of the hill and waved his hat at them, signaling them to join him.

"Let's go see," Walter agreed.

When Walter and his men joined Curtis one of the first things that they saw was Timbre sitting at the bottom of the hill with his back to them. The next thing they spotted, on the far side of the stream were three Comanche. Two of them were tied up and the third one appeared to be dead.

Jesse looked around and spotted the forth one lying on the hill with them in some brush.

"Where's Tess?" Walter asked, panic creeping into his voice when he didn't see her.

"There she is, downstream," Curtis informed his Uncle, pointing to a small figure that was sitting among the rocks.

Tess didn't give Timbre any indication that she was aware of his presence while he was cutting her loose. When she was freed she simply stood up and wondered off downstream as if she didn't have a care in the world. Tess stopped walking when she reached a stand of rocks and without looking around she walked into the stream and sat down in the cold water and began to hum some childhood tune.

Timbre took his bedroll from his saddle and freeing his blanket went and stood a few yards behind Tess, who still hadn't acknowledged his existence. He watched her as she scrubbed and hummed, just staring at the ripples in the stream. After some time passed and Timbre was fairly certain that she was going to freeze to death, he stepped into the stream and gently placing his hands under her arms he lifted her out of the water.

As soon as Tess had felt Timbre's hands on her she immediately stopped humming and became absolutely ridged. Timbre felt her tense-up and for a moment thought she was going to break wide open. As soon as he got her clear of the water he sat her on a rock and wrapped the blanket around her and then backed off.

After Timbre moved far enough away so that Tess could no longer feel his presence, she clutched the blanket tightly around herself and began to hum again. Timbre sadly looked at the young girl and knew that there was nothing he could do or say that would comfort her. The kindest service he could render to Tess at this time was to leave her be.

Timbre left Tess still humming to herself and walked a ways off to make a camp for himself. He was far enough away so as not to disturb her but close enough as to where he could keep an eye on her. Seeing her like that had put him in a black mood. Without saying a word to the two Comanche Timbre commenced to forcibly drag, kick, and punch them,

163

one at a time across the stream and out of sight of Tess. Of course they tried to resist, but that had pleased Timbre to no end.

After dropping the three Comanche where he wanted them, Timbre knew that he wasn't in any emotional condition to try and question them. If they gave him any crap there was no doubt in his mind that he'd kill them both before he got the answers he needed. But before he could allow himself that pleasure he needed them alive for a little while longer.

After applying tourniquets to their limbs so that they wouldn't bleed to death, Timbre then kicked them a few times just for the fun of it. He then left them to lie in their own filth. He then fetched Thor to help him drag the dead Indian pony out of camp. He didn't want the horse rotting there and stinking up the place. He thought of moving the dead Comanche out of camp too but then decided to leave him lying beside the other two so that they'd have something to look at and think about.

Having completed his tasks Timbre once again turned Thor loose to graze. He then sat with his back against the incline of the hill, making himself comfortable while waiting for Sloane and the rest to catch-up with him. There was only one way for Tess to leave the small canyon they were in and she'd have to pass him do to it, so Timbre felt safe in closing his eyes and taking a nap.

After about an hour had passed Timbre heard shouting coming from the top of the hill. Seconds later he heard Curtis yelling his name at the top of his lungs. A couple of minutes after that Timbre heard the men making their way down the hill.

Sloane rushed past him, without acknowledging him, and headed right for Tess. The rest of the men made their way to where Timbre was seated giving Walter plenty of space to be with his daughter. Standing, Timbre walked over to the wood he'd gathered earlier and started a fire. He was dying for a cup of coffee.

After the men had dismounted they each nodded to Timbre as they passed him bye and proceeded to where the Comanche's were tied-up. Some of them had never seen a Comanche before and wanted a closer look at what they had been chasing for so long—---- that is all except Jessie.

Most of the men shook their heads in disbelief as they stopped to stare at the two pathetic looking Indians who were just sitting there staring back at them with unmasked hatred on their faces.

"They don't look like much without their horses," Jesse said, dismounting and offering his hand to Timbre.

"They never do, but they were more than enough for me," Timbre nodded, squeezing Jesse's hand

"You did good. You still have your hair--- and I don't see you leaking anywhere."

"I got real lucky. Those assholes were drunk when they turned in last night," Timbre explained, releasing Jesse's hand.

"I'd say you got mighty lucky," Jesse agreed.

"What I could use now is a nice hot cup of coffee. I was in a bit of a hurry yesterday so I didn't think to bring any with me--- and those damn savages don't drink the stuff. How 'bout getting Curtis to make us some?" Timbre smiled.

"Give him a couple of minutes to get his fill of his first Comanche. In the meantime fill me in on how the girl is doing"

"Physically, I think she'll be alright but I doubt if she'll ever be right in the head again. She's shut herself off from the world and I don't think she'll ever let it back in---- and maybe that's for the best," Timbre sadly informed him.

"We've both seen it happen before--- but it's always harder to swallow when it happens to someone you know," Jesse commented, while fighting back the tears.

"Yeah, and it's even harder to take when you happen to love that person," Timbre expounded, placing his arm around Jesse's shoulders.

"It just don't make any sense---someone having to suffer that way--- but then it never did. Did it?" Jesse asked, rubbing his shirt sleeve across his eyes and not really expecting an answer.

"It never has to me," Timbre agreed. "But then again, I'm not the guy who calls the shots. Maybe all this makes sense to the big man up there. I'll be sure to ask him when I get back there."

"You do that," Jesse mumbled, walking away, wanting time to himself. "I'll get the coffee."

As Jesse walked away the rest of the men approached Timbre. All the men that is except Curtis who was still back at the stream staring at the Comanche's.

Tentatively, the men gathered around the fire facing Timbre. No one spoke, each man was waiting for someone else to speak first. Finally, after a long silence, Camilo asked: "We were wondering, how is the girl?"

"She'll live," Timbre told him, not going into details.

"Did they give you much trouble?" Frank asked next, their shyness starting to dissipate.

"Some, but those bullet holes slowed them down a mite."

"They don't look so tough," the one called Glen piped up.

"Would you like me to untie them and give them their weapons back so you can see how tough they are?" Jesse asked, coming back with a pot, some cups, and a bag of coffee.

"No. I rec'on I wouldn't," Frank smiled.

"Good. Now that you men have asked your questions your horses need tending to," Jesse strongly suggested.

"That they do," Pike agreed, taking the hint and leading the men away.

"I see that Walter is still alive so I assume that he didn't give you any trouble over Evelyn's grave," Timbre said, more than asked, while watching Jesse prepare the coffee.

"You assume right. As a matter of fact the subject never even came up, so I guess I still owe you."

"No you don't. You never did owe me. I apologize for acting poorly toward you. I called in a debt that wasn't due me. The only excuse I have is that I wasn't thinking right. I was thinking more about what was laying before me than our friendship. If there's anyone in this world that owes me nothing---it's you."

"Forget it. You had the right. I do owe you whether you think so or not. But for now I think it best if we just drop the subject. Let's just say that our viewpoints are a little different when it comes to that subject."

"You always were mule stubborn about somethings. Brothers just don't owe brothers---- and that's my last word on the subject," Timbre emphatically stated, sitting down to wait for the coffee to boil.

"Yeah," Jesse smiled, sitting opposite Timbre and changing the subject. "Did you find out anything useful from those two butchers?"

"I haven't gotten around to questioning them yet. By the way, how's your Comanche?"

"Poor, but serviceable."

"Then it's better than mine. After you have your coffee how about seeing if they'll answer a few questions for you?"

"I'll give it a try."

Seeing Curtis making his way toward them, Timbre commented: "Here comes Curtis."

"I've never seen anything like that!" Curtis exclaimed, as he joined them. "Shouldn't we bury that dead Comanche? He's starting to smell something awful."

"Did you or your Uncle think to bring along any of Tess's clothing from home?" Timbre asked, ignoring Curtis's question.

"Jesse suggested it to me, but not in front of my Uncle. I hid some of their clothing on one of the pack horses."

"Then you best bring them to your Uncle."

"Yeah. Good idea," Curtis agreed, heading for the packhorse, his concern for Tess driving out anymore thoughts of the dead Comanche.

"I've said it before and I'll say it again: He's a good boy," Jesse stated, as he watched Curtis fetch the clothes.

"Yeah. He's a little hot headed and asks too many questions-- but he'll do."

"He'll grow out of that."

"Or die trying," Timbre half-joked.

"Not if I have any say in the matter," Jesse stated, with deep emotion.

For the first time Timbre realized how much the Sloane family meant to Jesse and how hard it must've been for him not to have shown it when he found out about Evelyn. Now that the chase was over Jesse could let his emotions out without worrying about them interfering with his judgement.

"How's the coffee doing?" Timbre asked, giving Jesse something else to think about besides his sorrows.

"Should be ready," Jesse told him, pouring him a cup of it.

"Ummmm, that's good," Timbre said, sipping it. "Oh, oh, hold on to your hat, here comes Walter," Timbre mumbled, as he saw Sloane approaching them.

"Do you mind if I sit?" Walter asked, surprising Timbre with his new found manners.

"No, be my guest," Timbre offered, looking at Jesse who was also shocked by Walter's courteous request.

"Thank you," Walter said, sitting. "First off: I want to apologize to you Jesse. I've been acting like a fool treating you the way I have--- and I'm asking you to forgive me."

"Done," Jesse told him, without hesitation, knowing how hard that was for Walter to say.

"Secondly," Walter continued. "I thank you, Tim. Although you got there too late to save my Evelyn I do thank you for bringing her a bit of comfort during her last moments."

'I hope you never find out how much comfort,' Timbre thought to himself.

"I also thank you for my Tess's life. I know it will take a long time before she's well in the head again, but at least she's alive and I have you to thank for that. I'm also sorry for being so rude to you. My only excuse for being so stupid is that I was so preoccupied with my own hurt and worry that I wasn't thinking straight."

"Believe me when I say I understand that. Apology accepted."

Even though Timbre accepted his apology he knew he could never warm up to the type of man Sloan was. But, just knowing that after today he would most likely never have to deal with him again made it easier for Timbre to accept his apology.

"Where do you go from here?" Walter asked, taking the cup of coffee that Jesse offered him.

"There's still two white men out there that need killing," Timbre told him.

"You plan on hunting them down?" Walter asked.

"Yep."

"Why?" Walter wanted to know, curious as to what Timbre's motives were for continuing the chase. "It wasn't your life that they devastated."

"Let's just say they pissed me off."

"I would imagine they did, but that doesn't seem like enough of a reason to undertake such a dangerous mission."

"You sound as if you don't want me to run them to ground," Timbre stated, surprised by Walter's attitude.

"On the contrary. I want them more than dead. I want them to suffer the way they made my loved ones suffer. I just want to make sure that your motives are strong enough to keep you going if things get tough. If they're not, then I plan to take additional steps to insure that those animals pay for what they did."

"There's nothing you can do that will ensure their deaths, especially the two Comanche's that got away, short of killing them yourself. But, in all fairness to you I'll tell you that I'm not that concerned with the two Comanche, my main goal is to get the two whites that put them up to this. I'm going to hunt them down because they're deceased animals who need to be exterminated before they can do this again to anybody else---and rest assured they will kill and torture again if they're not stopped," Timbre declared, with venom dripping from his words.

"They didn't do anything that those Comanche didn't do, yet I do believe you hate those white men a lot more than you hate those Indians."

"You're right. I do. Don't get me wrong, nobody likes what the Comanche's are capable of doing but at least we know their nature well enough to guard against them. Sometimes our defenses are inadequate but at least we know enough to try to guard against them. But when whites start acting worse than the Comanche what kind of precautions can you take against them? It's like giving the fox the key to the henhouse."

"I see your point but I'm not totally convinced that that's your only motive for wanting to continue the hunt--- but I guess it'll have to do," Walter told him. "I'm going back to relieve Curtis, he's watching Tess," He stated, standing-up and walking away.

Jesse waited until Walter was out of earshot before saying: "He's dead? You and your Pa killed and buried him yourselves. You really don't have to go on this hunt. You ain't going to find what you're looking for."

"This is too much of a coincidence- and the one thing we've both learned the hard way was never trust in coincidence. I have to see for myself or I'll never have a moment of peace again."

Jesse nodded, he understood what was driving Timbre and almost agreed with him---- almost.

"I'm going to see if those savages are willing to answer any questions--- which I truly doubt they will," Jesse told him, standing.

"I'll wait here. I'm not ready to deal with them just yet. If they start to talk, call me."

"Will do," Jesse said, walking away and nodding to Curtis as they passed by each other.

"Where's he going?" Curtis asked, sitting by the fire and helping himself to some coffee.

"To question the two Comanche."

"Oh," was all Curtis said to that as he watched Jesse cross the stream and stop in front of the two Indians. Once Jesse started to talk to the Comanche, Curtis asked, "You think he'll get anything out of them?"

"Who knows. Anything's possible."

"I guess so. My Uncle told me that you're going after the four that got away. He wants me to go along with you," Curtis nonchalantly informed Timbre.

Curtis watched Timbre for his reaction to his statement while trying to act as if what he'd just said wasn't any big deal.

"Why? Doesn't your Uncle like you anymore?" Timbre smiled, knowing that this was one of the extra measures that Walter had mentioned on taking.

"Of course he still likes me. He just thinks that a member of the family should be along with you when you catch-up with those murderers."

"What for?"

"To help kill them. He can't go because of Tess, so that just leaves me."

Timbre kept his mouth shut while trying to find the right words to tell the boy what he thought of Walter's idea. Timbre didn't just come right out and laugh in Curtis's face, although the urge to do so was there. He was just about to try and explain the facts of life to Curtis when Jesse returned.

"I can't get anything out of those two, but I'm pretty sure that one or both of them speak American," Jesse added, as he sat. "They're in pretty bad shape. How they can stand the pain without screaming is beyond me."

"Well, since they won't talk they're of no further use to me. Curtis, go over there and slit their throats," Timbre ordered, looking directly at the young man.

"What!" Curtis exclaimed, sitting straight up.

"You heard me, go cut their throats. You can't very well shoot them, the noise would upset Tess."

"I don't understand?" Jesse said, as startled by Timbre's order as Curtis was.

"Oh, that's right, you missed it," Timbre explained to Jesse. "Walter says that Curtis should be there when I catch-up with his Aunt's murderers. He thinks that Curtis should take part in the killings. It's kind of a family thing that Curtis agreed to do. Isn't that right, Curtis?"

"Yeah," Curtis nodded. "But I wouldn't put it that way."

"What way? All I'm asking you to do is to kill those two savages. After all, didn't they take part in killing your Aunt and raping Tess? Somebody has to kill them, or do you plan on letting them go?"

"He's right you know," Jesse agreed, seeing where Timbre was heading. "If you're so anxious to kill you might as well start your killing here".

"I get the point! Layoff me!" Curtis angrily shouted. "I know I should be able to do it, but I can't. I guess I'm just too soft?"

"No," Timbre told Curtis, feeling bad for having put him on the spot like that. "You're not soft, you're just not a killer and that's nothing to be ashamed of. You should be proud of your Aunt for raising you to be more civilized than the rest of us."

"Thanks, but that doesn't help me with my Uncle. I don't know what I'm going to tell him. He won't understand."

"Tell him that you're going along with me," Timbre smiled. "I never said I wouldn't take you. Hell, I can use the company. I just wanted you to realize what you're capable of doing and what you're not capable of doing. You just trail along and I'll take care of what killing there needs to be done."

"You mean that?" Curtis excitedly asked.

"If Jesse says it's alright, then I mean it."

"It's not alright with me but I can't stop him from going, and maybe I shouldn't try to. Just try not to get him killed," Jesse ordered.

"I kept you alive for all those years until you learned to take care of yourself. Didn't I?"

"You didn't, your Pa did, but you keep him alive anyways."

"Jeeze! You'll never forgive me for that one little mistake, will you? I keep telling you that it wasn't my fault that you were shot by that old Indian," Timbre told him, for at least the hundredth time.

"Let's not go into that again. It was your fault and you damn well know it," Jesse stated, rubbing his shoulder.

"Okay, if that's the way you see it. Let's just drop the subject. Ya know, you don't ever hear me ball babying about the time you got my foot caught in that wolf trap. It still hurts like blazes when the weather turns bad," Timbre complained, rubbing his calf.

"No, not much. It's all you cried about for years. Besides, it wasn't my fault you stepped into that trap. If you weren't so----"

"Jess!" Curtis yelled, interrupting their bickering before it got out of hand. "Uncle Walt told me to tell you that he wants you to take the men and ride over to the Bar H Ranch and buy or trade for some fresh horses. He also told me to tell you that it's about forty -miles east of here, if memory serves. He also says for you to stop at Twin Creek on your way back and pickup some more supplies."

"I believe the Bar H is a lot closer than forty-miles," Jesse corrected him. "We'll leave right after I eat."

"While you're shopping for horses would you be so kind as to pick me up another pack animal and enough supplies to last me and Curtis for a couple of weeks. I seem to have left my pack animal back in Cotton Grove and it doesn't look as if I'll be going back there to retrieve him. That is if it wouldn't be too much of an inconvenience for you?" Timbre sarcastically asked Jesse.

"I'm going along with Jesse when he goes for the horses, I'll see to our supplies," Curtis volunteered before Jesse could answer.

"I'm going to fix me some food," Jesse declared, standing. "Anybody else hungry?"

"Some food sounds good to me," Timbre smiled.

"I thought it would," Jesse mumbled, walking away. "You always could eat."

"You think he's going to stay mad at you?" Curtis asked.

"Naw. He'll get over it soon enough, he always has. Ya know, the truth is that it was sorta my fault that he got shot. I was the one who talked him into exploring that seemingly deserted village- but don't tell him I said that. Oh, and one other thing: If you have a change of heart, don't go killing those two Comanche--- I still want to try talking to them."

"I'll go help Jesse with the food," Curtis said, standing and giving Timbre a strange look.

When Curtis caught-up with Jesse at the packhorse, Jesse informed him, "The boys are using the pans. They'll be finished with them in a couple of minutes and then we can have them."

"You think Timbre will stay mad at you?" Curtis asked, trying to pass the time while they were waiting for the cooking utensils.

"He'll get over it. He always has. Ya know, it was kinda my fault that he got his foot caught in that trap. I did sorta talk him into jumping over that log without looking first--- but don't you go telling him I said that."

"I'll see about the pans," Curtis told him, giving Jesse a strange look as he walked away.

Timbre awoke sometime during the night, sweating profusely, even though the air had a bit of a nip in it. He'd been dreaming of Evelyn again. In this dream she'd appeared to him all cut-up and bleeding, and begging him to avenge her. Timbre sat up, wide awake, knowing that any attempt to get back to sleep would be useless. He'd have to wait until he was exhausted again before trying. As he pulled on his boots, Timbre shook the vision of Evelyn out of his head. Standing, Timbre saw that the camp was nearly deserted, except for the two wranglers that were snoring by the fire. Jesse, Curtis, and the rest of the ranch hands had left around noon to fetch the fresh horses and supplies. Walter and his daughter were still downstream. The only time that Sloane had left Tess's side was to get them something to eat, or to relieve himself.

Grabbing his six-gun and shoving it into his belt Timbre climbed to the top of the hill. Standing on its windy summit and perusing the shadowy desolate panorama that spread out before him made Timbre feel small and insignificant. It was as if he were being dissolved into the landscape, slowly disappearing. The miles and miles of solitude made him want to doubt his own existence. He longed at that moment to hold a woman in his arms, any woman, just to prove to himself that he really did still exist.

Not allowing himself to dwell on those feelings, Timbre, with great effort forced those thoughts out of his head. His time at sea had taught him how overwhelming those emotions could become if allowed to linger. Taking a deep breath, that was close to being a sigh, Timbre made his way back down the hill. On reaching the bottom Timbre decided to check on the two Comanche. As he passed his bedroll he picked up his canteen and continued on. After crossing the stream the first thing that struck Timbre was the stench of decaying flesh. If the wind had been blowing toward him, instead of away from him, the camp would've smelled unbearable.

"Whew! Your friend sure does stink! I hope the stench isn't interfering with your rest," Timbre told them, wrinkling up his nose as he looked down at the two glaring men. "You guys want some water?"

The two thirsty Comanche's ignored Timbre so he took matters into his own hands. Forcing their heads back, one at a time, Timbre poured water down their throats.

"I wouldn't want you guys dying of thirst. What would your friends think of me?" Timbre asked, not expecting a reply. "Now listen fellas: You're starting to make me feel as if I'm boring you. Ya know, more than one person has told me that I've got a sparkling personality, so I can only assume that you two are purposely trying to hurt my feelings---- and that's not a very nice way to treat your host. I'll tell you what though, just to prove to you two that I'm really a swell guy I'm gonna overlook your rudeness, but for tonight only that is. But, later on in the day I'm afraid I'm going to have to insist that one or both of you take a more active role in our little get togethers. Now get yourselves some rest and think about what I just said. We'll pick this up again later on."

Timbre looked down at the two Comanche figuring that if they did understand American, like Jesse guessed they did, they must be convinced by now that he was crazy- and that suited Timbre just fine because Indians feared crazy people.

Gingerly he made his way back across the stream, hopping from one rock to another, careful not to get his feet wet. Reaching his bedroll Timbre pulled off his boots, put away his gun, lay back down, and dozed off again.

The next day was a lazy day and everyone just sat around wondering how long it would take for the others to get back. Timbre went through the motions of talking with the two Comanche again, who were slowly dying, with no luck. He again forced water down their throats and dropped some beef jerky down in front of them, which they didn't touch. Timbre had to admit, no matter what he thought of them, that they were the toughest men he'd ever met. He could see why they ruled the plains.

It was late on the third morning and Timbre was still in his bedroll sound asleep when he heard a voice telling him from a million-miles away. "Come-on, you can't sleep forever."

"What time is it?" Timbre mumbled, recognizing Jesse's voice as he slowly floated to the surface of consciousness.

"Close to eleven. We rode in about fifteen-minutes ago. If I'd been a Comanche your scalp would be dangling from my lance by now."

"You can have my hair just leave my body in the bedroll," Timbre told him, opening his eyes to the bright daylight. "God! That almost blinded me!"

"Come-on. Keep your eyes open. We don't have much time, we'll be pulling out shortly," Jesse informed him. When Timbre didn't respond, he added: "Damn you're getting old. You better find yourself a nice town with a nice soft bed in it and give up the trail."

"I had a nice town with a nice soft bed in it but you elected to drag me out of it, or are you getting too old and senile to remember that far back?" Timbre asked, opening his eyes again and throwing off his blanket. "Did you at least make coffee?"

"It's almost done, along with some biscuits and bacon."

"Why didn't you tell me that in the first place?" Timbre asked, pulling on his boots. "God, do I have to piss."

"The bushes are over there," Jesse pointed, walking away.

After Timbre relieved himself and washed at the stream he joined Jesse by the fire where there was coffee and food waiting on him.

"When are you guys going to start for home?"

"Right after we get a couple of hours sleep. We missed a great deal of sleep to get here by morning."

"You get my stuff? Where's Curtis?"

"Yep, and Curtis is talking with his Uncle"

"How much I owe you?"

"Nada. It's on the house with the compliments of Walter Sloan," Jesse told him. Then he added, "Listen: After I get Walter and the boys back home I'll try and catch-up with you and Curtis. Curtis is a good man and he can shoot better than any man I ever met, but he's green and you might need some seasoned help on this one."

"It's a good offer, Jesse, but I don't know where we'll be in three or four-weeks. And, in less than a week there won't be enough of a trail left for you to follow. But I appreciate the offer anyways."

"Ya know, Walter could find his own way home from here, he really doesn't need me anymore."

"Normally I'd agree, but you've seen him, he's off in another world with his daughter and you're on the fringes of Indian territory--- not to mention the outlaws that roam around these parts. No Jesse, you'll be needed. Plus you're not the type that starts a job without finishing it. Your duty lies in getting them home. If something should happen to them because you warn't there you'd never forgive yourself."

"As much as I hate to admit it, you're right."

"I know I am," Timbre smiled.

"I know I'm harping on this- but take care of the boy."

"If it'll put your mind at ease I give you my word that if Curtis doesn't make it back, neither will I. What more can I promise?"

"Nothing more. That's good enough. Here he comes now," Jesse said, nodding toward Curtis who was walking toward them.

"Uncle Walt is ready to leave," Curtis informed them. "But he wants to talk to Tim first."

"Well, there goes our sleep. I'll go inform the men while you go talk to him," Jesse told Timbre, leaving them to go round up the men.

"Let's go," Timbre said to Curtis, standing.

"He wants to talk to you alone," Curtis informed him. "I've already said my good-byes to him so I'll just go and say my good-byes to Jesse and the men.

"You do that," Timbre said, heading to where Walter was waiting for him.

"We'll be leaving shortly," Walter stated, as he emerged from the bushes. "I wanted to thank you again and to ask you to watch over the boy."

"I've already been told to do that, a number of times."

"By Jesse no doubt. He loves the boy too. But that's not all I wanted to tell you. I also wanted to inform you that I gave Curtis enough money to finance your trip. If you men run short and need more I told him to contact me at the ranch and I'll wire it to you."

"Good enough, but I don't think we'll need anymore money."

"The offer stands anyway. Oh, and one other thing: I thought long and hard about offering you money for what you've done for us---- but after realizing what kind of man you are I felt it would be an insult to you do to that. Besides, there's not enough money in the world to repay you for what you've done for Tess. What I will offer you though is my word that if anytime in the future you find yourself needing something, anything, you can come to me, or write to me, and I'll make sure you get it," Walter finished, grabbing Timbre's hand and shaking it.

"I'll keep that in mind," Timbre told him, as Jesse and the men approached, leading Walter's mount.

Walter went off into the bushes when he saw his men approaching and returned minutes later with his daughter who still didn't seem to be aware of where she was.

Not willing to mount the horse by herself, Walter was about to lift Tess onto the saddle when she broke away and to everybody's surprise rushed over to Timbre. Standing on a rock she looked him right in the eyes and then kissed him on the cheek.

For a brief second Timbre recognized a brief look of sanity on Tess's face--- and accompanying that look was a look of unspeakable agony. Then, as suddenly as the look had appeared it disappeared.

Facing reality, even for a brief moment, had been too painful for Tess so she'd swiftly retreated back into her shell. How many more times Tess would try to face the world before eventually giving up, no one could predict. The one thing that was certain though was the moment she stopped trying she'd be lost inside herself forever--- and nobody would ever see Tess again. Timbre handed Tess over to her father and sadly watched Walter lift her onto the saddle.

"She'll be alright once we get her home," Walter told him, climbing aboard behind her. Walter was kidding himself and most everybody knew it but him.

"Remember what I told you," Walter said to Timbre, just before he rode away.

"I will," Timbre said, knowing that he'd never ask Sloane for a thing.

After Walter left with his men trailing close behind, Jesse rode up alongside of Timbre. Bending over he took Timbre's hand, and said: "We've already said all that needs to be said, so I'll just say good-luck."

"End of trail, Jesse," Timbre smiled, squeezing Jesse's hand tightly and feeling Jesse place something in it.

"End of trail, Tim," Jesse nodded, releasing his hand and riding off without looking back.

CHAPTER

11

Timbre smiled as he watched one of the best parts of his past ride away and wondered if he'd ever get to see Jesse again. Opening his hand, Timbre saw what Jesse had slipped into it. It was a new cyanide shell.

"How come you and Jesse always say end of trail, instead of good-bye?" Curtis asked, standing by Timbre's shoulder.

Putting his arm around Curtis's neck, Timbre gently steered him toward the two Comanche, explaining to Curtis: "When me and Jesse were just young pups and doing some exploring on our own we ran across this dilapidated cabin high up in the Rockies. Being young and inquisitive we decided to explore the inside of that seemingly deserted relic. Upon entering it we found to our surprise that it wasn't as deserted as we thought. There was an old man lying on a bed who looked to be at a hundred-years old and he looked dead to us. From where we were standing we couldn't see any wounds that might've done him in, and he wasn't decaying yet, so we figured that he hadn't been dead very long. We also figured that he either died of old age or some sort of disease so we decided not to get too close to him, in case whatever done him in was contagious. That was about the same time that small pox was running rampart. We were just turning to leave when that dead man sat straight up and looked at us. Well Sir, let me tell you, me and Jesse damn near wet our pants. You see, at that time we were still young enough to believe in ghosts- and by God there we were face to face with one, or so we thought. If we warn't so damn scared I guess we would've bolted but our legs just wouldn't move. Of course later on neither one of us would admit to being scared, it wasn't the manly thing to do, but the truth of the matter is we'd both been scared shitless."

"Does any of this have anything to do with my question?" Curtis interrupted.

"Patience, I was getting to that part. After we'd calmed down a mite I asked the old man what was ailing him, figuring that maybe there was something we could do to help. He promptly informed us that there nothing we could do for him--- he was just plain wore out, or put more simply, he was just dying of old age.

'Being young and full of piss and vinegar there was no way that me and Jesse could understand how anybody could just die from wearing out--- and we told him so."

"Well," he just smiled at our foolishness and said: "Boys, when you reach your end I hope your trail has as many miles on it as mine had, and that you have as little to complain about your life as I have. I have lived a long and fruitful life and I have traveled as far as a man is allowed to travel on this road. My trail was a long one but I rode it proudly and with honor right to the end. A great deal of the time I had me plenty to eat and drink and except for a woman every now and then there is nothing more a man could ask for from life. Now, if one of you will hand me that there bottle of Redeye on the table there, we'll have a drink to my demise."

Jesse, being the closest to the table grabbed the bottle and handed it to the old man. Holding it up with shaking hands the old trapper ceremoniously toasted: "Here's to the end of my trail." He took a long pull from the bottle, then let it slip through his fingers and onto the floor, coughed a couple of times, laid back and passed away. We buried that old timer that day without ever knowing his name. Ya know, that's always bothered me some."

"So, what your saying is, you and Jesse are just wishing each other a long life when you part company?"

"That's the short version," Timbre smiled, placing the cyanide shell that he'd been fingering into his top pocket.

"What's that you put in your pocket?" Curtis asked, noticing the movement.

"Insurance."

"Insurance against what?"

"Carelessness and suffering for it."

"I don't understand?"

"I'll explain it to you later," Timbre told him. "Right now we have work to do."

"What do you want me to do?" Curtis asked, anxious to carry his share of the load.

"Go downstream and dig a grave big enough for three. Then come back and get that dead Comanche and throw him in it--- but don't cover him up yet."

"You want me to touch him? He's been dead for almost three days--and he stinks."

"Throw a rope over him and use your horse to drag him there. I don't care how you do it, just get it done."

"Talking about horses, have you seen my new horse?"

"I'd have to be blind not to have noticed that big Buckskin grazing over there?"

"He's a beauty, isn't he?" Curtis proudly asked.

"He sure is," Timbre agreed, without really taking a good look at the horse. Timbre's mind was preoccupied with more important matters than Curtis's new horse, but he forced himself to act interested when he saw how excited Curtis was about the dumb beast.

"Did you name him yet?" Timbre asked.

"I sure have. I---"

"Let me guess," Timbre interrupted. "You named him Buck."

"Buck? Why would I name him Buck?" Curtis asked, with a straight face.

"I don't know. It was just a wild guess," Timbre lied, not sure whether Curtis was putting him on or not. With Curtis it was sometimes hard to tell.

"Ye know, now that I think of it, Buck sure does fit him. Dang! I wish I had thought of it, but it's too late now."

"Just get on with it. Don't drag it out," Timbre demanded, not having the time or the inclination, to play games."

"I named him Leather. Clever, huh?"

"Very. Speaking of horses, did you happen to see mine anywheres around?"

"I haven't seen him since we got here, but neither was I looking for him. What are you going to do if he's run off?"

"Take yours of course," Timbre stated, looking away so Curtis wouldn't see the smirk on his face.

"Ya know you can't be saying that every time you think you've lost your horse."

"Say what?" Timbre innocently asked.

"That you're going to take my horse. You just can't go around taking other people's horses whenever it suits you."

"Oh! Maybe not. Let's discuss it later," Timbre told him, holding back a smile. "Right now we have work to do. You dig and I'll question those two one more time."

As Curtis started digging Timbre questioned the two suffering Comanche who were inches away from dying. Jesse's guess had been right, they spoke American. When he finished with them he turned towards Curtis who was still digging and decided to give him a hand in order to speed things along. Grabbing the dead Indian by the ankle he dragged him to where Curtis was still shoveling dirt.

"Here's a deposit!" Timbre shouted, dumping the body into the hole with Curtis.

"Jesus!" Curtis screamed, scrambling out of the ditch. "Why'd you do that?"

"Because if I didn't you'd still be in there digging. I asked you to dig a grave not a tunnel to China."

"I was just making sure it was deep enough," Curtis said, defensively.

"No you warn't. You were stalling, hoping that I'd drag the body over here so you wouldn't have to touch it," Timbre angrily accused him.

"Did you get anything useful out of those two?" Curtis asked, sheepishly, changing the subject and hoping that Timbre didn't guess how right he was.

"One of them talked."

"How did you get him to do that?" Curtis asked, surprised.

"It wasn't that hard."

Curtis waited for Timbre to continue and when he didn't, he asked, "Are you going to keep it a secret or are you going to tell me how you did it?"

"Better yet, I'll show you. That is if you really want to see?" Timbre asked, with an edge to his voice.

Not liking the sinister implication that he detected in Timbre's tone, Curtis asked: "I don't know. Do I?"

Timbre was feeling mean because he was about to do something that was distasteful to him, and he was about to take it out on Curtis. But after seeing the trust on Curtis's face Timbre realized how wrong it would be to try and hurt him.

Having a change of heart, Timbre confessed: "Probably not. I was making a bad joke. You stay here I'll handle this alone."

"What're you going to do?"

As Timbre walked away, he answered: "I'm going to make another deposit."

Curtis did what he was told and stayed where he was. Although he wasn't sure of what Timbre's intentions were he was certain that whatever Timbre was planning it wouldn't be anything he'd want to take a part in. Curtis tried not to look when Timbre reached the two Comanche's and pulled out his gun, but he was unable to avert his eyes. Without hesitating, Timbre shot Black-Face right between his eyes, relieving him of his agony. Curtis was shocked speechless. He couldn't even force himself to look away when Timbre dragged the dead Indian by him and dropped him in the hole with the other Comanche. He'd never seen anyone killed before- much less murdered in cold blood.

"It's still not too late for you to catch-up with your Uncle," Timbre told Curtis, after dumping the body into the grave.

"Did- did you have to kill- kill him like-like that?" Curtis stammered.

"Why? Did you have another way in mind?" Timbre inquired.

"No. It's- it's just that I don't understand how you could just shoot someone in cold blood like that."

"It had to be done and I didn't hear anybody else volunteering to do it. And, in case you forgot, that poor soul that your feeling so sorry for took part in mutilating your Aunt and raping your cousin--- and I'm getting tired of reminding you of that."

"You don't have to keep reminding me, I remember- and I'm not feeling sorry for him. I just never seen anything like that before. As much as I hate them I couldn't do what you just did. All I'm trying to do is to understand how you could bring yourself to do what you did. If the time ever comes that I have to do something like that I don't think I'd be able to, no matter how much I wanted to," Curtis rambled.

"Don't think about it so much. If you worry about pulling the trigger you're either not going to do it or the person you're facing will do it first. Either way you'll most likely be dead. Just remember this: The first kill is always the hardest, and God help us, the more killing that you do the easier it gets. After a while you just don't give much thought to it anymore, you just do it. Just make sure of one thing when you pull that trigger and it will make it easier to live with: Make sure that you're in the right when you do kill someone or it will haunt you for the rest of your life."

"But you didn't have to shoot him. It looked to me as if his wounds were infected and that he was burning up with fever. Eventually that would've killed him. It just wasn't necessary for you to help him along---- and the same goes for the other one. Unless of course you've come to enjoy pulling the trigger."

"There's lots of things we don't know about each other, Curtis, and since we'll be spending a lot of time together I figure we both have the right to ask questions about each other so I'm going to choose not to take offense at what you just said. Instead, I'm going to write your stupidity off to your youth and try to explain some things to you.'

'For starters: There are times when I do enjoy pulling the trigger, but this isn't one of those times. Also, you're probably right, he would've died from his wounds, but if it will soothe your sense of fair play, I shot him because that's what I promised him I'd do."

"What kind of a promise is that?"

"You asked me how I got him to talk. Well, you just saw how."

"By promising to kill him?"

"No. By promising not to kill them and leaving them to the buzzards to finish them off."

"As usual I don't understand. You're going to have to explain it to me," Curtis confessed, giving up trying to make sense out of it.

"Comanche's believe that without their eyes they won't be able to find their way into the hereafter- and the first thing that Vultures go for are the eyes."

"I didn't know that," Curtis proclaimed.

"That's why it's important to try and find out as much as possible about the animal, or person, that you're hunting. For instance: Comanche's also believe that unless all his parts are buried with him he won't be whole when he enters his happy hunting ground. That's why I also told them that I'd scatter there bones all over Texas after the vultures got through with them unless they told me what I wanted to know."

"What happens if a Comanche loses a limb, or something, while he's young? Does he save it until he dies so it can be buried with him?"

"If it's a finger or toe he might carry it around with him in his medicine bag tied around his neck, but for anything bigger he pays the local Shaman to ceremoniously bury it for him so that it's waiting for him in the hereafter when he gets there."

189

"Tell me, would you have scattered their bones all over Texas?" Curtis asked, wondering how far Timbre would've gone.

"Are you nuts? Why would I do that? I don't believe in their gibberish. I just told them I was going to do that to scare them," Timbre explained, not believing that Curtis actually had to ask him that question.

"Well, they believed you," Curtis defended himself, feeling foolish. Trying to point out that he wasn't the only gullible one there.

"They believed me because they think I'm crazy. Do you think I'm crazy?" Timbre asked, looking at Curtis closely.

"When are you going to kill the other one?" Curtis asked, thinking it wise not to answer Timbre's question.

"I'm not. White-Face won't talk. He's a tough one, but I think I'll have another crack at him before I give up on him," Timbre said, walking away, well aware that Curtis had ducked his question.

Again Curtis stayed put, he had no stomach for witnessing up close another possible murder. He watched as Timbre conversed with the Indian. He was too far away to hear what was being said but it didn't look as if Timbre was having much luck with him.

About fifteen-minutes passed and it still didn't look as if Timbre was making any headway with the Comanche. Curtis looked away for a moment to check-up on his horse and before he turned back around he was startled by the sound of a gunshot. Quickly snapping his head around Curtis caught sight of Timbre holstering his gun.

Once again Curtis stared at Timbre as he dragged the last Comanche by him and deposited him into the grave with the other two.

"You can cover them now," Timbre told him.

"I thought you said that you warn't going to kill him if he didn't talk?"

"Yeah- if he didn't talk, but he talked."

"How did you get him to do that?"

"Same way, but only this time I pointed out to him how foolish he was being. I explained to him how he wasn't going to be able to find the hunting grounds like his friends did---- and all because of white men. The same white men that'd deserted him and his friends and left them to die."

"Did they tell you that the whites deserted them?"

"No, but in his condition and with his intense hatred for all whites it wasn't too hard to convince him that that's the way it happened."

"So what did they tell you? Where do we head from here?"

"You cover them up first while I make coffee. Then we'll talk," Timbre told him, walking away.

"What about that Indian on top of the hill?"

"Let him rot up there. Unless you want to drag him down?"

"No thanks," Curtis grumbled, grabbing the shovel.

The coffee was still hot when Curtis joined Timbre by the fire.

"You want me to put rocks over their grave?" Curtis asked him, before sitting.

"What for?"

"So the Coyotes don't dig them up."

"Do you really care if Coyotes feast on them? I certainly don't give a damn. All I did was promise them that I'd bury them. They're buried. Promise kept. I didn't promise them that I'd stand guard over their carcasses for the rest of my life. Now sit down and have some coffee while it's still hot"

"I'll sit, but I think I'll skip the coffee," Curtis said.

"Suit yourself," Timbre told him, pouring some more for himself.

"So. Where are we heading from here?"

"According to those two our friends are heading for a Trading Post somewhere near where the Pecos meets the Rio Grande. It's a hangout for Comancheros. You know what a Comanchero is?"

"Yeah, it's an outlaw that trades guns and whiskey to Indians."

"He's also a scum bucket that would trade his Mother for a price and then laugh about it. If you ever run across one, and chances are you will before this trip is over, you best be thinking about how you're going to kill him. Give him half a chance and that's what he'll be thinking to do to you."

"So, these are Comancheros we're hunting?"

"No. Not according to those two braves. They told me that these men showed up at their village one day accompanied by a few of the local Comancheros. They asked their Chief for some men to go along with them on a raid. In return for the loan of his men and some ponies the Chief was to receive ten six-shooters, ten rifles, and all the liquor they could drink. The Chief agreed to that, no questions asked. Comanche's would sell their souls for six-shooters."

"But why did they ride hundreds of miles just to raid my Uncle's ranch? There are plenty of whites between here and there that they could've kidnapped."

"I don't know. The two Comanche's claim that they made that same point over and over again but never got an answer. Their leader, the white man, just kept insisting that it had to be that particular ranch. It was your Aunt that he wanted and nobody else would do. Your Cousin was just unlucky enough to be home at the time of the raid."

"If they're not Comancheros how come they're heading to the Trading Post?"

"I can't rightly say, but what I can say is this: Those two Comanche's were scared to death of their boss man. And I've never known a Comanche to be afraid of any white man before."

"They were afraid of you."

"They thought I was crazy but they warn't afraid of me. Hell, they wouldn't even describe this guy to me except to say that he had blond hair. He'd warned them that if they told anybody, especially me, what he looked like his spirit would swoop down and snatch their souls away from them. From what I was able to piece together this guy had buffaloed them with some magic tricks and so they believed everything he told them."

"For him to have threatened them not to talk to you means he must have known you were on his trail."

"That's what I figure because he also warned them I would find them and kill them if they left his protection. They thought that was funny and laughed at him. Jesse called that one right---Pete must've told them I was coming for them."

"Lucky for us the Indians didn't believe him," Curtis commented.

"Yeah. Ya know, I have to agree with Jesse about another thing. This guy either knows me, or knows of me and since he didn't want himself described to me then I must have seen him somewhere's before too."

"You think you know who we're after?"

"No!" Timbre quickly snapped, looking up at Curtis.

"So, when do we start after them?" Curtis asked, thinking it strange the way Timbre had snapped at him. But he let it lay. He was learning when it was best not to push an issue.

"In the morning."

"Why not now? We still have five hours of daylight left."

"Because I want to take a bath. I'm tired of smelling myself-and a shave wouldn't hurt either. There's no telling how long it'll be before we'll be able to bathe again--- and by the way---a bath wouldn't hurt you none neither," Timbre suggested.

"Sounds like a good idea," Curtis agreed, sniffing himself.

Timbre stood and whistled loudly. When he got no response to his whistle he walked toward the stream, mumbling something about Thor.

"You ain't taking my horse!" Curtis yelled after him.

"Ain't, ain't a word!" Timbre yelled back, without breaking stride, knowing that Thor would show up sooner or later.

CHAPTER

12

The first four days passed smoothly and quietly for Timbre and Curtis. Slowly they were winding down from the excitement of the last couple of weeks. The outlaws' trail was all but gone but that didn't concern Timbre because he had more than a fair idea of where they were heading. On the fifth morning however the reality of the situation hit Curtis hard. Timbre was shocked out of a sound sleep by what he assumed to be gunfire. Thinking that they were under attack Timbre's eyes flew open while he simultaneously grabbed for his revolver. With his heart pounding Timbre cocked his six-shooter and pointed it in the general direction of the ruckus. He was just about to pull the trigger when he recognized Curtis who was on his knees rummaging through the supply bag of pots and pans.

"What the hell are you doing?" Timbre angrily yelled.

"I'm looking for the biscuits," Curtis informed him, without looking up, but still throwing the pans around.

"What makes you think that the biscuits are in the same bag as the pots and pans?" Timbre asked, uncocking his revolver and putting it down.

"Because they've got to be someplace," Curtis answered, throwing the pots onto the pans.

"Curtis, if you don't stop that banging I'm going to shoot you," Timbre told him. "Every damn renegade in the territory must know where we are by now--- thanks to you and your damn biscuits."

"I'm sorry. I wasn't thinking," Curtis apologized, sitting heavily down amongst the mess he'd created, looking as if someone had deflated him.

"What's in that bag by your right leg?" Timbre inquired, standing.

Curtis picked up the bag Timbre was referring to and opened it. With a sheepish grin, he answered: "Biscuits."

"Okay Curtis, what's eating at you?" Timbre asked, knowing that something was bothering the boy.

"Nothin'," Curtis answered, taking out a biscuit and nibbling on it.

"Bullshit! Tell me what's chewing on you and let's get it out in the open," Timbre demanded, taking the bag out of Curtis's hand and helping himself to a biscuit.

"It's this whole stinking mess!" Curtis screamed, jumping to his feet and forcefully throwing his biscuit away. His sudden outburst of violence startling Timbre.

"Don't worry about this mess, I'll clean it up," Timbre volunteered, trying to calm Curtis down, thinking that he was referring to the pots and pans that were scattered across the ground.

"I'm not talking about this shit!" Curtis yelled, kicking at a pot. "I'm talking about my Aunt, my Cousin, tracking down men in order to kill them---- I'm talking about my whole God damn life! Everything's changed, nothing will ever be the same again. Why did those bastards do this to me? What did I ever do to them?" Curtis asked, pleading for

Timbre to make some sense out the chaos that had become his life.

Although Curtis hadn't been a first-hand victim, like his Aunt and Cousin had been, he was never-the-less a victim. Curtis's reaction to the violation of his life had taken sometime to surface——-but surface it did. In his own way he'd been acting somewhat like Tess--- retreating into his own little world. The only difference being that his private world had been wrapped around the adventure of the chase and the attempted rescue of his loved ones. With the death of his Aunt and the recovery of his cousin Curtis had nothing left to retreat into anymore. He was now coming to grips with what all victims eventually have to face and overcome--- uncontrollable rage.

"This is hard country we live in, Curtis. You should know that by now that nobody lives out here without being dealt a few bad hands. Admittedly some hands are worse than others but no matter how bad the hand you're dealt you best learn how to play it out if you expect to survive. And whether you believe this or not, losing hands can sometimes be turned into winning hands if played right. Remember this: Hardly anybody ever learns anything from their good times, it's the bad times that teach us the lessons in life that are important. You can't forge steel without fire."

"How the hell can this hand be turned into a winner?"

"I don't know, that's something you're going to have to work out for yourself. Maybe you'll never find the answers to all of this, but whether you do or not the fact remains that you're still going to have to learn how to deal with this without destroying everything in camp---and yourself."

"Words, they don't mean nothin'," Curtis said, starting to clean up the mess he'd made.

"You're right, words do seem to be inadequate at times---especially when you don't even hear them. Hand me the coffee pot," Timbre told him, knowing that he's speeches weren't doing any good at this time. Some things just have to be rode out.

For the next two-days Curtis lost himself in learning. He was like a human sponge absorbing everything that Timbre had to teach him. He figured that if he could just ask the right questions that Timbre would eventually give him the answers that would make his life whole again.

"I've been meaning to ask you," Curtis said, while riding alongside of Timbre. "What's that shell for. The funny looking one that Jesse gave you?"

"Insurance."

"Yeah, yeah, insurance, so you've said. You also said that you'd explain to me what you meant by that when you got the time. Well, we got the time now."

"The shell is filled with Cyanide," Timbre informed him, matter of factly.

"Rat poison?"

"Yep."

"Why?"

"To swallow in case it looks as if I'm going to be captured by Indians, or even worse."

"You mean it's for taking your own life?"

"You've got it."

Curtis remained silent for a while, mulling that one over in his mind; then he said, "I don't think I could take my own life. My Aunt read us from the Bible that it's against God's law to commit suicide."

"I don't mean any disrespect but those fellows that wrote that book were never captured by Comanche's."

"God wrote that book," Curtis corrected him.

"If you say so," Timbre replied, knowing better than to argue religion with anybody.

"You don't believe in God?" Curtis asked, catching on to the way Timbre had brushed his comment aside.

"I never said that. Don't go putting words in my mouth. Just for the record: I do believe in a greater power. If you choose to call it God, that's alright with me. It's just that I haven't met him yet and so I don't know what he likes to be called. Now, let's get back to the original subject: You were telling me how you didn't think you could ever take your own life."

"Well, I couldn't," Curtis stated. "My Aunt couldn't, my Cousin couldn't, and I can't."

"Maybe your Aunt would've if she'd had the means to do so at her disposal," Timbre suggested."

"No. No matter how much she was suffering I don't think she could have brought herself to end her own life."

"People do change their convictions given the right circumstances."

"Not my Aunt. She believed too strongly in the Good Book."

"You might be right. In any case, it's something that we'll never know for sure," Timbre relented, not wishing to alter Curtis's memories of his Aunt just to make a point.

"Jesse knew that I couldn't take my own life that's why he didn't give me one of those," Curtis declared, pointing to the shell in Timbre's top shirt pocket.

"Jesse didn't give you one of these," Timbre explained, patting the shell, "Because he knew that you wouldn't need one."

"How could he know that?"

"Because he knows me and knows that I'd see to it that you warn't captured."

"I appreciate the thought, but you can't guarantee me that."

"For God sakes Curtis, stop being so dense and use your brains! Of course I can guarantee you that!"

It took Curtis a couple of seconds to figure out what Timbre was trying to tell him, but finally it got through to him. Skeptical of his conclusion, Curtis asked: "Are you saying that you'd kill me if it looked as if I was going to be captured?"

"It doesn't take you too long to grasp the obvious. Does it?"

"Isn't that great!" Curtis loudly exclaimed. "Not only do I have to worry about outlaws and Indians murdering me but now I have to worry about being killed by you too."

"No need to thank me. It's shaping up to be my pleasure," Timbre smiled.

"Well, before you go blowing my head off you better be damn sure that at least five savages have their arms wrapped around me and that I'm tied down and unconscious.

"Of course. I wouldn't dream of jumping the gun," Timbre grinned.

"Doesn't the thought of death ever bother you? I mean, you treat dying so casually."

"It's according to what kind of day it is and how I'm feeling at the time. There are some days when death looks inviting and then there are days when I just don't care one way or another, and then there are days when I would give anything if I could just live forever. But in any case---I've already done that."

"Now what do you mean by done that?" Curtis inquired, perking up by that remark.

"Just about a little over a year ago some asshole shot me in the chest and left me for dead. Even the so called doctor pronounced me dead---- and I guess I was dead for a short time."

"Wow! What was it like to be dead?" Curtis asked in amazement.

"All I'll say about that for now is: It's nothing to be afraid of," Timbre told him, not wanting to go into details. He knew that if he did Curtis would be asking him questions until he showed him what it was like to be dead.

"So you think my Aunt and Father are happy where they are?" Curtis asked, full of hope.

"I'd say so. If they were good people."

"My Aunt was a good person so I reckon my Dad was too."

"How old were you when your parents died?" Timbre asked.

"As far as I know my Mom might still be alive," Curtis replied, not volunteering any of the details.

"If I remember correctly you told me both your parents died of Cholera. Now you're telling me that they're alive? If they're still alive how come you were raised by your Aunt and Uncle?"

"I guess it's no secret, I just don't like talking about it to strangers. That's why I told you they were both dead, but I guess you're no longer a stranger.'

'When I was six, my Mother abandoned me and my Pa. She left a note for my Dad stating that she was leaving him because she was tired of living out in the middle of nowhere's in constant fear for her life. She just couldn't bear it any longer and that she would send for me when she found some place to settle. My Father figured that once she sent for me he'd then know where she was and he'd go to her and try to reason with her to come home. But, after months passed without any word from her my Pa got tired of waiting. He dropped me off at his brother Walter's ranch and went in search of my Mother. That was the last that anybody ever heard from either one of them.'

'When neither of them returned my Aunt and Uncle kept me, raising me as their own. I'm pretty sure my Dad died because if he hadn't he would've come back for me. It worked out okay though because I couldn't have asked for better parents."

"It's hard to fault your Ma for leaving this part of the Country. Look what it finally did to your Aunt- and it was a hundred times worse fifteen-years ago. The only thing I'd fault your Ma for is not taking you with her when she left. But like you said, you didn't do too badly."

"No, I reckon I didn't; but someday I'm going to find out what happened to my folks."

"You do that, but I doubt that you'll have much luck finding them after all these years."

"How much further you figure till we get to that Trading Post?" Curtis asked, changing the subject before he started to hurt to much thinking about his folks.

"If we can find it you mean. They wouldn't have built it where an army patrol might run across it. It's probably hidden somewhere deep in the boondocks."

"Then how are we supposed to locate it?"

"First we find a town and then we ask questions. Somebody around here is bound to know where it is."

"You know an awful lot about hunting outlaws. Have you ever worn a badge? It seems to me that you would've made a good lawman."

"I did for a short time, when I was younger. I rode with the Texas Rangers very briefly. I found it to be a thankless job and the pay stunk. Besides, the job had too many rules---wearing a badge was too confining for me."

"Lately, I've been giving some thought to becoming a lawman. I want to help tame this country."

"Someday this country will be tamed. Honest men with guns have always outnumbered the outlaws---- and sooner or later the bad men lose. But I'm afraid it will be some time before you see this country civilized. Law is scarce around these parts, and besides, you're not ready yet to wear a badge. You have a lot to learn about hunting men and you still need a bit of toughening up."

"That I'm working on," Curtis laughed. "Ya know, this is the furthest I've ever been away from home?" Curtis commented. "You've been East. What are the people like back there?"

"People are a little more sophisticated. They're more complex in the big cities."

"What does so-phis-ti-cated mean?"

"More knowledgeable about how the world works. They tend to over complicate things--- more bullshit to contend with I guess. They don't have to raise or kill their food in order to eat. They just go to the store and buy it. Hell, they wouldn't even know how to skin a critter muchless butcher one. And when they go to bed at night they don't have to worry about being scalped in their sleep. Most don't even carry guns and they don't go around shooting at each other--- unless they're criminals. But there's no shortage of police to protect them from those types. That doesn't mean that they don't have their own brand of misery but their troubles are a whole lot different than ours. They consider themselves much more civilized than we are out here in the West, and maybe they are."

"Are there a lot of people and buildings in those big cities?"

"More people and buildings than you can imagine. They have things back there that you've never dreamed of, muchless seen. Maybe if we live through this we'll take a trip back there so you can see for yourself."

"That sounds great. It sounds like a fun place to visit. Why did you leave it?"

"After a while I got tired of all the people and noise and found myself hungering for the solitude and freedom of the mountains again--- not to mention missing my friends. Then after I'm out here for a spell I get tired of the hard life and the effort it takes just to stay alive. Plus, war was inevitable between the states so I decided to see the world. I headed to San Francisco, hopped aboard a ship, and traveled around Europe and Asia till the war was over. I guess I'm just plain fickle and can't stay in one place for very long."

"If you had to choose only one place to live, where would it be?"

"You mean between East and West?"

"Yeah."

"Out here somewhere. This is my home. This is where I feel the most comfortable at. I can't imagine living in a city for the rest of my life and not being able to roam around freely. Sometimes I thank God that I won't be alive to see the West tamed."

"Why? You're helping to tame it. You've tracked down hostile Indians and outlaws most of your life, and in case you haven't noticed--- you're still doing it."

"Yeah. I guess I am. But what choice do I have. I just hate to see people get hurt, even Indians, if I could prevent it. But a tamed West means more people and more people mean more cities. You do the math."

"How can you feel sorry for the Indians after what you've seen them do?"

"I don't feel sorry for all of them, just the ones that just want to be left alone in peace. The ones that just got caught up in the white mans greed for land. It's the war like tribes, like the Comanche, Kiowa's, Apaches, and some of the others that I don't feel sorry for. They're always looking for a fight, it's their way of life. It just so happens that they've finally met an enemy that's going to kick their ass. Like your Good Book says: If you live by the sword, you'll perish by the sword. No, it's not those tribes that I'll be sad to see go. But sadly, when they go so go all the others. And with them gone the freedom to roam around as one pleases will disappear along with them. As soon as it's safe to homestead the white men will begin to fence in this whole country."

"I never looked at it that way before."

"Well, for now that's not important. We got other things to think about- like finding us a town."

"While we're looking will you teach me how to use that whip of yours?"

"Sure. After we make camp I'll teach you. It should be amusing," Timbre smiled.

It was past noon, two-days later, when Curtis and Timbre rode into a small dusty border town--- and to call it a town was stretching the word a mite. The town didn't even have a name. Besides having no name it also had no streets, no sidewalks, and only four wooden stores that were haphazardly strung out and were in much need of repairs.

"You call this a town?" Curtis asked, looking around.

"I don't call it anything, but don't knock it these might be the only stores around for a hundred-miles or more," Timbre told him, as he nodded politely to the merchants who were all standing by their doors, watching them closely.

"Why are they all staring at us?" Curtis asked.

"They're waiting to see what we have in mind. I guarantee you that they all have their guns within easy reach. By the looks of these people I'd say that they've seen some tough times so I suggest that you mind your manners and let me do most of the talking," Timbre told him, pulling up in front of what passed as a general store.

Timbre knew that living this close to the border had made these people weary of all strangers. They probably couldn't keep count of all the outlaws that passed through their little settlement in one year.

"Howdy. How can I help you today?" the wiry looking storekeeper asked, as they dismounted.

"We could do with some supplies. You reckon you can be of some service to us?" Timbre asked, smiling.

"If you've got gold or silver I can," the storekeeper answered him, without smiling back.

"That I have," Timbre replied, pulling out a handful of cartwheels from his pants pocket.

"Well then, I'm just the man who can help you," the storekeeper informed him, smiling at the sight of the silver flashing in the sun. "You just tell me what you need and I'll sure do my best to accommodate you."

When the other town's people saw their neighbor smile and heard the sound of the Cartwheels clinking in Timbre's hand they relaxed and went back into their stores to get out of the sun. Fresh money was always a welcome sight in this run down little Hamlet. Even if Timbre didn't spend any money in the other stores the General Store owner would. It was a close knit community, being that they all depended on each other for their survival.

"I have a list here of everything that I'll be needing," Timbre told him, handing the storekeeper a piece of folded paper. "If you don't mind me and my partner would like to get ourselves a drink while you're filling out our order."

"No. I don't mind at all," the clerk smiled, happy to share the business with his friends. "The saloon's right across the street, serves the finest whiskey you can get for a hundred miles. Not like that rot gut that some other places try to pass off as whiskey."

"That's a pretty big boast for such a small town," Timbre smiled.

"It's no idle boast. Try it for yourselves and see if I ain't telling you the gospel truth."

"That we will." Then turning to Curtis, he said: "Curtis, let's go test out this gentleman's word."

"If you don't mind me asking: What happened to your friends face? Did he run into a bobcat or something?" the clerk asked, noticing Curtis for the first time.

"No, the lad is learning to be a bull whacker," Timbre laughed.

"Maybe he should take up another trade before he cuts himself to ribbons."

"I've suggested that to him a number of times but you know how stubborn young people can be."

"Don't I know it. In any case, your supplies will be waiting for you when you get back," the storekeeper told them as Timbre and Curtis left the store. They lead their horses across the street with them to the saloon but left their packhorse in front of the store so the store keeper could load it with their supplies.

"Why are we going for a drink? Why don't we just ask that storekeeper what we want to know and be on our way? He seems like a friendly enough fella," Curtis asked. "Besides, I don't drink."

"Sometimes things aren't always what they seem to be. Let's first find out which way the wind is blowing before we go shooting off our mouths. When we enter the saloon follow my lead and say as little as possible. Got that?"

"I hear you," Curtis answered, thinking that Timbre was being too overly cautious and wasting their time.

"Good," Timbre said, as he watched Curtis tie his horse to the railing.

"You're not going to tie-up your horse again?" Curtis asked, watching Thor start to wonder away. "He won't go far. Besides, don't you know it's not healthy for a horse to be tied to a railing by its reins. If I were you I'd use a lead rope to secure him with."

"Why's that?" Curtis asked, figuring that Timbre was setting him up for a joke.

"Have you ever seen a horse get spooked and try to yank away from the railing, only to be caught up short by his reins?"

"That's why I tie him up, so he don't runoff," Curtis smiled, waiting for the punch line.

"Well, three out of ten times that horse will dislocate his jaw doing that. He might not show it right off but sooner or later he'll start balking at taking the bit. His gait will be off and he'll stop eating. The pain will also turn him dirt mean."

"I've seen a couple of good horses turn bad like that for no apparent reason, at least no reason that I could see at the time," Curtis contemplated, starting to take what Timbre was telling him seriously. "Maybe you got a point. You think I should use a lead to tie him off with?"

"Gee Curtis, I don't know," Timbre answered, shaking his head. "You stand out here and figure it out. I'm going inside to get me a drink."

Timbre walked through the open door and stopped to look around. The place was empty except for a sweat stained, unshaven, fat man in a dirty shirt standing behind a long plank propped up by four sawhorses.

"What will it be?" the fat man bellowed. "It ain't the fanciest place in the territory but it's got the best liquor that you can find in these parts----or any other parts I might add."

"So I've been told," Timbre smiled, walking to the middle of the make-shift bar and throwing down a silver dollar. "If it's only half as good as you people say it is I'll be more than pleased. I hate to drink alone so I'd be obliged if you'd join me."

"It's past noon so I see no reason why I can't have a drink or two with you," the barkeep laughed, pouring two shots of whiskey into two clean glasses.

Timbre picked up his glass and held it up to the light, examining its contents. The whiskey had a nice smoky haze to it. He then sniffed it and was surprised to discover that it didn't smell like Kerosene, but instead it had a pleasant odor to it. Satisfied that he wasn't going to be poisoned, Timbre drank it down in one gulp.

Placing his glass down, Timbre admitted: "My friend, I've done my fair share of traveling and drinking and I can honestly say that I can't remember ever having tasted whiskey finer than this."

"That's what I've been telling ya," the bartender barked, downing his whiskey.

Curtis walked into the bar as the barkeep was pouring Timbre his second drink. Spotting Timbre right away, which wasn't very hard to do since he was the only man in the bar besides the barkeep, Curtis walked over and stood beside him.

"Barkeep! Another glass for my brother," Timbre ordered, smacking Curtis on the back.

"I took your advice and tied Leather to the railing with a rope," Curtis informed Timbre, as he watched the barkeep pour him a drink that he didn't want.

"Good-boy," Timbre said, squeezing his shoulder. "Curtis, I want you to meet my new friend Max," the bartender nodded to Curtis, acknowledging him.

"Glad to meet you Max," Curtis said.

"Likewise," Max answered, wiping the bar with a dirty rag. "If you don't mind me asking, what happened to your face?"

"I'm trying to learn how to use a bull whip," Curtis grumbled.

"Max, how long you been tending bar?" Timbre asked, changing the subject, while placing another Cartwheel on the plank.

"Fifteen, twenty-years, here and there. I own this place now, bought it about six years ago," Max answered, putting the Silver dollar into his pants pocket.

"Now in that length of time you must've seen hundreds of men tie their horses onto the railing out front?" Timbre asked.

"I've seen my share," the fat bartender replied cautiously, uncertain as to where these questions were heading.

"I bet you have," Timbre agreed. My question is: How many of those horses, tied to the railings by their reins, have you seen dislocate their jaws?"

Max rubbed his unshaven chin, pretending that he was really thinking hard when in fact he had no idea of what Timbre was talking about--- nor did he care. The only thing Max cared about was possibly insulting the only customer he'd had so far today.

Not knowing how to answer, Max blurted out: "I once saw a horse keel over from standing in the sun too long. I even saw a couple killed by stray bullets, but I can't recall ever seeing any get their jaw dislocated---- but that don't mean it didn't happen."

"I'm really disappointed in you, Max," Timbre told him, taking another drink and acting as if his feelings were hurt. "Now this young lad is going to doubt everything I tell him from here on in--- and all because you can't recall seeing something that must've taken place at least a dozen times right before your eyes."

"Come to think of it, I did hear a couple of cowboys talking, a few months back on how their horses' jaws were injured from the railing. It'd slipped my mind for a second," Max lied, trying to placate what he thought was a drunken fool.

"Now see there, Curtis. Didn't I tell you so?" Timbre said, pretending to perk up. "This calls for another round of drinks."

Even though Curtis hadn't touched his first drink that didn't stop Max from setting another full glass beside his still full one.

"The lad ain't much of a drinker, is he?" Max asked, as Timbre finished his drink.

"He's still young. It takes him a while to get started," Timbre laughed, grabbing Curtis's glass and downing it. "Tell me Max? Where can a man find something to eat in this town?"

"Right here," Max beamed. "Not only do I serve the best liquor in these parts but I also serve the best buffalo stew you ever wrapped your lips around."

"If that don't beat all," Timbre slurred. "Bring us a couple of bowls of your stew."

"Have a seat over there, Gents," Max offered, pointing toward a couple of tables in the middle of the room. "And I'll go fetch your food. I've had a pot of stew simmering on the stove since last night."

Timbre grabbed the bottle of whiskey and his glass and headed for the closest table as Max disappeared into the back room.

"Don't you think you've had enough?" Curtis asked in disgust, sitting across from Timbre.

"More than enough," Timbre answered, in a surprisingly sober voice. "Now try and get into the spirit of things so this guy will think were nothing more than a couple of dumb harmless cowboys."

Curtis was speechless, he had actually thought that Timbre was drunk. He hadn't had any idea that Timbre had been play acting.

"Here you go," Max yelled, coming out of the back room carrying two big bowls of steaming stew. Setting the bowls in front of Timbre and Curtis, he said: "I'll be right back with your knives and forks--- and some bread."

"Hey, Max!" Curtis yelled, as Max reached the bar. "You got any beer?"

"Coming up!"

The beer was warm, but the rest of the meal was as good as Max had said it was. It seemed like ages since either of them had eaten a sit-down dinner.

Finishing his bowl of stew, Timbre belched and poured himself another drink, saying to Max, who was standing behind the bar: "Now that was the best stew that I've ever eaten, even better than my Mama's. Who'd ever thought that a little town like this could boast of having the best drinks and eats in the territory. After we roundup our brother Fred we're going to drag him back here for some more of this good whiskey and food."

"You have another brother around these parts?" Max asked.

"I don't rightly know. I mean I have another brother, but I don't rightly know if he's still around these parts or not."

"I don't get it. I thought you said you were on your way to meet him?"

"We are, but we can't find the damn place that he wrote us to meet him at."

"What place would that be?" Max asked, getting suckered into Timbre's trap.

"It's right here in this here letter," Timbre stated, making a big pretense out of trying to find the letter. "I can't seem to find the damn thing. You got it, Curtis?"

"No, you had it last," Curtis answered, not sure if he was saying the right thing or not.

"Maybe I left in in my saddlebags. I'll go get it," Timbre said, almost falling over himself as he started to get out of his chair.

"It's okay, stay put. I don't need to see the letter," Max told him, shaking his head. "Just tell me what it said."

"What said?" Timbre asked, falling back into his seat.

"The letter, the letter!" Max yelled.

"Oh, the letter. Yeah. What was in that letter, Curtis?" Timbre slurred.

"Where we were supposed to meet Fred," Curtis answered, hoping that was what Timbre wanted to hear.

"That's it- Fred! We were supposed to meet Fred at some Trading Post along the Pecos, but I'll be damned if we can find it. I don't think there is such a place. He must've been drunk when he wrote us that letter," Timbre declared, letting his head droop slowly down, till it rested on the table.

After a couple of minutes went by, with Max studying Timbre closely, Max asked: "What's your brother doing around these parts anyways?"

"Did I tell you that I had a brother?" Timbre asked, lifting his head off the table.

"Yes, just a couple of minutes ago!" Max yelled, losing patience with the drunken fool. Then, quickly regaining his composure, Max gently reminded him. "You told me that you were supposed to meet him at a Trading Post, somewhere along the Pecos."

"Right. Now I remember," Timbre nodded, lapsing into silence as he starred at the wall.

"Well? What's your brother doing around those parts?" Max shouted, getting Timbre's attention again.

"Oh, he didn't say. All he told us in the letter was to meet him there and that he had a surprise waiting for us across the border. Damn if I know what the hell it's all about," Timbre said, dropping his head back down on the table.

"You mean to tell me that you two risked your lives riding through Indian and bandit territory without knowing why?"

"He's our older brother, whatever he tells us to do, we do," Curtis joined in, starting to enjoy the play acting.

"Well, seeming as you two appear to be harmless enough and I might add---- not to bright. No offense. I see no harm in helping you to solve your problem," Max cautiously volunteered.

"What problem?" Timbre asked, lifting his head and looking around.

"Go back to sleep, I'm talking to your brother," Max told him.

"Good," Timbre mumbled, pretending to go back to sleep.

"How can you help?" Curtis innocently asked, holding back the excitement he was feeling.

"I know where you can find that Trading Post," Max told him, moving closer to Curtis and lowering his voice. "But you got to swear that you'll never tell anyone that I told you how to get there."

"How come?" Curtis asked, wincing as Timbre kicked him under the table.

"That don't concern you, boy. You just give me your word that you'll keep your mouth shut?" Max demanded, his eyes narrowing, not knowing why Curtis's face screwed up like that.

If it wasn't for Timbre's promise to come back and spend more money in his bar Max would've forgotten the whole thing; but his love for silver had overcome his fear of the Comancheros who ran the Trading Post.

"You got my word on it. I won't breathe a word of it to anyone," Curtis agreed, while rubbing his leg.

"You best keep it too," Max warned him.

"I gave you my word on it," Curtis said, raising his right hand.

"Alright, I'll trust you," Max finally relented, moving closer to Curtis. "When you leave town head due West. In four or five-hours you'll come to a stretch of sand, cross over it, and when you're well out of it turn South until you hit the Pecos. At the river turn due South and keep going until you reach a grove of Cotton Wood trees. Turn left at the edge of the Cottonwoods and follow them around until you come to a mountain. There you'll find the Trading Post that you're looking for cut into the front of the mountain. And for God's sake don't hang around there any longer than you have to. It's not a safe place to be."

"I sure do thank you," Curtis said. "We would've never found that place by ourselves. How long did you say it'll take us to get there?"

"I didn't say, but figure on at least eight to ten hours of steady riding- and don't forget your promise to keep your mouth shut. Don't tell anybody that it was me who told you how to find the place. In fact, don't even tell anybody around here were you're heading."

"Mums the word," Curtis pledged, holding up his right hand again.

"That's good," Max said, walking to the door to make sure that nobody had overheard him.

"Did you hear that?" Curtis excitedly whispered to Timbre.

"Good work," Timbre told him, slurring his words. "Now let's get out of here."

Pushing back his chair, Timbre struggled to his feet and weaved his way to the door, all the liquor he drank was finally catching up to him.

"Max old friend," Timbre said, in a loud drunken voice. "My brother here says that we got to be going--- but rest assured that we'll be seeing you soon."

"Take care of yourselves--- and don't forget to come back," Max told them as Timbre staggered out into the sunlight with Curtis right behind him.

Shading his eyes from the sun, Timbre asked: "Curtis, where's my horse?"

"Standing in the middle of the street," Curtis answered, pointing Timbre toward Thor.

Timbre reached Thor and grabbed onto his saddle, resting his head on it.

"You can drop the act now," Curtis informed him. "Max ain't watching anymore."

"Ain't, ain't a word--- and I ain't acting," Timbre mumbled. "Go pay for the supplies while I stand here and die- and while you're at it, get me a nice colorful Poncho."

"What do you need a Poncho for?"

"Don't ask me anything right now. Just get me the Poncho. Please," Timbre begged.

Timbre didn't know how long he stood there, leaning against the saddle, but the next thing his fogged mind was aware of was Curtis asking: "You want me to help you up on your horse?"

"If you don't mind," Timbre mumbled.

Curtis struggled to get Timbre aboard Thor. Finally, after a couple of attempts he managed to get it done. He then mounted his own horse and headed West out of town, with Timbre trailing behind him.

About three-miles out they came across a small stream where Timbre declared: "This is as far as I'm going for today."

Attempting to dismount, Timbre fell to the ground. Staggering to his feet and brushing himself off, Timbre struggled to regain his bearings. Curtis was just about to ask him if he needed any assistance when Timbre rushed into the bushes and became violently ill.

"You feeling better?" Curtis asked, with a big smile of his face, when Timbre staggered out of the bushes.

"Shut up," Timbre mumbled, leaning his face against his saddle again. "You're enjoying my misery a little too much."

"That's what you get for just not asking directly what we wanted to know. You didn't have to play act and drink a whole bottle of whiskey. Now you're paying for it."

"I'm going to tell you this just once--- and after I tell you this if you open your mouth again today-- I swear I'll shoot you," Timbre threatened, without looking up. "That rinky-dink town that we were just in only exists because the Comancheros allow it to. Hell, they probably get the stuff that they sell to the Indians from that place. Those people are so scared of those outlaws that they wouldn't have told us shit if we'd asked straight out."

"You mean that Max is a Comanchero?"

"No. Max and the rest of them are just doing what they have to do to survive. By the looks of them I doubt if they even make much of a profit from what they sell to that Trading Post we're heading for."

"Why do the Comancheros bother buying from them anyway? Why don't they just leave them alone and order their supplies from the same place that the town's people get their goods from?"

"It's safer for them to let the town's people order their goods for them. It draws less attention to their operation that way."

"How do you know that?"

"Because I've seen things like that before. Now be quiet and make camp. I need to sleep this off."

Curtis had some more questions for Timbre but thought it wise to leave him be- at least for the time being.

CHAPTER

13

"There it is," Timbre told Curtis, who was standing alongside of him at the end of the grove of Cottonwood trees. "If it hadn't been for Max we could've searched forever and never have found this place."

The Trading Post was about fifty yards directly ahead of them. It looked to be damn near impenetrable if attacked. The only part of the Post that stuck out of the mountain was its porch. Even its thick wood door and closed shuttered window were built into the face of mountain. To the right of the porch ran a stream and about twenty-yards beyond the stream stood a corral which contained four Indian ponies.

"We could've been here yesterday if you hadn't had to soak your head in the stream all day," Curtis accused Timbre, still mad because a whole day had been wasted waiting for Timbre to recover from his hangover,

"Stop your bellyaching. The horses needed the rest and we needed a bath. Why are you in such a hurry to get yourself killed anyway."

"I'm not in a hurry to die. I just want to get this thing over with and go home."

Timbre looked at Curtis and could see the strain on his face. The tension was getting to the boy but he looked to be still game.

"I'll bet my last dollar that those are the Indian ponies that we've been tracking all across Texas," Timbre commented.

"Do you think that the men we're after are still in there?" Curtis asked, with a slightly shaky voice.

"No. They're probably long gone. If they were still here their saddle horses would be out front. This is where they made the switch though."

"Then what are we waiting for? Let's get in there and find out which way they're headed," Curtis urged, some of the tension leaving his body.

"Easy does it. I've got a bad feeling about this place. Something just isn't right about it, but I can't quite put my finger on it," Timbre warned him.

"Come-on! We've wasted enough time! Every minute we spend out here gives those killers more of a lead on us. Except for those ponies, there ain't no other horses in sight. You said yourself that the men who were riding them are long gone. There's probably nobody in there 'cept the storekeeper."

"Okay," Timbre relented against his better judgement. "First let me get somethings together."

Timbre turned to Thor and reaching beneath his bedroll he pulled out a double-barreled shotgun. Then, from his saddlebags he retrieved a leather pouch.

"What are you going to do with that?" Curtis asked, as Timbre reached into the bag, pulled out two shells and loaded the shotgun.

"Nothing- I hope. It's just a precaution," Timbre explained, tying a leather thong to the stock of the shotgun and the other end of it around his shoulder so that it's triggers hung within easy reach of his hand. "Fetch me that Poncho you got for me."

Curtis retrieved the red and yellow Poncho from the pack horse and handed it to Timbre who then slipped it over his head, concealing the Shotgun hanging on his side.

"How much money you got left?" Timbre asked.

"A hundred-dollars or so. Why? Do you need some?" Curtis inquired, fishing through his pockets.

"Keep five-dollars and give me the rest," Timbre ordered, sticking out his hand.

"What do you need this much money for?" Curtis asked, reluctantly handing the money over to Timbre.

"I don't. I just don't want to take the chance of you losing all of it in there," Timbre explained, as he lifted his stirrup and stashed the money in a hidden compartment that was hidden beneath it.

"I didn't know that was there," Curtis exclaimed.

"That's the whole idea of it. There are a lot of things you don't know."

"Like what?"

"Like my boots. Inside of my left boot you'll find a knife and inside of my right boot you'll find a Derringer. I only tell you this in case something happens to me and you find yourself in need of a weapon."

"What could happen to you?" Curtis asked.

"Who knows? It's been my experience that it's the things that you don't plan for that are the things that are most likely to bite you in the ass. Some of the tightest spots that I've ever been in are the ones that I hadn't foreseen happening. And, like everyone else who's gotten themselves into a tight fix I've always lamented: 'If only I had this, or if only I had that.' Well, I learned my lessons the hard way. You might not always know what's going to happen but it doesn't hurt to be prepared for anything."

"What else do you have hidden?" Curtis asked.

"I thought that you were in a hurry." Timbre smiled, mounting.

"I am," Curtis remembered, also mounting. "Wouldn't it be wiser to sneak up on that place and take whoever's in there by surprise?"

"There's no way we can sneak up on that place without getting our heads blown-off. The best way to handle this is to act as if we've got nothing to hide and ride straight in. After all, it is a Trading Post. Don't forget, let me do most of the talking," Timbre cautioned him, nudging Thor forward.

"So, what else is new?," Curtis flippantly remarked. "You plan on getting drunk again?"

"Not in this place. Besides, my stomach couldn't take it."

As they dismounted in front of the sign that read PECOS TRADING POST Curtis asked, "You think they know we're here?"

"You bet," Timbre softly said. "Just keep in mind that we're dealing with some cunning and dangerous men. You're not going to no church social."

"I'm well aware of that," Curtis nervously replied. "What's the plan?"

"No plan. We'll play it by ear. Just follow my lead. Okay? Here we go," Timbre told him, climbing the porch steps and opening the door.

Even though it was still daylight outside the lamps were lit inside. The place smelled just like it looked, like a moldy old cave with the smell of liquor thrown in for good measure. To the right of where Timbre was standing was where the bar stood and behind the bar was shelves full of liquor bottles. He couldn't see the whole place because at the rear of the bar was a black curtain covering a tunnel entrance leading to God knows where.

"Boy, this place is big and spooky!" Curtis commented, from behind Timbre.

"Try not to sound as if you just left the farm," Timbre whispered.

"But I just did leave the farm," Curtis smiled. "Look at that bar. I bet Max would love to have that beauty," Curtis commented, gesturing towards the long Mahogany Bar with it's brass foot rails running all along the front of it.

"He probably did at one time- and don't mention him or that town again."

"Gotcha."

"What can I do for you boys?" a squeaky little voice asked, as the curtains parted and a squeaky little man walked out to stand behind the bar.

Timbre looked at the man and immediately disliked him. The man's sharp pointy features reminded Timbre of a rat. Even the hairs on his face randomly sprouted out here and there and looked more like whiskers than they did a beard. His thin oily, mousy brown hair on the top of his head looked as if it hadn't been combed or washed in years.

Timbre and Curtis stepped up to the bar and Timbre noticed Rat Face's dark beady eyes nervously dart from him to Curtis to the front door and then back to him again.

"We'll have a shot of Rye, if you got any," Timbre ordered.

"I got it," Rat Face said, sounding very unfriendly. "What are you two doing around these parts anyways?"

Timbre thought to himself, 'Looking to crush your pointy little head beneath my boot,' but instead forced himself to smile, and say: "Me and my brother just crossed the border and happened to run across your place. We almost rode by it, it's not an easy place to spot. I bet not many folks know you're even here. I'm guessing you don't do much business. Anyway, it's been sometime since we've tasted good American whiskey and we kind of hoped that you'd have some."

"If you two just crossed the Sabine how come you ain't still wet?" Rat Face suspiciously asked.

"I said that we just crossed over from Mexico, I didn't say that we were just born. We've crossed rivers before and we've learned to take our clothes off before doing so. We don't like riding wet."

"Oh," Rat Face squeaked.

"What's with all the questions? I'd think you'd be glad to get our business, wet or dry, considering that this place ain't in the heart of Kansas City," Timbre commented.

"Sorry," Rat Face apologized, trying to act like a concerned store keeper. "But a man way out here alone can't be too careful. What with being so close to the border and all."

"Apology accepted," Timbre smiled. "Now how about those drinks?"

"Coming right up," Rat Face told him, pulling out two glasses from beneath the bar and placing them in front of Timbre and Curtis. "What's your names?"

"I'm Tim Bree and this is my brother Curtis Bree," Timbre lied, watching Rat Face pour what looked like Max's whiskey into their glasses.

"This looks like some fine stuff," Curtis said, also recognizing the whiskey.

"It's the finest whiskey in the West. It comes all the way from Kentucky. The one thing I'm most proud of is my stock of good liquor."

Slowly sipping the whiskey, Timbre confirmed that it was indeed the same stuff that Max had served them.

"You and your brother ain't drinking like you've been dry for a spell," Rat Face suspiciously remarked, watching them slowly sip their liquor.

"I never said that we've been dry. What I said was that we hadn't had American whiskey for a while. You don't listen too well. In fact, we tied one on just the other night but only with Tequila. Ain't that right, Curtis?"

"Don't remind me. After drinking that stuff it's going to take my stomach a little time to get used to this good stuff- but once it does--- watch out," Curtis smiled.

"Well, while you're waiting for your stomachs to get used to my liquor you can pay for what you've already had."

"Fair enough. How much do we owe you?" Timbre asked.

"A dollar. Each."

"A dollar each! That's a lot of money. Even for this," Timbre complained.

"It might be a lot of money elsewhere but not here. Either pay up or get out," Rat Face demanded, not acting like a man who was all alone, seventy-miles from nowhere.

"Now don't go getting yourself all riled up. I didn't say I wasn't going to pay, I was just making an observation. You are the most unfriendly barkeep that I've ever run across," Timbre told him, throwing down two silver-dollars.

Rat Face picked up the money and put it in his shirt pocket without saying a word. There was something about the way Rat Face was acting that had Timbre's nerves screaming for him to get the hell out of there. But since he'd already committed himself to this course of action he forced himself to continue on with it.

"Those Indian ponies out there, are they for sale?" Timbre nonchalantly asked, without looking up from the bar.

"Why?" Rat Face wanted to know, his eyes narrowing.

"If they are, and if the price is right, we might be interested in buying them," Timbre told him.

"Why would you want to buy Indian ponies?"

"Any horses will do. Ours are plum wore out and we need some fresh mounts. If you got any others hanging around I'd be more than happy to have a look at them."

"No. Those are the only horses around here but I can't sell them. They don't belong to me."

"Who do they belong to? I'll negotiate with him."

"They're his," Rat Face said, pointing to the front door, as it banged open.

Timbre and Curtis both looked toward the door but all they saw was a huge shadow blocking out the sunlight.

"Come-on in boys," the huge silhouette bellowed, sounding as if his voice was coming from inside of an empty barrel. "Cecil has company."

Timbre and Curtis stared transfixed as the huge object moved toward them. The closer it got, the larger it got, until it eclipsed everything else from their view.

"Oh shit," Timbre mumbled under his breath.

When the giant stepped into the light Curtis saw that the man stood over seven-feet tall and weighed in about four-hundred pounds. His face was covered with long gray dirty hair, as was his head, except for the scar that ran down his left cheek. Although it was warm outside the monster was covered with furs and smelled as if he hadn't taken a bath in his entire life---which he probably hadn't. Just looking at that hulking pile of filth made Curtis's knees turn week.

"Mountain," Cecil squeaked. "This here fella calls himself Tim Bree and claims that the young one is his brother Curtis. They be interested in buying your Indian ponies."

"Is he now," Mountain bellowed, stepping up to the bar, about ten feet away from Timbre.

"Mountain Muntean," Timbre proclaimed, looking up into the huge man's insane looking eyes. "It's been a long

226

time. I was kinda hoping that you'd be dead by now. What are you doing in these parts?"

"That's none of your business," the big man growled, showing his rotting teeth. "You calling yourself Tim Bree now?"

"Now and again," Timbre forced himself to answer calmly, knowing that he and Curtis were in deep shit.

Mountain Muntean was the biggest and craziest trapper that had ever roamed the Rocky's. At first he'd worked for the Northwest Fur Company, as their bullyboy, but even they had to finally let him go when he became uncontrollable. Trappers who generally feared no one traveled out of their way just to avoid having any contact with Muntean. Even the Indians dreaded his visits to their villages. It was rumored that Mountain had once broke a Grizzly's back with nothing more than his hands--- and Timbre had no reason to doubt that.

"Boys," Muntean smiled, his mood instantly changing. "I want you to meet the best tracker that ever lived. If he ever takes up your trail you can save yourselves a lot of time and trouble by just surrendering to him."

"He might be able to find me but is he man enough to bring me in?" a voice asked from behind Mountain. Muntean stepped to the side and Timbre saw four men standing behind him. A quick glance showed Timbre that three of them were scummy looking men but the fourth person grabbed and held his attention.

Timbre was surprise to see standing among that rabble a beautiful blond-haired girl. He guessed her age to be between twenty and twenty-five years old. It was hard to be exact because of all the dirt that was covering her.

Quickly Timbre scanned her torn yellow dress and lithe body and then raised his eyes and made contact with her pleading blue eyes. Without her having to say a word Timbre knew that the girl was Mountain's captive. There was nothing that Timbre could do for her at the moment so he quickly sized up the three filthy Comancheros that were bordering her. The first thing that Timbre inspected was their weapons. Each of the men had ball and cap six-shooters hanging from their sides, plus their knives. Timbre saw no shotguns or rifles and this made him feel a bit more confident that he might make it out of this place alive. Him and Curtis were outnumbered but when it came to firepower he had the edge. The next thing that Timbre looked at were the men themselves.

The man standing to the left of the girl had long greasy black braids trailing out from the bottom of his black Stetson. He had the facial features and coloring of a half-breed. The hombre standing to the right of her was a Mexican. He wore a big Sombrero that covered most of his face. The outlaw standing behind the woman wore an eye-patch over his left eye and had filthy blond hair. Those three were normal size and lean. Compared to Mountain they looked like they could fit in his pocket.

"You don't have to be much of a man to bring you in, you Squirrel," Mountain told the half-breed, while looking directly down at Timbre. "But just to prove to you how dangerous this man is I know for a fact that he once hunted down and killed five Blackfoot braves all by himself. Five braves that knew he was coming and were lying in wait for him. I know this to be true because those braves were my friends. It was a feat of such grandness that I forgave him and so did not kill him myself for that. I know of nobody, besides myself of course, who could have accomplished such a feat. You kill anymore Indians lately?" he asked Timbre.

Timbre looked up into Mountain's eyes, taken by surprise by the question and saw the insane rage building up in him. Knowing that he'd have to kill Mountain if he wanted to get out of there alive, Timbre answered: "Two or three, here and there, but that's beside the point. You don't expect anybody here to believe that you ever had "A" friend--- Indian or white, much less five of them? Nobody-----" Before Timbre could finish what he was about to say Mountain moved faster than any man his size had a right to. A huge hand shot out and encircled his neck. His air was immediately cutoff and his eyes started to bulge out of his head as his feet slowly left the floor.

Everything happened so quickly that Curtis didn't realize what was taking place until it was too late. By the time he was aware of the situation he was already being covered by three guns.

As Timbre was slowly being strangled, Curtis's mind franticly raced for a solution to Timbre's deadly predicament. Running out of time and options Curtis was about to draw his gun and go for broke when he saw Mountain gently lower Timbre back down to the floor.

"If you don't let go I'm going to blow your balls out through the roof of your head," Timbre croaked, with the front of his shotgun jammed between Mountain's legs.

"Go easy," Muntean pleaded, releasing Timbre and backing-off to stand with his men. "You do not really want to pull those triggers."

"You want to bet," Timbre grimaced, in a hoarse whisper, rubbing his throat with his left hand. "Tell your men to holster their guns."

"Put them away men. He won't go and kill us in cold blood," Mountain ordered, becoming braver now that the barrels of the shotgun had been removed from his privates.

"Don't go betting your balls on that, Big Boy. I didn't live this long by being squeamish about pulling the trigger. Blowing you four to hell won't spoil my supper none. You! Sis! Come stand next to my partner."

"She ain't going nowhere!" Mountain bellowed, grabbing her by the arm. "You pull that trigger and you bring her down with us-- and I do not think you'd want to do that."

"You're right, I don't want to do that- but I will. She's better off dead than being with you. Now, you only got two ways to go, either tell your men to back off and let the girl go, or get your ass's blown-off."

"You're bluffing," Muntean laughed.

"Times up," Timbre said, raising the shotgun. "Bye-bye, Shitheads."

"Wait!" Mountain bellowed, when he saw Timbre's finger start to tighten on the trigger. "Back off men. And you," he told the girl shoving her toward Curtis. "go stand over there."

The three men holstered their guns as the girl fell into Curtis's arms.

They were all surprised to see fear on Mountain's face, something that they'd witnessed only one other time, and that had been just recently.

"Now you've gone and taken all the fun out of my day," Timbre told him. "I was so looking forward to blowing your head off. Oh well, the day's still young. Maybe later."

"What is it that you want from me?" Mountain asked, frustrated with the way things were going for him.

"For starters: I want the girl."

"Like hell!" Mountain roared, causing some dirt to fall from the ceiling. "I risked my life to get her! She's mine!"

230

"She was yours," Timbre informed him, poking Mountain hard in the stomach with the barrels of the shotgun. "Unless you're prepared to risk your life for her again."

"Do not push me too far," Muntean snarled, hardly feeling the blow from the gun. "Or shotgun or no I will tear your guts out and choke you with them."

"Is that so. Well I'm pushing," Timbre told him, nudging him with the shotgun again. "Anytime you get tired of me pushing you go ahead and make your move. The only reason that you're still breathing is because I need some information. If you tell me what I want to know I might not splatter your guts all around the room. On the other hand if you as much as look at me cross-eyed I'll be more than happy to blow your big ugly body into a lot of little ugly bits."

Muntean was crazy, but he wasn't stupid. He knew that Timbre would've liked nothing better than to have killed him years ago and was now just looking for an excuse to pull the trigger on him. Mountain had no intention of giving him such a reason. He would play along with Timbre for now but silently vowed to make him pay later for yet another humiliation.

"Now, now, Mr. Bree," Muntean started, in a soothing voice, his face cracking into a smile that looked more menacing than friendly. "We two should not be fighting among ourselves. After all, there is not many of us old trappers left. You want the girl? She's yours. Consider her a gift for old times' sake. Now put the scattergun away. We are all friends here."

"This is very generous of you Mountain. I guess old age does mellow us all, but just to make sure that you remain mellow I'll keep the shotgun where it is. It has such a soothing effect on you."

"I can understand why you don't trust me, although it saddens me. I am a victim of past lies."

"Yeah. You were always misunderstood. My Father even misunderstood you when he carved up your face."

"I was a mere boy then," Mountain spat, his hand shooting to the scar on his left cheek that was hardly noticeable under his beard, his temper briefly flaring. With supreme effort Mountain regained control of himself. "I fell under the influence of some very bad men. It's no longer worth mentioning."

"Okay, we won't mention it. What about you selling white women and children to the Indians? Should we mention that?"

"If you are referring to the incident concerning your little friend Jesse, that also was a misunderstanding. If you and your Father had stayed a little bit longer you would have discovered the truth for yourselves. I severely punished those men when I learned about the evil lies that they had spread about me."

"Pity we didn't hang around longer and straighten it all out. If we did we might not be having this conversation today, but we had other business to attend to at the time. But that's all water under the bridge. Today's topic is: Who was riding those Indian ponies out front? And how long ago did they leave here? And where are they heading to?"

"Let's all have a drink while I tell you what you want to know," Mountain suggested. "I have nothing to hide. I care nothing for the men who rented my animals. I can only assume that those men were up to no good, or why else would you be hunting them?"

"A drink sounds like a good idea-except the us part. My throat is a little sore, so I'll do the drinking while you do the talking," Timbre ordered, reaching his hand back, without taking his eyes off of Mountain and his men. "Rat Face! Put a drink in my hand."

In less than a minute Timbre felt a glass being placed in his hand. Glancing at it quickly, Timbre downed the whisky. Within seconds of drinking the shot of whiskey Timbre felt his head begin to float. His vision rapidly blurred and his legs started to buckle.

"You bastard," Timbre muttered, realizing that he'd been drugged.

Instinctively, without being able to focus, Timbre yanked on both triggers of the shotgun. The recoil from both barrels going off at the same time threw him back against Curtis and the girl, knocking them all to the floor. Everything turned black as Timbre fell deeper and deeper into what felt like a well with no bottom.

After God knows how long Timbre felt himself floundering toward consciousness. There'd been times, especially after some toots he'd been on, that he'd felt like dying when he awoke, but none of those times had ever compared to this one. His head felt like it was being slowly crushed and he could've sworn that his body had been disassembled and then put back together, using defective parts. He hurt in places that he hadn't known he had. Everything ached so bad that he was afraid even to open his eyes. If being semi-conscious hurt this much, he thought, what would consciousness feel like.

"You awake?" a voice whispered, close to his ear.

Something inside of Timbre told him that he should recognize the voice, but the effort it took to identify it was too much for him to handle.

"It's me, Curtis. If you can hear me, give me some sort of a sign," the voice said, intruding once again into his painful head.

The name Curtis started Timbre's brain formulating thoughts again. Little by little the previous day's events started to take shape in his mind. When Timbre reached the part where he passed out he moaned softly.

"Good. You can hear me," Curtis said. "Listen. We're in big trouble. I think they're going to kill us."

"You mean I'm not dead yet? Pity," Timbre whispered, using herculean effort to open his eyes. "How come?"

Timbre had been right. The light was a bitch. His vision was still blurred and he had to fight down the urge to vomit.

"I don't know. I think they're saving us for something special. Can you sit-up?" Curtis asked, seeing his eyes open.

"I don't want to sit-up. I never want to sit-up again. Where are we?"

"On the front porch. They tied us up and dragged us out here early this morning."

"What happened after I passed out?" Timbre asked.

"Shhhh. Later. Here comes Mountain."

"Well," Muntean bellowed, sending waves of pain through Timbre's head. "Look who's awake, Boys!"

A huge hand grabbed Timbre by his shirt front and yanked him into a sitting position. Timbre's stomach rebelled at the sudden movement. Lowering his head he puked all over the front of Mountain's boots.

"Are we feeling a little under the weather, Mr. Bree?" Muntean asked, looking down at his boots. "Patch! Fetch me a bucket of water before this shit dries!"

Timbre forced himself to study the situation while Mountain waited for the water.

Looking down, Timbre could see that his hands were tied with rawhide, but his feet were still free. Turning his head to the right he saw that Curtis's hands were also tied, but unlike himself, Curtis's feet were also tied. Timbre then looked at

Curtis's face and saw a bloody bandage wrapped around the boy's head. Examining Curtis's eyes and seeing that they were clear told Timbre that Curtis wasn't badly hurt.

Before Timbre could talk to Curtis the outlaw with one eye, the one called Patch, appeared with the bucket of water. Mountain grabbed the bucket and splashed half of the water over his boots, washing them clean, the rest of it he set in front of Timbre, telling him: "Go ahead. You look like you need it."

Timbre grabbed the bucket and drank his fill through what felt like cut and swollen lips. He then cupped his hands and threw some water on his face, the cool water stinging his cheeks.

"Why so generous?" Timbre asked Muntean, after he was finished.

"Generous?" Mountain repeated, not understanding Timbre's question.

"The water. The fact that we're still alive," Timbre explained.

"Oh, that. The men did want to kill you. Especially after you blew that poor Mex to hell and took a chunk out of my leg with that scattergun of yours. In fact, you managed to put some buckshot in all of us. We all hurt like hell but only the Mex was fatal. They were so furious with you that I had to stop them from stumping you to into a mud puddle," Mountain informed him, showing Timbre his bandaged leg.

"Sorry about that," Timbre apologized, holding back a grin. "It was a reflex."

Timbre was sorry alright. He was sorry that he hadn't blown his ugly head off his shoulders but he didn't think that this was the right time to tell Mountain that.

"You are not truly sorry--- yet that is. But believe me when I say you will be. A little more than two days walk from

235

here there's a very nasty Comanche war chief named Talon. He is at this moment impatiently waiting for something. Can you guess what it is that he is waiting for?" Muntean asked, starting to enjoy himself.

"For you to show up and carry him away from all this," Timbre answered, knowing that it was not the thing to say even before he said it, but he wasn't able to stop himself.

"You always did have a smart mouth," Mountain told him, cuffing Timbre on the side of the head. "That was what I always hated most about you. If it wasn't for your damn father I would have ripped out your tongue a long time ago. It's a pity that he can't save you now."

"You're right," Timbre agreed, trying to clear his head. "I do have a smart mouth. I deserved that smack. Untie me and let me go and I promise you that I'll never smart off to anybody ever again."

"Go ahead and make all the little jokes you want, but it's no joke that Talon is waiting for his youngest son to return from his first raid."

"So? What's that have to do with me?" Timbre asked, knowing the implications of Mountain's words.

"You killed his son and the other three braves that were with him. I know that they're lying somewhere out there rotting," Muntean stated, sweeping his tree trunk of an arm in a half-circle.

"What makes you think that I killed them?" Timbre asked.

"Because you are here--- and they are not," Mountain reasoned.

"I tracked those ponies here, but I never saw any Comanche's. About three-hundred miles north of here some tracks veered off but I was in too much of a hurry to bother with them," Timbre lied, knowing that Curtis and he were headed for a Comanche barbeque.

"I don't believe you, but it makes no matter. Even if I did believe you I would still have to give you to Talon. If I don't give him someone to take his anger out on he might take it out on me- and you know what an angry Comanche is like. I think he'll enjoy you two very much. Don't you?"

"You remember what you told me yesterday, well it was all true. We never did like each other, but were the last of our kind. There aren't many of us ol' mountain boys left. You don't really want to hand me over to the Comanche--do you? If you do that who'd be left to tell the tails of the great Mountain Muntean?" Timbre desperately lied to him. He knew what was in store for them if he couldn't talk Mountain out of turning them over to Talon and he'd do anything to avoid that---even kiss the big jerks ass.

"You are right. In a strange way I will miss you. I have always dreamed of killing you myself- and now I'll have nothing more to look forward to," Muntean told him, softening up a little. "But, as you can see my hands are tied in the matter. You're a reasonable man, try and see it from my point of view."

Timbre knew that anymore pleading would be useless. Pretending to scratch, he reached down into his right boot.

"If you're looking for your little toys, don't bother," Mountain laughed. "We took them all away from you."

"Son-of-a-bitch was a walking arsenal," Patch snarled, talking for the first time.

"Prepare yourselves. We leave in ten-minutes," Muntean said, reaching down and cutting Curtis's leg straps.

"You won't change your mind?" Timbre asked.

"Watch them," Mountain told Patch, as he limped away and entered the Post, not bothering to answer Timbre.

"I don't see Thor," Timbre said, looking around as Curtis helped him to his feet.

"When the half-breed went to get him Thor bit off two of his fingers and then ran off," Curtis informed him.

"That's one for Thor," Timbre laughed, hurting his face.

"I wouldn't laugh in front of Bonner if I were you. He's half Comanche--- and all mean. If he ever catches your damn horse he'll have him for lunch. Now let's get going," Patch ordered.

"Nice gun you have there," Timbre said to Patch, noticing his '45 in Patch's holster, as he struggled to get his balance, still feeling a little dizzy.

"Yeah, she's a beauty. I want to thank you for this," Patch half laughed. "Mountain gave the other one to the half-breed to help calm him down. He figured you wouldn't mind since you'll be dead soon anyways."

"Well I hope you two enjoy them as long as you can because I'm gonna want them back."

"You must be crazy. What would a dead man want with guns?" Patch asked, with a confused look on his face. "Hey, boy! How did you ever get mixed up with this fool?"

Before Curtis could answer, Timbre asked, "Yeah, how about the boy? Was it really necessary to bash him in the head?" Timbre asked.

"We never laid a hand on him," Patch said defensively. "It was you who put that gash in his head. You and that stupid shotgun of yours."

"What the hell are you talking about?" Timbre asked, confused.

"When you let go with both barrels you went flying back and your head smashed into the boy's head. Then you both went down like a bag of flour--- which was a lucky thing for the boy. If he had reached that gun he was going for he would've been shot full of holes. So, in a way he owes you his life---temporally that is. Now get moving, you've done enough palavering."

As Timbre stepped off the porch he checked his shirt pocket to see if they'd overlooked his cyanide shell. They hadn't. He'd intended to share it with Curtis if things started to look hopeless.

After looping ropes around their necks Patch handed Curtis's leash to the half-breed that was already mounted. The Bred looked really pissed-off as he nursed his bloody left hand that was wrapped in a cloth. Keeping Timbre's rope for himself Patch also mounted.

"Why can't the boy ride?" Timbre asked Patch, noticing that they were bringing Leather along.

"His horse is another present for Talon--- and Mountain wants the horse to be at his best when we get there. Besides, the walk will clear his head," Patch laughed.

A few minutes later Mountain came limping out of the Trading Post with Cecil and the girl. Stopping by his horse he turned to Cecil and said: "I'll be back in a week or so. Take good care of the girl. If you harm or touch her in any way I'll rip that nose right off your face. Do you understand me?"

Timbre noticed Patch unconsciously touch his eye-patch when Mountain mentioned ripping something from Cecil's face.

"You can trust me," Cecil squeaked, watching Mountain mount his horse. It was the biggest horse that Timbre had ever seen—--it had to be to carry that load.

"I know I can," Mountain smiled, looking down at him. "And you my Sweet, you can sit around and dream about how glorious it is going to be for you when I get back. Pity I don't have more time to show you what you are missing." Kicking his suffering horse hard in the flank and leading Leather and the Indian ponies, Mountain bellowed: "We go!"

CHAPTER

14

With tears running down her cheeks Carlene Braff watched the two men being dragged away. She was crying as much for them as she was for herself. For a brief moment last night Carlene had believed that she'd been rescued when the nice looking older man had taken her away from the Monster. That's how Carlene thought of Mountain, not as a man, or an animal, but as a monster. A monster straight out of her worst nightmare.

A shiver ran through Carlene's body when she thought of what fate awaited the two men at the end of their walk. Like everyone else who traveled through the Southwest she'd heard all the gory tales of what the Comanche did to their captives. Carlene didn't know which was worse: being slowly killed by the Comanche or being taken by the monster.

Carlene stared at the backs of the two men as they faded into the dust. When she saw Curtis stumble her heart stumbled with him and she suddenly realized that she had deep feelings for the young man. He was young and handsome and the way that he had held her so protectively last night made her feel so safe and warm.

Carlene had never loved a man, other than her father. This was an entirely new emotion that she was experiencing. Carlene wasn't quite sure what it was that she was feeling. She wasn't even sure what she felt was even real and not something out of desperation. She let her thoughts drift back to the night before in an attempt to sort out her true feelings.

Everything had happened so fast that Carlene had trouble putting it into perceptive. One minute the two men were talking-- and it was obvious that they had some history and clearly didn't like each other. Then, suddenly the Monster had grabbed the other man by the throat and was slowly chocking him. Somehow, the man had gained the upper hand and the Monster had let him go. Then, the next thing she remembered was being roughly pushed into Curtis's arms. She was so relieved at the prospect of being saved from a fate worse than death that she almost fainted with relief. She lost track of time then and also of what the men were saying until there was an ear splitting explosion. She turned around quickly and was met with the horrible sight of the Mexican being blown almost in half. At the same time as she was witnessing that Tim came flying back into her and Curtis. She could hear the monster bellowing in pain as the three of them hit the floor getting all tangled up together.

Then, for what seemed the longest time there was absolute silence, even though in reality only seconds had passed--- and in those seconds the scene permanently etched itself into her memory. She could see it as clearly as if it had just happened: Timbre lying on the floor unconscious gasping for air, the two outlaws frozen in shock as they stared at the Mexican who'd been blown back about ten-feet. His body was barely visible in the shadows, except for the great volume of blood that poured from what used to be his belly. The monster was just standing there holding his leg with blood seeping out from between his fingers, grimacing in pain and cursing under his breath.

Curtis was gripping her arm tightly and mumbling something as blood streamed from a cut over his right eye. He was barely conscious. Then time began moving so fast that the following events became a blur in her mind.

The outlaws, all except Cecil who'd disappeared to somewhere, rushed over and started to kick Tim who was lying motionless. Curtis who had been forgotten in their haste to get at Timbre barely could make out them stomping on him. Wiping the blood from his eyes Curtis shoved Carlene to the side and started to draw his gun. In a loud voice he ordered the outlaws to get away from his partner. The Commanchero's immediately stopped kicking Timbre and all faces turned toward Curtis. A second later they began to laugh.

"You plane to shoot us with that, Boy?" Mountain roared, almost hysterical with laughter.

Curtis heard their laughter through a haze and wondered what was so funny. Looking at his gunhand he vaguely saw that his gun was still in his holster and that he was pointing his finger at them. With a sheepish grin on his face--- he passed out.

Carlene kneeled over the unconscious Curtis to inspect his wound but Mountain yanked her away and ordered Cecil, who had miraculously appeared again, to get some rawhide to tie him up with. Then he ordered Carlene to see to his leg. There wasn't much to be done for Mountain's leg, the shot hadn't entered his leg but had just ripped a chunk of meat out of the outside of his thigh. After bandaging the monster's leg Carlene was ordered to check out the other outlaws. After bandaging their minor wounds and almost puking from their disgusting stench, she was allowed to see to Curtis.

Curtis' had a gash over his right eye but it didn't look too serious. Carlene was allowed to stitch up his cut and bandage it before they dragged him off to the side.

It didn't take Curtis very long to regain consciousness and when he opened his eyes he found Carlene shivering up against him. With all the confusion and burying going on Carlene and Curtis were all but forgotten. Toward dawn they were disturbed when Rat Face and Patch separated them and dragged Curtis outside and dumped him on the porch beside Timbre.

Like most strangers who are thrown together in a life threatening situation Curtis and Carlene had become very close. They had whispered to each other things that they wouldn't have confided to even a close friend. It was like confessing to a priest just before you died. By the time they were separated each knew most of the other's life story.

Carlene Braff was born into a semi-wealthy family, in New York City. Her father, Philip Braff, spent his childhood in comfort. His family was better off than most and he was pampered for most of his childhood. At the age of eighteen he had decided to study medicine; and at the age of twenty-three Philip had became a doctor. At twenty-four, by arrangement by his family, Philip Braff married Grace Shillinglaw, who also came from a prominent New York family.

From the moment they were married Philip and Grace disagreed on almost every aspect on how their lives should be led. Philip, on the one hand, insisted on giving up his affluent Manhattan practice, he wanted to dedicate his life to the care of the less fortunate. Grace, on the other hand thought that Philip was mad for even harboring such a notion. It was a humiliating position that Philip was placing her in. It was hard enough trying to explain to her friends why Philip insisted on practicing medicine in the first place instead of doing something more fruitful, like raising horses, or traveling through Europe, but to try and defend his desire to administer medicine to the scum of the city was simply too much for Grace to endure.

Philip, in his own way was as stubborn as Grace and was used to doing as he pleased. It wasn't long before he gave up his plush practice and moved his office to the poor part of town. This did not sit well with Grace and soon after Philip's move she made a move of her own--- Grace moved out of their communal bedroom and into one of the spare bedrooms.

Although Grace locked her door against her husband's affections, it didn't matter--- the damage had already been done. One-year and three-months after they'd married Grace and Philip Braff had a baby girl---who they named Carlene.

Within months after Carlene's birth Grace declared that she desperately needed to get away. Motherhood was too much for her to bare. She was utterly exhausted from her nine-months of pregnancy and the horrors of labor. Grace decided that what she needed most was a long ocean voyage. Of course taking the baby along was out of the question. How could she possibly regain her strength with a crying infant in tow? So, off Grace sailed into the sunset, leaving Carlene behind to be looked after by Philip.

Eleven-years later Grace was still recuperating in Europe and it was rumored that she was doing it in the arms of some Duke from some nominal kingdom; And, it was also rumored that as far as Philip was concerned, he barely noticed her absence.

While Grace was in Europe Carlene and her Father became as close as a father and daughter could become. Every chance that Philip got he took Carlene with him to the clinic and it wasn't long before she became indispensable to him.

Philip relied on little Carlene as if she were a grown woman, and in many ways Carlene was. Out of necessity she'd become self-sufficient and now looked after her Father more than he looked after her. Their lives were closely intermingled and ran smoothly, that is until the day that Grace came storming back into their lives.

Grace's love affair had ended. She'd been dumped by the Duke for a younger woman. She felt humiliated. Too humiliated to allow her to stay any longer in Europe--- she couldn't possibly face her friends there any longer. Catching the first ship home, she rumbled into Philip's and Carlene's lives-- like an unexpected cyclone.

Reunited with Carlene for the first time in almost twelve-years and seeing the way that she was being raised sent Grace straight up the wall. No daughter of Grace's was going to publicly disgrace her with her shameful ignorance of social etiquette. People would think that she'd neglected her daughter and Grace couldn't have that. Within three-weeks of Grace's arrival Carlene was shipped off to boarding school to learn the niceties of being a lady.

At first Philip had protested, as did Carlene, but the more he thought about it the more he realized that a formal education wouldn't do his daughter any harm. Philip admitted that for once Grace was right and that he had indeed neglected his daughter's refinements. Carlene being smart enough to realize that there was nothing she could do to prevent her Mother from sending her away to school capitulated but not before extracting a promise from her father. She made Philip swear that as soon as she graduated from finishing school that she be allowed to come back and continue to work with him, which he readily agreed to. But, unbeknownst to them Grace had other plans for her daughter.

After her daughter finished with this school Grace planned on sending Carlene to a boarding school in Europe. After all, Grace couldn't have a teenage daughter following her around giving away her age. This was also a way for her to get even with Philip because Grace had come to the conclusion- and only God knows how- that it had been Philip that had destroyed her love affair with the Duke. She'd come to believe that it was the fact that she was married that had driven the Duke away, or so she fantasized.

When she had realized how much sending Carlene away to finishing school was hurting Philip she vowed to herself to keep on hurting him, like she'd been hurt. Using Carlene as a weapon Grace's vengeance might've worked except for one slight oversight: It was Grace's love for the spotlight that finally was her undoing for her quest to hurt Philip.

Carlene's sixteenth birthday and her graduation from finishing school gave Grace an excuse to throw a lavish party, the kind that she so loved. She made sure that all the right young men were in attendance, not for Carlene's sake but for her own. Grace loved to flirt and thanks to her beauty and charm she always managed to become the center of attention at all the gatherings. This party was to be no different, Grace planned to steal the spotlight from her daughter and have all the young men crawling at her feet.

The night of the party Grace thought she looked stunning and couldn't understand why the young men weren't flocking to her. She soon became aware that she was being ignored by all the men in favor of her daughter. Instead of being a proud parent, she was devastated.

Watching Carlene twirl around the dance floor with one man after another Grace realized for the first time that Carlene had become a rare beauty. A deep pang of jealousy struck Grace deeply when she realized that her beauty paled in comparison to her daughter's. The very thought that her daughter had surpassed her and that she had been partly responsible for it by sending her to finishing school was too much for Grace to handle. It wasn't a realization that Grace was equipped to deal with--- and so she dealt with it the only way she knew how.

Two-weeks later Grace was aboard a steamship heading back to Europe and far away from her rival--- for that's how she regarded her daughter now. Grace's vanity had been stronger than her quest for vengeance against Philip. A week after Grace's departure Carlene was back again working alongside of her Father.

Carlene and Philip worked side-by-side for almost a year until one day Philip decided that he was going to Mexico to help the peasants there. He'd heard that there were only a few qualified doctors south of the border and that the people there were in dire need of medical assistance.

At first Philip had refused to take Carlene with him, claiming that the land was much too uncivilized and therefore much too dangerous for a young lady. But, after much arguing and persuading, Carlene wore her Father down and he reluctantly agreed to take her along.

For two-years they labored night and day in Mexico, administering medical treatment to the poor. Then one day Philip decided that he'd had enough. Mexico had too many sick even for him to care for. He himself became ill from the lack of medical supplies, the squalid living conditions, and the heat. It was a broken man and an older and wiser girl that started on their long Journey home.

Carlene and her Father were in route to the nearest seaport to catch a ship back to New York when the stagecoach they were on was ambushed fifty miles from the Texas border by Mountain and his men. The outlaws killed everyone on board---- all except Carlene. Mountain had taken one look at Carlene and was instantly in lust with her. If he was capable of love one could even say he loved her, but the truth was he desired her like he'd never desired anything in his whole life. He desired her so much that he was almost sorry that he'd killed her father--- almost.

Gently placing a near hysterical Carlene on a horse, handling her as if she were a Princess, he started back to Texas with his prize in tow. Mountain swore to himself not to touch the girl until they reached the Trading Post even though every bone in his massive body cried out for him to take her right there and then. But, for the first time in his life he showed some constraint because he wanted everything to be just right, so that he could savor every moment when he finally took her. It was only Timbre's timely intervention that'd saved Carlene from what she considered to be a fate worse than death.

Carlene remembered how she'd felt at seeing the two men standing at the bar after Mountain had dragged her into the Trading Post. At first she'd been drawn strongly to the older man because he'd reminded her of her Father, although he was a bit younger and more handsome than her Father had been. Something about him told her that he'd protect her from this Monster who was tugging on her. And, if he did indeed rescue her she knew that she'd love him forever--- that is until she spotted Curtis who was standing behind him. Young, tall, very handsome, with piercing green eyes that never left her face. Just by looking at him she knew he'd die for her.

Curtis, she discovered later on, was everything that she'd ever wanted in a man. He was kind, naive, gentle, young, handsome, brave, and vulnerable. He listened and sympathized with her through the long night and when she'd cried on his shoulder he'd cried with her. Curtis was a man who could sympathize with the hardships she endured and wasn't afraid to show his feelings. The world hadn't hardened him yet, like it had his friend, Tim.

Carlene could see that Timbre could be hard as nails. He was so hard that he'd been willing to sacrifice her life in order to kill the monster, but strangely enough she didn't fault him for that. In truth, she'd much prefer being dead to having to lie with that huge, ugly, filthy beast. The more she thought about it the angrier she got at Timbre for not doing her the kindness of ending her life--- something she wasn't sure she had the guts to do for herself.

"Well Missy, your little boyfriend is gone for good now," Cecil squeaked, breaking into Carlene's thoughts. "You won't be seeing him again so you best get him out of your head."

Cecil surprised Carlene, she hadn't thought anybody knew how she felt about Curtis, much less this ratty little creature. Cecil was smarter and more observant than she'd given him credit for. She'd have to keep a closer eye on him, Carlene thought to herself.

"You didn't think anybody saw the way you two were carrying on last night. Did you? All nice and cuddly and whispering to each other," Cecil continued, when he saw the way Carlene had reacted to his comment, so he added: "If Mountain had seen the way you two were carrying on that boy wouldn't be on his way to Yellow-Jacket now, he'd be dead. You were lucky that Mountain was hurting too much last night to take notice."

"You're his flunky? Why didn't you tell him?" Carlene asked, looking down at him.

"Because I didn't want to see anything happen to your boyfriend."

"What do you care what happens to him?"

"I don't, but it might've upset you and I didn't want you to be upset," Cecil told her, with a leer in his eyes. "The way I figure it, you owe me now."

"The way I see it, I don't owe you a thing. You didn't do us any favor. Curtis would've been better off dying quickly by Mountain's hand than being tortured by those Indians."

"What do you know about being tortured?" Cecil smiled.

"I have to look at you, don't I?" Carlene snapped.

"When Mountain gets back you'll pray that you were mine and not his," Cecil smirked.

Carlene looked at Cecil and shivered. He probably was right. She silently vowed that she would do whatever it took to escape---and failing that she swore to take her own life.

"Get moving now," Cecil ordered, giving her a slight shove.

Carlene walked slowly to the steps of the Post, trying to hold back the tears without a lot of success. The warm wind gently blowing from the south helped to dry them before Cecil could see her crying. She didn't want to let that little rat see her breaking down.

"Wait a minute!" Cecil squeaked, just before Carlene started to climb the steps. "Give me your clothes."

"What?" Carlene exclaimed, not believing what she'd just heard.

"Give me your clothes," Cecil repeated, with a big leer on his face.

"I will not," Carlene told him, contemptuously.

"You will to!" Cecil screamed, in a voice so high that it could've shattered crystal. "Mountain left me orders to clean you up and that's just what I'm going to do."

"I also heard him say that if you touched me he'd pull that stupid nose off your ugly face," Carlene smirked, thinking that she'd gained the upper hand.

"So he did," Cecil admitted, acting as if he were in a quandary.

Raising his hand, as if to scratch his head, Cecil changed its direction in mid-scratch and like lightening grabbed the front of Carlene's tattered dress and ripped it off.

"You sneaky little bastard!" Carlene screamed, instinctively covering her breasts with her hands. "You just wait till Mountain gets back."

"He didn't say I couldn't look," Cecil snickered, holding up part of Carlene's dress and waving it just out of her reach. "Now if you want something to wear I suggest that you go to the stream and scrub off all that dirt."

Although Carlene had never been naked in front of a man nudity was nothing new to her. Working with her father she'd seen it all. Being naked didn't bother her as much as it would've bothered any other young woman in her position. Besides, after seeing so many naked bodies as a nurse Carlene knew, with all humility, that she had one of the great ones. Maybe, just maybe, she'd be able to use it to escape she thought.

Taking a deep breath and stealing herself Carlene dropped her hands to her side.

"Oh, my Lord," Cecil hoarsely whispered, his tongue dropping out of his mouth.

"Take a good look, you pig," Carlene told him, defiantly. "This is something you'll never have."

Cecil stared at the blond beauty with saliva dripping from corners of his mouth. He had never seen anything as beautiful as her. She was a Goddess. The mere sight of her sent ripples of pain down through his belly. Without even being aware of what he was doing, Cecil's hand slowly rose toward Carlene.

"Lay one finger on me you freak and Mountain will kill you," Carlene warned him, with fire in her eyes after she noted the effect that her nakedness was having on him.

"Please," Cecil croaked, still reaching out for her.

"Maybe I can do something for you. That is if you're willing to help me get away from here before Mountain returns," Carlene softened, letting his fingers trail across her breast.

"I can't do that," Cecil almost cried. "He'd kill me."

"Then there's no reason for me to be nice to you. Is there?" Carlene said, slapping his hand away.

"I'll give you anything you want, anything but that," Cecil swore, reaching for her breast again.

"What good would anything do me after that monster gets back?" Carlene asked, slapping his hand away again and sticking her chest out further.

Cecil didn't answer but she could see the turmoil raging within him. With a supreme effort Cecil tore his eyes away from Carlene's chest and without looking at her, murmured: "Wait here." He then raced up the stairs and into the Trading Post.

As soon as Cecil went stomping off Carlene knew that she'd lost. The little man's fear of the giant was stronger than his desire for her-- and she could hardly blame him for that.

Carlene didn't feel as if she'd lost her bid for freedom by much so she decided to keep on working on Cecil. Fifteen-minutes later Cecil came back out carrying a bar of soap and a towel. He thrust them into Carlene's hands without looking directly at her.

Taking the towel and soap Carlene took a step forward and rubbed herself up against Cecil; saying: "You sure you want to hand me over to Mountain?"

Cecil couldn't remember wanting anything as badly as he wanted her in his entire life. As far as he was concerned he'd as much right to her as Muntean did- maybe more. It'd been him who'd brought Mountain into this setup. It'd been his brains and money that'd started the Trading Post. The only reason that he'd brought that stupid giant in on his deal in the first place was so he could trade with the Indians. Cecil feared the Indian's and the Comanche's had sensed it. They'd used his fear to take advantage of him during their dealings.

Cecil didn't know Indians well enough to realize that they wouldn't have harmed him, they needed him more than he needed them. The only thing that Cecil knew was that they didn't like him and that he was being cheated by them; so, he'd recruited Mountain to handle the trading for him.

At first the arrangement had worked out fine. Even after giving Muntean and his men their split Cecil was still making a bigger profit than before. The trading was more equitable and plus Mountain was ranging out further, bringing in a lot more business. Not to mention that the towns people had considerably lowered their prices to him also. Things just couldn't have been going better for Cecil until he woke up one morning to find that he was now working for the Mountain--- and not the other way around.

Cecil looked at the girl and saw that she was enjoying seeing him suffer. This was his place and he deserved her. He ought to teach her a lesson, he thought. But then he remembered Mountain's warning and the time that Patch had crossed him. To punish the outlaw the giant had plucked out his eye and crushed it beneath his foot. Cecil had become ill with fear when he'd witnessed that barbaric act. After that he'd never mention again who's place this was.

Remembering that incident made Cecil realize that he was just kidding himself. He no more had the nerve to take the girl than he did to take his business back. She had the upper hand for now and they both knew it.

"Go take your bath," Cecil ordered, his voice breaking up. "There's nothing I can do for you."

Carlene knew by the tone of Cecil's voice that it was over. She almost felt sorry for him and knew that tormenting him any further wouldn't do any one of them any good. Wrapping the towel around herself Carlene headed for the stream to bathe as Cecil went back into the Post, leaving her alone. Cecil wasn't worried about leaving Carlene unguarded because he knew that there was no where she could escape to, especially without any clothes.

Carlen lay in the cool water for what seemed like hours, forgetting where she was and what had happened. It was the sound of Cecil's voice that dragged her back to reality.

"Come-on, Missy. It's time to get out now," Cecil told her, standing by the stream and trying not to look at her naked body.

"Must I?" Carlene asked, too relaxed to argue with him.

"Yes," Cecil said, laying the brush and comb beside her towel. "When you're finished come back into the Post."

Carlene watched Cecil walk away slumped over and dragging his feet while he climbed the porch steps. After the door closed behind him, Carlene climbed out of the water and began to brush her hair. She stood in the sun naked letting the warm breeze dry her body. Once in a while she'd look toward the Post and would catch Cecil peeking at her through the one small window cut into the mountain.

Carlene didn't know how long she stood there combing her long thick blond hair and enjoying the sun but she knew that she couldn't stall for much longer. If she didn't go inside soon Cecil would come out and fetch her.

What Carlene didn't realize was as far as Cecil was concerned she could've stood there letting the breeze caress her body for the rest of the day. He hadn't thought it possible but Carlene was even more beautiful now that she was cleaned and her hair was combed than she'd been before. He couldn't get his full of looking at her.

Leaving the sunlight for the darkness and gloom of the Trading Post was not an easy thing for Carlene to adjust to. Forcing herself to pick up the towel she wrapped it around her body and walked into the gloom of the cave. Cecil was standing by the door when Carlene entered. Even in the semi-darkness she could see that his face was flushed and that he was breathing hard.

"Here, put this on," Cecil ordered, handing Carlene a slinky, low-cut red dress.

"You have something a bit different?" Carlene asked, holding up the dress with one hand and examining it.

"Mountain personally picked that one out for you. It's either this one or nothing," Cecil told her, regaining the former nastiness to his voice which reminded Carlene of how much she disliked him.

With a sigh, Carlene dropped her towel and while looking directly into Cecil's little lustful eyes she slowly stuffed herself into the dress.

"Well? What do you think?" Carlene asked, twirling around, deciding to torture him again, the top part of the dress barely covering her breasts.

"I'm going to make us something to eat," Cecil once again croaked, leaving the room quickly. She was more desirable partially dressed than she was naked---if that was possible.

"Let me help," Carlene offered, following him and enjoying the pain that she was inflicting on him.

Carlene always knew that she was pretty, her father had told her so a thousand times, but she'd never before known the power her beauty had over men--- that is until now. She was becoming intoxicated with her new found power and who safer to try it out on and to make suffer at the same time but Cecil. After all, if it hadn't been for that little weasel drugging Tim she'd be free now along with Curtis and Tim.

"We have to make a lot of food," Cecil squeaked, almost fainting as Carlene walked up behind him and pressed her breasts into his shoulder as he was stacking a bunch of dead chickens on the table.

"Why?" Carlene asked, in a sultry voice, blowing her warm breath into his ear.

"Mountain will be hungry when he gets back and there's no telling when he'll be back!" Cecil nearly screamed.

"I make great chicken," Carlene told him, reaching over his shoulder to fondle a chicken leg.

"Then do it!" Cecil screamed, running out of the room.

A couple of hours later Carlene called Cecil in to eat and then proceeded to tease him unmercifully all through dinner. Once or twice she even had to remind him of Mountain's existence. Finally, when Cecil couldn't take anymore, because he was either going to go insane or explode, he grabbed Carlene by the arm and forcibly dragged her down the hall and threw her into an empty bedroom. It took all of his will power to lock the door from the outside and leave her by herself.

Once she was alone Carlene pulled out one of the kitchen knives that she'd concealed under her dress and hid it under the filthy pillow on the bed. Cecil had been in such a state that he'd forgotten to search her for any weapons.

At first she'd thought to lure Cecil into the bedroom and use the knife on him, even though her long training with her Father had taught her that all life was sacred. Suddenly, and with complete surprise, she realized that she'd changed drastically and was now capable of murder. But, she also surmised that even if she could kill Cecil where would she go? She had no idea where she was and without a horse Mountain would track her down within a couple of days. She thought of killing the monster when he tried to take her but she doubted that the knife she had would be enough to finish him off. And even if she did manage to kill him then she would belong to Cecil, or one of the other brutes, which was just as bad. She finally concluded that her situation was hopeless and the only way out for her was to use the knife on herself.

As Carlene lay on the bed everything came flooding back to her: Her Father being killed by the Monster, Curtis and Tim being led away to their deaths and her now a slave to something that she didn't even consider human. It seemed like years had passed since all of this had transpired.

Before this had happened she couldn't have possibly imagined that life could be so unfair and that people could be so cruel. Now, she was no longer the naive girl that she had been a few short weeks ago, she was now a fully grown hardened woman without any illusions about life being fair. What usually would've taken years for a person to change as much as she had, due to circumstances, had only taken less than ten days. Carlene started to cry, as much for herself as for the one's she'd lost. She finally fell asleep, exhausted from crying.

Sometime during the night Carlene was awakened by the sound of somebody trying to get into her room. Knowing that it wasn't Cecil, because he wouldn't dare try to molest her, she reasoned that it must be Mountain returning early. Muntean's return could only mean one of two things: either Curtis and his friend were already dead, or they were now being tortured to death, either way it was the end for her too.

Carlene, with nothing more to lose, calmly reached under the pillow and retrieved the knife she had hidden there. Sitting on the edge of the bed she gripped the handle with both hands and placed the point of the blade against her chest at the spot that she knew her heart to be. She sat there terrified waiting for the door to open before plunging the blade into her breast. Carlene wanted the monster to suffer. She wanted him to know how close he'd come to having her before he lost her.

CHAPTER

15

As Timbre and Curtis were being led away from the Trading Post Curtis kept looking back at the young girl standing in the yard.

"Mind where you're walking," Timbre told Curtis, when he tripped and almost fell. "Stop worrying about her and start worrying about yourself."

"Do you think she'll be alright?" Curtis asked.

"No," Timbre answered, "But she's going to be better off than we're going to be."

"We're in for a rough time, aren't we?" Curtis asked.

"That's putting it mildly. What we're experiencing now is a rough time. I don't want to scare you so I won't describe what we're in for."

"Well then, if you're going to keep your promise to Jesse and kill me--- this is as good a time as any. I give you my permission," Curtis smiled, half-joking.

"You giving up already?" Timbre asked.

"Not if you have a way that'll get us out of this?"

"It's still early, the games hardly begun."

"So, what's your plan?" Curtis asked, in a whisper, with hope in his voice.

"I haven't thought of one yet, but I'm working on it," Timbre whispered back.

"Great," Curtis mumbled, his chin falling down onto his chest.

"My poncho and hat doesn't look as good on that hombre as it did on me," Timbre commented, referring to Patch who was wearing some of his gear."

Timbre could see the despair that Curtis was feeling written all over his face. He tried to kept the boy talking in order to keep his mind off of their immediate problems.

"What the hell happened yesterday after I hit the floor?" Timbre asked.

Curtis explained everything that had taken place once again after Timbre was drugged and ended it by saying: "Mountain lied to you, he never stopped them from stomping you. In fact if it hadn't been for his shot up leg he probably would've mashed you into the floor himself."

"Well that explains why I feel like mush. Do I look as bad as I feel?" Timbre asked,

"Worse."

"You're only saying that because you aren't in my body," Timbre winced, when he tried to smile.

"You're walking, aren't you? If you felt as bad as you looked you'd still be unconscious."

"Then I'm glad that I don't have to look at me. Now, tell me about the girl."

"You mean Carlene?" Curtis asked, perking up a bit at the mere thought of her.

"No. The other one."

"What other one?" Curtis asked, confused.

"Right."

"Oh!" Curtis smiled.

"Hey, you two!" Patch yelled back. "No talking!"

"Piss-off!" Timbre yelled back at him. "What are you going to do about it- kill us?"

"He has a point," Mountain's huge voice rang out. "Let them be. They cannot escape with talk."

Turning his attention back to Curtis, Timbre asked: "What were you saying?"

"I was about to tell you about Carlene." "Well go ahead," Timbre urged.

"Her name is Carlene Braff. She was born in New York City----". Curtis rambled on about the girl for close to an hour, telling Timbre everything that she'd told him--- well, almost everything that is. When he was finished there was no doubt in Timbre's mind that Curtis was in love.

"Does she love you too?"

"How do you know how I feel about her? Curtis asked, surprised by Timbre's question.

"Just a lucky guess, but that's not what's important right now. What is important, is that she's rich."

"Why's that?"

"Maybe, just maybe mind you, we can use that to bargain her way out of this mess."

"How?"

"Give me time to think on it. I'll get back to you after I've thought it through."

"Before you start thinking on that," Curtis inquired, visibly happier now that there was a chance to save Carlene. "Tell me: How did you know that it hadn't been Mountain and his men who'd been riding those Indian ponies?"

"Easy. Look at the tracks his horse is leaving. Have you ever seen tracks cut so deep? Not even a fully loaded

261

packhorse leaves prints that deep. Speaking of pack horses what happened to ours?"

"Last I seen of him he was being unloaded in the back of the corral. And, I see what you mean," Curtis agreed, looking at the crater like impressions left by Muntean's horse. "Lugging Mountain around must be one hell of a strain on that poor creature."

"He isn't going to win any races, that's for sure," Timbre chuckled. "But, to get back to your question. Another reason why I was sure that Mountain wasn't in on the raid is because torturing woman isn't his style, unless you count lying with them. Don't get me wrong, he wouldn't think twice about killing a woman but he wouldn't murder her the way your Aunt was murdered- that's just not him."

"What about Carlene?" Curtis asked, thinking about what Mountain had in store for her.

"It's not a pretty picture but you got to think like Muntean. In his mind what he plans to do to that girl isn't torture. He really believes that she's going to enjoy being with him."

"He's got to be crazy to think that!" Curtis exclaimed.

"Now you're catching on."

"You've got to think of something to get her out of this," Curtis implored, starting to panic at the thought of Mountain and Carlene together.

"I'm trying, but it's hard to think with you talking at me. Try to get your mind off of the woman for a while and be quiet. When I come up with something I'll let you know."

"Okay," Curtis reluctantly consented, closing his mouth.

A couple of hours passed and Curtis was slowly giving up hope that Timbre would ever come up with an idea. Suddenly, Timbre turned to him and whispered: "I think I've come up with something. It just might save all our asses. Let me do the talking."

"So what's new?." Curtis mumble sarcastically.

"Hey!" Timbre yelled. "You! Whale-Shit!"

Mountain stopped his horse and the two outlaws followed suit. Twisting his head around Muntean stared at Timbre with fire in his eyes.

"You sure got a way about you," Curtis whispered, seeing the way Mountain was looking at them.

"I got his attention, didn't I?"

"Can't argue with that. But just off the top of my head I'd say that there might've been a better way of doing it."

"You could be right," Timbre agreed, watching Mountain dismount and limp menacingly toward them.

"What did you call me?" Mountain demanded to know, grabbing Timbre by the front of his shirt and pulling him up to his face.

"Forget it. A slip of the tongue. How would you like to be rich?" Timbre asked, smiling.

"Is this going to be one of your stupid tricks?" Mountain asked, not yet ready to let Timbre down.

"No trick. I'm making you a legitimate offer," Timbre told him, getting tired of balancing on his toes.

The possibility of making money always interested Mountain, so he asked: "What is your offer?"

"If you let us and the girl go I'll show you how you can lay your hands on fifty-thousand dollars."

"Tell me first how I can get this huge amount of money. Then I will consider releasing you all," Mountain consented, letting Timbre down.

Timbre knew that after he told Mountain how he could get his hands on the money the big man would still turn them over to the Comanche's. But his first priority was to try and save Carlene. Then he'd work on freeing himself and Curtis.

"Okay, fair enough. The girl just happens to be filthy rich. If you hold her for ransom her people should pay at least fifty-thousand for her return. You might even get more if she's unharmed and untouched. You know how picky those rich people can be about damaged goods."

"Ummm," Mountain grunted, rubbing his chin. Only a huge amount of money would let him consider giving the girl up---and fifty-thousand dollars was more money than he'd ever seen in his life. "If what you say is true it is certainly worth thinking about. But why should I let you two go? I don't need you two to ransom her off."

"True," Timbre agreed, ready to play his second hole card. "But you do need me if you want to multiply that fifty-thousand dollars by ten."

Mountain didn't know how much money that was but he did know that if he couldn't add it up it must be a fortune. Since Timbre had been so easy to trick the first time into revealing how he could get the fifty-thousand dollars Mountain figured that he shouldn't have any trouble fooling him again.

"I'm listening. If what you say is true, we can make a deal," Mountain agreed.

"You've no doubt heard the rumors that I'm a rich man. That me and my Dad found gold somewhere out there. Let me be the first to tell you that those rumors are true. We did find gold, a whole mountain of it. Since that gold is of no use to me if I'm dead I'm willing to tell you where to find it--- in exchange for our freedom of course."

"That sounds like a fair bargain, but how do I know that you won't lie to me?"

"I have no reason too. I have enough gold put away to last me two life times. I don't need anymore. I just want to live to enjoy what I have."

Mountain made believe that he was thinking hard on the deal and after a few moments passed said, "Done. Now tell me where the gold is and I will set you all free."

"First: To show me your good faith untie us and give us food and water. Then I'll tell you what you want to know."

"Do it," Mountain ordered his two men. "But watch them until he tells us where the gold is."

Patch and Bonner, who were listening closely, dismounted and did as they were ordered.

As soon as Timbre and Curtis were untied they rubbed their wrists, forcing the blood back into their hands. When they'd regained feeling in their fingers Bonner handed them a canteen of water and Patch gave them each a slab of beef-jerky. Sitting in the dirt Timbre and Curtis attacked their meal as if it were the finest meal that they'd ever eaten.

"Okay, you got your food and water. Now, where can I find the gold?" Mountain impatiently inquired.

"Relax. Give us some time to rest and eat. Go sit in the shade and have something to eat yourself. The golds been there for thousands of years, it isn't going anywhere."

"If you are playing me for a fool I will hurt you badly," Mountain threatened, putting his foot softly on Timbre's leg and pressing down.

"Ouch!" Timbre yelled, pushing Mountain's foot away. "Don't worry, I wouldn't cross you."

"I am not worried," Mountain told him, letting Timbre push his foot away. Turning, he ordered: "You, half-breed, make us something to eat: And you, Patch--- don't take your eyes off of these two."

With that Mountain walked away and sat in the shade while the other two outlaws tended to their duties.

Although the two Comancheros were close enough to guard Timbre and Curtis they weren't close enough to hear what they were saying.

"Do you think he'll ransom Carlene back to her people?" Curtis asked, in a low voice.

"Not if I tell him were the gold is," Timbre answered, also in a low voice.

"If you don't tell him then he won't set us free, Curtis reasoned. Then as an afterthought he added. "Well, if our lives are the price we have to pay for Carlene's safety then so be it. I say you don't tell him where the gold is," Curtis voted.

"You're being awfully caviler with my life. I'm not the one who's in love with her so why should I sacrifice myself?"

"What's caviler mean?" Curtis asked.

It means you're playing fast and loose with my life."

Curtis thought hard on that and in desperation told him, "Because it's the right thing to do."

"Maybe, maybe not, but it doesn't matter. Even if I told him the truth he wouldn't let us go. He'd take the gold, keep the girl, and still turn us over to the Comanche's."

"So what you're telling me is that no matter what, we're going to die?"

"Did I ever tell you about the time that I was captured by the Crows?" Timbre asked.

"No offense but I'm really not in the mood to listen to one of your stories," Curtis stopped him.

"That's too bad because I was going to tell you about the time that I was in kinda the same fix as we are now," Timbre shrugged.

"How did you get out of it?" Curtis eagerly asked, anxious to hear the story now.

"My Dad and Jesse bailed me out."

"Oh. I was kind of hoping that you got yourself out of that one," Curtis said, his eagerness deflated.

"I could've if I'd just had something to cut my bonds with. But they'd taken everything away from me, except my pants that is. I guess they didn't want to see me naked."

Curtis looked at Timbre, barely hearing him, he was thinking that he wasn't ready to die. There was so much he hadn't done yet, or experienced. He still had his whole life ahead of him. He thought of Carlene and how he wouldn't have the chance to make love to her. Then, a nagging thought came tiptoeing into his brain. Lifting his head he looked at Timbre, who was staring at him.

"What are you trying to tell me?" Curtis asked.

Timbre smiled and after looking over to make sure that the outlaws were still out of earshot, he said: "It's about time you caught on. Listen carefully and don't ask questions. I've got a knife and when the time is right I'm going to cut my hands free. Then I'll pass it over to you. After you cut your thongs do nothing until I make my move. Now this part is important so pay close attention. Chances are we'll be pulled along by our necks again. At some point I'm going to purposely fall and when I do your job is to makes sure that I'm not dragged and strangled to death."

"How am I supposed to do that?"

"If Patch doesn't see me fall you yell and get his attention. They don't want to deliver me to Tallon dead so they'll stop long enough for me to regain my feet. Just remember this: Whatever you do don't let Bonner stop and wait for Patch to catch-up. My whole plan rests on the fact that you two be in front of me when I get to my feet. You got that?"

"How am I going to keep him from stopping?"

"Jeez! It's a good thing I told you not to ask any questions or else we'd really be in trouble. I don't know. Walk up his back, smack his horse in the rump, you'll think of something. Just make sure you're in front of me when I get up."

"One last question," Curtis whispered.

Anticipating Curtis's inquiry, Timbre explained: "I had compartments added into the back of my belt. The only way you can see them is if you take my belt off. I have a couple of small razor sharp folding knives in the compartments- along with some other things."

"You never fail to amaze me," Curtis commented, shaking his head.

"Don't I though," Timbre smiled. "Be quiet now, here comes the ugly trio."

"Now that we've all rested and eaten tell me where I can find this gold," Mountain demanded, looming over Timbre.

"Just one more thing," Timbre added, struggling to his feet. "Who was it that was riding those Indian ponies that your leading?"

"I can't tell you that," Mountain told him, starting to get angry.

"Even for the location of the gold?" Timbre asked.

"Like you said: What good is gold to me if I am dead?" Mountain said, parroting him. "Besides, that was not part of our bargain."

"I never thought I'd see the day when Mountain Muntean would fear any man," Timbre truthfully stated.

"I fear no man, but I do fear evil spirits," Mountain said, looking around nervously.

"What are you talking about?" Timbre asked, never having seen Mountain act this way before. He was acting as spooked as the two Comanche he'd killed a couple of weeks ago.

"I've said to much already. Now, where's the gold?"

"You know where Sutter's Mill is, in Northern California?" Timbre asked, knowing that he wouldn't get anything more out of Mountain and not wanting to push his luck too far.

"What kind of trick is this?" Mountain asked, his eyes flashing. "Everyone knows that they have already found gold there years ago."

"There yes, but not the gold that's buried fifty miles north of there, in the Klamath Mountain Range," Timbre lied, knowing that Mountain would guess he was lying but wouldn't be absolutely positive of it.

"You lie," Mountain hissed. "There is no gold there. Men have searched those mountains for years and have found nothing. I ought to beat you until you tell me the truth," Mountain said, grabbing Timbre by his already sore neck.

"I'm telling you the truth," Timbre gasped. "Beating me won't make it any different. All you'll have is a dead captive--- and Talon won't like that."

At the mention of Talon Mountain let Timbre go; saying: "You are lucky. If I did not have the girl and if I did not need you, you would regret the day that you played me for a fool."

"Are you so sure that I lied?" Timbre asked, rubbing his neck.

After staring at Timbre for a few seconds, Muntean bellowed: "Tie them. And this time tie their hands behind their backs. I've been too easy on them up till now."

Timbre and Curtis's hands were tied with rawhide thongs and the ropes were slipped over their heads once again. They were rested and refreshed as they started out again and ready to put their plan into action.

As soon as the Comancheros backs were to them Timbre retrieved the knife from the compartment in his belt. He wanted to cut his bindings as quickly as possible, before his fingers became too numb to feel them.

Cutting his hands free, which was easier said than done, Timbre then inched his way toward Curtis. When he was sure that nobody was watching he slipped the knife into Curtis's waiting hand.

Curtis worked on his thongs for over a half-hour. Finally, to Timbre's relief, he cut himself free and then slipped the knife back to Timbre. Both men then continued on, side by side, waiting for the right moment to strike.

It took over two-hours before the right spot presented itself. Timbre saw that Mountain was heading for a gully and that they'd have to enter it single file. As mountain started to descend into the wash Timbre caught Curtis's attention and then threw himself to the ground. The rope immediately tightened around his throat, digging through the skin and cutting off his air. It took all of Timbre's willpower not to reach up and grab the line with his hands. If he allowed himself to do that the game would be up.

"Hey stop!" Curtis yelled. "You're killing him."

Everybody stopped and looked back. Timbre very slowly struggled to his feet. Curtis, remembering what Timbre had told him to do continued to walk. He was almost touching the rump of Bonner's horse when the outlaw looked down and saw him. Startled by Curtis's closeness Bonner nudged his horse forward. When Mountain saw Timbre get to his feet and Bonner start to close in on him he also began to move again- entering the gully.

Timbre watched Mountain, who was leading Leather and the four ponies disappear into the wash followed closely by Bonner and Curtis.

Slipping the noose from around his neck, but holding it taunt with his hand, Timbre quickly shortened the gap between himself and Patch. Just as Patch felt that something wasn't quite right Timbre took a couple of running steps and vaulted onto the back of his saddle. Wrapping his left arm around the outlaw's mouth Timbre jammed the small knife into his throat so that he couldn't yell out. Then he snatched his gun out of the outlaws holster and ramming the gun into the struggling man's side he pulled the trigger. Shoving the dead man off the horse Timbre scooted the rest of the way onto the saddle and kicked the already spooked mount into a run. As Timbre raced into the gully and around the bend he saw that it had widened some.

Having been alerted by the gunshot the half-breed was facing toward him when he came around the bend with his gun drawn. About twenty-five feet beyond him Muntean was trying to get Leather out of his way so that he too could whirl around and fire.

Timbre and Bonner spotted each other at the same time and simultaneously fired at each other. If it wasn't for Curtis yanking back on the rope that was tied around his neck and attached to Bonner's saddle Timbre might've come out second best. As it was Bonner's aim was thrown off when his horse stumbled a bit. Bonner's bullet ripped off a chunk of meat from Timbre's side but Bonner wasn't so lucky, Timbre's bullet took off the top part of the outlaws head off.

Timbre didn't have time to stop and admire his work as Mountain's bullet wheezed right by his ear. Swinging his gun around Timbre saw that it was too late to fire again, he was already on top of Muntean and to late to turn aside. The two horses slammed into each other and both men went tumbling to the ground.

Timbre was momentarily stunned after hitting the ground so hard. His body ached and felt like lead. He was slowly struggling to his feet when a huge hand slammed him back down. Rolling over onto his back Timbre lashed out with his foot only to have it caught in midair.

"I knew I should have killed you the moment that I laid eyes on you," Mountain raged, with his eyes blazing while holding on to Timbre's foot. "Now I am going to make you wish that I had turned you over to the Comanche's."

"Wait a minute!" Timbre yelled, as Mountain put one foot on his belly and started to twist his leg off.

"For what?" Muntean asked, smiling, slowly putting more pressure on the leg.

"Can't we talk about this," Timbre screamed.

"You talk. You are so good at it. You may even say something that I want to hear before I finish pulling your legs off and I start on your arms," Mountain insanely laughed.

"Let him go!" Curtis shouted, from behind Muntean.

Both men were momentarily stunned when they heard the command. They'd completely forgotten Curtis.

"I said let him go! And I ain't going to tell you again," Curtis ordered in an authoritative voice.

Mountain let go of Timbre's leg and turned toward the voice. Curtis was standing about fifteen-feet away and pointing Timbre's shotgun at him.

"Put that gun down before I get mad at you," Muntean told him. "I can see that you have never shot a man before and I doubt that you're capable of doing it now. If you had the guts for it you would have done it already. Do yourself a favor, be a good little boy and put that thing away before Mountain has to take it away from you---and you will not like how I do that."

"You're right--- I should've shot you in the back, it was a mistake on my part, but that doesn't mean I won't pull the trigger now, so I suggest you back off," Curtis warned him, as Muntean slowly advanced on him.

Timbre rolled over to his hands and knees and started to search for his gun. Like Mountain, he didn't think that Curtis could pull the trigger either. Timbre was still searching when he heard the roar of his shotgun going off. Looking around he saw Mountain just standing there with blood splattering the ground.

"You shot me," Mountain said, more in surprise than anger. Turning to Timbre, he said to him: "The little Cockroach has killed me---- me the Great Mountain Muntean."

"He said he would," Timbre commented, not knowing what else to say. He was as surprised as Mountain was.

"But who thought...?" Mountain asked, still refusing to believe it.

"Not me- and sure as hell not you," Timbre answered, watching him bleed to death while trying to hold his guts from falling out with his hands.

Staggering to the side of the gully Mountain put his back to the dirt wall and slid down into a sitting position. Timbre slowly got to his feet while trying to ignore all the pains that were attacking his body. He shuffled over to Curtis who seemed rooted to the ground as he watched Mountain die.

"Come-on. We don't have time for you to brood over this," Timbre warned him.

"I never killed a man before," Curtis mumbled, without blinking.

Timbre understood the emotional changes that Curtis was experiencing but what he'd told him about not having the time was true.

"I sympathize with you but we got to get moving--- and I mean like now!" Timbre yelled, knowing that he wasn't getting through to him. In desperation, Timbre added: "I don't know where those Comanche's are but I'll bet they've heard those shots. If you want to live long enough to save Carlene you best snap out of it."

At the mention of Carlene's name Curtis came out of his trance, and asked: "What do you want me to do?"

"Get all our gear together and roundup the horses. I'm going to get the rest of our guns."

"Right," Curtis said, moving quickly.

Timbre walked over to Mountain, who was still breathing and looked down at him. Although he had always disliked the man Timbre still felt sadness at his passing. There was only one Mad Mountain Muntean, and for good or bad, it would be a long time before the world would see the likes of him again.

"I'd like to get our guns," Timbre requested of him, still leery of the strength that lay in those hands. "Will you hand them over peacefully?"

"Take them. I do not have the strength to argue with you. I'll be dead in a short time anyway," Mountain told him in a whisper. Then looking Timbre in the eyes, he continued: "The man you seek is the one they call The Count."

"It can't be, I buried him myself," Timbre blurted out, his eyes opening wide.

"Yes, but you can not bury his spirit. It is his ghost that now walks the Earth. That is why I was frightened to talk of him before, but now that I am to be a spirit also I no longer fear him."

"If he's a ghost why did he need your horses? Ghosts don't ride horses," Timbre asked, trying to make sense out of what Muntean was telling him.

"I do not know why spirits act as they do. I do not question ghosts."

"Why are you telling me this now?" Timbre demanded, not believing what he was hearing.

"Because, if the Comanche's don't get you, and I do not think they will, I want you to continue your hunt. I want you to catch this evil spirit so that he can kill you and carry you to hell where we can continue our fight," Mountain laughed, blood spilling from between his lips. "The Weasel, at the Trading Post, knows where the Count is going. Now, before I die and for old times- shot me. I do not want it to be said that the Great Mountain Muntean was killed by a child. Let it be said that the cunning Timbre brought him to his end."

Reaching down and pulling out Curtis's pistol from Muntean's belt, Timbre smiled, and told him: "See you in hell--- but don't wait up for me." With that he shot Muntean between the eyes--- for old time's sake.

"Why the hell did you do that?" Curtis asked, when Timbre joined him, after searching through Mountain's pockets.

"For old time's sake," Timbre answered. "Now drop it."

"Here's all your stuff," Curtis told him, handing Timbre his gun belt, guns, hat, knives, derringer, and poncho.

Timbre put all his weapons away, except one, which he handed to Curtis. The Poncho he threw on the ground, declaring: "It's got blood all over it."

"So do you," Curtis informed him, looking down at Timbre's side. "Jeeze, you look awful. I better see to that wound."

"Forget it. It looks worse than it is. We got to get out of here. How many horses do we have?"

"Three, counting Leather. The horse you used as a battering ram broke his leg. We'll have to put him down. The Indian ponies took off somewhere."

Timbre looked over to the side and saw the horse hobbling on three legs.

"Shit. Okay, you ride Bonner's horse and I'll ride Mountain's. Lead Leather and put Patch's out of its misery."

"Why can't I ride Leather?" Curtis asked.

"Because, I think it would be a good idea to keep him fresh," Timbre said, pulling himself aboard Mountain's horse with help from Curtis. "Do me a favor and adjust these stirrups," Timbre asked, his feet a good five inches above them.

"Right," Curtis nodded, doing it for him. "After Mountain, you must feel like a feather to this horse."

"I bet I do," Timbre smiled. "Now take care of that injured pony."

"Okay, hand me my gun."

"I gave you a gun, how many do you need?"

"But that's your gun," Curtis stated, looking confused.

"Used to be, it's yours now."

"You mean it---you're giving me your gun?" Curtis asked, surprised at the handsome gift that Timbre was offering him.

"You earned it. After you finish with that horse round up some ammunition for it and let's be on our way."

Timbre waited for Curtis while he went over and shot the lame horse and then searched the dead men for more ammunition. He even stripped off Patch's fancy holster rig to fit his new gun. Putting it around his waist he came back and mounted Bonner's horse.

"Take a last look before we go. Except for possibly of one or two, other men you just killed the most dangerous man in the West."

"I didn't kill him, you did," Curtis commented, as Timbre started forward.

"No. He was as good as dead before I finished him off."

"Then why did you do it?"

"It's personal."

"Then tell me, if it ain't too personal: Who is the most dangerous man in the West?" Curtis wanted to know.

"The man that we're hunting," Timbre answered, riding ahead.

"And who might that be?" Curtis yelled.

"Later, we got no time for that now. Follow me and be ready to move fast."

As they came out of the gully Timbre looked around carefully and then turned left.

Curtis, coming out behind him, spurred his horse until he was siding him, asking: "Why are we heading this way? The Post is in the other direction."

"Too many hiding places in that direction. I don't know where those Comanche's are but I got a feeling that they're close by. If they jump us I want to see them in plenty of time to make a run for it. We'll make for that hill over there," Timbre told him pointing at a rise a little ways off. "We'll swing back after we cross over it."

"I don't see anything. I think you're being overly cautious again," Curtis said, anxious to get back to Carlene.

"The last time I let you talk me into something it almost cost us our lives. If you don't like the way I'm doing things go it alone," Timbre admonished him. "Just don't expect me to save your ass if you get into trouble."

"You don't have to get so mad," Curtis sulked.

"Just keep your eyes open," Timbre ordered, feeling the hairs on the back of his neck begin to tingle. "And also keep an eye out for Thor."

"You think Thor is around here someplace?"

"Yeah. He hates to be away from me for too long---since I'm the only one that will put up with him. He's around here somewheres."

"Why don't you just whistle for him?"

"Why don't I just whistle for the whole Goddamn Comanche nation?"

"You won't have to--- here they are now," Curtis told him, pointing behind them and to their left.

Timbre looked to where Curtis was pointing and saw about twenty or thirty warriors watching them from the top of a rise.

"Okay, here's the plan," Timbre said, talking quickly. "We make a break for that hill I pointed out to you. It's a fairly good distance from here so when your horse starts to tire transfer over to Leather- and don't stop to do it."

"What about you?"

"Don't worry about me. No matter what happens you keep on going. You still have a girl to rescue."

"But what if they capture you?"

"My guns aren't the only thing I took back from Muntean," Timbre told him, tapping his top pocket. "Here they come! Let's eat up some ground!"

Curtis looked over his shoulder and saw the Comanche's charging down the hillside. Kicking his horse into a gallop he heard Timbre whistle.

"That horse you're riding isn't going to outrun them!" Curtis yelled, holding his mount back in order not to leave Timbre behind.

"Don't wait for me- keep going!" Timbre yelled, whistling again.

"I don't think Thor is around!" Curtis yelled.

"That damn horse is going to be the death of me yet!" Timbre mumbled, whistling again.

They rode hard for well over an hour and every time Timbre looked back he could see that the Comanche's were gaining on them. He could feel his horse tiring fast. The big bronc wasn't built for speed or endurance, Mountain had picked it for its strength.

"They're gaining fast!" Curtis screamed, looking back at the yelling Indians who were less than three-hundred yards away and gaining.

"How's your horse doing?" Timbre asked, looking ahead.

The hill that they were making for was now only about five-miles away. Five-miles that his horse couldn't possibly make.

"I'm going to have to change soon!" Curtis told him.

"Okay. This bronc is just about done in. After you change horses don't bother to look back. Put your spurs to Leather and get the hell out of here."

Curtis didn't answer, he knew that there was nothing he could do or say. Somebody had to stay alive to rescue Carlene. He wouldn't be of any use to her by staying behind and dying with Timbre. With great sadness Curtis pulled Leather alongside of him and without slowing down changed mounts.

Doing as he was told Curtis put his spurs to Leather without looking back and felt himself leaving Timbre behind. Timbre watched Curtis transfer horses and then pull away from him. He didn't think badly of him for saving himself, it was the right thing to do.

As his horse started to falter Timbre took the cyanide shell out of his pocket and placed it between his teeth. He then checked his guns making sure that they were in easy reach. Timbre figured on dying, but he also figured on taking a bunch of Comanche's with him.

Looking back over his shoulder to check his lead on the Indians, Timbre was surprised to see Thor trotting along behind him.

"You bag of shit," Timbre shouted, taking the shell out of his mouth to do it. "Get over here!" he shouted at Thor.

Thor came up beside Mountain's exhausted horse and Timbre, calling on what remained of his strength, grabbed his mane and started to switch over. Timbre's body which had been drugged, beaten, and shot in the last twenty-four hours was now rebelling against his attempted acrobatics. The pain and the effort it took to change horses was too much for him. Just when Timbre was sure that he wasn't going to be able to complete the transfer he felt a hand pushing him from behind.

"You finished playing around?" Curtis smiled, stretching over Mountain's horse and pushing Timbre into Thor's saddle.

"For now," Timbre smiled back, as the bullets started to wheeze pass them.

"Then let's get the hell out of here!" Curtis yelled, putting the spurs to Leather.

Timbre kept up with Curtis easily and their fresh mounts quickly out distanced the Comanche's tired ponies. They reached the hill in no time and the two fresh horses took the steep climb without breaking stride.

"Slow down! We're safe," Timbre yelled, once they reached the other side of the hill. "They've had it."

Curtis looked back at the top of the hill and saw a bunch of Comanche's on winded horses looking down at them.

"They know they can't catch us now and they aren't about to kill their mounts trying," Timbre explained, after they slowed their horses to a walk.

"We made it!" Curtis yelled, waving his hat. "Go to hell, you bastards!"

"Up yours, White man!" A voice drifted down to them from the top of the hill. "Next time!"

Timbre and Curtis looked at each other, then to the top of the hill, then back at each other, and then started to laugh uncontrollably as the Comanche's watched the two laughing white men until they were out of sight.

CHAPTER

16

"What did you see?" Timbre asked Curtis, as Curtis came running back from the Trading Post.

It was night and they were in the grove of Cottonwood trees again in front of the building.

"Somebody was kind enough to cut a small window in the front wall that I could peek into. I couldn't see much but I'm sure that the front room is empty. I tried the door but it's sealed tighter than a can of paint. I guess we'll have to wait till Cecil opens up before we can get in. You think Carlene will be alright until morning?" Curtis asked, breathing hard.

"Yeah. Rat Face doesn't know Mountain is dead and he wouldn't dare touch her while he thinks he's alive. But we can't wait till morning to get in. I figure those Comanche's are going to be showing up here in the very near future. I for one want to be long gone when they do."

"What makes you think they'll turn up here?" Curtis asked.

"After losing us if I were those Bucks I would've doubled back to the gully to find out what all that shooting was about. Then, I would've hightailed it to my chief and informed him of what I'd found. Now, if I were Talon, after finding out that Mountain and his men were dead I'd head for here. I'd want to know if my supply of guns and ammunition were still available and I'd want to find out if there'd been any word on my son.

"Sounds right. When do you figure they'll get here?"

"Taking into consideration that their horses were tired I'd guess the soonest they could be here is by first light, the latest noon and anytime in-between. It depends on whether they travel at night or not."

"Do you think they will?" Curtis asked.

"Personally, no. Indians don't like to travel at night if there isn't a full moon---and there isn't a full moon tonight. But then, I could wrong? Hopefully it'll take those braves sometime to get back to their village and then some more time for Talon to decide on his next move. They'll probably start out just before sunrise, but I wouldn't stake my life on it. Either way I intend to be long gone before they arrive here."

"What makes you think that Talon wasn't with that bunch that jumped us? If he was that'll throw your whole time table off."

"Because if he had been they would've been here by now."

"I'll buy that. But how are we going to get into the Trading Post before morning?"

"I've been doing some thinking on that. Do you remember when we were standing at the bar yesterday and then Mountain suddenly appeared?"

"Yeah."

"Well, just before Muntean barged in I remember thinking that Rat Face was acting mighty brave. It was as if he knew that Muntean was right outside ready to come to his aid if need be. My question is: How did he know Mountain was out there? I didn't hear any horses ride up. Did you?"

"Come to think of it, no," Curtis answered, giving it some thought. "If you're right- how did he know?"

"I've got a hunch that Mountain was somewhere close by all the time. He was just waiting to find out who we were before making his move. After all, we could've been anyone--- rangers, soldiers, even other outlaws. I have a feeling that he knew it was me before he came through that door. And, if I'm right about that then that means there's another entrance hidden somewhere around here."

"Maybe Mountain and his men saw our horses standing out front when they approached the Post. If that's the case then they could've left their mounts in the trees, walked the rest of the way and peeked inside?"

"The way that bar is in the shadows? There's no way he could've made us out from the outside. When you just peeked in could you have made out any faces in the dark?

"No, I could hardly tell if anybody was in there."

"Okay, but let's assume that he was able to recognize me. That still doesn't explain the fact that Rat Face knew he was out there?"

"Put that way I'm inclined to go along with your reasoning. You haven't been wrong yet," Curtis agreed.

"Isn't that wonderful," Timbre smiled. "We finally agree on something. Well, we aren't accomplishing anything standing around here and flapping our jaws. Let's start looking for another way into that joint."

"Where do you suggest we start looking?"

"We'll start by searching along the mountain face. Look for anything that might be concealing another entrance."

"Like what?" Curtis asked, following behind Timbre.

"I don't know, just keep your eyes open. Aren't I in enough pain without having to listen to your dumb questions?"

"I don't know. Are you?" Curtis giggled.

"Jeeze. I should've let the Comanche's have you--- after spending time with you that would've taught them a lesson about who they capture in the future. They'd most likely never take another white man captive again," Timbre told him, scanning the face of the mountain, as they walked.

About twenty yards to the right of the Trading Post porch they found the other entrance they were looking for. It had been poorly concealed and was wide enough for a horse to enter. Finding it had been easier than Timbre had expected. Mountain, or one of his men, hadn't covered the ingress properly when they'd exited it. They must have been in a hurry.

"That wasn't hard," Timbre proclaimed. "Somebody did us a favor and forgot to put those bushes and tree limbs back in front of the entrance. You have any matches on you?"

"No. but I have some in my saddlebags. You want me to go get them?" Curtis asked, while trying to peer into the dark cave.

"First feel around inside of the entrance, there might be a lantern or some matches lying close by. Most miners leave a light by the opening."

"Okay," Curtis said, entering the dark cave. Curtis banged around in the dark for a few minutes and then emerged carrying both a lantern and a box of matches. "You were right. Here they are. Now what?" Curtis asked.

"Light the lantern," Timbre told him, sighing. "And then led the way back in."

"Right," Curtis nodded, lighting the lantern.

Curtis and Timbre entered the cave and the first thing that they saw, to their right, were a bunch of stalls. Two of the stalls contained horses and hanging from a nail on one of the stall posts was another lantern. Timbre lifted the lantern off it's peg and getting a match from Curtis lit it.

"No wonder we didn't see any horses when we rode up. They were hidden in here," Timbre commented, "There's our packhorse. The other one must belong to Rat Face. You get those cayuses ready to travel. In the meantime I'm going to have a look around."

"Right," Curtis said, hanging his lantern up and grabbing the saddle by the little black mare.

When Curtis was finished securing the tack on their pack animal and saddling the mare he looked around for Timbre who was no where to be seen.

"Where are you?" Curtis hissed, in a controlled yell, taking his light and shining it around the cave.

The squeaking sound of a door opening, or closing, caught Curtis's attention. Drawing his gun and raising his lantern higher Curtis slowly made his way to the other side of the large cave, toward where the squeaking sound had emanated from.

"Get in here," Timbre whispered, his head quickly popping into view from behind a door that Curtis hadn't noticed before.

Curtis holstered his gun as he walked through the door and into a network of tunnels.

"They must've been in quite a hurry yesterday to get to us--- they forgot to lock the door," Timbre informed Curtis, nodding to the thick Cottonwood door that Curtis had just passed through.

"Maybe they just figured nobody would be snooping around," Curtis said.

"Could be that too, but I like to believe that we had something to do with them being sloppy. That is if you don't mind?" Timbre asked, looking at him.

"No, I don't mind," Curtis smiled. "I kinda like being thought of as a dangerous man."

"That you are," Timbre seriously said, raising his lantern. "This place is a maze of tunnels but I believe that if you follow the tunnel that branches off to the left you'll come out in Rat Face's back rooms."

"Me?" Curtis softly asked. "Where will you be?"

"Out front. Making a racket."

"Why? Why don't we both follow the tunnel and take Rat Face by surprise?"

"Because we don't know where he, or the girl. We might walk smack into the both of them and if he starts shooting the girl may catch a stray bullet. I also need Rat Face alive. I don't want to take the chance of having to shoot him."

"Okay. What's your plan?" Curtis asked.

"I'm going out front and fire some shots into the main door to get Rat Face's attention. While he's busy checking out the gunshots you come in by the back and get the drop on him. Simple."

"But what if you hit him, or me?

"I won't. I'll be firing high and I doubt if my bullets will go through that door anyway. You just be sure to let me know when you get the drop on him so I can stop firing."

"Don't worry, I'll be sure to yell out."

"Good. Now remember: Don't make your move until you hear my shots."

"What if I can't hear them from inside the tunnel?" Curtis asked.

"I didn't think of that. You might have a point. Let's do this: Start counting as soon as I leave here. If you haven't heard any shots by the time you reach- let's say- five-hundred, go ahead and make your move. Got that?"

"Five-hundred. I got it," Curtis confirmed.

"Good. Oh, and one more thing. I'm taking the mare and the packhorse out front with me and tying them with our horses back in the trees. See you in a little bit," Timbre told him, leaving Curtis to start his count.

Timbre gathered up the two horses as he left the cave. He then led them to the grove of trees were their other horses were. All the while he was doing this Timbre kept count along with Curtis--- hopefully.

Timbre was up to four-hundred and twenty by the time he fired the first shot high into the Trading Post door. Waiting for a couple of more minutes he then placed another bullet into the top of the door.

Timbre did this another time and was just about to fire his forth round when a bullet whizzed by his ear- less than an inch away from his head. A split second later Timbre saw and heard an explosion come from the Trading Post window.

"You little bastard," Timbre mumbled, ducking behind a tree, his heart racing. "You almost split my melon with that one."

Timbre stayed hidden behind the tree. He saw no reason to expose himself to anymore danger, he'd accomplished what he'd set out to do, he'd gotten Rat Face's attention. Without exposing himself Timbre fired into the air. He was in the process of reloading when he heard Curtis yell out: "It's all clear! You can come in now!"

Timbre gathered up their horses and limped slowly to the Post. The front door was now unlocked and upon entering Timbre saw that Curtis had Cecil standing up against the bar with his hands in the air.

"Nice work," Timbre complemented Curtis. "Where's the girl?"

"I don't know. I haven't had time to look for her yet," Curtis answered, anxious to start his search for her.

"Where's the girl?" Timbre asked Cecil.

"Last room on the right," Cecil squeaked, more than willing to cooperate. "I have the key right here in my pocket. I took good care of her, she'll vouch for that."

Cecil figured, and rightly so, that if these two men were back that meant that Mountain was dead. Fumbling the key out of his pants pocket, Cecil offered it to Timbre,

"Give it to him," Timbre ordered.

"Yes Sir," Cecil said, sliding the key down the bar to Curtis.

"By the way," Curtis commented, grabbing the key. "In case you're interested: I couldn't hear the shots from inside the tunnel. In fact, I didn't hear them until I was halfway down the hall. You're lucky that Cecil was on his way to get himself a drink or else you'd be out of ammunition by now."

"I was born lucky," Timbre told him.

"I believe that," Curtis agreed, turning and disappearing through the curtains behind the bar.

"I'm very angry with you," Timbre told Cecil, as he walked to the bar. "First you were rude to me, then you drugged me, and then you damn near put a bullet through my head just now. Just what am I going to do with you?"

Cecil hadn't been frightened by the boy when he'd gotten the drop on him, but this dirty bloody man scared the hell out of him the same way that the blond man, who Timbre has been tracking, had scared the hell out of him.

The Count had warned them that Timbre was on his way and that they should be very concerned about that. Mountain hadn't said much about it but Cecil could tell that it had worried him some because he did take some precautions by setting up an ambush for him.

At the time Cecil couldn't understand why everyone was so worried about one man. He'd thought to himself: What could one man do against Mountain and his men--- except die. He had considered Muntean invincible, but now that he was dead and Timbre was back, Cecil figured he had plenty of cause to be scared of this man.

Cecil couldn't begin to imagine how Timbre had accomplished the killings of Mountain and his men but he wasn't about to grieve any over it. He was now the sole owner of his business again; And, if he played his cards right these men might leave without killing him. His only regret was that he wouldn't get to keep the girl now that Mountain was dead: But he figured, you can't have everything--- or can you?

"I'm sorry. I was just doing what Mountain ordered me to do," Cecil cowered. "And if I knew that was you outside I never would have shot at you."

"I'm inclined to believe that," Timbre told him, leaning on the bar. "You don't seem like such a bad sort. I can understand how Mountain scared you into doing things that you wouldn't normally do. Just to show you that I don't hold a grudge, let's have a drink together. I can sure use one."

Timbre watched Rat Face scurry behind the bar. When he reached down for glasses, Timbre said: "Not that I don't trust you, but why don't you hand me the guns that you have stored under there-- and be real careful about it."

"I only have the one," Cecil told him, placing a Navy Colt gently on the bar top. "I wouldn't have used it anyway."

"Of course you wouldn't have, but why let temptation trouble you," Timbre told him as he picked up the gun. "Tell me, Cecil: Do you enjoy breathing?"

"Yes Sir," Cecil answered, his legs starting to quiver.

"Good. Then we shouldn't have any problem coming to an understanding," Timbre told him, cocking the gun.

"What is it you want?" Cecil asked, staring at the Colt, which was pointed at the far wall.

"First, pour us a drink, and while you're doing that you can tell me when the Count left here and which way he was traveling," Timbre ordered, slowly turning the business end of the revolver so that it was now aimed at Rat Face's head.

Cecil looked down into the barrel of the gun and his hands started to shake. They shook so badly that when he tried to pour the drinks he spilled most of the liquor all over the top of the bar. Cecil had only managed to fill one small shot glass before the bottle was empty. Still shaking, Cecil held up the bottle so that Timbre could see that it was empty; and said: "This is empty, I'll get another one."

Cecil reached under the bar top and came up with a half filled bottle of Rye. With steady hands he then proceeded to fill Timbre's glass. It was strange how his hand had all of a sudden stopped shaking. Putting the bottle back he then grabbed a rag and nervously began to wipe the bar; asking: "Is Mountain really dead?"

"As dead as he's ever going to get," Timbre informed him, patiently waiting for answers to his questions.

Cecil hadn't believe any of that spirit shit that Mountain had been spouting and didn't fear that the blond man would come back for him--- in any form. But he did believe that Mountain was dead and that if he didn't want to join him he'd best tell this man anything he wanted to know.

"They left here some hours before you arrived. The blond man, the one they called Count, said that they were in a hurry and that they couldn't hang around here any longer waiting for you to show up. He ordered Mountain, who'd just gotten back from a raid in Mexico, to make sure that your hunt for him ended here," Cecil blurted out. "If you ask me this Count fella was mighty relieved when Mountain turned up. He couldn't wait to dump you in his lap and hightail it out of here before you arrived."

"Where were they heading?" Timbre asked, fingering the glass.

"They didn't tell me direct but I heard them talking about going to Montana," Cecil said, as he watched Timbre play with his drink.

At the mention of Montana Timbre's attention increased twice fold. That was where he was headed before all this happened. He didn't believe in coincidences and so that bit of news worried him but he didn't know why yet.

"One more question," Timbre asked, uncocking the gun and laying it on the bar. "What did this Count look like?"

"I'd say he was about your age, your height, but slighter in build. He had long slinky blond hair, almost as pretty as a woman's, but the thing that gave me the willys was his----"

"Eyes," Timbre finished for him.

"Yeah. You knew what I was going to say. You must've seen him before."

"Maybe," Timbre mumbled, deep in thought.

"His eyes reminded me of molded cheese," Rat Face said, shivering.

"I never heard them described quite like that, but I guess it fits," Timbre nodded, raising his glass.

"Yeah. Well, drink up," Cecil smiled, showing his pointy little teeth.

"First, let's play a game," Timbre declared, setting his glass back on the bar without drinking from it. "You like games Cecil?"

I don't know what kind of game you got in mind?" Cecil asked, suspiciously.

"It's a guessing game." Covering both glasses with his hands, Timbre rotated them around a couple of times, then ordered: "Now pick one."

Cecil, who hadn't been paying attention because he hadn't known what Timbre was up to now looked down at the two glasses, and asked nervously: "You still don't trust me? Even after I just told you everything you wanted to know?"

"Of course I trust you," Timbre smiled. "I just like playing games. Come-on, humor me."

Cecil stared at the glasses and licked his dry lips. Things warn't going as he'd planned. It was supposed to have been easy, given the condition that Timbre was in. The switching of the bottles had been a work of art. Cecil had figured that once he'd taken care of Timbre the boy wouldn't have been much of a problem for him to dispose of. Then he would've had everything- his business, plus the girl.

Realizing that his plan had backfired and that he didn't have a choice if he wanted to keep on living, Cecil picked up the glass nearest to him. Calculating that he had a fifty-fifty chance of winning the game Cecil downed the drink with one gulp.

"There," Cecil smiled after a few seconds had passed and he knew that he'd made the right choice. "You didn't seriously think that I'd be fool enough to try the same trick on you twice? Do you think me that big a fool? Give me more credit than that."

"No, I never thought you were a fool- just greedy," Timbre told him, picking up the Colt again and using the barrel of it to push the remaining drink closer to Cecil. "Have another."

"But that's not fair!" Cecil protested, almost in tears. "It's your turn. You got to play the game by the rules."

"I am," Timbre smiled. "You see, the rules state that the person with the gun gets to make the rules. I just made up the rule that says you get to drink twice. Any arguments?" Timbre asked, cocking the gun again.

"It's just not fair," Cecil pleaded, beginning to cry, as he slowly brought the glass to his lips.

"You're right, it isn't fair," Timbre agreed, pointing the gun at Cecil's tiny little heart. "But you got to learn to take the bad with the good. Now drink up."

Cecil looked at the gun, weighed his options, and then slowly drank the whiskey. Ten seconds later he was crumpled up on the floor behind the bar.

"And you said you could be trusted," Timbre smiled, to the unconscious figure. "Now, if you'll excuse me I have some things that need attending to."

Carlene gripped the knife more firmly in her hands when she realized that the monster had inserted the key into the lock and was opening the door. The handle of the door slowly turned and then the door itself began to swing open. Carlene moved the point of the blade an arm's length away from her body. Closing her eyes she took a deep breath, tensed her arm muscles, and prepared to plunge the knife into her heart.

"STOP!"

Carlene recognized the voice a half-second before she started the knife on its fatal journey. Checking her death stroke Carlene opened her eyes and saw Curtis standing in the doorway with a horrified look on his face.

"What are you doing?" Curtis asked, refusing to believe what he almost was forced to witness.

"I.. I.. I..," Carlene stammered, staring at the knife in her hands and feeling like puking.

"Give me that," Curtis ordered, crossing the room and gently removing the knife from her hand and throwing it away.

"I thought you were the Monster," Carlene stammered, beginning to cry.

Curtis sat beside the crying girl and enfolded her in his arms; saying: "You needn't worry about him anymore- he's dead."

A wave of relief swept over Carlene. Pulling her head away from Curtis's shoulder she looked up into his eyes and asked: "How--- how did you do it?"

Curtis wiped her tears away with the sleeve of his shirt and began to tell her everything that'd happened to them since they'd been led away that morning.

It took Curtis over a half an hour to tell Carlene everything and by the time he'd finished her eyes were dry and shinning. A part of Carlene knew that everything that Curtis had told her actually took place and was for real, but another part of her felt as if she were reading a book- a book written especially for her. Curtis's tale was the most exciting story that she'd ever heard and as far as she was concerned, Curtis was her true hero.

Hardly able to contain her excitement, anxious to find out what the next chapter held in store for them, Carlene asked: "What now?"

"I don't know for sure. We better find Tim and see what he thinks," Curtis told her.

"Lead the way," Carlene jubilantly urged him, taking his hand and squeezing it tightly.

They found Timbre sitting in the kitchen gobbling up the chicken that Carlene been forced to cook for the monster.

"Hey. I see you found her," Timbre said, looking up and biting into a chicken wing as they entered,

"Yeah. She was where Cecil said she'd be. Talking about Cecil, where is he?" Curtis asked, looking around for him.

"He's taking a nap in the other room," Timbre informed him. "Have something to eat, this stuff is great. I might keep that little rat around just to cook for us."

"No need for that. I prepared the chicken," Carlene smiled, as Curtis helped himself to the food.

"Well Sis, anybody who looks like you and can cook like this is a most welcome companion," Timbre complimented her, admiring the way she looked in her red dress. "But you did cook a tad to much for just us."

"That was supposed to be for the Monster," Carlene corrected him.

As soon as Carlene said the chicken had been meant for Mountain, Timbre turned his head and spit the chicken out onto the floor; asking Carlene: "Tell me that you didn't poison this"

"No. I didn't think of that," Carlene answered, laughing and wondering why she hadn't thought of that.

"Thank God you don't have a villainous heart," Timbre sighed, very painfully getting to his feet.

"What happened to you?" Carlene asked in as concerned voice, getting a good look at Timbre for the first time.

"Just about everything," Timbre answered, trying to smile.

"Curtis," Carlene ordered in her Doctor's voice. "Go find my medical bag. It's out front somewheres."

"Yes, Ma'am," Curtis answered, jumping to his feet and leaving the room.

"You take off that shirt and I'll have a look at your wound," Carlene ordered, advancing toward Timbre.

"Not right now. It's stopped bleeding. If I pull the shirt off it'll tear the scab open and I'll start bleeding again and I don't have time for that," Timbre told her, putting his hand on her shoulder and holding her off.

"Don't be a hero. You need attention," Carlene insisted, trying to push his hand to the side.

"Believe me, the last thing that I'm trying to be is a hero. All I'm trying to do is to keep us all alive. There's a very good chance that there's a mess of pissed off Comanche's making their way here at this very moment. And, if I'm unable to travel we're going to be in for a lot of trouble."

"But I'm just trying to make you feel better," Carlene insisted, trying to reason with him.

"That's just it, I don't want to feel better. I'm in pain and the pain keeps me awake and moving. If I felt better I might not be able to stay awake. Just throw a bandage over my shirt for now and clean up my face. At least I won't look so bad and we can worry about the rest of me later," Timbre told her, trying to appease her healing instincts.

"If that's the way you want it?" Carlene capitulated, her need to help satisfied.

Just then, Curtis entered the room carrying a black bag; and asking: "This it?"

"Yes. Thank you," Carlene smiled, taking the bag from Curtis and then rummaging around in it.

"Curtis," Timbre said, watching Carlene lay out what she needed on the table. "While she's doing this load the packhorse with whatever supplies you think we'll need. Grab whatever you want from out front and don't forget to take along plenty of water. I thought I saw canteens and water skins hanging out there somewhere. Oh! And pack me some extra shirts."

"Got it," Curtis said, leaving the room again.

Carlene stepped close to Timbre and wrapped a bandage around his shirt, then told him: "Sit down so I can tend to your face."

As Carlene opened a bottle of antiseptic and bent over to apply it to his cuts and bruises, Timbre felt a stirring beginning low in his belly. The girl was even prettier now that she was cleaned up than he thought she'd be, in fact she was down right beautiful. It'd been a long time between woman for Timbre. He was starting to feel the effects of his abstinence.

"Are you trying to kill me?" Timbre hoarsely asked, pushing Carlene away when the liquid started to burn and his abdomen began to ache. Her female scent was filling his being with desire.

"Stop being such a baby," Carlene admonished him, half guessing that it wasn't only the antiseptic that was troubling him.

"Baby my ass. Tuck yourself back in and finish what you were doing," Timbre told her in a strained voice, indicating where her milk white breast had popped out of her low cut dress.

Carlene looked down at where Timbre was pointing and instead of being embarrassed, as she would've been less than a day ago, she smiled and asked: "Don't you like what you see?"

Since driving Cecil half mad with desire she'd realized that she liked teasing men until they were half crazed. But, she was also smart enough to realize that that sort of behavior could only lead to trouble. So, after seeing the pain on Timbre's face, she silently vowed to control her impulses before they caused Timbre any more discomfort.

"I love what I see," Timbre truthfully replied. "But that young man out there happens to be in love with you- and he's my friend."

Blushing, at the mention of Curtis, Carlene tucked herself back into her dress, mumbling: "I don't know what's come over me lately. I've never acted like this before."

"You were inches away from the worst days of your life. For all intent and purposes your life was over and you had resigned yourself to death. Now you've been given a second life and it isn't very real to you just yet. For the moment you're still high on adrenaline and you're using your beauty and desirability as an escape from reality. Sooner or later you'll come down from that high and most likely feel shame for what you've done. I suggest that you prepare yourself for those feelings, even though you haven't done anything yet to be ashamed of. As a trained healer you should know all that."

"I guess you're right," Carlene agreed. "But why do I find you so attractive, even though I love Curtis? Carlene asked, still blushing. "This is all so new to me. I just don't understand any of it."

"Because you're young and don't know the difference between love and desire yet. As we go through life we'll meet people that we'll feel desire for-- but truly only love one."

"I've worked with enough people to know that there is a difference between love and lust, but I've never personally experienced either one before."

"Well you are now and I suggest that you work it out quickly. I'm too old and randy to be playing games with you."

"How do you know so much about woman?" Carlene asked, curious about this killer with such a gentile manner with the ladies.

"Because they're people and I always could feel what other people are feeling. It's a gift I was born with," Timbre confessed, looking directly into Carlene's eyes.

Carlene thrilled under Timbre's direct stare, and asked: "You can tell what people are thinking?" Not quite believing him.

"Sometimes, but most of the time I just feel what they're feeling. There's a big difference between the two."

"I guess so. Sometime in the future I'd like to explore this subject deeper with you, as a Doctor that is, but for now I better just finish cleaning you up. I've had enough confusion for one day."

"Haven't we all," Timbre smiled, trying to ignore her closeness.

Carlene was just finishing cleaning Timbre's face when Curtis came back in. "That's it. Anything else you want done?" Curtis asked, grabbing another piece of chicken.

"Yeah. I want to destroy this place? Any suggestions?" Timbre flippantly asked.

"That's easy. Just use the barrels of gunpowder that are in the cave. There's enough there to blow this place to hell and gone," Curtis answered, between bites.

"You found kegs of gunpowder?" Timbre asked, incredulously.

"Yeah. Back there in the tunnel," Curtis reaffirmed, pointing with a chicken leg.

"Show me," Timbre ordered, standing.

"Come-on," Curtis offered, leading the way.

Timbre and Carlene followed Curtis down the tunnel until they came to a wooden door. Curtis stopped for a moment, opened the door, and then bent over to pick up a lantern that he'd left burning there. He then resumed walking for about twenty-five yards until the tunnel suddenly opened up into a large chamber.

"Here it is," Curtis declared, holding his lantern high.

Timbre looked around and saw that the cave was indeed filled with kegs of gunpowder; And, in addition to that there were boxes of guns and ammunition stacked up against the walls.

"Wow! There's enough explosives here to start a war. I wonder where they got it all from?" Timbre asked, to no one in particular.

"I noticed that a lot of those cases have Mexican writing on them. I'd guess they were robbed from Mexican miners," Curtis volunteered.

"If the Comanche's knew that all this stuff was here Mountain and his men would've been dead a long time ago. We've got to destroy all of this before Talon finds it. He can damn near win Texas back with this much powder and guns," Timbre warned.

"How do we go about it?" Curtis asked.

"Carlene," Timbre said. "You go back to the front and get yourself something practical to wear. Me and Curtis will join you shortly."

"Okay, but I'll need a lantern to find my way back," Carlene told him.

"No problem," Curtis smiled, walking over to the wall and pulling down another lantern that was sitting on a ledge. Lighting it he handed it to Carlene. "There you go."

"Thank you, Darling," Carlene said, quickly kissing him on the lips and then abruptly turning and leaving.

"Okay," Timbre began, looking at the blushing Curtis. "Put down that lantern and give me a hand. Let's pile all the kegs of gunpowder and ammunition in the center here."

Without waiting for a reply Timbre painfully started to roll the kegs of gunpowder into the center of the cave. A few seconds later Curtis was doing the same.

They were almost finished, when Timbre yelled: "Look what I found!"

Curtis stopped what he was doing and looked to see what Timbre was holding.

"Isn't this a beauty?" Timbre asked, holding up a Sharps 44/90. You don't see many of these around anymore. They only made a couple of thousand of these--- if that many. Buffalo hunters would sell their Mama's for one of these. This thing can shoot for over 800 yards. I even found ammunition for it," he smiled, shaking a sack full of rounds.

"You already have a rifle. What are you going to do with another one?" Curtis asked.

"It's for you. To replace that crappy one that you're carrying," Timbre told him, proudly presenting Curtis with the rare piece.

"I guess you were too busy bleeding to notice that I took Bonner's rifle. I grabbed his rifle while I was retrieving your gear. I didn't think he'd need it anymore," Curtis confessed, examining the Sharps that Timbre had handed to him.

"Then give it back," Timbre told him, snatching the rifle out of his hands. "I'll keep it for myself."

"What are you getting so mad about?" Curtis asked. "All I did was to tell you that I already have a good rifle."

"I'm sorry," Timbre apologized, not wanting to make an issue out of it. He didn't feel like teaching the boy that it was impolite to turn down a gift. "I guess it's just that I'm tired and I hurt. Let's finish up here and vamoose. Open one of those barrels of powder and pour it over the other ones. Then break open another one and use it to leave a trail as we go."

"Right," Curtis said, doing as he was told.

It took them about fifteen-minutes to back out of the tunnel and onto the front porch, leaving a steady stream of gunpowder as they went.

"You got everything you need?" Timbre asked Carlene, who was standing out front waiting for them. She was now wearing a tan leather skirt, a heavy white cotton blouse, and brown boots.

"I think so," she answered, watching Curtis set the barrel down.

"Good, then mount up," Timbre told her. Turning back to Curtis, he said: "I don't think I'm going to be able to ride very fast and once you light that powder we're going to have to vacate this place in a hurry. If Talon is anywhere in the vicinity the explosion will surely hurry him along. Not to mention that if we aren't far enough away when that stuff goes off it will hurry us along--- permanently. What me and Carlene will do is to start riding now. In about fifteen-minutes light that fuse and ride like hell. You shouldn't have any problem catching up with us."

"What about Rat Face?" Curtis asked. "Should I get him out of there?"

"He treated me alright," Carlene intervened. "I see no reason to kill him."

"Okay. If you want to drag him out and put him someplace where he'll be safe, go ahead. You'll find him behind the bar," Timbre informed Curtis, struggling to mount Thor. "And Curtis, any sign of trouble light that powder and get the hell out of here. Got that?"

"Got it," Curtis answered, as Timbre and Carlene slowly started North.

Thirty-minutes later, Carlene asked Timbre: "What's taking him so long?"

"It sounds like him coming now," Timbre told her, hearing a horse quickly overtaking them in the darkness. Minutes later Curtis came galloping out of the dark to join them.

"Did you put Cecil someplace safe?" Carlene asked.

"I carried him into the woods. I think he'll be safe enough there," Curtis assured her.

At that moment the loudest and biggest explosion that any of them had ever heard shattered the night air. The ground rumbled and everything shook.

The horses spooked and Curtis reached over and grabbed Carlene's pony's bridle just before she lost control of him. Timbre was busy himself hanging on tightly to Thor and the bucking packhorse at the same time.

They were finally getting their mounts under control when a second explosion made the ground shake again. This time they saw flames shooting up into the blackness of the night. The bright fire was coming from miles away, where the top of the mountain used to be.

"There must've been another store of powder somewhere in those tunnels," Timbre shouted to them.

"You think Cecil lived through that?" Carlene shouted back.

"Maybe, but we aren't going back to find out. Every Comanche within fifty miles has been alerted. We have to put some distance between us and that place," Timbre yelled, turning a fidgety Thor North again. The faint rosy glow of dawn was just beginning to bud when they finally rode out of the sand. The desolate wasteland had stretched out further Northbound than it had Westbound.

"The horses are about done in," Curtis stated to Timbre, who looked to be 'all done in' himself.

"We'll stop when we get to those boulders," Timbre told him pointing to a stand of rocks maybe a mile away and stacked maybe thirty feet high.

By the time they rode their ponies through an opening on the side of the rocks they were all bone tired. Once inside they saw that the boulders formed a complete circle, forming a natural windbreak. The interior of the rock cropping was filled with clean white sand that looked as if it hadn't been disturbed for at least a hundred years.

Timbre had to ask Curtis to help him dismount because he'd become too stiff to get down by himself.

"You don't look so good," Curtis commented, helping Timbre take off his gun belt and then to sit with his back resting against a boulder.

"I'm getting tired of hearing that," Timbre grimaced. "You don't look much like any dandy yourself."

"Maybe not, but at least I can walk."

"Sure. Rub it in," Timbre moaned, removing his hat and sailing it away from him. "Since your making such a big deal out of walking, walk over to the horses and unsaddle them. Then give them all the water they want and fed them. We'll be staying here for a while. Oh, and before you go, do me a favor and pull off my boots."

"I still think we should've headed for that town," Curtis grumbled, pulling off Timbre's boots. "A bed wouldn't have hurt you any."

"Like I said before: Why bring misery down on their heads? Talon and his braves are tracking us and I'm guessing he wants our skins real bad. I can't see where getting innocent people killed would help us any."

"What makes you think that they're after us?" Carlene asked, joining them after she'd retrieved her doctor's bag from the packhorse. "We haven't seen hide nor hair of anyone since leaving the Post."

"They're coming. I can feel them," Timbre told her, matter-of-factly.

"If he says they're coming, they're coming," Curtis told her. "I don't know how he does it but he hasn't been wrong yet."

"If you say so, Darling," Carlene conceded, in a patronizing manner. "Now, will you please get me some water so I can attend to his wounds?"

"Okay," Curtis answered, ignoring her skepticism but loving the way she called him Darlin'.

"I see that you've started bleeding again," Carlene commented, knelling in front of Timbre,

While Carlene was rummaging through her medical bag Curtis dropped off the water and then left again to attend to the horses.

"Yeah. I think it ripped open while I was dismounting," Timbre informed her, looking down at the blood seeping through the bandage.

"Well then, I guess you won't mind if I have a look at it now?" she asked him sarcastically while unwinding his bandage.

Once the bandage was removed she then took the canteen and poured the water all over where the shirt was stuck to him. Then she slowly cut it away from his body.

"God! How did you get that?" Carlene asked, pointing at the big ugly puckered scar right below where Timbre's heart was located.

"Bullet," Timbre answered simply.

"Why arn't you dead?" Carlene incredulously asked, examining the old wound. "Being shot that close to the heart would've been enough to kill most men."

"That's what everyone else said, even the doctor who dug the bullet out. Amazing, isn't it? Clean living and a pure soul, that's the ticket to a long and healthy life," Timbre jokingly replied.

"If that's the way to a long life you would've been dead a long time ago. The truth is, it probably didn't kill you because you're too ornery to die," Carlene smiled, examining the rest of his torso. "What are these other scars from?"

"A couple were made from arrows, a few from knives, and some from near misses, well not near enough misses----and the four long ones on my back I got from one mean Cougar," Timbre explained.

"Near misses. What do you consider a hit?"

"A hit is when I'm killed."

"I don't understand why you'd set out to ruin what was probably a fine body at one time," Carlene commented, shaking her head. She saw no reason for this kind of devastation to a human body.

305

"Yeah. I purposely set out to have all this done to me because I thought it would look attractive to the ladies," Timbre sarcastically told her. "Can you just get on with what you were doing and keep your stupid remarks to yourself?"

Carlene's eyes flashed fire. Without replying she picked up the bottle of antiseptic and generously splashed it into his open wound.

"AHHHHHHH!" Timbre screamed, pushing Carlene away, the burning pains bringing tears to his eyes.

It took sometime before Timbre could form words again and when he could all he could think to say, without pissing Carlene off again, was: "That wasn't a very professional thing to do."

"Maybe not, but it was immensely satisfying," Carlene smiled. "Now as soon as I wash my hands and clean you up a little bit more, I'll stitch that shut."

"I hope you're referring to my wound," Timbre groaned.

"Maybe."

"What happened?" Curtis asked, walking over. "Why did you scream?"

"Whatever you do, don't get shot around her," Timbre warned him.

Curtis looked at Carlene, saw the look in her eyes, and figured it wasn't worth pursuing.

"What now?" Curtis asked, yawning.

"I figure we got maybe a four or five hour lead on Talon and his braves. After Carlene finishes patching me up you two rest for a couple of hours and then hightail it out of here."

"What about you?" Curtis asked.

"I won't be able to ride for a day or two so I'll stay here and hold them off. That'll give you two time to get away."

"Still trying to be a hero?" Carlene asked, dabbing at his wound.

"No, just being practical," Timbre winced. "Why should we all risk our lives. You two can ride and I can't. If I could ride I'd be getting the hell out of here too. But since I can't, the smart thing for you two to do is to save yourselves. Don't worry, I'll catch-up in a week or so."

"And how do you plan to do that if you're dead?" Curtis asked.

"I don't plan on being dead," Timbre told him, grinding his teeth, as Carlene put in the first stitch.

"You plan on killing all those Comanche's by yourself?" Curtis asked, watching the needle go in and out of Timbre's flesh.

"Jesus, woman!" Timbre agonized, trying not to move. "Hold it a minute and let me catch my breath before you do anymore or I'll be long dead before the Indians even get here."

"I'm nearly finished. Be still and stop acting like a baby," Carlene ordered, putting in the last three stitches and wondering how Timbre had managed to sit through all that pain.

"Answer my question," Curtis reminded him. "How do you expect to hold off all those Indians?"

"Luck," Timbre stated, breathing hard from the exertion of fighting off the pain. "You know how lucky I am. Something, or somebody, will most likely come along to save my butt. Besides, maybe Talon didn't bring many warriors with him. Why should he? There's only the three of us."

Curtis studied Timbre's face for a moment and then said: "You really do believe that you're that lucky, don't you?"

"Of course," Timbre affirmed, leaning back and relaxing now that Carlene was finished bandaging him.

"What if nobody comes along this time to save your skin?" Carlene asked. "Without Curtis around to help pull your fat out of the fire you'd be lost."

Timbre looked at Curtis, who averted his eyes and was blushing. He didn't know what Curtis had told Carlene, but it didn't matter. The truth-of-the-matter was that Curtis had saved his ass when Mountain was about to yank off his leg.

"I haven't quite thought of it that way," Timbre said with a straight face.

"Well, it doesn't matter," Carlene stated. "Because we're not leaving you. Are we Curtis?"

"Well, I'm not," Curtis told her. "But there's no reason why you should stay."

"And just where am I supposed to go in this wilderness by myself? How long do you think I'd last out there all alone. I'm an Easterner not a frontiersman. I'd get lost out there by myself."

"She's got a point ya know," Timbre agreed. "You got to go with her. She wouldn't last the night out there by herself."

While Curtis was thinking about what Timbre had said, Carlene made up his mind for him by declaring: "You can leave if you want but I'm staying. You can't make me go and if you try I'll fight you. Nobody owns me. I have a right to live or die anyplace that I please to."

Timbre hated to agree with her again but he'd fought most of his life for that very same right and couldn't see any reason for denying Carlene that privilege too--- even if it did mean her dying.

"She's right again, Curtis."

"But if she stays she'll be killed- or worse," Curtis argued, hoping to get Timbre to back him up."

"He's right you know," Timbre agreed, turning back to Carlene.

"He may be but it's my life and I'll do with it as I please," Carlene flatly stated.

"But why would you want to stay and possibly die with me? You hardly know me. Did it ever occur to you that I might not be worth it," Timbre asked, genuinely wanting an answer.

"You risked your life for Curtis's Aunt and Cousin, who you didn't know. You risked your life for me, who you didn't know. You could've run out and left me with Cecil, but you didn't. Should I be expected to do less simply because I'm a woman. Woman have honor and courage too--- in case you're not aware of that."

"What makes you think I was willing to risk my life for you?" Timbre asked, taking a new approach to the problem.

"Because you came back for me."

"It wasn't my idea to do that," Timbre explained. "It was Curtis's. He forced me to go back with him and rescue you."

"I believe that Curtis would've come for me, with or without you, but I don't believe that Curtis forced you to go back with him. I may not know you well but I know you well enough to know that you're not the type of man who's forced into doing anything he doesn't want to, and no amount of talking is going to make me think differently."

"If I had the strength to put you both on your horses and make you leave, but I don't, so I give up. What say you, Curtis?"

"I don't like it, but I guess we're all staying."

"Carlene, hand me my shirt, please," Timbre requested of her.

"It's ruined. I'll get you a new one," Carlene told him, picking up the tattered and bloody shirt and showing it to him.

"I don't want to wear it, I just want to get something out of the pocket," Timbre explained, taking the shirt from her hand and removing the cyanide shell from the bloody rag.

"What's that?" Carlene asked.

"Take it," Timbre offered, placing the cartridge into her hand. "Put it someplace where you can get at it fast."

"What's it for?" Carlene asked, rotating it around in her fingers, inspecting it from all angles.

"It's insurance against pain," Curtis told her, not able to continue because he didn't want to think of Carlene using it.

"I still don't know what you two are talking about," Carlene said, looking at Curtis, mystified.

"It's filled with cyanide," Timbre stepped in, letting Curtis off the hook. "If it doesn't look like we're going to make it, bite on the end of it, suck the wax out, and swallow the poison. Believe me, it'll be a whole lot quicker and a lot less painful than what the Comanche will do to you."

"What if I swallow the wax? It'll probably make me sick if I do," Carlene asked, looking at Timbre.

Timbre studied Carlene's face for a few seconds and then began to laugh when he came to the conclusion that she wasn't joking.

Carlene and Curtis at first were puzzled by Timbre's sudden outburst of laughter and thought that he'd slipped over the edge. Then, almost simultaneously they realized the ridiculousness of Carlene's question and both of them joined in laughing with Timbre. The tension that had been building up in them was now being released and so they laughed harder than the situation might have called for.

Holding his side where the stiches were, Timbre choked: "It's optional." That remark caused them to laugh even harder.

"If I don't stop laughing I'm going to bust open my side," Timbre said, wiping his eyes and forcing himself to stop laughing. Extending his hand, he asked: "Help me up, Curtis. I have to go to the privy,"

Everyone thought for some reason that Timbre having to relieve himself was hilarious and so they began to laugh even harder.

"Me too!" Carlene gasped, holding her stomach.

Finally, when their laughter was beginning to border on insanity they regained control of themselves. Curtis first helped Timbre to his feet and then Carlene. Then they each disappeared behind separate boulders while still chuckling to themselves.

When they emerged again they realized that they hadn't eaten since last night so Carlene dug out the left over chicken she'd packed from the Post. After they'd finished eating, Timbre said to Curtis: "One of us should stand guard, but you look as worn-out as I feel."

"I can do it," Carlene volunteered. "I got some sleep last night before you two showed up."

"You sure?" Timbre asked.

"If you're asking me if I'm sure that I got some sleep last night, the answer is yes. If you're asking if I'm sure I can stand guard, my answer is: Just because I'm a woman dosn't mean that I can't see. Woman have eyes just like men," Carlene chastised Timbre, becoming angry again.

"You being a woman had nothing to do with it. My concern was that you were tired and might fall asleep," Timbre defended himself, too exhausted to want to argue.

"Well I won't," she stated, standing.

"Fine. In my saddlebag you'll find a spy scope. Get it and climb to the top of those rocks. They'll be coming from the same direction as we came from. As soon as you spot anything, even if it's only a dust cloud, wake us."

"Yes, Sir," Carlene acknowledged, starting to walk away.

"One more thing. If you feel like you're going to fall asleep wake Curtis and he'll take over," Timbre told her, laying back onto the soft warm sand and closing his eyes.

Timbre's last conscious vision before drifting off to sleep was of Curtis climbing the boulders carrying his rifle in one hand and pulling Carlene along with the other.

"WAKE UP!" A voice yelled, penetrating deep into Timbre's pain racked sleep.

Groggily, Timbre tried to comply with the order but couldn't force his mind to break through the thin barrier of sleep. His conscious mind refused to take charge even though it struggled hard to do so.

Half of Timbre was still fighting sleep when he felt the sudden shock of water rushing into his mouth and nose. Instinctively, to save himself from drowning, his body snapped awake dragging his consciousness along with it.

"What!" Timbre yelled, sitting up, the sudden shock of being awakened so quickly making him feel mentally sluggish and physically ill, not to mention the pain that shot through his side.

"They're coming!" Carlene warned him, not bothering to apologize for throwing the water in his face.

"Does Curtis know?" Timbre asked, letting Carlene help him to his feet and hand him his gun belt.

"Yes. He was sleeping up there beside me while I was keeping watch. I woke him when I saw a cloud of dust off in the distance, just like you said to. He's still up there keeping watch," Carlene filled him in, talking quickly as she assisted Timbre in pulling on his boots.

"Good job," Timbre complimented her, limping toward where Curtis had stowed all their gear.

The first thing Timbre did was to pick up his Sharps and the bag of bullets. The Sharps he hung over his shoulder and the bullets he stuffed into his pocket.

"Can you help me up there?" Timbre asked her.

"I think so. I'm getting quite good at climbing up and down those rocks."

"Great," Timbre moaned, as started the climb with Carlene pushing him from behind.

Timbre and Carlene quickly joined Curtis, who was nestled among the top boulders looking out toward the sand.

"They just came off of the flats and unto the mound of sand," Curtis told him. "Can you see them?"

"I can make them out some, but not much," Timbre answered, straining his eyes. "Hand me my spyglass."

"It's lying on the rock right next to you," Curtis told him. Before Timbre could reach for it Carlene picked it up and handed it to him.

"Thanks," Timbre said, focusing his spyglass on the spot where he reckoned the Comanche's were. "I count about twenty of them."

"Eighteen," Curtis corrected him. "And that's including Talon"

Recounting, Timbre said: "You're right, eighteen."

"I wonder why the Chief is named Talon?" Curtis asked.

"I imagine he took his name from the Hawk who swoops down and kills swiftly with his talons" Timbre guessed.

"Oh yeah. I didn't think of that," Curtis agreed.

"Why do they always paint their faces when they're out to kill?" Carlene asked.

"Indians are a superstitious lot. They paint their faces because they believe that the ghosts of those that they've killed will come back to haunt them. If their faces are painted their victims won't know who to look for. They'll just move on to the next life without seeking revenge," Timbre informed her.

"They sure are painted up today," Curtis remarked.

Slowly, as if a light was being lit in his head Timbre began to realize something, and so he asked: "Curtis, can you see them clearly from here- without the use of the spyglass?"

"Yeah. Can't you?" Curtis asked, surprised at the question.

"No," Timbre answered him, astounded by the boys eyesight. "I can just barely make them out with the glass."

"Without the glass I can barely see them myself," Carlene added. "You must have remarkable eyesight, Curtis."

"I guess I do. I never gave it much thought."

"If you can see them from here do you think you can hit any of them from this distance?" Timbre asked.

"How far you figure they are?" Curtis asked, trying to judge the distance.

"Give or take, seven or eight hundred yards," Timbre guessed.

"If they stood still long enough and I had something that could shot that far- maybe."

"Here," Timbre said, handing him the Sharps and then placing the ammunition on the rock in front of him. "This should do it. Now let's see how good you are with it."

Curtis watched as Timbre showed him how to load the rifle. Taking the rifle back from Timbre he examined its sights. When he was satisfied with them he rested the barrel on the boulder in front of him and sighted on the led Indian, which he assumed was Talon.

"Put your fingers in your ears if you want to hear again in the near future," Timbre cautioned Carlene.

"What about me?" Curtis asked, laying down the Sharps.

"Rip up your bandana and stuff bits of it into your ears," Timbre told him.

Curtis ripped pieces off of his kerchief and stuffed them into his ears as Timbre had instructed him to do. Then, picking up the rifle again he steadied the front of it on the boulder once more and carefully sighted it on the Indian again.

They sat there with their fingers in their ears for what seemed to be a very long time. Finally, Timbre heard the muffled explosion of the Sharps going off and saw the front of the rifle lift off the boulder.

Grabbing up his spyglass and placing it to his eye, Timbre saw a red spot magically appear and spread over the War Chief's yellow torso. He then watched as Talon slowly tumbled from his pony and onto the ground.

"By God! You hit him dead center," Timbre stated in awe. "I've never seen shooting like that--- and I've seen some of the best. That sure stopped them dead in their tracks for the time being."

Timbre was right. The Comanche's had stopped advancing and were frantically searching around trying to discover where the shot that had killed their Chief had come from. They couldn't comprehend that the bullet had originated from the rocks- almost a three quarters of a mile away.

"Can you do that again?" Timbre loudly asked, reloading the rifle.

"I can try," Curtis said, having trouble hearing him because he still had the cloth in his ears.

"Okay," Timbre shouted, handing him the rifle back. "Take out that young buck in the red paint. The one that's waving his arms around and pointing toward us."

A couple of minutes passed before Timbre heard the muffled explosion again. Quickly picking up the spyglass he was in time to see the bullet smack into the young bucks shoulder, sending him spinning to the ground.

"Unbelievable," Timbre murmured.

"What?" Curtis asked.

Reaching over and pulling the clothe out of Curtis's nearest ear, Timbre yelled: "UNBELIEVABLE!"

"You don't have to yell," Curtis smiled. "Anybody else you want me to shot?"

"Yeah. All of them, but I'm afraid that this beauty is finished- the barrel is cracked," Timbre informed him, taking the rifle out of Curtis's hands and examining it. "Whoever loaded these cartridges put a lot of powder in them for extra distance. It's a pity, it was a fine piece of art."

"What now?" Carlene asked.

"We sit back and wait. It's their move now," Timbre told her, tossing the Sharps aside and doing what he advised them to do.

"What do you think their next move will be?" Curtis asked.

"No telling with Comanche's. The way they're powwowing I'd guess that most of them want to go home and the rest want to keep coming. Without a Chief to lead them it could go either way."

"If they keep coming what do you think our chances are?" Carlene asked.

"I think we'll take out a bunch of them," Timbre smiled.

"But they'll eventually get to us. Is that what you're saying?" Carlene clarified.

"We ain't dead yet," Timbre shrugged. "Anything can happen."

"They're pulling out!" Curtis yelled, sitting up straight and watching the Comanche's as they collected their dead and wounded and started back the way they'd come. "I wonder why? They must know that they have us cold."

Timbre scanned all around with his spyglass and then announced: "Dust cloud moving this way from the North."

"I don't see anyone," Curtis said; looking at the little puff of dust way off in the distance.

"Me neither, but it's enough to send the Comanche's racing for home," Timbre told him, keeping his glass focused on the moving dirt. "I hope that whoever, or whatever it is, is friendly."

"You mean that we're not safe yet?" Carlene asked.

"Not till we know who or what is coming our way," Timbre told her.

"How long before we'll know?" she asked.

"We should be able to tell within the next fifteen or twenty-minutes."

"What if it's more Indians---or outlaws?" Carlene asked.

"I doubt if it will be more Indians, not from that direction, but it could turn out to be outlaws heading for the Trading Post," Timbre guessed, not taking his spyglass off of the cloud of dust. "If it is outlaws they might just pass us buy. If not, we fight. I can tell you this much: The dust isn't being kicked up by cattle or wild horses. It's definitely being made by men on horseback. Can you see them yet, Curtis?" Timbre asked, handing him the spyglass.

"I can just make out the horses but I can't tell anything about the riders, not just yet" he answered.

"You should he able to see them soon. In the meantime Carlene how about you climbing down and getting us some biscuits and beef-jerky? My stomach is starting to talk to me," Timbre requested. "I'd do it myself, but I barely made it up here the first time."

"Yeah. I'm hungry too," Curtis declared, standing and stretching. "I'll get them. You sit tight Carlene, I can use the exercise. Unless you want to come along?"

"No thanks. I had my exercise for the morning. Besides, I can't see how you two can eat at a time like this. We can be killed at any time now and all you two can think about is your stomachs. I'll wait here and see if we're going to live through this day or not--if you don't mind," she weakly smiled.

"Right. I'll be right back," Curtis smiled at her, making his way down the rocks.

"Aren't you worried?" Carlene asked Timbre, after Curtis was out of earshot.

Putting down his spyglass, Timbre looked at her and said: "That's a silly question, of course I'm worried. I wouldn't be human if I wasn't. What made you ask that question?"

"I was watching you while the Comanche's were out there. There presence didn't seem to have much of an affect on you. Even the other morning, after you were captured by Mountain and you were being marched off to your death, you didn't seem to be very worried about it, in fact you were still making jokes. I could see that Curtis was scared, but you warn't. I want to know why. I've been scared ever since my Father was killed and I'm tired of feeling that way. You know what's going on, you're not a fool. What do you know that I don't know? What's your secret?" Carlene demanded to know, almost in tears.

"No secret. You have every right in the world to be scared. It's only natural. I don't know what to tell you," Timbre truthfully replied.

"I'm starting to have a tough time coping with all this and I'm beginning to unravel. The only thing that kept me together this long is Curtis. I don't want him to think that he's fallen in love with a hysterical woman. A woman who comes apart every time things get a little tough," Carlene confessed.

"You certainly don't strike me as an hysterical woman, and under the circumstances nobody would blame you for coming apart," Timbre told her, trying to soothe her.

"But that's just it, I'm not a woman who normally folds in a crisis, but I can feel myself becoming one. If you don't tell me how you handle the pressure I'm going to start screaming- and I don't think I'm going to be able to stop any time soon," Carlene desperately pleaded, with tears running down her cheeks.

"Okay, I'll try to explain it- if I can," Timbre began in a soft voice. "The reason that I wasn't too scared is because I never doubted for a minute that I wouldn't be alive by this time next week. Don't get me wrong, I was afraid, but I was afraid of being hurt, not of being killed. Believe me, lesser degrees of fear are manageable."

"But how could you really be sure that you wouldn't be killed?" Carlene wanted to know, puzzled.

"Ever since I was a kid I've always felt that when my time was up I'd be aware of it long before it happened."

"You really believe that?"

"Yes I do. Tell me? Did you feel like you were going to die yesterday, or today-- or tomorrow for that matter?"

"I was too scared to think about it but common sense told me that my situation was hopeless and I was going to die," Carlene confessed.

"But, in spite of all your common sense you didn't die. Your common sense was wrong."

"But, how can you go against reason," Carlene protested.

"Easy. I'm not saying that you should throw caution to the wind but what I am saying is: There are days when you know that you're going to prevail no matter how much the odds are stacked against you. And even if you're wrong and you lose at least you didn't waste your time with thoughts of dying," Timbre smiled. "To put it simply: Don't let yourself think about losing."

"I'll have to give that one a lot of thought," Carlene said, a bit confused

"You're problem is that you've been around sick people too long. People that were so sick that no matter how hard you tried, they died anyway. You've come to except death--- I haven't," Timbre told her, without turning around.

"How can you not accept death after all of it that you've witnessed?"

"Because those were other people's deaths, not mine. I have no control over how other people live or die. They either made a mistake or they warn't as lucky as I am. If you believe that you're lucky, you are. It's when you stop believing in your own luck that death and bad times creep up on you."

"I don't even know what luck is," Carlene stated, not knowing how to react to Timbre's philosophy to life.

"Me neither, but that doesn't mean it doesn't exist. Hell, I don't know what air is but that doesn't mean that I'm going to stop breathing just because I don't understand what it is."

"My father used to say that people make their own luck," Carlene reminisced.

"That's one philosophy, and in part I guess it's true. You have to go after what you want and work hard at it, but there's still that little piece of something that makes you or breaks you in the end. Like the luck we had today with the Comanche's."

"But that wasn't luck, that was Curtis's shooting ability."

"Yeah. Lucky for us he could shoot that good, huh? Lucky for us I found that rifle," Timbre chuckled.

"I see what you're saying but I'm still not sure that I agree with you. I'll have to think on it some more," Carlene smiled, feeling better.

"I wonder where Curtis is with that food? My stomach is starting to eat at my backbone," Timbre asked.

320

"He's probably down there practicing with that stupid gun you gave him."

"I don't think so, I didn't hear any shots. Did you?"

"He isn't practicing shooting it. He was up half the night seeing how fast he could get it out of his holster. He's like a big kid with a new toy," Carlene chuckled.

"And I'm getting darn good at it too," Curtis said from behind them, handing them biscuits and jerky.

Timbre thought to himself that he must be hurt worse than he thought because he hadn't heard Curtis coming up the rocks.

"So what were you two talking about while I was gone—-besides me that is?" Curtis smiled.

"Death and fear," Carlene softly said.

"Oh, was he telling you about the time he died?"

"WHAT!" Carlene shouted.

"Didn't you tell her about the time you were dead for a while?" Curtis asked Timbre.

"No. It must have slipped my mind," Timbre answered, giving Curtis a hard look.

"Here I am pouring my heart out to you about being afraid of dying and that little bit of news just slipped your mind? Carlene quietly yelled. If looks could kill Timbre would've been dead again.

"What do you make of them now?" Timbre asked, handing Curtis the spyglass while biting into a biscuit and trying to ignore Carlene's stare.

Curtis studied the riders for a couple of minutes, then declared: "It's the Calvary."

"You sure?" Timbre asked.

"As sure as their buttons are made of brass," Curtis smiled.

321

"Lucky us," Timbre stated, winking at Carlene. "You two stay here till you can count their teeth. I'm going down and make us some coffee."

"Not so fast, Buster! You have some explaining to do," Carlene hissed, stopping him while trying to control her temper.

"Okay, but can I do it over a cup of coffee?"

"After you," Carlene told him, making way for him to pass her.

"See you in a little while," Curtis said, watching as Timbre made his way slowly and painfully down the rocks and knowing that his big mouth had started something that he didn't want any part of.

Timbre was on his second cup of coffee by the time he finished explaining his death to Carlene. He didn't understand why, but he told her the whole story. He could tell by the look on her face, and her silence, that she was digesting what he had told her. Whether she believed him or not was a different story.

Before she could register what he'd told her and start to ask the hundred questions that was racing through her mind Curtis came down and ran over to them.

"They're almost here," he panted, out of breath.

"Take her and get behind those boulders and cover me until we're sure that they're friendly," Timbre ordered him.

Without asking any questions Curtis grabbed Carlene's hand, hoisted her up, and dragged her behind the far boulders. Minutes later twenty or so blue uniformed troopers, with one civilian in the lead, rode into camp.

"Howdy, Hoss," the smiling, gray-haired, wrinkled civilian said. Dismounting, he walked toward Timbre with his spurs jingling and his badge shinning in the sun. He extended his hand toward Timbre and said: "Haven't seen you in a Coon's age. What brings you back to these neck of the woods---- and in such dire condition?" he asked, looking Timbre over.

"Hi ya, Meeks," Timbre smiled, shaking the blue-eyed man's hand. "Long story. You quit the Rangers and join the army?"

"Naw. Ever since the end of the war they've been sending more and more of these blue boys in to do some of our work for us," Meeks told him, letting go of Timbre's hand and looking around. "I've been temporarily assigned to this here new Lieutenant to teach him how to fight Injuns."

"Well tell them to light down and make themselves comfortable," Timbre smiled.

"I will if you tell those people hiding behind the rocks to put their guns away and come on out," Meeks consented, looking directly at the boulder that was concealing Curtis and Carlene.

Hearing what had transpired between Timbre and the man called Meeks, Curtis stepped out from behind the rock with Carlene following behind him.

Jack Meeks was one of the Texas rangers that Timbre had ridden with years ago when he was tracking Mexican bandits and Comanche's around these parts.

Timbre broadly smiled and said: "Time hasn't slowed you down any. You're still as sharp as ever."

"I wouldn't have gotten to this age if I hadn't stayed awake---and neither would you have," Meeks replied. Then turning his head he looked back and yelled: "Lieutenant! Why don't you give the men a break? Come on over I want you to meet someone."

Timbre saw the young Lieutenant nod and then issue orders to his Sergeant. He then dismounted and handed his reins to the old grizzled veteran before making his way toward Meeks and Timbre.

The Lieutenant removed his hat, uncovering his long well-kept brownish blond hair. Ignoring everyone else he fixed his light gray eyes on Carlene. With a pronounced Southern accent, he said to her: "Ma'am. You ar' indeed a welcome vision fa' these tired eyes."

Timbre saw Curtis's face start to turn red, and if the truth be known, so did his a mite.

"Stow it, Soldier Boy," Timbre threatened, with an edge to his voice.

The young officer turned his sparkling eyes on Timbre and smiling, said: "No disrespect intended, Suh. I was just pleasantly surprised ta see such an attractive young lady in these here parts."

Before Timbre could reply, Meeks interjected: "Lt. Forrest Dodge, meet Timbre. He's the best tracker, red or white, that I've ever had the pleasure of working with."

"How fortunate for us that we've run into ya, Suh," Lt. Dodge proclaimed.

"And why is that, Lieutenant?" Timbre asked, not liking him much.

"May we sit down and have some coffee while I explain our predicament ta yah?" the young soldier asked, still flashing his white teeth at them.

"Be my guest," Timbre offered, not trusting anybody who smiled that much.

When they were all seated and having coffee Dodge got on with his story.

"My men and I ar' out of Fort Craig. We've been sent ta find and destroy whoever is supplying the Comanche's with weapons. In particular, a very nasty war chief named Talon. We've been roaming these here parts now fa' close ta three

weeks without so much as a clue as ta his were-a-bouts----
that is until last night when we heard a very formidable
explosion. Given the direction that the sound came from
we judge it to be twenty or thirty miles somewhere South of
here. If you're as good as Meeks says you ar' maybe you can
help us locate where this horrendous noise originated from?"

"The man you're looking for is Mountain Muntean,"
Timbre informed him. "And the place you heard blowup last
night was called the Pecos Trading Post. It's about thirty-
miles South of here. It was hidden in the side of a mountain,
that's why it was so hard to locate."

"Mountain Muntean," Meeks whistled. "Now there's a
bad one. He's killed many a good man. I sure wouldn't like to
run into him and his men without a detachment of rangers
backing my play. You say he's the one that's running the
guns to Talon?"

"He was," Timbre stated. "He's dead now- and so is Talon."

"How do ya' know all this?" Dodge asked, suspiciously.

"Because Curtis, here, slowed Mountain up a mite
yesterday with a blast from my shotgun and then I blew
him to hell shortly afterwards. As for Talon, Curtis shot him
dead about two-hours ago with the prettiest shot that I ever
did see," Timbre told them, without batting an eye.

"That's most likely the shots that we heard, the ones that
directed us here. Maybe you better start from the beginning,"
Meeks said to Timbre, while sizing up Curtis.

Timbre talked for about hour, trying only to hit on the
highlights of their adventures and filling him in on why they
were in these parts in the first place. When he was finished,
Meeks and Lt. Dodge were flabbergasted.

It was Lt. Dodge who finally broke the silence, by saying:
"I guess ya all did our jobs fa' us. Texas is eternally grateful
ta the both of ya fa' that- an' so am I."

For some reason Timbre didn't feel that Dodge was sincere in what he was saying. Timbre had the feeling that Lt. Dodge resented them for robbing him of his chance at glory.

"I'm especially distressed ta hear of your hardships Ma'am," Dodge continued, flashing his white teeth at Carlene. "If there is anything I can do ta ease your grief, please don't hesitate ta prevail upon my services. I am forever your devoted servant."

Before Carlene could reply Curtis spoke up for the first time. Fixing Dodge with a hard stare, he stated: "We didn't do it for the state of Texas, or for you. We did it to stay alive. And, as far as the lady is concerned she doesn't need any help from a Johnny-come-lately. She's gotten along just fine without you."

"My offer was ta the lovely lady," Dodge rebuked Curtis, with an edge to his voice but with a smile still on his lips. "But if she doesn't need my services for the moment I believe I had better go and catch some Comanche's before they get clean away."

Meeks, seeing the rage on Curtis's face butted in. Standing, he said: "It was a pleasure meeting you, Son. If you ever decide on becoming a Texas Ranger you come see me. The Rangers can use men like you."

"Thank you, Sir," Curtis replied, standing and shaking Meeks' hand while ignoring Dodge. "I'll sure give it some thought."

"You do that," Meeks told him, letting go of his hand and then turning his attention to Timbre. "The men you're hunting are about three days out in front of you--- and pushing hard. We ran across them North of here. They more than likely heard that explosion last night too. My guess is that they now have a pretty good idea that your still coming and that you'll be pushing just as hard. I'm sure sorry I didn't know who they were else I could've saved you a lot of time and trouble."

"Not your fault," Timbre told him, shaking his hand.

"Nice ta have met ya'all," the Lieutenant chimed in, still smiling. "And especially you, Ma'am. If ya find yourself anywhere in the vicinity of Fort Craig, please don't hesitate ta drop in an' say hello."

"Don't hold your breath, Lieutenant," Carlene smiled, in her most seductive voice while watching the smile disappear from Dodge's face.

As Dodge turned in a huff and stormed off, Timbre said to Meeks: "There's one thing I didn't mention before: Yesterday, me and Curtis were chased by at about thirty Comanche but today, like I already stated, we saw only eighteen of them. I don't know where the others got to but if I were you I'd watch my back- especially with that glory hound Lieutenant leading you. He'll most likely get you killed if you let him-- so don't you let him. Texas wouldn't be the same without you."

"Ain't that the truth," Meeks smiled. "But don't you worry none about me, Hoss. I've been around his type before- and I'll still be around when he's sitting on his ass somewhere down South, if he lives that long."

"You make sure of that."

"That I will," Meeks smiled, taking his horse from the soldier who handed him the reins.

"You best be going before that soldier boy leaves you behind. All of a sudden he looks mighty anxious to be on his way," Timbre commented, seeing Lt. Dodge impatiently sitting astride his horse, while nervously avoiding their eyes.

"He'll wait. He just can't handle rejection very well. It makes him a mite uncomfortable," Meeks smiled, taking his time mounting. Then looking down, the smile vanishing from his face, he said: "You and the boy did good, real good. I owe you a big one. You make sure you heal yourself proper before you try taking on those fellers that you're after. The world wouldn't be the same without you roaming through it and stirring things up a might."

"Ain't that the truth," Timbre smiled, starting to feel tired.

"See ya in a better life," Meeks waved, leading the soldiers out of camp.

"Your friend Meeks is alright, but that Lt. Dodge leaves a whole lot to be desired," Curtis said, from behind Timbre.

"You really should learn to control your jealous nature," Timbre told him, turning back toward the small fire. "It'll get you in trouble someday."

"I noticed that he rubbed you the wrong way, too," Carlene noted, sitting between them.

"That wasn't jealousy. I was just being protective of you. Besides, he was an arrogant bastard," Timbre laughed.

"But in a roundabout way he did save our skins," Carlene commented, giving the devil his due. "He did run off the Comanche's."

"If it wasn't him it would've been somebody else," Timbre flatly stated.

"The 01' Timbre luck. Is that it?" Carlene asked.

"We're alive," Timbre told her. "I rest my case."

"I must admit I'm not nearly as scared as I was before," Carlene smiled.

"What are you two talking about?" Curtis asked, feeling left out.

"We're talking about luck," Carlene informed him. "And how if you feel you have it, you do."

"I don't rightly follow what you're saying but if you're telling me that we've had our share of good luck, I couldn't agree with you more," Curtis nodded.

"That's what I'm saying," Carlene said, stretching over and kissing Curtis on the lips, causing him to blush again.

"I'm truly happy to see that you're feeling better," Timbre sincerely told her.

"Thank you," Carlene smiled, kissing Timbre on the cheek. "What was that for?" Timbre asked, surprised.

"That's for being my friend," Carlene told him. "That is if you have room in your life for another one?"

"There's always room for one more," Timbre assured her, reaching out and stroking her hair.

"You sure do know a lot of people," Curtis declared. "Is there anyplace in this country that you can't go without bumping into somebody you know?"

"Not many, but there are a lot of people who I'd rather not run into, like Mountain for instance," Timbre chuckled.

"You know, when I was a kid, Jesse filled my head with so many wild tales about you that there came a time when I didn't really believe that you actually existed. I came to think that he'd made you up, sorta like a fairy tale.

"Why's that?" Timbre asked.

"I reasoned that if you were for real you'd be a famous man. Wrote up in books and all. But now that I know that you are for real and those stories Jesse told were true I can't understand why you're not famous, like Kit Carson, or Bridger, or Johnson?"

"Lucky I guess," Timbre shrugged, adding: "Speaking of Liver-Eating Johnson, I remember a time in the Bitterroots when----"

"Liver-Eating? Why do you call him Liver-Eating?" Curtis asked, interrupting his story.

"It wasn't me who gave him that name. He came by that nick name honestly. He used to cut out and eat the livers of his enemies--- after he'd killed them of course. Most called him Biscuit-Eating Johnson, though. Now there's a man who could make biscuits."

"That's disgusting," Carlene stated.

"What? Making biscuits?"

"No! Eating people's livers!"

"To most folks no doubt, but you can't judge mountain folks by other people's standards. You got to winter up there in the high country all by your lonesome before you can claim the right to do that. In any case, it sure got his enemy's attention."

"I'm sure it did," Carlene agreed. "But you're changing the subject again. Why wouldn't you want credit for all the good deeds that you've done?"

"Because fame is just something else that'll rob a man of his freedom. Once you become known people start pestering you for all sorts of reasons. I've worked long and hard to avoid fame- and I'll shot the first person who tries to make me famous. Besides, I doubt if I deserve all that praise. Most of what I did was just a matter of luck."

"But how were you able to avoid it with so many people knowing about you?"

"Hell! There were a couple of times when I had to up and leave the territory because some damn fool was trying to find me and write about one of my adventures. Thank you anyways, but I like my life just the way it is. Most of the time that is."

"But think of the money you could make from being famous," Carlene pointed out.

"Don't need it, but what I do need is something to eat. If ya all wouldn't mind slapping somethin' together I'd be forever in your service, lovely lady," Timbre smiled, imitating Lt. Dodge.

"I give up," Carlene laughed. "Come on Curtis, let's fix something to eat for this poor starving man."

"Sure," Curtis sighed, slowly getting to his feet, feeling the last couple of days activities catching up with him.

Carlene cooked beans and biscuits and they ate and talked some more until Timbre retired to his bedroll and fell asleep.

Timbre sleep through the rest of the day and night. Once during the night he awoke to discover that Curtis and Carlene were not in their bedrolls. At first he was alarmed but then it occurred to him, with a twinge of envy, that they were two young people in love and had gone off to be alone. Groaning, he rolled over and went back to sleep.

The next morning, Timbre awoke first. His body was sore all over, but he'd been sore for so long now that he'd forgot what it felt like to feel normal. Rolling over he saw that Curtis and Carlene were back in their bedrolls and sleeping soundly.

Quietly, he got to his feet, making sure to not wake them. Timbre silently walked over and watered and fed the horses and then he re-started the fire and let yesterday's coffee reheat while he left camp to take care of his morning business.

Timbre was bent over the fire, cooking bacon and biscuits, when Carlene opened her eyes and looked at him. Smiling, she asked: "How are you feeling this morning?"

"A little stiff, but better than yesterday. I think I'll be able to do a little riding today," Timbre told her in a low voice, not wanting to wake Curtis.

"Hmmmm. That smells good," Carlene declared, throwing off her blanket and jumping to her feet. She moaned loudly, as she stretched not caring if she disturbed Curtis or not.

"Sit," Timbre told her, indicating to a spot next to him. "The food will be done in a few minutes and the coffee, such as it is, is ready."

331

"Save that seat for me," Carlene smiled. "If you'll excuse me for a moment, I need to wash up."

"Of course, but watch out for snakes," Timbre warned her, as Carlene disappeared behind the rocks, taking a canteen of water with her.

"What snakes?" Curtis asked, sitting up and rubbing his eyes.

"Any snakes," Timbre murmured, pouring a cup of coffee and bringing it to Curtis. "I was talking to Carlene."

"Where is she?" Curtis asked, taking the cup from Timbre's outstretched hand and looking around for her.

"Washing," Timbre told him, taking his place again in front of the fire.

"Oh," Curtis nodded, sipping some coffee. "God! This stuff tastes like panther piss! I hope you cook better than you make coffee."

"The coffee is from last night and if you don't want any of my food, don't eat it," Timbre chided him, helping himself to some bacon and biscuits.

"I'm too hungry to be choosy," Curtis told him, joining him by the fire and helping himself.

"Is that for me?" Carlene shouted, emerging from behind the rocks.

"Here," Curtis offered, handing her his plate of food and then fixing himself another.

"Thanks," Carlene smiled, sitting down between him and Timbre.

"We have a lot to iron out today," Timbre informed them, between mouthfuls of food.

"Like what?" Curtis asked.

"Like, what are we going to do with Carlene, Curt?"

The only one who'd ever called him Curt had been Jesse and that'd only been occasionally. He liked to be called

Curt, it made him feel grown-up, which he felt he now was. This little excursion with Timbre had forced him to mature rapidly.

"We discussed that last night while you were asleep," Curt began.

"And?"

"And, we figure that she can ride along with us until we reach my Uncle's ranch. I'll drop her off there and then go on with you."

"You don't think that'll be putting her in danger? Have you forgotten about the men we're tracking?"

"The way I see it they've got at least a three day lead on us, or maybe even more, so the chances of us catching them before they get out of Texas is pretty slim."

"Is that so?" Timbre asked. "What if they decide to stop running and decide to make a fight of it? Would you want to take the chance of Carla falling into their hands?"

"What makes you think that they'd stand and fight now?" Curtis asked. "All they've done so far is run."

"Because, no matter what they've done, and no matter what you think of them, these men that we're chasing aren't cowards. They're choosing to run for their own reasons, which at the present I'm not aware of, but they may choose to stop running and take us on at any time."

"You talk as if you know these men and that this isn't the first time that you've had dealings with them. I think I've earned the right to know what's going on," Curtis stated, putting down his empty plate.

Timbre thought for a while on what Curtis was asking, then informed him: "I wasn't holding out on you, or was I trying to keep something from you. I was keeping my mouth shut because I refuse to believe what all the evidence is pointing at. All that talk about ghosts and spirits that we've been hearing about, is as far as I'm concerned, all nonsense. Made-up fairy tales to scare the ignorant savages. But, on the other hand I have to admit that there's a lot going on that I don't have an explanation for. But since you're neck deep in this chase I guess you have a right to make up your own mind about it. I warn you though, the story begins way back, when I was a boy of about nine or ten."

"We're listening," Curtis told him.

Timbre set down his coffee cup, stared into the fire for a couple of minutes to collect his thoughts, and then began: "It was the beginning of Spring. My Dad, our traveling companion Jake, and me had just come off the mountain after an exceptionally hard winter. When we hit the flat country the first thing that we ran into was a Cheyenne village. Those were the days when the Cheyenne were still more or less friendly toward whites. But, like I was saying: It'd been a hard winter and we'd lost a couple of our pack animals to the cold so we'd decided to spend some time in the Cheyenne town and trade for new ones. That was the first time that I laid eyes on Raven.

Raven was the most beautiful girl that I'd ever seen up until that time. She was older than I was, somewhere in her early teens. She had long black-hair that shinned like a Ravens wing in flight. I guess that's where she got her name from. To this day I can still see her running through the village with her gleaming hair tied back with white thongs, which matched her white beaded doe skin dress that her Mother had made for her. Around her neck, wrists and ankles she wore colored beaded necklaces that made a tinkling sound whenever she moved. Her big round eyes were almost as black as her hair and seemed to reflect the light whenever she looked at me. In fact, when she danced it seemed that her whole body was made of nothing but sunlight. I fell madly in love with her the moment I saw her, as only a young boy, that had never been in love before, could. During our stay in that village I did very little but follow Raven around, like a new born calf follows his Mama. I was fortunate though because she was just as fascinated by my white skin as I was by her beauty, so she put up with this young puppy always lapping at her heels.

At first trying to talk with her was difficult because I couldn't speak Cheyenne and she couldn't speak American, but we got along as most people will do if left to their own devices. Weeks went by and we became fairly close friends. I'm pretty sure she saw me as her younger brother even though I didn't regard her as my older sister. Then one day my Dad announced that it was time for us to move on. Of course I was devastated, I didn't think I could leave her without my heart being broken. The only way my Pa could get me to leave was by him promising me that we'd visit the village on a regular basis.

My Dad wasn't a stupid man and had seen how attached I had become to Raven. He also knew that I was too young for her at the time but told me that I'd be older the next time we came through and things might then change between her and I. I remember how much that had cheered me up and how I couldn't wait to grow up and make Raven mine.

Their trading with the Cheyenne had gone much better than they'd anticipated. It seemed that my Dad and Jake had come to the conclusion that they could make more money swapping our furs for ponies and then selling them at the trappers yearly gathering. But of course I didn't care about all that, I left the trading up to them. The only thing that concerned me was when I was going to see Raven again.

After we left the village Jake revealed to us that I wasn't the only one who had other reasons besides trading for wanting to stop back at that village again, Jake had also had been smitten by an Indian maiden named Clear Sky and was anxious to see here again.

It was the very next year when we were on our way to visit that village again that we hooked up with Jesse and he became part of our extended family. It was also the year that Jake decided to marry Clear Sky.

For the next six years Jake still traveled with us but he made sure he visited his wife at least three to four times a year, which I didn't mind because it gave me a chance to see Raven, who became more beautiful every time I visited her.

Jesse had been traveling with us for about eight years when he decided that he wanted to see if he could make it on his own. At least that's what he told us, but I think he just wanted to be near Raven. He also had been taken by her and we competed for her attention constantly, but in a friendly way. But since I knew her first I had a slight edge on him. He built his camp near the village so he could see Raven regularly and hopefully win her heart. We still occasionally trapped with Jake and Jesse but that was just for fun and old time's sake.

After Jessie and Jake left our little group me and my Dad mostly roamed the high country together. Sometime along the way we accidently stumbled upon a fortune, but I'm getting ahead of my story. The getting rich part has nothing to do with what happened.

Now that I've set up the story I have to go back a ways. It was shortly after our first encounter with that Cheyenne village that a couple of strange white men started to show up around those parts. One of them went by the name of The Count. I don't think he really was a Count, although he sure tried to act like royalty. The other one was a gunsel that always accompanied him. I didn't get his name at the time but I know it now--- Fargo. He did all of The Count's dirty work for him. Fargo was, and still is, the fastest man I'd ever seen with a handgun.

Each year around the end of summer these two mysterious men would appear at the trappers' summer rendezvous, even though they weren't trappers and no one ever could remember inviting them. And, every year like clockwork they'd suddenly disappear after a couple of days without having said more than a couple of words to anyone. It was always shortly after they disappeared that one or two young Indian maidens would turn up murdered. Not just murdered, but horribly mutilated. Somebody was snatching them out of their villages at night and then doing terrible things to them.

The Count, being a very peculiar man, what with those ugly eyes and that quiet evil smile was suspected right-off by the trappers. But those who were foolish enough to link his name to the murders soon found themselves facing Fargo's guns. Like I said before, Fargo was the fastest man that I'd ever seen with a hand gun and many a man fell before his six shooters to prove it. But I believe even without Fargo backing him most of the men were afraid of The Count anyways. There was something very spooky about that man. I been told that he never spoke but just smiled his evil smile whenever somebody said anything to him--- which was rarely. Fargo, besides doing his shooting for him, also did his talking for him. But since I never had an occasion to speak to the man I couldn't swear to that. Another peculiar thing about that man was that every time I got within thirty yards of The Count I would get physically ill. I never could figure out what caused that reaction in me so I kept my distance from him.

One thing for sure though: There came a time when no one mentioned the murders and The Count in the same sentence anymore. It wasn't that those men were cowards, far from it, they were simply men who'd worked their whole lives at minding their own business and felt that life was dangerous enough without risking it for something that was of no concern of theirs. Besides, there was not a shred of evidence that The Count was guilty of anything but their suspicions. As far as they were concerned it was up to the Indians to take care of their own--- and the Indians didn't complain to them none about it.

"At first, the different tribes banded together and sent out their best trackers to find the killer of their woman. The Braves would always find tracks leading away from the mutilated body's but after following them for a couple of miles the tracks would simply vanish into thin air. It was as if a giant bird had swooped down and lifted the killers from the Earth. This was something that the Indians couldn't understand. The only explanation that made any sense to them was that an evil spirit was responsible for carrying off their woman- and in a way they were right.

Terror and fables quickly spread from village to village. No matter what precautions the Indians took they couldn't catch, or stop, whatever or whoever was doing these terrible things to their woman. Little-by-little the power they attributed to their demon-spirit increased. They finally came to believe that only powerful magic could stop it; and they as mere mortals could do nothing to prevent the massacre of their woman. Believe me when I say that their medicine men worked overtime on that one.

Of course Dad and I had heard all the tales about The Count and the murders but having no evidence of his being guilty of anything we also minded our own business. We did run across him once, outside of the rendezvous. It'd been in a little town in Colorado, we ignored him then figuring that he was of no concern of ours.

What I remember the most about that encounter was the way that he looked at me, from across the street, and the way my stomach turned being that close to him. I had the feeling that he was aware of my capabilities and was eager to test them out. Little did I know how right I was. We could've saved ourselves a lot of grief if we'd just shot him right there--- Fargo or no Fargo.

It was a couple of months later, after we rode into the Cheyenne village, that I realized what a big mistake not shooting him had been. Sometimes turning your back on a problem because you don't think it's any of your concern has a way of coming back to haunt you, and this one took a big bite out of my ass.

As soon as we entered the village we could tell that something was wrong. It didn't take long to find out that Raven had just been found murdered, horribly mutilated. I can still remember the rage that I felt at that moment, and especially the pain. I had finally decided to ask her to choose who she wanted, me or Jesse, and I was going to do it on that very visit. Although my heart felt like it had been ripped out of my chest it was the rage that held back the tears and enabled me to set out after her killer. Within hours of her death Dad and I were on their trail. Jesse and Jake were already out there searching for sign.

The first thing that I discovered was that the Indians were right, the tracks did just vanish three or four-miles after we found them. But what really set me back was that I couldn't even get a feel for the men I was tracking. In the past I'd always been able to grab onto something- a whim, a hunch, a guess--anything. But when I needed my gift more than any other time in my life, I couldn't find it. Maybe it was the grief that was stifling it. Even though I was frustrated I was too filled with rage to give up so we just kept riding. We rode deep into the mountains.

We were on top of a ridge skirting a little valley when that sickness in my stomach took hold of me. I looked down toward the valley floor. At first I didn't see anything, but the feeling that I needed to up-chock kept getting stronger so I kept searching. Then suddenly, like he was riding out of a mist, there he was--- The Count. He was just nonchalantly riding along, seemingly without a care in the world, and unaware of our presence. And, as luck would have it without his gunny Fargo.

I whispered over to Dad that there he was, as I pointed at him. I don't know why but my Father didn't see him right off and wanted to know what I was pointing at. I kept trying to point out to my Dad where he was but for some reason he still couldn't see him. I think he thought I'd finally went around the bend with grief. Finally, I got tired of trying to get my Dad to see him, so without saying another word, I grabbed my long gun and dismounted. I knelt, took careful aim, and proceeded to put a .50 caliber slug through The Counts body.

By the way he flew off his horse I'd say he died instantly----and that's when my Dad finally saw him. But killing him wasn't enough to satisfy the rage that I felt. I wanted to go down there and cut off his head and mount it on a pole but my Father was against that. He said that he didn't raise any barbarian and no matter how mad I was he wasn't going to allow me to cut off his head and mount it. As usual I gave in to my Father's wishes. But we did make our way down to where The Count was laying just to make sure that he was dead. We thought of burying him but my Dad convinced me to leave him for the Buzzards and Coyotes because that would be as good as cutting off his head.

After The Counts death the mutilations stopped--- until now that is. Now everything I've heard and seen points to the fact that he's back, even though that goes against everything I believe. But what's confusing me is that Mountain, who'd known him from way back when, believed that it was him and that he was back from the dead," Timbre finished, still staring into the fire and not looking at either of them.

After a considerable time of silence, Curtis said: "Maybe it wasn't The Count that committed all those murders. Nobody ever saw him do it. You said so yourself. Maybe it was Fargo, or somebody else entirely. Maybe you just killed the wrong man back then."

"I don't believe that for a second," Timbre sneered. "After I killed him I found Ravens necklace on him. I know it was hers because I'd given it to her. Also, the killings of the Indian woman abruptly stopped after his death. No, I'm convinced that I got the right man. Besides, how do you explain Mountain's insistence that it was The Count who rented those horses from him?"

"Do you really believe that you're dealing with a ghost?" Carla asked, her eyes getting wider.

"No. I've heard my share of ghost stories but I've never actually seen one. Until I do I'm not about to start believing in them now," Timbre answered her. "There has to be a rational explanation for all of this."

"What do you think it is?" Curt asked.

"You're guess is as good as mine," Timbre shrugged.

"Did you ever see Fargo again?" Carla asked, looking at Timbre as if she were seeing him for the first time.

"Yeah. About a year ago."

"Where?"

"It was in a little Cantina about fifteen-miles north of Los Angeles. When I walked into the place, there he was, waiting for me. I didn't recognize him at first, that is until he spoke," Timbre explained. "Said he'd been looking for me for a lot of years to pay me back for what I'd done to his boss."

"Is that all he had to say?" Carla asked.

"No, we chatted for a bit but nothing worth mentioning. Unless you count him telling me that I was about to die mentioning. The next thing that is worth mentioning is that we both drew our guns."

"And you shot him," Curt finished.

"Not even close. He killed me. And that's how I got that big ugly scar that Carla admired so much," Timbre smiled. "I don't think that I cleared leather before he dropped me. I was lucky, though..."

"No kidding," Carla interrupted, feigning surprise.

"I was lucky, though," Timbre continued, ignoring her snide remark. "After he left me for dead a friend of mine placed me in his cart and drove me to another friend in Los Angeles where I was attended to by a real Doctor. That's the doc who told me that I had no right to be alive."

"And I agree with him," Carla confirmed. Not mentioning the conversation her and Tim had, about the afterlife, in front of Curtis. She figured they'd have that talk sometime later on.

"That may be so but I hope you'll excuse me if I don't lay down and roll over."

"I guess I can forgive you for that," Carla smiled.

"Did you ever find out why nobody was ever able to stop The Count from stealing those Indian women? And why he couldn't be tracked, or seen?" Curt asked.

"Nope. Never did. He took that secret to the grave with him. But if it is his ghost that we're chasing remind me to ask him how he did it when we catch-up with him. I've been mighty curious about that myself."

"Do your instincts tell you anything about who we're chasing, or are they a blank like last time you chased him?" Curt inquired.

"My instincts tell me one thing and my reasoning tells me another. But if Mountain was telling me the truth and it is the Count back from the grave I can tell you this much: He's left most of his skills in hell. Not only did he leave a trail all across Texas but I could feel his evil when I first started tracking him."

"Aren't you afraid of catching up with them?" Carla asked. "After all, Fargo almost killed you once before."

"That did occur to me. But I figure this time I'm not going to try to match hand speed with him."

"You going to shoot him in the back?" Curt asked.

"If I'm lucky. Why? Does that bother you?"

"No. It just seems a shame that he won't know that it was you who put him under."

"If you saw them you'd probably think twice about facing them too," Carla informed him, looking into the fire. "Shooting them in the back sounds like a very good idea to me.

"That's right! You saw them!" Timbre exclaimed, remembering that Carla had been at the Trading Post at the same time that they were there.

"Yes. I remember there was a man named Fargo, who dressed all in black, and he called the one who led them, the one with the milky gray eyes, Count. They match everything that you told me about them. Is it possible that they could be the same ones? God! Just thinking that gives me the creeps. After what you just told me about them I guess I owe Mountain some thanks."

343

"Why's that?" Timbre asked, looking up from the fire.

"Because, the one you call The count wanted to buy me from Mountain. When Mountain told him no he got angry and said that he wished he'd had the time to change his mind. Then he looked at me and said something about how much pleasure I'm going to miss out on. Then he smiled that evil smile that you talked of," Carlene shivered, hugging herself. "If anybody could come back from the grave I'd put my money on him."

"What are you thinking?" Curtis asked, seeing a peculiar look on Timbre's face.

"I'm thinking about how much Muntean must've wanted Carla for him to go against The Count like he did. He was always scared to death of him. I'm also thinking how nice it would be if it really was The Count that we're after."

"Why's that?" Curtis asked, puzzled.

"So's I can have the pleasure of killing him all over again," Timbre told him, with hate flashing in his eyes. "The last time was way too fast."

"Did you really want to cut-off his head?" Carla asked, in a whisper.

"Yep. It would probably still be hanging in some Cheyenne village now if I did, and there'd be no doubt if it was him or not that we're chasing," Timbre smiled, making Carla shiver again.

"You never did say how Jesse took Raven's death," Curtis asked.

"We both took it hard. Jesse just up'd and disappeared and me and my Dad headed for Montana. Well, we better break camp and do some riding," Curt said, throwing his cup of cold coffee on the fire and standing up without looking at Timbre.

The look that he'd witnessed on Timbre's face after Carla had asked him if he really would've cut-off The Count's head had sent a shiver through his body. Curtis had no desire to see that insane look of hatred again.

"Yeah. Let's do that," Timbre agreed, not able to get the vision of Raven and Evelyn out of his head.

CHAPTER

17

Jesse climbed the three steps to the back door of the ranch house. Knocking once, and not waiting for an answer, he entered into the kitchen.

"Help yourself to some coffee," Walter Sloane offered, while sitting at the kitchen table.

As Jesse poured himself a cup of coffee he had a strong feeling that his ranching days were just about over- which was fine with him. Things just weren't the same anymore since Evelyn's death. It wasn't that Jesse had expected life to go on the way it had forever, but given the type of man Walter was he didn't expect it to get as bad as it did. Since their arrival home Walter had totally neglected the ranch. The men rarely saw him anymore, he spent all of his time looking after Tess, who gave no sign that she was aware of his presence. If it wasn't for Jesse taking charge the ranch would have fallen into shambles.

Even though Sloane hadn't discussed his intentions with him, Jesse, never-the-less had become aware that Walter was trying to sell the ranch. Something as important as that was hard to keep a secret. Now, standing by the stove, Jesse reasoned that Walter wouldn't have summoned him in the middle of the day unless he had something imperative to tell him--- and the way things were going lately it couldn't be good news.

"What can I do for you, boss?" Jesse asked, sipping his coffee and sitting across from Sloane

"I sold the ranch," Sloane stated, coming right to the point. "As much as I love this place it just ain't the same anymore."

"Yeah," Jesse agreed, having reached the same conclusion.

"I feel it will do Tess good to get far away from here. Maybe one of those fancy doctors back East can help her."

"Hopefully," Jesse nodded.

"Jenking owns the place now. He wants you and the rest of the boys to stay on. You'll still have a job, that is if you want one."

Jenking owned the spread to the west of them and Jesse knew him to be a decent man. Jesse also knew that for years Jenking and Walter had been trying to buy each other out, now it looked as if Jenking had finally gotten his wish. Knowing Walter though, Jesse figured that Jenking had payed dearly for the privilege of owning Sloane's spread.

"No. I think I've had enough of ranching," Jesse told him, declining the offer of staying on. He'd seen the handwriting on the wall weeks ago and had given the matter a lot of thought, he had already made-up his mind to move on.

"That's what I thought you'd say," Walter nodded, correctly surmising what Jesse's answer would be. "I got a good price for the ranch so you won't be walking away empty handed. I'm giving you enough money to tide you over until you decide what you want to do next. It's my way of letting you know how much I appreciate everything you've done for me over the years."

347

"I thank you, but what about Curtis?" Jesse asked.

"I've given the boy a lot of thought," Walter replied. "Since you're not going to be working for Jenking I was hoping that you wouldn't mind working for me a bit longer."

"In what way?"

"I'm leaving quite a bit of money for Curtis in the bank. He can use it to join me or use it anyway he sees fit to- the choice is up to him. I don't know when he'll be coming back but when he does I don't want him to think that I just up and deserted him. That's where you come in."

"You want me to wait for him, to tell him where you've gone?" Jesse surmised.

"If you wouldn't mind," Walter affirmed.

"What if he doesn't come back?" Jesse asked, not liking the question but knowing that it had to be asked.

"I've also thought about that," Walter sadly stated. "He's been gone now for close to two months without so much as a word. I realize the possibility exists that he might not be coming back. I now wish that I never sent him with your friend, but I wasn't thinking clearly at the time."

"He'll be back," Jesse declared. "Tim will see to that."

"I pray you're right. I feel toward Curtis as if he were my own son. But in the event- God forbid- that he doesn't make it, I put the money in both of your names. When the time comes that you believe that Curtis is...lost, withdraw the money, keep five-percent for your trouble, and send the rest on to me."

"It'll be taken care of," Jesse promised, not wanting to dwell on the possibility that Curtis was dead. "Is there anything else?"

"Yes. When you see Curtis make sure he writes to me. That is, if he chooses not to join me."

"Done," Jesse acknowledged; then he asked: "Do you want me to get the men together so you can tell them what your plans are."

"No. I was hoping you'd take care of that for me. I don't feel up to it. Tell them just before I leave, while you're handing out the bonus's that I'll be giving them. That should ease some of the news that they'll be riding for a new boss, if they choose to that is. That will be my way of saying good bye and thanks for their loyalty."

Jesse looked at Walter and didn't see the man he used to know. The man he used to know would've never asked him to do his job for him, Sloane had lost more than his wife to the Comanche. Maybe it was time for him to get out of Texas, Jesse thought.

"Yes Sir," Jesse nodded, not liking it, but agreeing to do it.

"Thanks. Oh, and one other thing: I'd like to be away from here by the end of the week. I don't see any sense in dragging this out," Walter told him, looking old and tired. "I figure to just take our clothes for now. And if you wouldn't mind have the boys pack the rest of my belongings and send them on to me. I'll leave you the address as to where to send them before I leave."

"Yes Sir," Jesse nodded again, feeling too depressed to say much more.

"And Jesse," Walter added.

"Yes."

"If you ever get tired of the West and want to come live with us I'd be more than happy to have your company. You've been the only true friend that I've ever had; and even though I've never said it, I've always valued your friendship highly."

"Thank you, Walt. I feel the same way toward you. You've all been like family to me, but I've lived in the East and I never did take to it much. I might visit from time-to-time but out here is where I belong," Jesse told him, wanting to add, 'and so do you, but didn't say it.

"I understand," Walter stated, as he stood. "I better check on Tess, now. You stay and finish your coffee."

Jesse watched Walter slowly walk out of the kitchen, humped over like he was carrying the world on his shoulders. No matter how hard and tough a person was there was always something just around the bend just waiting to break them. Thank God, Jesse thought, that he hadn't run into his breaker yet. Although he was feeling powerfully low just about then.

They'd been traveling for almost two weeks and Timbre was beginning to become concerned with the lead that the outlaws were accumulating on them. Carla wasn't used to hard riding and they frequently had to stop to let her rest. Plus, Timbre's wound kept opening up and some stiches had to be replaced from time to time. Then there were the times that they had to stop because Carla began crying for no apparent reason and had to be consoled. Calming her down delayed them even further.

Curtis hadn't understand Carla's mood swings and that worried him. Also, lately at night when they made camp she'd been turning him away. Curtis figured that it was something that he'd done in order for her to act that way. Not being able to figure out what he'd done to make her act that way, he too started to become moody.

Finally, to control a situation that was rapidly getting out of hand, Timbre had to explain to Curtis what it was that woman went through once a month; and, coupling that with the loss of her father that she was still trying to cope with, Timbre pointed out that there was nothing they could do but to be patient with her- something he was fast becoming short on.

The trail Timbre was following eventually faded away, but by stopping in the few towns along the way he was able to pick up bits of information about the men they were chasing. The one constant that kept popping up was the fact that the killers didn't seem to be in any hurry anymore. They weren't pulling ahead of them as much as Timbre had fretted they were. Finally, after three-weeks on the trail they reached the cutoff that led to Sloane's ranch. Timbre could now deposit Carla someplace safe and start to gain some ground on his quarry.

"How far to your Uncle's from here?" Timbre asked Curt.

"I'd say sixty miles," Curtis estimated.

"If we delivered Carla to the ranch that would mean the loss of at least three-days, if were lucky," Timbre told Curt. "And I figure we're almost four-days behind now. If they get a seven-day lead on us they'll be as good as gone--- if they aren't already."

"What choice do we have?" Curt asked.

"Isn't there a town close by where you can drop me off?" Carla volunteered. "You can send word to your Uncle from there and maybe he can send someone to fetch me. I'll be just fine alone, for a couple of days."

"There's a town about thirty-miles west of here where I can drop you off. I can hire someone from there to take you on to the ranch," Curtis figured out loud.

"That sounds alright," Carla agreed.

"We'll still lose two-days," Timbre told him. "Tell you what: You escort Carla to the ranch and I'll push on from here. I know what route our friends have to take to cross the mountains. I'll give you the directions and you catch-up with me when you can."

"Why can't you wait a couple of more days?" Curtis asked. "We can make-up the time once we drop Carla off."

"Because, if Cecil told me the truth, I have friends where they're most likely heading. The town that my friends live in is where they'll likely have to stop to resupply," Timbre informed him, looking toward the Rockies with a worried look upon his face. "I'm thinking that it's too much of a coincidence as to where those animal's trail is heading. If I don't keep pressing them they might linger there longer than I'd like."

"It sounds as if you have a young lady waiting for you up there," Curtis smiled.

"What makes you say that?" Timbre asked, wondering how Curtis surmised that.

"Because you've never voiced your concern about the people in any of the other towns that we've passed through."

"You're getting sharper kid," Timbre smiled back. "There is a lady waiting for me up there, although I've never been smart enough to make a commitment to her- at least not out loud."

"What does she look like?" Carla asked, with a slight twinge of jealousy in her voice.

"What does it matter?" Curtis smiled, placing his arm around Carlene's shoulders, immediately catching the infliction in her voice. "You're already spoken for."

Curtis had known for a while how Carla felt about Timbre. He knew that after him Timbre was next in line for her love. At first that had bothered him, but when he realized that he too had grown to love Timbre, although he'd never admit that out loud, he reasoned that it was alright for Carla to feel the same way.

"I'm just being protective," Carla smiled.

"You'd approve of her," Timbre told her. "After all this is over we'll take a trip up there and you can meet her for yourself."

"I'd like that," Carla agreed, and meaning it. Carla was smart enough to know that she couldn't have both men- and Curtis was her first choice.

"Good. Now that that's settled we best get on with it," Timbre stated, anxious to leave. "Oh, and Curt, while you're at the ranch pick yourself up some winter clothing. Summer is over where we're going."

"What about you?" Curtis asked. "You want me to pick you up some winter gear too?"

"No thanks, I have winter gear waiting for me up there. I'll be alright until I get to it," Timbre informed him. "Now listen up, here's how to find me, and keep in mind that you'll be passing through some hostile country. They'll be Kiowa, Apache, Cheyenne, Arapaho, and Crow. Travel light and try to stay close to towns and well used trails whenever possible. Keep your camp fires small and your eyes open." After a pause, Timbre re-thought the whole plan. "Maybe you better not make the trip alone, I don't think you're ready for it," Timbre concluded, worried for him now that he thought about it.

"I think Tim is right," Carla chimed in. "I know you can take care of yourself but you've never made a trip like this before. From what you've told me there's so much more you have to learn about the trail. Please, don't be offended, and please don't let your pride get you killed. Please, for me."

Curtis looked at her for a long time, thinking, and trying not to let his pride get in the way of his judgement. He knew that they both were right and he wasn't ready to make a eleven hundred mile journey through hostile country by himself.

"You're both right, but I still want to be there when you finally catch-up with them. There are two of them so you might need the help," Curt conceded. "How about this? I'll drop Carla off at the ranch and hook-up with Jesse. Then he can come along and show me the way? Will that work for the both of you?"

"Thank God you're not stubborn," Carla sighed with relief. "That's another reason I love you. You're smart enough to put your feelings aside when you see the truth of things. Yes, that will work for me but I hope you don't mind if I still worry about you?""

"That will work for me too," Timbre agreed. "Jesse knows the way and I'm sure he'll be glad to make the trip. Plus, you'll travel faster and safer with him guiding you, he knows the territory and where I'm going. I guess it's settled then so I best be getting started. You don't mind if I take the packhorse, do you? I've got a longer way to go than you two," Timbre smiled, hugging Carla and kissing her on the cheek as she hugged him back.

At first Carla wouldn't let go of him and Timbre had to gently pry her loose. Looking him in the eyes she softly told him: "I owe you my life. I can never repay you for what you've done for me, except love and pray for you. You just better not get yourself killed, and for that matter you better keep Curtis alive too. And don't forget to change that bandage every couple of days. You're mostly healed by now but be mindful to keep it clean anyway."

"End of trail," Curtis whispered in Timbre's ear, as he gave him a quick hug.

As they watched Timbre ride off, Carla asked Curtis "What does that mean? End of trail."

"I'll tell you while we're riding," Curtis answered, hugging her.

They were both feeling the void that the departing Timbre had left in their hearts and Carla had the strangest feeling that she'd never see Timbre again---at least in this life. With tears running down her cheeks, she mounted-up and followed behind Curtis.

CHAPTER

18

Without Carla slowing him down and his wound just about healed Timbre was able to make good time. Although he was in a hurry he didn't push Thor to hard, he averaged about thirty miles a day, give or take a few miles either way.

Along the way he was able to avoid the hostile Indians and the ones he couldn't avoid luckily turned out to be Cheyenne. Although the Cheyenne braves he encountered were mostly hostile now to the white man a lot of them remembered him as a friend, or had heard of him. After he explained his mission to them they gave him safe passage and even accompanied him part of the way in order to see that he was kept safe. Most of them either remembered, or heard tales, about the evil spirit that he had banished those many years ago. He had become a legend among their people, he had done what no other Cheyenne had been able to do.

Finding out that the evil spirit had returned and Timbre was on his way to dispose of it again they were more than happy to help him. Before they left him to travel on alone Timbre asked them to be on the look out for Jesse, who would be along shortly, and to give him as much help as they could, which they readily agreed to do.

A little over a month later, and a few harrowing adventures, an exhausted Timbre sat on a hill overlooking a picturesque little community called Thermopolis. He had lost the tracks of the two killers weeks back and hadn't seen hide or hair of them since.

Thermopolis was a beautiful little town in Montana, nestled in a valley between the Big Horn mountains and the Worland's. A little clear green lake lay to the left of the tiny village and in front of it ran a calm bubbling stream. A meadow surrounded the town and surrounding the meadow were stately Spruce Pines, which towered into the sky.

Beyond the pines Timbre could see the snow topped peaks of the mountains. The sight of mountains always took his breath away. He always preferred the mountains over the windy flat nothingness of the great plains.

The residents of Thermopolis made their living by catering to settlers who passed through on their way to Canada, or from Canada to Wyoming. If supplies or repairs were needed Thermopolis was the last place to obtain them before entering the only pass that went through the mountains for at least fifty-miles in either direction. The town even had a little hotel for the pilgrims who arrived to late to make it through the snow laden pass.

Thermopolis was a cozy and safe little town to winter in. It was a peaceful little community and the only trouble that ever came its way was from strangers who wintered over and even that was rare. Thermopolis didn't even have a sheriff and the people that lived there weren't equipped to handle any major trouble, only the little disturbances.

As Timbre sat his horse with a blanket wrapped around his shoulders he realized how much he loved this place- especially some of the people in it. He thought how ironic it was that the chase should lead him here, but deep down he knew that it wasn't dumb luck that brought the chase to this town but a carefully calculated plan by The Count. This was The Counts very destination from the beginning, before this whole nightmare had begun. This was the town that housed the people that he'd intended to say good-bye to if he decided to go on to Africa.

Looking at the town brought back memories. When he was about twelve-years old, he, Jesse, Jake, and his Dad had done a good deed for the town's blacksmith, Oleg Kaluzny. A deed that had changed all their lives for the better.

Oleg Kaluzny was as big as a grizzly and in many ways resembled one. But despite his formidable size and appearance Oleg was one of the gentlest, kindest, loving, individuals that Timbre had ever had the good fortune to run across. Oleg's two loves were his wife Trinna and his daughter Catlene. Catlene had been the catalyst that brought Timbre into their lives. She'd been about nine-years old when she embarked on that fateful adventure.

It started when Catlene, wanting to show-off her knowledge of the area to two older boys whose parents were having their wagon repaired by her daddy, volunteered to act as a sight-seeing guide for them. Being a cocky nine year old she had led them deep into the tall pines to places that even she hadn't been to before. Trusting their guide and being caught up in the adventure of it all the two boys didn't notice how late it had become. Tired and hungry they all decided it was time to go home. It was then that Catlene learned her first lesson in woodsmanship; and that was that one tree looked just about the same as any other tree.

Catlene had gotten them thoroughly lost, she had no idea in which direction the town lay. As the sun began to set the children headed the wrong way, away from the town. Deeper and deeper into the woods they traveled. If there's such a thing as a lucky day for getting oneself lost that was Catlene's lucky day.

At the same time that Catlene was getting herself lost, Sam, Timbre and the others were spending the night in the Thormopolis Hotel. They were sitting in the hotel dining room just finishing their dinner when they heard a commotion taking place outside the restaurant.

Strolling outside to investigate what all the excitement was about Sam and Timbre overheard the men telling Oleg and the parents of the other two children that it was useless to start the search for them until morning. It would be dark within the hour and they were merchants, not trackers.

Sam knew that the odds of all the children surviving the night in the cold of the wilds were not very good so he volunteered their services. The worried parents snapped up his offer in a heartbeat. Jesse and Jake opted to stay behind and let Sam and Tim handle the rescue. They both knew that Sam and Tim were more than capable of locating the children so they strolled back into the dining room to finish their meals. No sense all of them freezing out there if it wasn't necessary.

Three-hours later Sam and Timbre found the three missing children. They found them scared and hungry huddled together in a deer bed under a Pine tree. Sam had to calm the crying children down before he could lift them onto the back of their horses. Catlene, who was mounted behind Timbre, clung tightly to him, her dirty face was pressed tightly against his back. Timbre was her knight in shining armor, just like the ones she'd dreamed about from her story books. He was her hero.

For Sam and Timbre finding the children hadn't been that big of a deal but for Oleg and Trina it had been the greatest thing that anybody could ever had done for them. From that day forth they treated Timbre as if he were their own son and Sam as if he were their blood brother.

Once a year after that incident Timbre and Sam would stop and visit Oleg, Trina, and Catlene for a week or so, dragging Jesse along until his departure from them. If for some reason they missed a visit Oleg would get very angry with them---and nobody wanted that huge Russian angry with them.

It was impossible for Timbre not to grow to love those warm, generous caring people. They became his, Jesse, and Sam's family. They were the ones who helped him get over Raven's murder and then his Father's death. In fact, Oleg's home was where Timbre retreated anytime he needed to heal, inside or out. At first Cat was like a sister to him but gradually he started seeing her differently as she grew and Raven faded from his heart.

Years later, after Sam was killed, Timbre spent a year with Oleg and his family before he decided to roam the world. It was mostly his missing them, especially Cat, that made him quit his wonderings and head West again. If Timbre called anyplace on Earth home, it was Thermopolis-where the Kaluzhny's lived.

Nudging Thor, Timbre slowly drifted down the hill, across the stream, and into the town---keeping alert for any signs of strangers. Pulling up in front of the big barn that was Oleg's blacksmith shop, and stable, Timbre sat there listening to the clang of metal-on-metal that was coming from behind the half-closed doors.

"You are late," a bellowing gravelly voice with a heavy accent, rang out. "Are you going to come in or are you going to sit there and freeze your ass off?"

Timbre smiled at the sound of that voice. Dismounting, he led Thor through the doors.

"I zee dat you have a new horse. Something you picked up overseas? Oleg asked, admiring Thor. Then, putting down his hammer he spread his arms wide and ordered Timbre. "Come to Oleg!"

Oleg was a huge man with arms like oak trees. He wasn't as tall as Mountain but close to it. He might not have been as big as mountain but he was packed with more muscle and Timbre wouldn't want to bet on who'd come out on top if he and Mountain ever clashed. Oleg had a heavy beard and plenty of dark hair but it was neatly trimmed and his grey eyes were clear and friendly.

Timbre took a step forward and was immediately engulfed by Oleg's huge hairy arms. The power in that hug squeezed the air out of him, reminding him for a moment of Mountain. Timbre emitted a funny little noise as the air rushed out of him.

"You are still nutting but skin and bones," Oleg laughed, releasing Timbre before he passed out.

"I wish you wouldn't be so glad to see me," Timbre told him, taking a deep breath.

"Vhy? Are you not also glad ta see Oleg?" the big man asked, with a hurt expression on his face.

"You know I am," Timbre smiled, hugging Oleg back.

"So? Vhy are you so late? Dah nice summer is over and dah cold is already come. You get yourself in trouble again?" Oleg guessed, looking Timbre over.

"I've been busy for the last year. First: I was healing at Jake's place for some months and then Jesse roped me into chasing two men all across Texas and back again," Timbre told him. "Their trail led me here. Have any strangers come through here in the last week or so?"

361

"Da. Dhey leave only dhis morning- early, after buying supplies. Dhey look like very bad men. I vas glad ta see dhem go. I did not like the way one of dem looked at my Catrina. If they did not leave this morning somebody would have been hurt."

"This morning! That means that they must've waited somewhere around here for three or four-days, which also means that they must think that I'm dead, or they're purposely waiting on me," Timbre stated, more to himself than to Oleg.

"Dhey stay four-days," Oleg confirmed. "Vhat do dhese men do dhat you chase after dhem?"

"They raided a ranch where Jesse was working, kidnaped the two woman who were there, Mother and daughter, and then tortured the Mother to death. The daughter witnessed her Mother's death and then was given to four Comanche's who raped her repeatedly. When I finally caught up with the Comanche's she was already quite mad."

"Sum-a-bitches. If I know dhat I give dhem somethin' they never forget," Oleg angrily said, picking up his hammer and hitting it forcibly against the anvil. "How you get involved?"

"The women were friends of Jesse's. You remember Jesse?"

"Da. Does it look like I get so old dat I can't remember dhat little cyclone. Why does he not come and see Oleg anymore?"

"I can't say. Maybe he was too busy," Timbre said, shrugging-

"No one should ever get so busy dhat dhey do not have time for friends," Oleg told him, fixing Timbre with an accusing stare.

"Don't I always have time for my family?" Timbre smiled.

"Not enough. My Trina she is all the time worried for you. And Catlene, she misses you like crazy. But enough about dhat for now. Do dhese animals dhat you chase have names?"

"You won't believe this, but one of them calls himself Fargo and his boss calls himself The Count."

"The same animal you and your Daddy kill a long time ago. Da, now I see dhe resemblance."

"When did you ever see The Count?" Timbre asked, surprised by Oleg's remark.

"Once, twice, from a distance. When him and his shadow pass through here years back, before you kill him."

"You never told me back then that they'd passed through here?"

"You never ask. You dhink I tell you about every person dhat I see?"

"But weren't you worried about Catlene?"

"Why? At dhat time only Indian girls were being murdered. Nobody know for sure who was doing dhose terrible dhings."

"I guess your right," Timbre agreed, remembering that he'd said almost the same thing at one time. "Well, it's white girls who he's butchering now so keep Catlene close to home for the next couple of days."

"You talk like dhis is dhe same man you kill years ago," Oleg remarked.

"Some say it is," Timbre admitted, looking for Oleg's reaction.

"Dhen dhere is somedhing wrong with dhere heads. People who are dead, stay dead. Who told you such a dhing?"

"Mountain Muntean. He saw this guy up close and even talked to him. He swore that it was The Count."

"Muntean! A gaint half-wit. I dhought he vas dead. It saddens me to hear dhat he still valks dhe Earth," Oleg declared, shaking his head.

"Cheer up, he doesn't anymore," Timbre informed him.

"I am glad, but I am not so glad if it vas you who kill him. I do not like you killing people. It is no good for your soul."

"It would've been worse for my body if he wasn't shot, but don't fret none, I only partially killed him," Timbre smiled.

"Who kill his other parts?" Oleg asked.

"A young kid that I'm traveling with."

"Where is dhis young man?" Oleg asked.

"He'll be along in a day or two with Jesse. It's a long story. I'll tell it to you later," Timbre told him.

"Tell me dhis now," Oleg demanded of him. "Do you believe dhat dhis man dhat you kill years ago is dhe same man you chase now?"

"Truthfully, I don't know what to believe anymore," Timbre confessed.

"Lots of people look like each other," Oleg commented, seeing the confusion on Timbre's face. "Brothers, fathers, sons, cousins, an' sometimes even strangers."

"Your right," Timbre agreed, giving that theory some thought. "It has to he something like that. Dead men don't just get-up and ride away."

"Now you make sense. Go put dhat horse in dhe last stall and feed him."

"Huh." Timbre grunted, coming out of his deep thoughts, as Oleg's words sunk in. "I can't. I need him."

"For vhat?"

"I have to go after those men."

"Not on him you are not. He is almost as tired as you. Dhu tin air hurts his lungs. He needs time to rest and adjust to dhese mountains--- just the same as you do," Oleg said, concerned for Timbre's health.

"But I've almost got them.".

"You almost got nutting. If you catch dhem, dhey vill put many holes in you. Dhey are rested and you look like vhat comes out of da back end of your horse. No! I vill not allow my son to do such a foolish dhing," Oleg declared, ready to stop Timbre from leaving, even if it meant using physical force.

"I guess you're right," Timbre sighed, feeling the fatigue starting to settle in. Oleg was making a lot of sense, more sense than his tired brain was. "I'll put Thor in the stall and come back later to shoe him--- he needs them badly."

"You go vash for lunch, I shoe him later."

"No, I better do it. He can be contrary at times."

"I vill do it. If he gets smart vith me, I vill make him vish dhat he never saw Oleg," Oleg grinned, tapping his hammer lightly on the anvil while Thor sized him up.

"Okay, but I better skip lunch. I need a bath and change of clothes more than I need food."

"Trina and Catlene vill be disappointed dhat you do not come ta eat. Dhey vill blame me for dhis," Oleg told him, looking past the back of the barn, toward his house.

"They'll be more disappointed if I do come," Timbre laughed. "I smell like a goat."

"No, a goat smells much better," Oleg laughed with him. "You go vash, but you be sure ta come here after you smell sveet."

"Don't you worry about that," Timbre told him, leading Thor to the back stall.

Timbre unsaddled Thor and then rubbed him down. He put feed in his box; saying: "Behave yourself around here. You've got a nice warm place to stay, plenty of food, and in a little while Oleg is going to come and fit you with new shoes. And don't mess with that man he might cave your thick skull in." With that said Timbre picked up his gear and headed for the front doors.

Ever since Timbre had come to this little hamlet those many years ago he'd stayed at the hotel. Not that Oleg and Trina didn't want him to stay with them but during his absence Cat had become a full grown woman, and the way their relationship was progressing he felt it wise not to stay under the same roof with her at night. He didn't think that he had that much control when it came to her and she wasn't the type to take no for an answer. Plus, he didn't want to test Olef's love for him if they were caught doing something they shouldn't be doing.

"I'm going now!" Timbre yelled to Oleg on his way out.

"Without saying hello to me?" a smooth silky voice asked, from the shadows.

Timbre turned and saw Cat step out into the light and his heart skipped a beat. Every time that Timbre saw her she looked better and better and his need for her was becoming stronger and stronger.

Catlene was five-foot-eight-inches tall with long thick chestnut colored hair, and Timbre swore that her green-eyes glowed in the dark. At first glance her strong smooth face didn't seem to be that pretty but the more you looked at her the prettier she got until she was downright beautiful. Her face was so interesting that it took a while before it would all register in your brain. She was the most fascinating and desirable woman that Timbre had ever known. Whereas Carlene was beautiful Cat was exotic looking and desirable as hell.

"I, I didn't see you there," Timbre stuttered, watching her glide toward him.

"But I knew you were here," she glowed, wrapping her arms around his neck. "I always know when you're close," she finished, kissing him on the mouth.

Timbre felt Catlene's full body press up against his and his loins instantly reacted to her. Blushing, Timbre looked over at Oleg who was pretending not to be watching them.

"How are you, Cat?" Timbre asked, hoarsely.

"You can feel how I am. How about you?" Cat asked, pressing against him harder, while laughing at him with her sparkling eyes. She was totally enjoying his discomfort.

"Vhy do you not stop driving each other crazy and get married like normal people do?" Oleg asked, without looking up from his work.

"That's what I've been asking him ever since he first found me, Papa, but he won't do it," Catlene pouted, starring directly into Timbre's eyes and making him nervous.

"Can't you control your daughter?" Timbre asked Oleg, while trying to push Catlene away from him. "She has no shame."

"Vhy should I control her vhen I dhink she is right?" Oleg said, putting down the piece of metal he was heating and looking at them. "It is vay past due dhat you settle down and raise children-- and who better dhan to do dhat vith dhan my Catlene."

"I'm not ready to settle down," Timbre whined.

"You dhink you are getting any younger? Look at you! In another year or two if you keep going dhe vay you are going no woman vill vant you!" Oleg shouted. "You are all dhe time beat up, or someone is shooting you. You should kiss my Catlene's feet for still vanting to marry a broken down man like yourself. My God! You can hardly valk in dhe mornings anymore because of all dhe time sleeping on dhe hard ground."

"When you're right, you're right," Timbre agreed, looking into Catlene's eyes.

"Does that mean you'll marry me?" Catlene asked, wearily.

"I guess it does," Timbre smiled.

"When?" Catlene asked, her eyes narrowing.

"Let me think about it. I'll let you know."

Timbre knew that everything that Oleg had said was true. He wasn't getting any younger. Besides, worrying about Cat all the way up here had made him realize how much he really did love her. Now that he was holding her, why he ever thought that he could leave her and go to Africa was beyond his comprehension. His only explanation was that it seemed like a good idea at the time.

"Don't you think about it for too long," Catlene warned him, without smiling. "I've just about fed up with waiting around for you. I want somebody who's going to stick around and love me. If you don't want the same thing I'll find somebody who does."

"But I'm the one you love," Timbre smiled, trying to make light of the situation.

"Yes, and you're the one I'll always love. But that doesn't mean I can't live without you if you force me to. I've been doing a good job of it so far"

"That's funny because I don't think I can live without you," Timbre said, hugging her tightly.

"You mean that?" Cat asked, not knowing if Timbre was making fun of her or not.

"I mean that with all my heart," Timbre sincerely told her, kissing her quickly on the lips. "Now, let me go get cleaned-up."

"I'll walk you to the hotel," Catlene offered, with a big smile on her face.

"No you won't. You'll stay close to your Father," Timbre ordered her.

"Why?" Catlene asked, not liking to be told what to do.

"Your Father will explain most of it to you and I'll fill in the rest of it tonight," Timbre promised, pushing her gently away.

"Okay. I'll do as you say--- but just this once," Catlene smirked.

"Thank you," Timbre sighed, knowing that she was going to be a handful after they were married.

"You're welcome," Catlene smiled, stepping away from him so that he could leave.

Before Timbre turned to leave, he told her: "Don't forget to tell Mama that I said hello and that I'll see her for dinner." Then shouting over Catlene's shoulder, he yelled: "Oleg! I'll see you for dinner!"

"Da. Trina vill be so happy vhen she hears dhat you are going to finally marry our Catlene, she von't be able to stop crying," Oleg said, with tears in his eyes.

As Timbre walked away he looked back and saw Catlene standing by the barn doors with Oleg's big arm wrapped around her. Seeing them standing together like that made Timbre realize how right it felt to be marrying Catlene. She was going to make him one hell of a wife.

CHAPTER

19

"That was a wonderful meal, Mama," Timbre groaned, after stuffing himself with roast-beef, corn, and mashed-potatoes.

"Good. I am glad you enjoy it," Trina smiled. "Catlene, she help me to cook it."

"You don't have to sell her to me, Mama, I already said I'd marry her," Timbre joked.

"Now he is doing my daughter a favor," Oleg commented, to no one in particular.

"Now Papa, leave Elmo alone," Catlene teased, grinning wickedly at Timbre as she stood to help clear the table.

Except for Jesse and Jake, the Kaluzhny's were probably the only people still alive who knew Timbre's real name.

"Don't ever call me Elmo. Not even as a joke," Timbre warned her, the smile vanishing from his face.

"Oooh, I'm sorry. I promise I'll never do that again," Catlene apologized, stepping behind his chair and bending over his back so that she could wrap her arms around his neck. "I forgot how sensitive you are about that."

"Yeah," Timbre grunted, not believing her. "Just, please, don't do it again. Okay?"

"I already promised I wouldn't. Don't you trust me?" Cat asked, mischievously.

"Leave dhe man alone," Trina ordered. "At least until after you two are married."

"That's right. Do as your Mama says and stop picking on me," Timbre smiled.

"Okay, but only if you tell us the story you promised," Cat bargained.

"First ve clear dhe table, dhen he vill tell us," Trina ordered, gathering up the dishes.

Timbre watched Trina clean the table with Cat's help. When mother and daughter stood side-by-side it was easy to see where Catlene had inherited her beauty from. Even though Cat was taller than Trina, had a fuller figure, lighter hair, and naturally looked younger, they still had the same pretty facial features and color eyes.

"Dhere! Dhat is done," Trina declared, as she placed the cups down in front of them and Cat poured the coffee. "Now you begin your story."

Timbre told them the whole tale, starting it in California and ending it here. The only two things he omitted was his notion to go to Africa and the gory details of Evelyn's death. They got the idea without going into all of that.

"You did right, chasing dhose animals," Trina declared after Timbre had finished.

"Mmmm," Oleg agreed, nodding, as he puffed on the pipe that was sticking out of his grayish shaggy beard.

"Is she as pretty as me?" Cat demanded to know, her eyes scrutinizing Timbre's face for any wrong doing.

"Who?" Timbre asked, making believe he didn't know who she was referring to.

"You know who," Cat snapped. "Or maybe you think I mean your friend Curtis?"

"If it matters any, she's beautiful," Timbre admitted, knowing that Cat would detect a lie. How she was always able to tell when he was lying was a mystery to him. "But not as beautiful as you," he quickly added.

"Good," Cat said, satisfied. "Because she sounds like someone I'd like but I couldn't if you thought she was prettier than me."

"That's dumb," Timbre commented, not understanding her.

"That may be so but that's the way I feel about it."

"Well, you can stop worrying because I think you're the most beautiful woman in the world, except for your Mama of course," Timbre smiled, winking at Oleg.

Catlene beamed, but before she could respond, Trina asked: "Vhat do you plan on doing about dhose men now?"

"I plan on finishing the job I started," Timbre flatly stated.

"All by yourself?" Oleg asked.

"No. Jesse and Curtis should be here in a day or two. They'll wait till then. I have a feeling that they've stopped running and will be waiting on me somewhere up there."

"Swear to me that you'll not go after those men until Curtis and Jesse arrive," Cat demanded, wiggling herself between Timbre and the table so that she could sit on his lap and face him eye to eye. "I mean it, I don't want you going after those killers by yourself."

"I promise," Timbre swore. He'd planned on waiting for Curtis and Jesse anyway, even before Cat made him promise to do so.

"I wouldn't want to lose such a rich future husband," Cat laughed, hugging him.

"So! That's why you want to marry me! For my money," Timbre declared, feigning shock.

"Vhy else would she marry a dilapidated old man like you?" Oleg joined in. "She wants her Papa to retire in luxury."

"Well, if that's the price I have to pay for her I guess she's worth it," Timbre said, hugging her back.

"You better believe I'm worth it," Cat whispered in his ear.

"Good. Dhat is settled," Oleg laughed, standing. "Now it is time for us to get some air while dhe vomen clean."

"Not for me," Timbre yawned. "I'm beat. I can hardly keep my eyes open."

"You see how old you are getting," Oleg pointed out.

"Don't I know it," Timbre agreed, lifting Cat off his lap and standing. "Oleg, would you mind if I use the spare bedroom tonight? I'm to tired to walk to the hotel"

"You know you are always velcome to it, but vhy tonight? You don't fool me with the too tired excuse," Oleg asked, suspiciously.

"I'll sleep better knowing you're all close by."

"You really think those men are still somewhere around here?" Cat asked.

I can't swear to it but I have a strange feeling that they are, so I'm not going to take any chances," Timbre shrugged. "Before turning in make sure that all the doors and windows are locked--- just to be on the safe side."

"I close and lock all the shudders and doors tonight," Oleg told him. "Nobody is going to get my Trina and Catlene."

"Good, nobody is safe as long as those two animals are roaming about. Remember: Evelyn was a mother too," Timbre warned.

"I do not forget."

"Okay. If you need me for anything wake me--- and don't hesitate to do that," Timbre emphasized.

"Don't worry, we won't hesitate," Cat told him. "You got me scared if that's what you intended to do."

"I'm just trying to alert you to the possible danger that exists and to get you to act with a little extra caution--- at least for the next couple of days."

"Well, it worked," Cat informed him.

"Good, then I can sleep easy."

"You vill find your winter clothing at dhe foot of your bed, in dhe cider chest. Dhey are all cleaned and pressed," Trina told him.

"Thank you, Mama," Timbre smiled. "See you all in the morning. Good-night."

"And do not vorry. I lockup everything good and tight," Oleg reassured him.

"You get your rest," Trina added.

"I'll wake you early," Cat said, kissing him. "I love you."

"And I love you- but not too early," Timbre warned, turning and heading for his room.

Timbre alerted his senses to respond to any strange noises during the night and as a result of that his sleep was a restless one. In the morning, true to her word, Catlene tiptoed into his room to wake him.

"That's a good way to get yourself shot," Timbre cautioned her, without opening his eyes. "Trying to sneak up on a man like that."

"How did you know I was here?" Cat asked, jumping on him and kissing his cheek. "I was trying to be so quiet."

"Because you move like a Buffalo," Timbre joked, stealing himself for the blow that he knew was forth coming.

Timbre wasn't disappointed. A second later Cat yanked his pillow out from under his head and shouted: "Why you---" and then proceeded to repeatedly hit him with it.

"I give up," Timbre laughed, grabbing her arms and wrestling her down.

Timbre felt Cat laying half under him. Her firm breasts were heaving and her thick hair was fanned out on the white sheets. She looked extremely beautiful and very desirable and Timbre's body reacted appropriately to her.

"You going to do something about that?" Cat asked, feeling his hardness pressing against her leg.

"Yeah, throw you the hell out of here," Timbre croaked, rolling off of her.

"Not until you apologize for calling. me a Buffalo," Cat told him, reaching down and fondling his discomfort.

"Oh God!" Timbre moaned, trying desperately to remember where he was. "I didn't call you a Buffalo, but I apologize anyways. Now get out of here before you get us both in trouble."

"What trouble?" Cat smiled, gently stroking him.

Before Timbre could answer, two things happened. First: His whole body tensed and he exploded while trying to stifle a moan. Second: Trina called for Catlene from the kitchen.

"Catlene! Breakfast is ready!" Trina yelled.

"Coming Mama! I was just waking Tim!" Cat yelled back, rolling out of bed. "That's what happens when you stay away from me too long," Cat whispered, smoothing her dress. "Now you better clean yourself up before coming to breakfast," she told him, quickly turning and swishing out of the room.

This was the very reason why Timbre had made the decision to stay in the hotel when he was in town. Cat loved to tease him, but always managed to stop just short of the ultimate act. Timbre wasn't complaining too much though, but it always made him nervous when she played around in the house. Cat loved to live a bit dangerously, it excited her but Timbre figured that just trying to stay alive was all the excitement he needed.

Timbre felt like going back to sleep. He hadn't felt so relaxed in months, but he knew that he had to get-up and get washed---and so he did.

Timbre and Catlene spent the whole day together. They went shopping in the morning and then walking in the afternoon. The evening was spent with Catlene's parents making plans for their upcoming wedding. By the time that they were ready to turn in for the night it had been agreed by everyone that he and Cat would be married in the Spring.

The next morning Timbre awoke feeling rested. He ate a hearty breakfast and then accompanied Oleg to the stables to check on Thor.

"How're you feeling today?" Timbre asked Thor, looking him over. "I see you have a new shoes-- and you're groomed. Who gave you the haircut?" he asked, not expecting an answer while carefully stroking Thor's head. "And a nice big lump on your head to go with the new look," Timbre added, feeling the bump under Thor's mane. "I told you not to mess with that man-- but thanks for not killing him," Timbre whispered in his ear.

Walking to the front, to where Oleg was hammering away, Timbre said: "I warned you that he'd try to take a chunk out of you."

"I betcha he no try again," Oleg stated, without looking up from his work.

"I know I wouldn't," Timbre agreed. "You think he'll be okay to travel today?"

"He not hurt bad. Just a little bump. You cannot hurt dhat one by hitting him on his dhick head."

"Probably not," Timbre agreed. "You need any help here?"

"No. Business is starting to get slow. You go and spend time with Catlene. I'll keep an eye out for your friends."

"I'm starting to worry about them," Timbre commented, looking out the front doors.

"I vould not vorry none about dhat fella, Anyone who can kill a man like Mountain can take care of himself."

"I hope you're right," Timbre said, starting back to the house.

At eleven a.m. there was still no sign of Curtis and Jesse and Timbre was becoming restless. Cat and Trina were busy getting things ready for their upcoming wedding even though it was months away, so Timbre found himself with nothing to do.

"I'm going down to McClone's for a beer," Timbre announced, not able to sit around doing nothing.

"Okay," Cat said, stopping what she was doing to look at him.

"I'm sorry I haven't been better company but you know how Mama is, everything has to be done right now."

"It's okay," Timbre said, forgiving her. "I understand. But if Curtis and Jesse don't show up soon I'm going to go crazy."

"Then I'll marry a crazy man. Just don't forget your promise to wait for them," Cat reminded Timbre, with a worried look on her face. She could feel his impatience.

"I won't," Timbre sighed, strapping on his guns and leaving the house.

"Be home in time for dinner!" Cat yelled after him. "And sober!"

Timbre sat at one of the few tables in McClone's tavern, sipping a beer and frequently glancing at the door. It was still early so there was nobody in the room except him. Even Ion McClone, who was also the owner of the restaurant and hotel was off somewhere attending to business.

Timbre was putting his empty glass down when he felt as if a bucket of evil was being poured all over him. Snapping his head up and quickly looking towards the door he saw a man enter who was completely dressed in black and glided, more than walked, silently into the barroom.

The man wore his wide-brimmed black hat pulled down low on his forehead. He walked past Timbre without so much as a glance in his direction and strolled up to the bar and quietly stood there with his back to Timbre, patiently waiting for someone to serve him. What game Fargo was playing eluded Timbre at the moment-- and frankly he didn't care what the game was. Death had just walked into the room.

Timbre saw that Fargo's long black winter coat had slits running up both sides of it. Black handled Colts hung low on his hips, protruding from those slits. His tall rail-thin shape made Timbre think of a Spector. Slowly, Timbre started to pull out his forty-five.

"If you want to die quickly keep on doing what you're doing," a soft voice without any emotion to it warned him. The voice brought to one's mind a picture of a tombstone. Timbre relaxed his grip and let his gun slide back into its holster.

"So, you're still alive," the man in black said, still not turning around.

"It would seem so."

"We didn't think that Mountain would fail to kill you, but I'm glad he didn't," the man stated, with a slight smile to his voice.

"I appreciate your concern- Fargo."

"Don't bother. I'm glad he didn't kill you because I want to be the one to do it. You're the only man that I ever shot that lived. You made me look bad."

"I'm sorry about that. My only hope is that I can make you look bad again."

"Can't fault a man for hoping, but in this case hoping ain't going to be good enough."

Fargo, tired of waiting for someone to come and serve him reached over the bar and grabbed a bottle of whiskey and a glass.

"Ain't, ain't a word. Where's your friend?" Timbre asked, looking out the door for any sign of The Count.

"He's waiting for me up there," Fargo answered, jerking his thumb toward the mountain. "I just came back to fetch something."

"Oh! Like what? Some lingerie. Doesn't The Count find you attractive enough just the way you are anymore?"

Fargo spun around, his eyes blazing. For a second Timbre thought that he might've pushed him a little too far. He'd finally hit a nerve and looking into Fargo's blazing eyes was like glimpsing a piece of hell.

"You always did have a smart mouth," Fargo hissed, barely able to control himself. "So that's where I'm going to put my first bullet- right in your big smart mouth.

"That's just about what Mountain told me. I guess he was right. It's my biggest flaw. I just can't control my big mouth. Sorry if I've offended you," Timbre lied. Pissing Fargo off before he found out what he wanted to know was not the brightest thing he could do. "So tell me: What is it you came back for?" Timbre asked.

"That big lummox of a blacksmith's daughter," Fargo calmly told him, knowing that she was Timbre's girl. "My boss took a fancy to her while we were in town, so I rode back here to fetch her for him."

Timbre's stomach tightened. It took all of his self-control not to reach for his gun.

"Why didn't he just take her with him when he left?" Timbre asked, trying not to act too concerned.

"We were waiting on you to arrive. My boss wanted you to know what was going to happen to her before I killed you. You really shouldn't have pissed him off so much."

"How is The Count?" Timbre asked.

"I was wondering when you'd get around to asking that," Fargo told him. "That's the only reason why I haven't killed you yet. I wanted to see your face when I told you that he's alive and doing well."

"Bullshit! He's dead and you know it. I don't know who's up there but it isn't The Count. Not unless you learned how to bring the dead back to life."

"Maybe I have, but in any case, I said what I had to say," Fargo spat. "You know, I'm fairly sick of you so it's time for dying. Do you want it here and get this nice clean floor all filled with blood or would you prefer to die outside in the street?"

"One more thing before we get at it."

"Make it quick, I'm getting impatient."

"How did you know about this place?"

"Oh, did I neglect to tell you? Your friend Jake furnished us with your destination. We took a little detour in Texas but we figured we'd find you here after we were through with that other business. The one thing that threw us is that we never expected you to get involved in our other enterprise. Goes to show you how you can't plan for everything. But, as you can see things worked out rather nicely anyway."

"You're lying, Jake wouldn't tell you squat."

"Don't blame him, he truly didn't want to, but you know how persuasive the Count can be. Jake lasted quite a while before he finally broke. I have to give that tough old fool credit for that."

"So he's dead?" Timbre whispered.

"As dead as you're going to be in a minute. You ready now?"

"After you," Timbre elaborately gestured, standing and waving his arm toward the door.

"I think not," Fargo grinned. "I don't care to be gunned down from the behind. You had your chance to do that and you blew it. You go first."

"I'm hurt that you don't trust me," Timbre smiled, determined to stop Fargo from going after Cat--- no matter how many bullets he had to absorb to accomplish that.

"I see you've made another friend," a soft Texas voice commented from behind him.

Timbre turned toward the voice and there stood Curtis. He'd been so distracted by Fargo that he'd failed to hear Curt come in.

"Where the hell have you been?" Timbre asked.

"We had to take a detour or two, Indians and all that," Curtis shrugged.

"Well, you've arrived just in time to meet one of the men who helped to butcher your Aunt," Timbre informed him, turning his attention back to the gunman. "Curtis, meet Fargo. We were just on our way out to meet Mr. Death."

"So I heard," Curtis grinned.

"You picked a bad time to show up, boy," Fargo told him, in his monotone voice. "Now I'm going to have to kill you too. Right after I take care of your friend that is."

"You'll settle with me first, you turd. That is if you got the guts for it," Curtis growled, the smile vanishing from his face and his hand poised over his six-shooter.

Things happened fast after that. Both men cleared leather in a heart beat, faster than the eye could follow, their guns discharging at what sounded like the same time.

An amazed Timbre watched wide eyed as a big red hole appeared on Fargo's chest, as his gun fell to the floor.

"Holy shit," Timbre mumbled, letting the Derringer he'd been cancelling fall out of his sleeve and into his hand. Cautiously, he approached Fargo.

"It's not possible," Fargo mumbled, as blood trickled from his mouth. "The son-of a-bitch killed me." With that he crumbled to the floor.

"Is he dead?" Curtis groaned.

Timbre turned towards Curtis and saw him struggling to his feet with his left shoulder covered in blood.

"Yeah. You shot him dead," Timbre informed him. "I didn't think anybody could match his speed with a gun."

"I've been practicing," Curtis winced, as he stumbled into a table.

Timbre rushed to Curtis's side and grabbed him around the waist and helped him onto a chair. Timbre sat him down and examined his shoulder; saying: "It looks like the bullet passed clean through your shoulder. It's not fatal but you won't be traveling for a while."

"But----"

"But nothing. Like it or not you're going to be down for quite a bit. That was a damn fool thing you did," Timbre scolded him. "Did it ever occur to you that I had the situation under control?"

"He beat you before so I figured that I had a better chance of beating him than you did," Curtis stated, staring at his wound.

"Not likely," Timbre informed him, tossing the Derringer on the table. "He would've never made it to the door."

"Oh," was all that Curtis could think to say.

"What happened here?" McClone asked, slowly emerging from the backroom.

"That fella, laying on the floor was trying to rob you. This gent stopped him," Timbre lied, not feeling like explaining the whole story to him.

McClone looked around and saw the whiskey bottle and glass on the counter. Knowing that he hadn't put them there, he bought Timbre's story.

"Aye. That evil looking man was in here just the other day with some other gent in tow," McClone commented, in his Scottish brogue. "I didn't trust them then and it seems my opinion of them was justified. Now, don't be misunderstanding me, I appreciate what the lad did but a bottle of whiskey hardly seems to be worth killing over."

"I agree, but he didn't give the lad a choice. He went for his gun when the boy told him to leave the money on the bar for his drinks," Timbre explained, as he stuffed Curtis's kerchief into his wound.

"Aye, but why would your friend concern himself over my problem?"

"He's a born do gooder," Timbre answered, taking Curt's right-hand and making him hold the kerchief tightly against the hole in his shoulder.

"Why're you lying to him?" Curtis whispered.

"Because, McClone is a little on the dense side. If I tell him the truth you'll bleed to death before he grasps it all. Now, you think you can stand?"

"I think so-- with a little help," Curtis answered, allowing Timbre to pull him to his feet.

"Where would you be taking the lad?" McClone asked.

"Oleg's," Timbre told him, steadying Curtis.

"Aye. Trina will know how to tend to him. Be sure to tell her to inform me if the lad needs anything. That's the least I can do for him."

"I will."

They were slowly making their way to the front door when Oleg burst in carrying a rifle. Seeing Timbre half-carrying Curtis, he asked: "Vhat happen here?"

Timbre gestured behind him with his head, saying: "The boy gunned downed Fargo."

"I'm not a boy," Curt declared, through clinched teeth.

"Killing people don't make you a man," Timbre told him. "Now shut up and save your strength."

"Here," Oleg offered, putting his rifle down. "I vill carry him." With that Oleg picked Curtis up like he would a child and left the saloon.

In front of the saloon the fifteen or twenty residents of Pine Ridge were milling around waiting to find out what the shooting had been about. Timbre and Oleg pushed their way through them, ignoring their questions and quickly made their way to Oleg's house.

"What happened to him?" Cat asked, opening the door for them and stepping aside. "For God's sake he just got here less than twenty-minutes ago."

Timbre explained the whole thing to them as they carried Curtis to the bedroom. Curt was just about unconscious by the time they laid him on the bed.

"I vill need hot vater, clean towels, my sewing kit, bandages, and some of dhat pain killer I use on duh horses," Trina said, while cutting off Curtis's shirt. "You three go fetch dhem for me," she ordered.

Once they were out of the room, Cat turned to Timbre; declaring: "You're going after the count alone now--- aren't you?"

"Where's Jesse?"

"Curtis told me Jesse's horse came-up lame about three miles out of town and that he sent him up ahead while he walked his horse in and to tell you that he'd be here real soon."

"I can't wait for him. If the Count finds out what happened here he'll be in the wind and I might never get him. And if I don't get him we'll never feel safe again. So what choice do I have?"

"You promised!"

"I promised that I'd wait for Curtis. Well I did. It's not my fault that he can't go on with me. Besides, he killed Fargo and Fargo was the only one of them that I was truly worried about."

"I still don't want you going alone," Cat pleaded.

"I'm not crazy about it myself, but I'm also not crazy about waiting around here till The Count decides to come for you. Besides, as soon as Jesse shows up tell him the direction I went and to catch-up. He should be along in about an hour or so," Timbre told her.

"I know you're right," Cat agreed, burying her face in his chest. "But for God's sake, be careful."

"For my sake too," Timbre joked, kissing her. "Now go help your Papa fetch that stuff for your Mama. I'll be back sometime tomorrow."

"If you're not, I'm coming looking for you," Cat threatened.

"Promise me you won't do that," Timbre ordered, grabbing Cat roughly by her arms. "I'm not going through all this just so you can go out and get yourself killed by that animal."

Seeing the fear in Timbre's face and knowing that he was right again, Catlene vowed, "I promise. But if you don't come back I'll never forgive you," she threatened, kissing him long and hard.

Breaking the kiss, Timbre smiled; saying: "Me neither. Don't worry, I'll be back. I love you too much not to be."

"I love you too," Catlene said as Timbre disengaged himself from her embrace. Picking up Curtis' gun off the table he then turned and left.

As Catlene watched Timbre walk to the stables she had a strong feeling that she should do something to stop him- but she just didn't know what.

Thor was well rested and loped along with no problem on the inclined road that led to the pass. There wasn't another gap through the mountains in any direction for at least fifty-miles so Timbre didn't bother searching for sign. Though while riding through the pines he did occasionally spot Fargo's tracks going in the opposite direction towards town. Two-hours later, just before reaching the edge of the snow line, Timbre stopped and dismounted. Whispering to Thor, he said: "He can't be much farther ahead. I don't believe he'd leave the cover of the trees."

Timbre held onto Thor's bridle as he slowly walked along while studying the ground for sign. The trees loomed up on either side of the road, casting him in shadow. This high up he was quickly running out of daylight.

"Look! This is where Fargo came out onto the main road," Timbre said to Thor, pointing to the tracks that disappeared into the trees on his right. The thin trail that meandered off through the pines brought to Timbre's mind a tributary flowing from a river.

"Well. What do we do? Do we follow his tracks now or do we wait till morning when there'll be more light and hopefully Jesse?"

Timbre didn't really expect Thor to answer but it was comforting to talk to something, even if it didn't talk back- it also helped him to think clearer. "In my opinion I think it's too damn cold to camp the night here without a fire, so let's push on and put an end to this once and for all. Then we can go home to our nice warm beds," he told Thor while taking his whip off his saddle.

Had Timbre been listening to his inner-voice, the voice that'd kept him alive for all these years, the voice that was screaming at him now to pay attention, he wouldn't have gone any farther. But, as it was he was too busy thinking about Cat and his up-coming marriage and his nice warm bed to pay any attention to his nagging inner voice. He had broke the first rule of hunting--- he took his head out of the game.

Timbre was nonchalantly following the path that weaved serpent like through the pines. Finally, his inner-voice, that was in an absolute panic now, and the nausea that he was suddenly felling, made it near impossible for him to ignore the warnings any longer--- but it was too little too late.

"That's as far as you go!" a voice rang out from across a small clearing.

Timbre was immediately aware that he'd been caught with his pants down. He knew that he had only a second to decide on what to do. If he waited too long to make his move he wouldn't have a prayer of surviving.

Judging that the voice had come from about twenty-yards to his right, Timbre quickly drew his .45 from his belly holster, spun and fired. All hell broke loose then. It was like the fourth of July. Bullets began to whiz all around him, some of them plucking at his clothing.

Timbre forced himself to ignore those near misses and to keep firing. Everything was happening so fast that his mind wasn't able to register it all. Timbre was working on pure instinct. While firing at a shadow to his right and

387

trying to retreat back into the Pines at the same time he felt a sharp burning pain in his left leg. He knew he'd been hit but he didn't have time to worry about it, or to slow down. Emptying his six-shooter into the Pines of where the shots where coming from, Timbre threw it aside and drew his other gun. Staring hard into the trees he saw an outline of a body suddenly appear.

Thinking that Timbre had to reload, The count exposed himself for a brief moment. Timbre rapidly fired three-shots at him and saw him quickly vanish behind a tree. He was certain that he had hit him, but how bad he was shot Timbre couldn't tell. Timbre carefully started to circle around to get behind the Count when a bullet took out a chunk of his left arm. He quickly fired back despite the pain as the killer ducked behind another tree. Hearing a scream, Timbre knew that another one of his bullets had found it's mark. A second later, and taking him by surprise, The Count darted out from behind the tree and fired again at the same time that Timbre did.

It was as if a giant fist hit him in the gut. Timbre was knocked over backwards with the wind knocked out of him. Vaguely he felt himself land. Timbre waited for his brain to become somewhat operational again and to get his wind back before he struggled to his feet--- all the time expecting another bullet to come crashing into him at any second.

Feeling as if he were floating on a cloud Timbre forgot all about The Count. He felt something warm all over the front of his shirt and looking down he saw his blood flowing out from a hole in his belly.

"That ain't good," Timbre mumbled to himself, feeling detached from the situation. Timbre was in shook, the pain hadn't registered in his brain yet. Looking around, he yelled: "Where the hell are you horse? It's time to go home now!"

When Thor didn't turn up, Timbre searched the area with only his eyes, not moving anything else. Not seeing him, he said to himself, "I guess I went and got us both killed."

Thinking that Thor had taken a stray bullet brought Timbre back to reality. He suddenly remembered the outlaw and he wondered what had become of him. Bending over to pick up his empty gun Timbre discovered that his left arm wouldn't work. Since he couldn't reload his six-shooter with one hand he abandoned it and reached for his whip.

"Jeez! What now?" Timbre groaned as he tried to walk and almost fell.

Looking down at his left leg, which was almost numb, Timbre saw blood dribbling out of a hole in his thigh-- then he remembered being shot there.

Dragging his leg Timbre finally made it to where he'd last seen the outlaw. It was almost dark now and visibility was poor, but not to poor to see a gun barrel poking out from behind a tree. Quick as a rattler's strike Timbre's whip lashed out and wrapped itself around the barrel of the Navy Colt.

Owww!" a voice screamed, as Timbre yanked back on the whip and the gun flew past his head.

"Come-on out of there," Timbre ordered.

As the man slowly stepped out from behind the tree Timbre's eyes opened wide with disbelief. Because there, standing right before him, was The Count.

"Well, we finally meet face to face," the blond-haired man moaned, clutching his bleeding belly. He was obviously in great pain and Timbre could see the blood seeping out from between the man's fingers. His last bullet had found it's mark, just as the outlaw's had found his. They'd managed to belly-shoot each other.

"You sure do look like his double, but you can't be The Count that I killed all those years ago."

389

"What makes you say that?" the man inquired, leaning heavily against a tree.

"Because ghosts don't shoot guns."

"I'm not a ghost, I'm as real as you are. And I am the one they called The Count."

Impossible. I saw you dead." Timbre said, slowly lowering himself to the ground as the pain started to take over.

"I might say the same about you. Is there no killing you?" The Count asked, as he too slowly slid down the tree and onto the ground.

"I believe you just did," Timbre declared, feeling himself becoming weaker by the minute. "At least I have the satisfaction of taking you with me. Tell me the truth since we're both dying anyway, who are you? And don't tell me you're 'The Count' returned from the dead. I'm not buying that load of crap."

"Have it your own way," the bleeding killer sighed, to weak to argue. "But if you think this is the end of me you're sadly mistaken. I'll be back as soon as I heal."

I doubt that you're going to heal from those wounds. How many times did I hit you?" Timbre smiled.

"Three times, but the one in my gut is the one that did the most damage. It hurts like the dickens, but it will heal. Unlike yours that will kill you."

"How do you figure that?"

"Do you really think I killed all those woman for fun. Well, it was kinda fun, but that wasn't the whole reason. See this?" The count asked as he ripped open his shirt.

"What the hell is that?" Timbre asked.

"It's called chain mail. While it won't completely stop a bullet it stops it enough from penetrating to deeply. As long as a bullet doesn't reach my heart or brain I can rejuvenate. It will take me some time, like the last time you shot me, but it will heal."

"Supposing I believe you. What does killing all those woman have to do with it?"

"Since you're going o die I'll tell you. Remember what the Apaches believe?"

"They believe a lot of things. Can you be more specific?"

"When they torture people they try and absorb their energy as they're dying. They believe that they can absorb their power. Believe it or not, they're on the right track. The only thing that they were missing was the chanting and the crystals."

Slowly reaching into his pocket he brought out a big white crystal. By using the right vowel sounds I can get the crystal vibrating and as the life force is slowly being released from a body the crystal absorbs it and then transfers back into me. While you're dying I'm planning to take your life force and transfer it to me. After that's done I'll be strong enough to leave this place and properly heal myself. To bad you killed Fargo I could use him about now. But, no matter, I'll make do."

"What makes you think that Fargo is dead?"

"Because he's not here and you are."

"For your information I didn't kill him. Eve's nephew did the job for me."

"Who's Eve?"

"The woman you butchered in Texas," Timbre informed him, surprised that he didn't know her name.

"I rarely bother with names. Knowing their names makes it to personal and confuses the work I have to do on them."

"Tell me. How do you choose your victims? Why go all the way to Texas to get Eve?"

No special trick to it. When I see someone I can tell how much energy I can get out of them. If they seem weak

I can't use them. Eve, as you call her, was just bristling with strength and energy. A rare find even for me. She really did last a long time. If you hadn't interrupted me I could have gotten so much more out of her."

"Why did you take off? You could've waited around and killed me and then finished what you started."

"Because you're too good. We might've been able to kill you but you most likely would have held us up long enough for your friends to catch up with you. Why take the chance? You know, you're the only one that ever got close enough to me to almost do me in. If your bullet was a hair over to the right you would've succeeded. How you even saw me was quite a feat, nobody else ever had, not even your sharp eyed Indian friends. You were the most dangerous man I've ever come across. That's why I was hunting you for all those years. I couldn't take the chance that our paths wouldn't cross again--and, as it turned out it seems I was right to do so. You are quite a mystery to me. To bad I won't have time to study you."

"I'm curious, how did you make yourself invisible so nobody could see you? And how did you cover your tracks?"

"I never was invisible, as you say, I learned a little trick a couple of hundred years ago on how to distort light so it broke around me and only made me seem invisible. As far as my tracks go, they never disappeared because they were never there. I just moved to the side and watched your Indian friends just pass me by and get confused when the tracks ended. It took me centuries to master that trick-- but I had the time."

"How come you didn't use that trick on me just now?"

"What makes you think I didn't? For some unexplained reason it doesn't work on you. You really did take me by surprise. I didn't think you were crazy enough to draw and fire when I had you cold."

"If you say I didn't kill you back then, then where were you for all these years? Why haven't I heard about you killing any more women until now?

"Like I said, you came close to killing me last time and it took me years to heal. And then there was that little war going on and all my killing went unnoticed, especially if I stuck to the wounded and dying. It was a regular smorgasbord. Too bad that little fracas had to come to an end."

I thought you only killed woman?"

"The truth being I do prefer men. They have more power to give but they die quicker than woman--- and where's the fun in that? Plus, woman don't put up as much of a fight as men tend to do. I prefer not to have to fight if I don't have to, chances are you'll wind-up killing your intended victim before you can extract their power from them."

"And what about Fargo, did you share your victims with him? Was he hundreds of years old too? Will he be coming back to life also?"

"No, poor lad, I raised him to protect me while I was doing what I was doing but I didn't share any of my secrets with him."

"What do you mean you raised him? He looked about the same age as you."

"Didn't you understand anything that I was telling you, are you that dense? There have been dozens of Fargos throughout my life and there will most probably be dozens more. I'll let you in on a little secret: I'm three-hundred and eighty years old, and as soon as I get home I'll find another little orphan and train me another Fargo."

"Bullshit. Nobody lives that long," Timbre exclaimed.

"Believe it or not, makes no never mind to me. Are you going to try and kill me now?" The Count asked, nodding at the knife in Timbre's hand.

"I thought about it, but for some reason my arm won't work," Timbre told him, struggling to get his arm up.

"Doesn't matter, you wouldn't have the strength to pierce this chain mail anyway"

"Shit!" Timbre exclaimed as he struggled to get his arm to work.

"You know, I didn't think anybody could out draw Fargo," the outlaw commented, almost as an afterthought, but not sounding overly heartbroken over Fargo's death.

"Me neither," Timbre admitted groggily, as he felt himself slipping into darkness.

"I guess it's time," he heard The Count say from what seemed far off. "You won't mind if I start sapping your power from you. You have so little left, but hopefully just enough to enable me to get out of here and find your pretty girl friend. Now there's one with enough power to heal me completely." Silence fell over them except for this annoying humming coming from The Count.

Timbre started to float away, knowing he had failed to save Cat. He was just about unconscious when felt something wet touch his face. Opening his eyes slightly he looked into Thor's eyes.

"So you aren't dead. Good for you," Timbre whispered, unable to put any strength into his voice.

"Nice horse," The Count told him, stopping his chanting for a minute. "I don't imagine you'll mind if I keep him since you won't be needing him anymore?"

"Tell me something Count, did you say that the only way you can die is a bullet in the head or the heart?" Timbre asked softly. An idea forming in his fuzzy brain.

"That's what I said. Not that it will do you any good," The Count answered him as he fondled the crystal. "I can feel your life energy slipping away and starting to fill me."

"If that's true, then it's time for you to die," Timbre told him. "Thor, would you please stump his head in for me?" Timbre asked, hoping that Thor would understand him.

Thor looked over at the Count with murder in his eyes and the Count saw it and terror took hold of him. He had nowhere to run and nothing to protect himself with. He tried desperately to scramble away and felt his ankle being smashed as Thor's hoof made contact with it. He screamed loudly, cursing Timbre, as Thor's teeth grabbed hold of his ass and pulled him back.

"Stop playing with him and finish the job," Timbre ordered, in a chocked voice.

Thor let go of The Count and looked back at Timbre with what looked like a smile on his face. Then he looked down at the Count, who had turned over on his back to face Thor. With tears running down his cheeks The Count looked up into Thor's fiery face not believing that he was about to die. He was thinking that this couldn't possibly be happening to him, not after all these years. He opened his mouth to say something but before the Count could get a word out a half ton of muscle stomped him hard in the chest, driving the crystal through his breast bone and making the Count's eyes bulge out of his head. When Thor was satisfied that The Count was beyond feeling any more pain he finished the job by making mush out of the Count's head.

"It's starting to snow," Timbre moaned, half conscious, but smiling at the mess that Thor had made of The Count. "Thanks Thor-- I'm going to miss you."

Looking at the big soft white flacks falling on him he thought to himself: 'This should speed things up a bit.' The cold had numbed his body and in doing so chased away the pain that he had been in. He figured he should be frozen solid within a couple of hours.

"No sense both of us dying," he said to Thor, who was standing over him. "Why don't you go home and get warm?" Thor remained where he was, just staring at Timbre. "At least go to the head of the trail and guide Jesse here when you see him." With that Thor turned around and headed for the main trail.

He barely saw the rider pull up within a few feet of him and dismount. Timbre was sure that it was Jesse, but then decided that it couldn't be. Last time he'd checked Jesse was still alive.

"I kinda thought that you'd be a bit more tickled to see me," Jesse said, bending over Timbre.

"I would be if I wasn't so disappointed that you went and got yourself killed," Timbre informed him, deliriously.

"I'm not dead yet, Pard, and neither are you," Jesse told him.

"I'm not? Good, because I have things I want to tell you before I pack it in. So listen good because I don't have the strength to repeat this."

"You're not going to die," Jesse told him starting to examine his wounds.

"Stop it Jesse. We've both seen enough bullet wounds to know when someone is going over," Timbre told him. "But I'm glad you're here at the end. I always thought it fitting that you be by my side when I reached the end of my trail."

"You ain't reached your end of trail yet. Soon as I get you off this mountain, Trina we'll patch you up good as new. You should see what a fine job she did on Curtis," Jesse told him with tears running down his cheeks.

"You always were a bad liar, Jesse. Even when you were a kid you couldn't lie worth a damn. I'm not going anywhere and you know it. In my saddlebags you'll find a letter stating that I've left everything I own to you and Cat. In there you'll also find instructions on how to get to it. I've been carrying that letter around with me for quite a spell now. I figured that it was just a matter of time before the famous Timbre luck would run out."

"That's a load of crap. You took out one of the baddest men that ever lived, you did things that no one else could do. I grant you that you're shot-up pretty bad but you're still alive and you're going to stay that way. If that isn't the famous Timbre luck then what the hell is? No my friend, you still have it, believe that and hang on to it. And, if that ain't enough to get you up and moving think on this: Do you really expect me to go down that mountain and tell Cat that you're dead? If you do you're crazier than that mad man lying over there. She'd skin me alive."

"She's a tough one alright," Timbre smiled, thinking of Cat and how much he was going to miss her. "Do me a favor and tell her that I'm sorry that I couldn't keep my promise. She'll know what I mean."

As Timbre watched Jesse tie a tourniquet around his leg he knew that trying to argue with him was a waste of time. Once Jesse made up his mind on something there was no changing it. Jesse was determined to get him down the mountain no matter how much pain it caused him.

"Jesse, take care of Thor for me. I give him to you. He'll make you a good companion. Jake's ranch is now yours. Take him there and breed him. You'll have the best horse ranch in California."

"You think Jake will have anything to say about that?"

Jake's dead. The ranch is mine now and in a couple of minutes it's going to be yours," Timbre informed him. He then turned and looked up at Thor. "You hear me Thor, you go with Jesse now and take care of him."

"Okay. That should hold you till I get you to Trina. You got some frost bite, but there's nothing I can do about that here," Jesse told him. "You sit tight, I'll go make you a travois so I can get you out of here."

"Jesse! The only thing dragging me behind your horse is going to do is rip me open some more. Please! Let me be and let me die here in peace. At least here I'm too numb to feel any more pain. You know damn well that I ain't going to make it anyways," Timbre pleaded with him, trying to change his mind.

"Ain't, ain't a word. Besides, I'm not planning on dragging you. I'm going to connect poles between our horses, sorta like a hammock. You'll be so comfortable you'll think you're in a St. Louie cathouse."

"Yeah," Timbre sighed, knowing better than to argue.

Jesse took a good look at The Count for the first time and asked: "What the hell did you do to his head, or what's left of it? Even his own Mama wouldn't recognize him now."

"Wasn't me. Big boy did it for me," Timbre groaned, nodding toward Thor.

"Remind me not to piss him off." Jesse stated, starting to walk off to make the travois.

"Jesse," Timbre grunted, stopping him from leaving for a moment. "Find my guns, there somewhere over there by that tree. One belongs to Curtis and you keep the other one, it might come in handy for you someday."

"I'll find them, but you'll be able to use them soon yourself," Jesse told him, continuing to walk away.

It took Jesse close to twenty-minutes to construct Timbre's special rig and to find his guns. After he finished he lead the two horses close to where Timbre was lying. Stooping over Jesse placed his hands under Timbre's armpits.

"Remember: Dead men don't feel pain. That privilege is only reserved for the living," Jesse whispered in Timbre's ear, while he braced himself to lift him.

"Dandy."

"Get set, here goes," Jesse warned, jerking Timbre to his feet.

"Hey Jesse, I don't feel any pain. See you at the end of trail, Partner." With that Timbre passed into darkness.

CHAPTER
20

"Hi Dad. Is this time for real or am I going back again," Timbre asked, as his vision focused in on his Father.

"I'm afraid this time it's for real, Son. But if it's any consolation to you, you did a great job, an extraordinary job. You got a little sloppy at the end but you accomplished your task. It's a shame that you didn't get to reap your reward and get to marry Cat. But to tell you the truth we never expected you to get as far as you did. You were against a man that had great powers and has been wreaking havoc on Earth for hundreds of years."

"So all that crap that he fed me was true? Who the hell was that guy?"

"That guy is you."

"What the hell does that mean, he's me?"

"I should say, he's what you're going to be."

"You better explain that. So far I'm not liking what I hear."

"You remember when I told you that you'll be trained to help put things right that went wrong?"

"Keep going."

"Well, that's what he was trained to do, and he did it well, that is until the powers he'd gained up here turned him evil. You know that old saying: Power corrupts and total power totally corrupts. Seems as if he fell in love with his powers and it corrupted him. He thought that he had become a God."

"I never heard that saying before, it must've been said after my time."

"Maybe so."

"So, what do you think turned him, besides his love of power?"

"No one really knows. His job was to get in, correct the problem, and get out. Sometime on his last mission he decided he didn't want to leave the Earth ever again. Why? Nobody knows for sure. And, the only way he could live forever--- well, you're aware of how he accomplished that.

Oh, they sent a number of men to take him out but he always defeated them---that is until you came along and stumbled into him. After the first time you shot him they saw their chance to possibly eliminate him, even though it was a slim chance. They didn't have much faith that you'd succeed but they were desperate so they took a chance on you. They brought you back to life, which they rarely do, to try and finish the job. You can't imagine how pleased they are that you succeeded."

"So, where is he now?" Timbre asked.

"Somewhere dark and deep. Somewhere that nobody wants to end up in."

"So what you're telling me is that I'm his replacement?"

"More or less. You certainly don't have to go around torturing people. Your job will be to get in, correct the problem, and get out.

401

I know that it's hard for you to take it all in but in time you'll understand. After your training you'll understand it all."

"What do you mean training?"

"Like I told you before: The powers that be have singled you out to right their mistakes. It will all be explained to you after you rest up for a while. What I can tell you now is that you're going to have a very interesting after life."

"What about Cat, Jesse, and Curtis. How did their lives turn out?"

"Don't know yet, they're still living it. When their time is up you can ask them yourself."

"Have you seen Jake? Did he make it up here? I heard that he was killed. Is that true?"

"Yeah, he made it up here but he's still asleep. He had a hard death and needs time for it to fade from his memory. All those that died a horrible death don't wake up as fast as you did. The pain and agony that they suffered is to fresh in their consciousness for them to be happy. They wont wake-up until the memory of their death fades away."

"So now what?" Timbre asked.

"Now we go see your Ma, she's been waiting on you. Damn near busting at the seams to see you. You'll stay with us until you get over the loss's that you're still grappling with. When you feel up to it you can start your training. How does that sound?"

"I don't know if I'll ever get over losing Cat, but seeing Ma sounds good."

"You'll see Cat again when it's her time to move on. Oh, there's someone I want you to meet before we go," Sam smiled, as a little man walked out of what seemed to be a fog. "Tim, meet Sly."

"Hello Sly," Timbre nodded to him, wondering who he was.

"You don't recognize me do you?" he asked in a voice deeper than Timbre would've imagined it to be.

"No, I reckon not, should I?"

"You tell him Sam, he won't believe me," Sly said, looking over at Sam.

"Tim, meet Thor," Sam laughed.

"What! Thor was my horse, this guy is not a horse," Timbre said, totally confused.

"Yes, but Sly was doing the thinking for Thor. He entered him as soon as you took a cotton to him. It was the only help we could give you. Curtis and Jesse were just a lucky bonus, a very lucky bonus. Sly here volunteered to do that so you should thank him. It's not easy to pretend to be a horse. Didn't you find it strange that a horse could be so smart?"

"If you were Thor why did you give me such a hard time and throw me when I tried to ride you?" Timbre asked, looking at Sly, more confused than ever.

"A guy has to have some fun. After all I couldn't make any jokes so I did what I could to amuse myself. As far as throwing you goes, I was testing out what kind of a rider you were, plus, it was fun. Hey, you don't get many chuckles being a hay burner," Sly laughed. "You got to get your kicks where you can. Get it, kicks," Sly laughed even harder.

"Okay, but how about you wondering away all the time?"

"When you didn't need me I'd do a little sight-seeing. I always came back when you were ready to ride, didn't I?"

"Yeah, I guess so. But you were a little late when the Indian's were after my scalp."

"I wasn't in that damn horse all the time, like on the ship and sometimes in the stables. After you were captured and hog tied I figured that you were done for and saw no reason to stick around, I had other business to attend to. But as soon as I was told that you'd escaped and needed me I hopped

LOU SCAFIDI

right back into that maniac and rushed to your rescue. It took some time to get to you because that mule headed horse was wondering around the hills stomping on things."

"I see," Timbre told him, not blaming him for wanting out of Thor.

"Well, I have to be on my way now. I'm pretty sure we'll work together again. See ya."

"Hey Sly," Timbre stopped him for a moment. "Thanks for everything. I couldn't have done it without you, especially at the end there."

"No problem. I wanted to crush that bastards head in for a long long time. Thanks for giving me the opportunity to do it."

"So does that mean that without you Thor is going to be as crazy as he was when I first met him?" Timbre asked, worried about Jesse.

"I stayed with Thor until ya'll got back to the barn. After that, who knows, maybe I rubbed of a little on him, either way he's Jesse's problem now," Sly smiled. With that, he waved and vanished back into the mist.

"Okay then. Are you ready?" his Father asked, standing up.

"As ready as I'll ever be. Led the way."

The End?